BLOOD
RED
ROAD

DUSTLANDS: BOOK ONE

MOIRA YOUNG

DOUBLEDAY CANADA

FOR MY PARENTS AND FOR PAUL

Copyright © 2011 by Moira Young
Paperback edition published 2012

Doubleday Canada and colophon are registered trademarks

Library and Archives Canada Cataloguing in Publication is available upon request

ISBN: 978-0-385-67185-9

Printed and bound in the USA

Published in Canada by Doubleday Canada,
a division of Random House of Canada Limited

Visit Random House of Canada Limited's website: www.randomhouse.ca

10 9 8 7 6 5 4 3 2 1

CONTENTS

LUGH GOT BORN FIRST. ON MIDWINTER DAY WHEN THE SUN hangs low in the sky.

Then me. Two hours later.

That pretty much says it all.

Lugh goes first, always first, an I follow on behind.

An that's fine.

That's right.

That's how it's meant to be.

Becuz everythin's set. It's all fixed.

The lives of everybody who's ever bin born.

The lives of everybody still waitin to be born.

It was all set in the stars the moment the world began. The time of yer birthin, the time of yer death. Even what kinda person yer gonna be, good or bad.

If you know how to read the stars, you can read the story of people's lives. The story of yer own life. What's gone, what's now an what's still to come.

Back when Pa was a boy, he met up with a traveler, a man who knew many things. He learned Pa how to read the stars. Pa never says what he sees in the night sky but you can see it lays heavy on him.

Because you cain't change what's written.

Even if Pa was to say what he knew, even if he was to warn you, it would still come to pass.

I see the way he looks at Lugh sometimes. The way he looks at me.

An I wish he'd tell us what he knows.

I believe Pa wishes he'd never met that traveler.

If you seen me an Lugh together, you'd never think we was the same blood.

Never think we grew together in the same womb.

He's got gold hair. I got black.

Blue eyes. Brown eyes.

Strong. Scrawny.

Beautiful. Ugly.

He's my light.

I'm his shadow.

Lugh shines like the sun.

That must of made it easy fer them to find him.

All they had to do was follow his light.

SILVERLAKE

THE DAY'S HOT. SO HOT AN SO DRY THAT ALL I CAN TASTE IN my mouth is dust. The kinda white heat day when you can hear th'earth crack.

We ain't had a drop of rain fer near six months now. Even the spring that feeds the lake's startin to run dry. You gotta walk some ways out now to fill a bucket. Pretty soon, there won't be no point in callin it by its name.

Silverlake.

Every day Pa tries another one of his charms or spells. An every day, big bellied rainclouds gather on the horizon. Our hearts beat faster an our hopes rise as they creep our way. But, well before they reach us, they break apart, thin out an disappear. Every time.

Pa never says naught. He jest stares at the sky, the clear cruel sky. Then he gathers up the stones or twigs or whatever he's set out on the ground this time, an puts 'em away fer tomorrow.

Today, he shoves his hat back. Tips his head up an studies the sky fer a long while.

I do believe I'll try a circle, he says. Yuh, I reckon a circle might be jest the thing.

Lugh's bin sayin it fer a while now. Pa's gittin worse. With every dry day that passes, a little bit more of Pa seems to . . . I guess disappear's the best word fer it.

Once we could count on pullin a fish from the lake an a beast from our traps. Fer everythin else, we planted some, foraged some, an, all in all, we made out okay. But fer the last year, whatever we do, however hard we try, it jest ain't enough. Not without rain. We bin watchin the land die, bit by bit.

An it's the same with Pa. Day by day, what's best in him withers away. Mind you, he ain't bin right fer a long time. Not since Ma died. But what Lugh says is true. Jest like the land, Pa's gittin worse an his eyes look more'n more to the sky instead of what's here in front of him.

I don't think he even sees us no more. Not really.

Emmi runs wild these days, with filthy hair an a runny nose. If it warn't fer Lugh, I don't think she'd ever wash at all.

Before Emmi was born, when Ma was still alive an everythin was happy, Pa was different. Ma could always make him laugh. He'd chase me an Lugh around, or throw us up over his head till we shrieked fer him to stop. An he'd warn us about the wickedness of the world beyond Silverlake. Back then, I didn't think there could be anybody ever lived who was taller or stronger or smarter'n our pa.

I watch him outta the corner of my eye while me an Lugh git on with repairs to the shanty roof. The walls is sturdy enough, bein that they're made from tires all piled one on top of th'other. But the wicked hotwinds that whip across the lake sneak their way into the smallest chink an lift whole parts of the roof at once. We're always havin to mend the damn thing.

So, after last night's hotwind, me an Lugh was down at the landfill at first light scavengin. We dug around a part of it we ain't never tried before an damn if we didn't manage to score ourselves some primo Wrecker junk. A nice big sheet of metal, not too rusted, an a cookin pot that's still got its handle.

Lugh works on the roof while I do what I always do, which is clamber up an down the ladder an hand him what he needs.

Nero does what he always does, which is perch on my shoulder an caw real loud, right in my ear, to tell me what he's thinkin. He's always got a opinion does Nero, an he's real smart too. I figger if only we could unnerstand crow talk, we'd find he was tellin us a thing or two about the best way to fix a roof.

He'll of thought about it, you can bet on that. He's watched us fix it fer five year now. Ever since I found him fell outta the nest an his ma nowhere to be seen. Pa warn't too happy to see me bring a crow babby home. He told me some folk consider crows bring death, but I was set on rearin him by hand an once I set my mind on somethin I stick with it.

An then there's Emmi. She's doin what she always does, which is pester me an Lugh. She dogs my heels as I go from the ladder to the junk pile an back.

I wanna help, she says.

Hold the ladder then, I says.

No! I mean really help! All you ever let me do is hold the ladder!

Well, I says, maybe that's all yer fit fer. You ever think of that?

She folds her arms across her skinny little chest an scowls at me. Yer mean, she says.

So you keep tellin me, I says.

I start up the ladder, a piece of rusty metal in my hand, but I ain't gone more'n three rungs before she takes hold an starts shakin it. I grab on to stop myself from fallin. Nero squawks an flaps off in a flurry of feathers. I glare down at Em.

Cut that out! I says. What're you tryin to do, break my neck?

Lugh's head pops over the side of the roof. All right, Em, he says, that's enough. Go help Pa.

Right away, she lets go. Emmi always does what Lugh tells her.

But I wanna help you, she says with her sulky face.

We don't need yer help, I says. We're doin jest fine without you.

Yer the meanest sister that ever lived! I hate you, Saba!

Good! Cuz I hate you too!

That's enough! says Lugh. Both of yuz!

Emmi sticks her tongue out at me an stomps off. I shin up the ladder onto the roof, crawl along an hand him the metal sheet.

I swear I'm gonna kill her one of these days, I says.

She's only nine, Saba, says Lugh. You might try bein nice to her fer a change.

I grunt an hunker down nearby. Up here on the roof, I can see everythin. Emmi ridin around on her rickety two-wheeler that Lugh found in the landfill. Pa at his spell circle.

It ain't nuthin more'n a bit of ground that he leveled off by stompin it down with his boots. We ain't permitted nowhere near it, not without his say so. He's always fussin around, sweepin clear any twigs or sand that blow onto it. He ain't set out none of the sticks fer his rain circle on the ground yet. I watch as he lays down the broom. Then he takes three steps to the right an three steps to the left. Then he does it agin. An agin.

You seen what Pa's up to? I says to Lugh.

He don't raise his head. Jest starts hammerin away at the sheet to straighten it.

I seen, he says. He did it yesterday too. An the day before.

What's all that about? I says. Goin right, then left, over an over.

How should I know? he says. His lips is pressed together in a tight line. He's got that look on his face agin. The blank look he gits when Pa says somethin or asks him to do somethin. I see it on him more an more these days.

Lugh! Pa lifts his head, shadin his eyes. I could use yer help here, son!

Foolish old man, Lugh mutters. He gives the metal sheet a extra hard whack with the hammer.

Don't say that, I says. Pa knows what he's doin. He's a star reader.

Lugh looks at me. Shakes his head, like he cain't believe I jest said what I did.

Ain't you figgered it out yet? It's all in his head. Made up. There ain't nuthin written in the stars. There ain't no great plan. The world goes on. Our lives jest go on an on in this gawdfersaken place. An that's it. Till the day we die. I tell you what, Saba, I've took about all I can take.

I stare at him.

Lugh! Pa yells.

I'm busy! Lugh yells back.

Right now, son!

Lugh swears unner his breath. He throws the hammer down, pushes past me an pratikally runs down the ladder. He rushes over to Pa. He snatches the sticks from him an throws 'em to the ground. They scatter all over.

There! Lugh shouts. There you go! That should help! That should make the gawdam rain come! He kicks Pa's new-swept spell circle till the dust flies. He pokes his finger hard into Pa's chest. Wake up, old man! Yer livin in a dream! The rain ain't never gonna come! This hellhole is dyin an we're gonna die too if we stay here. Well, guess what? I ain't doin it no more! I'm outta here!

I knew this would come, says Pa. The stars told me you was unhappy, son. He reaches out an puts a hand on Lugh's arm. Lugh flings it off so fierce it makes Pa stagger backwards.

Yer crazy, you know that? Lugh shouts it right in his face. The stars told you! Why don't you jest try listenin to what I say fer once?

He runs off. I hurry down the ladder. Pa's starin at the ground, his shoulders slumped.

I don't unnerstand, he says. I see the rain comin. . . . I read it in the stars but . . . it don't come. Why don't it come?

It's okay, Pa, says Emmi. I'll help you. I'll put 'em where you want. She scrabbles about on her knees, collectin all the sticks. She looks at him with a anxious smile.

Lugh didn't mean it Pa, she says. I know he didn't.

I go right on past 'em.

I know where Lugh's headed.

✝ ✝ ✝

I find him at Ma's rock garden.

He sits on the ground, in the middle of the swirlin patterns, the squares an circles an little paths made from all different stones, each their own shade an size. Every last tiny pebble set out by Ma with her own hands. She wouldn't allow that anybody should help her.

She carefully laid the last stone in place. Sat back on her heels an smiled at me, rubbin at her big babby-swolled belly. Her long golden hair in a braid over one shoulder.

There! You see, Saba? There can be beauty anywhere. Even here. An if it ain't there, you can make it yerself.

The day after that, she birthed Emmi. A month too early. Ma bled fer two days, then she died. We built her funeral pyre high an sent her spirit back to the stars. Once we'd scattered her ash to the winds, all we was left with was Em.

A ugly little red scrap with a heartbeat like a whisper. More like a newborn mouse than a person. By rights, she shouldn't of lasted longer'n a day or two. But somehow she hung on an she's still here. Small fer her age though, an scrawny.

Fer a long time, I couldn't stand even lookin at her. When Lugh says I shouldn't be so hard on her, I says that if it warn't fer Emmi, Ma 'ud still be alive. He ain't got no answer to that cuz he knows it's true, but he always shakes his head an says somethin like, It's time you got over it, Saba, an that kinda thing.

I put up with Emmi these days, but that's about as far as it goes.

Now I set myself down on the hard-packed earth so's my back leans aginst Lugh's. I like it when we sit like this. I can feel his voice rumble inside my body when he talks. It must of bin like this when the two of us was inside Ma's belly together. Esseptin that neether of us could talk then, of course.

We sit there fer a bit, silent. Then, We should of left here a long time ago, he says. There's gotta be better places'n this. Pa should of took us away.

You ain't really leavin, I says.

Ain't I? There ain't no reason to stay. I cain't jest sit around waitin to die.

Where would you go?

It don't matter. Anywhere, so long as it ain't Silverlake.

But you cain't. It's too dangerous.

We only got Pa's word fer that. You do know that you an me ain't ever bin more'n one day's walk in any direction our whole lives. We never see nobody essept ourselves.

That ain't true, I says. What about that crazy medicine woman on her camel last year? An . . . we see Potbelly Pete. He's always got a story or two about where he's bin an who he's seen.

I ain't talkin about some shyster pedlar man stoppin by every couple of months, he says. By the way, I'm still sore about them britches he tried to unload on me last time.

They was hummin all right, I says. Like a skunk wore 'em last. Hey wait, you fergot Procter.

Our only neighbor's four leagues north of here. He's a lone man, name of Procter John. He set up homestead jest around the time Lugh an me got born. He drops by once a month or so. Not that he ever stops proper, mind. He don't git down offa his horse, Hob, but jest pulls up by the hut. Then he says the same thing, every time.

G'day, Willem. How's the young 'uns? All right?

They're fine, Procter, says Pa. *You?*

Well enough to last a bit longer.

Then he tips his hat an goes off an we don't see him fer another month. Pa don't like him. He never says so, but you can tell. You'd think he'd be glad of somebody to talk to besides us, but he never invites Procter to stay an take a dram.

Lugh says it's on account of the chaal. We only know that's what it's called becuz one time I asked Pa what it is that Procter's always chewin an Pa's face went all tight an it was like he didn't wanna tell us. But then he said it's called chaal an it's poison to the mind an soul, an if anybody ever offers us any we're to say no. But since we never see nobody, such a offer don't seem too likely.

Now Lugh shakes his head. You cain't count Procter John, he says. Nero's got more conversation than him. I swear, Saba, if I stay here, I'll eether go crazy or I'll end up killin Pa. I gotta go.

I scramble around, kneel in front of him.

I'm comin with you, I says.

Of course, he says. An we'll take Emmi with us.

I don't think Pa 'ud let us, I says. An she wouldn't wanna go anyways. She'd rather stay with him.

You mean you'd rather she stayed, he says. We gotta take her with us, Saba. We cain't leave her behind.

What about . . . maybe if you was to talk to Pa, he might see sense, I says. Then we could all go to a new place together.

He won't, Lugh says. He cain't leave Ma.

Whaddya mean? I says. Ma's dead.

Lugh says, What I mean is . . . him an Ma made this place together an, in his mind, she's still here. He cain't leave her memory, that's what I'm sayin.

But we're the ones still alive, I says. You an me.

An Emmi, he says. I know that. But you see how he is. It's like we don't exist. He don't give two hoots fer us.

Lugh thinks fer a moment. Then he says, Love makes you weak. Carin fer somebody that much means you cain't think straight. Look at Pa. Who'd wanna end up like him? I ain't never gonna love nobody. It's better that way.

I don't say naught. Jest trace circles in the dirt with my finger.

My gut twists. Like a mean hand reached right inside me an grabbed it.

Then I says, What about me?

Yer my sister, he says. It ain't the same.

But what if I died? You'd miss me, wouldn't you?

Huh, he says. Fat chance of you dyin an leavin me in peace. Always followin me everywhere, drivin me nuts. Since the day we was born.

It ain't my fault yer the tallest thing around, I says. You make a good sunshade.

Hey! He pushes me onto my back.

I push him with my foot. Hey yerself! I prop myself up on my elbows. Well, I says, would you?

What?

Miss me.

Don't be stupid, he says.

I kneel in front of him. He looks at me. Lugh's got eyes as blue as the summer sky. Blue as the clearest water. Ma used to say his eyes was so blue, it made her wanna sail away on 'em.

I'd miss you, I says. If you died, I'd miss you so much I'd wanna kill myself.

Don't talk foolish, Saba.

Promise me you won't, I says.

Won't what?

Die.

Everybody's gotta die one day, he says.

I reach out an touch his birthmoon tattoo. High on his right cheekbone, jest like mine, it shows how the moon looked in the sky the night we was born. It was a full moon that midwinter. That's a rare thing. But twins born unner a full moon at the turnin of the year, that's even rarer. Pa did the tattoos hisself, to mark us out as special.

We was eighteen year our last birthday. That must be four month ago, near enough.

When we die, I says, d'you think we'll end up stars together, side by side?

You gotta stop thinkin like that, he says. I told you, that's jest Pa's nonsense.

Go on then, if you know so much, tell me what happens when you die.

I dunno. He sighs an flops back on the ground, squintin at the sky. You jest . . . stop. Yer heart don't beat no more, you don't breathe an then yer jest . . . gone.

An that's it, I says.

Yeah.

Well that's stupid, I says. I mean, we spend our lives doin all this . . . sleepin an eatin an fixin roofs an then it all jest . . . ends. Hardly seems worth the trouble.

Well, that's the way it is, he says.

You . . . hey Lugh, you wouldn't ever leave without me, would you?

Of course not, he says. But even if I did, you'd only follow me.

I will follow you . . . everywhere you go! When I say it, I make crazy eyes an a crazy face becuz it creeps him out when I do that. To the bottom of the lake, I says, . . . to the ends of the earth . . . to the moon . . . to the stars. . . !

Shut up! He leaps to his feet. Bet you don't follow me to skip rocks, he says an runs off.

Hey! I yell. Wait fer me!

✝ ✝ ✝

We run a fair ways out onto the dry lakebed before we find water enough to skip stones. We pass the skiff that Pa helped me an Lugh build when we was little kids. Now it lies high an dry where the shoreline used to be.

We walk till we're outta sight of the shanty, outta sight of Pa an Emmi. The fierce noonday sun beats down an I wrap my sheema around my head so's I don't fry too much. I wish I took after Ma, like Lugh, but I favor Pa. It's strange, but even with our dark hair, our skin burns if we don't cover up.

Lugh never wears a sheema. Says they make him feel trapped an anyways the sun don't bother him none. Not like me. When I tell him it'll deserve him right if he drops dead from sunstroke one day, he says, well if that happens you can say I told you so. I will, too.

I find a pretty good stone right off. I rub my fingers over its flat smoothness. Feel its weight.

I got a lucky one here, I says.

Lugh hunts around to find one fer hisself. While he does it, I walk up an down on my hands. It's about th'only thing I can do that he cain't. He pretends he don't care, but I know he does.

You look funny upside down, I says.

Lugh's golden hair gleams in the sun. He wears it tied back

in one long braid that reaches almost to his waist. I wear mine the same, only my hair's black as Nero's feathers.

His necklace catches the light. I found the little ring of shiny green glass in the landfill an threaded it on a piece of leather. I gave it to him fer our eighteen year birthday an he ain't took it off since.

What did he give me? Nuthin. Like always.

Okay I got a good one, he calls.

I go runnin over to take a look. Not as good as mine, I says.

I'm gonna skip eight today, he says. I feel it in my bones.

In yer dreams, I says. I'm callin a seven.

I whip my arm back an send the stone skimmin over the water. It skips once, twice, three times. Four, five, six. . .

Seven! I says. Seven! Did you see that?

I cain't hardly believe it. I ain't never done more'n five before.

Sorry, Lugh says. I warn't lookin. Guess you'll hafta do it agin.

What! My best ever an you didn't . . . you rat! You did see! Yer jest sick with jealousy. I fold my arms over my chest. Go on. Let's see you do eight. Betcha cain't.

He does seven. Then I do my usual five. He's jest pullin his arm back fer another try when, outta nowhere, Nero comes swoopin down at us, cawin his head off.

Damn bird, says Lugh, he made me drop my stone. He gits on his knees to look fer it.

Go away! I says, flappin my hands at Nero. Shoo, you bad boy! Go find somebody else to—

A dustcloud's jest appeared on the horizon. A billowin orange mountain of dust. It's so tall, it scrapes aginst the sun. It's movin fast. Headed straight at us.

Uh . . . Lugh, I says.

There must be somethin in my voice. He looks up sharpish. Drops the stone in his hand. Gits slowly to his feet.

Holy crap, he says.

We jest stand there. Stand an stare. We git all kinda weather here. Hotwinds, firestorms, tornadoes, an once or twice we even had snow in high summer. So I seen plenty of dust storms. But never one like this.

That's one bastard of a cloud, I says.

We better git outta here, says Lugh.

We start to back away slow, still starin. Then, Run, Saba! Lugh yells.

He grabs my hand, yankin at me till my feet move, an then we're runnin. Runnin fer home, fast as wolfdogs on the hunt.

I look over my shoulder an git a shock. The dustcloud's halfways across the lake. I never seen one move so fast. We got a minute, two at most, before it's on us.

We cain't outrun it! I yell at Lugh. It's comin too fast!

The shanty comes into view an we start to shout an wave our arms.

Emmi's still ridin around on her two-wheeler.

Pa! we scream. Pa! Emmi! Dust storm!

Pa appears in the doorway. Shades his eyes with his hand. Then he makes a dash fer Emmi, snatches her an runs full pelt fer the unnerground storm cellar.

The cellar ain't more'n fifty paces from the shanty. He hauls up the wooden door set into the ground an drops Emmi inside. He waves his arms at us, frantic.

I look back. Gasp. The great mountain of orange dust races towards us with a roar. Like a ravenous beast, gobblin the ground as it goes.

Faster, Saba! Lugh yells. He rips off his shirt an starts wrappin it around his face.

Nero! I says. I stop, look all around. Where's Nero?

No time! Lugh grabs my wrist, pulls at me.

Pa yells somethin I cain't hear. He climbs into the storm cellar an pulls the door to.

I cain't leave him out here! I pull myself free. Nero! I yell. Nero!

It's too late! Lugh says. He'll save hisself! C'mon!

A fork of lightnin slashes down an lands with a almighty crack an hiss.

One Missus Ippi, two Missus Ippi, three—

There's a sullen rumble of thunder.

Less'n a league! Lugh says.

Everythin goes black. The cloud's on us. I cain't see a thing.

Lugh! I scream.

Hang on! he yells. Don't let go!

The next thing I know, a tingle runs across my skin. I gasp. Lugh must feel it too becuz he lets go my hand like he's bin scalded.

Lightnin's comin! he yells. Git down!

We hunker down, some ways apart. We crouch as low to the ground as we can git. My heart's stuck in my throat.

One more time, Saba. If lightnin catches you out in the open, whaddya do?

Crouch down, head down, feet together, hands on knees. Don't let my hands or knees touch the ground. That's right, ain't it, Pa?

An never lie down. Don't ferget that, Saba, never lie down.

I hear Pa's voice loud an clear in my head. He got struck by lightnin as a boy. Nearly got killed from not knowin the right thing to do, so he's made damn sure we all know what to—

Crack! The darkness splits open with a bright flash an a slam boom. It sends me flyin. I bang my head aginst the ground—hard. Try to pull myself up but fall back. Dizzy. My head spins round an round. I groan.

Saba! Lugh shouts. Are y'okay?

Another flash an boom splits the darkness. I think it's headed away from us, but I cain't be sure, my head's so muddled. My ears ring.

Saba! Lugh yells. Where are you?

Over here! I call out, my voice all thin an shaky. I'm here!

An then Lugh's there, kneelin beside me an pullin me up to sit.

Are you hurt? he says. Are y'okay? He slips his arm around me, helps me to stand. My legs feel all wobbly. Did it hit you?

I . . . uh . . . it . . . knocked me offa my feet, is all, I says.

Then, as we stand there, the dark rolls away.

An the world's turned red.

Bright red like the heart of a fire. Everythin. The ground, the sky, the shanty, me, Lugh—all red. Fine red dust fills the air, touches every single thing. A red red world. I ain't never seen nuthin like it before.

Me an Lugh stare at each other.

Looks like the end of the world, I says. My voice sounds muffled, like I'm talkin unner a blanket.

An then, outta that red dust haze, the men on horses appear.

† † †

There's five of 'em. Ridin sturdy, shaggy coat mustangs.

Even in normal times we don't git folk passin by Silverlake, so it's a shock to see strangers blowin in on the tail of the worst dust storm in years. The horsemen pull up near the shanty. They don't dismount. We start over.

Let me do the talkin, Lugh says.

Four of the riders is dressed in long black robes. They got on heavy leather vests strapped over top an sheemas wrapped round their heads. They're dusted head to foot with red earth. As we git closer, I can see the fifth man's our neighbor, Procter John. He's ridin his horse, Hob.

As we come in earshot, Lugh calls out, Strange kinda day fer a ride, ain't it, Procter John?

Nobody says nuthin. Their sheemas cover the riders' faces so's we cain't see their expressions.

Now we're right up near 'em.

Procter, Lugh nods. Who's yer friends?

Procter still says naught. Jest stares down at his hands holdin the reins.

Look, I whisper to Lugh. Blood trickles out from unner Procter John's hat, snakes down his face.

What's goin on here? says Lugh. Procter? By the sound of his voice, I can tell he thinks somethin ain't right about this. Me too. My heartbeat picks up.

Is this him? says one of the men to Procter John. Golden Boy here? Is he the one born at midwinter?

Procter John don't look up. He nods. That be him, he says in a low voice.

How many years you got, boy? the man says to Lugh.

Eighteen, says Lugh. What's it to you anyways?

An you was fer definite born at midwinter?

Yeah. Look, what's all this about?

I told you he's the right one, says Procter John. I should know. I bin keepin a eye on him all this time like you told me to. Can I go now?

The man nods.

Sorry, Lugh, says Procter John, still not lookin at us. They didn't give me no choice.

He clicks Hob an makes to leave. The man slides a bolt shooter from his robe. I know he must be movin fast, but it all seems to go so slow. He pulls the trigger an shoots Procter. Hob rears in fright. Procter slides off an lands in a heap on the ground. He don't move.

A cold jolt runs through me. We're in trouble. I grab Lugh's arm. The four men start movin towards us.

Fetch Pa, Lugh says. Quick. I'll draw 'em away from the house.

No, I says. It's too dangerous.

Move, gawdammit!

He turns. Starts runnin back towards the lake. The men heel their horses an head after him. I run like stink fer the storm cellar, fast as my feet'll carry me.

Pa! I yell. Pa! Come quick!

I look over my shoulder. Lugh's halfways to the lake. The four riders is spreadin out to make a big circle. Lugh keeps runnin, but he's caught in the middle. They start to close in, tighten up. They're trappin him. One unhooks a rope from his saddle.

I pound my foot on the door of the storm cellar.

Pa! I scream. Pa! Open up!

The door creaks open. Pa's head appears.

Are they here? he says. Have they come?

You seen this comin. You read it in the stars.

Four men! I says. Quick! We gotta stop 'em!

Emmi, stay here! Pa scrambles outta the cellar. They cain't be stopped, Saba. It's begun.

His eyes look flat. Dead.

No, I says. Don't say that.

Now Lugh's trapped by the circlin horsemen. He darts at a gap. They block it. He stumbles, falls, picks hisself back up agin. In the dusty red haze, it don't look real.

Don't jest stand here! I yell at Pa. Help me!

I dive into the shanty. Grab my crossbow, sling my quiver on my back. Grab Pa's bolt shooter. Empty. I throw it down with a curse. Snatch up his crossbow an quiver.

I come runnin out.

Pa! I yell. They got Lugh! I grab his arm, give him a hard shake. This is real! You gotta fight!

Then it's like he comes to life. He pulls hisself tall, his eyes spark an the Pa I remember's back. He hauls me to him, holds me so tight I cain't hardly breathe.

My time's nearly up, he says quickly.

No, Pa!

Listen. I dunno what happens after this. I could only see

28

glimpses. But they're gonna need you, Saba. Lugh an Emmi. An there'll be others too. Many others. Don't give in to fear. Be strong, like I know you are. An never give up, d'you unnerstand, never. No matter what happens.

I stare at him.

I won't, I says. I ain't no quitter, Pa.

That's my girl.

He takes the crossbow. Slings the quiver on his back.

Ready? he says.

Ready, I says.

We start runnin. Runnin towards Lugh an the men on horseback.

One of the riders is loopin his rope into a lasso.

Load! yells Pa. We each snatch a arrow. Load.

The roper twirls the lasso once, twice. Throws.

Aim! yells Pa.

The lasso grabs Lugh's leg. The roper yanks on it, brings him down.

Fire! yells Pa.

We let fly. The arrows land short.

Load! Pa yells agin.

The roper an another rider leap offa their horses. They flip Lugh onto his back. One sits on him. Th'other one yanks his arms over his head, ties his wrists together, then his ankles.

Stop! says Pa. Let him go!

We're still runnin. We take aim. One of the mounted

riders turns. Sees us comin at 'em. He raises his bolt shooter. He fires.

Pa cries out. His arms fly up in the air.

Pa! I scream.

He staggers. He falls.

Pa! I throw myself down beside him. The bolt's gone right through his heart. I grab his shoulders, pull him up. His head flops forwards.

No! I shake him. No no no no no no no! Don't do this, Pa! You cain't die! Please don't die!

I give him another shake. His head lolls back.

Pa, I whisper. I'm froze. I cain't move. He's dead. They've killed my pa.

A wild rage rises up in me. Red hot. Floodin me. Chokin me. I grab my crossbow. Leap to my feet an start runnin towards the men. As I run, I load my bow.

Aaaaaah! I scream. Aaaaaaah!

I take aim. I shoot. But the red hot's makin my hands shake so much that I shoot wild. The arrow flies wide.

A shot comes whistlin at me. Sharp pain. Right hand. I cry out. My bow flies from my hand.

I keep runnin.

I burst past the horses, throw myself at the man tyin up Lugh. We roll on the ground, over an over. I kick at him, punch at him, screamin. He pushes me off. He's on his feet. Grabs my arm, hauls me up, slams me down. I land on my back. I gasp.

Gasp. Cain't breathe. Cain't breathe. Cain't git my breath.

Then. Then.

I pull myself to my feet an face 'em, swayin.

The four horsemen's all down on the ground now. On foot. They surround Lugh. They don't even look my way. It's like I ain't here. Like I don't exist.

I hold my bleedin hand to my chest. Let him go, I says.

They don't pay me no heed.

Lugh raises his head. Eyes wide. Face white. Terrified. Like I ain't never seen him before.

I step closer. Take me with you, I says.

The one in charge jerks his head. They lift Lugh an sling him over one of the horses.

Please, I says. Please . . . take me with you. I won't give you no trouble. Jest don't leave me here without him.

They tie him to the horse. The rider holds the horse's reins an jumps on behind one of th'other men. They start to move out in a swirl of red dust.

Lugh! I cry. I run alongside him. I gasp. Cain't git a breath.

Lugh lifts his head. Our eyes meet. Lugh's eyes. Blue as the summer sky. I grab his hands.

I'll find you, I says. Wherever they take you, I swear I'll find you.

No, he says. It's too dangerous. Keep yerself safe. You an Emmi. Promise me you will.

They grab Hob's rope as they pass. They're takin him too.

They break into a canter.

I cain't keep up. My hand slides away from Lugh's.

Promise me, Saba, Lugh says.

I keep runnin after 'em.

I'll find you! I scream.

They disappear into the red haze.

Lugh! I scream. Lugh! Come back!

My legs go out from unner me. I fall to my knees.

Emmi comes runnin outta the storm cellar. She stops. Stares at the hazy red world. At Procter John, lyin next to the hut. Then she sees Pa.

Pa! she screams an goes runnin towards him.

I cain't speak. Cain't breathe.

Lugh's gone.

Gone.

My golden heart is gone.

I kneel in the dust.

The tears roll down my face.

An a hard red rain starts to fall.

† † †

There's a knife in my gut.

It twists, rips me open. With every heartbeat, it slides in

a bit further. I cain't feel such pain an live. I wrap my arms around my body, double over. My mouth opens in a silent scream.

I stay there a long time.

The rain don't let up. Around me, the parched earth turns into a churnin sea of mud.

Look, Pa, it's rainin.

Too late.

Nero flaps down an lands on my shoulder. Tugs at my hair. I straighten up. Move slow. I'm numb. I don't feel nuthin.

Git up. You got things to do.

My hand. I look at it. Seems like it's a long ways off. Like it belongs to somebody else. The shot scraped the skin off in a long strip. It must hurt.

I stand. Make my feet move. Right. Left. So heavy. I wade through the mud to the shanty. Nero flies off to huddle unner the eaves.

Hand. Clean yer hand.

I pour water over it. Pack it with fireweed leaf an tie a cloth around it.

Pa's dead. You gotta burn him. Set his spirit free so's it can journey back to the stars where it come from.

I look in the wood store. There ain't enough to build a proper pyre. But I gotta burn him.

Think. Think.

I find our little handcart. Wheel it towards the lake. Shove it through the mud till I come to where Emmi's standin by Pa.

She's got bare feet. She's soaked to the skin. Her hair hangs in wet rat's tails. They drip down her face, her neck.

She don't move. Don't look at me. She stares at nuthin.

I grab both her arms, give her a shake.

Pa's dead, I says. We gotta move him.

She leans over an retches into the mud. I wait till she's finished. She looks at me sidewise, wipes a shaky hand across her mouth. She's cryin.

All right? I says. She nods. Take his feet, I says.

I take him unner his armpits an pull. Emmi takes his feet. Pa's got skinnier the past six months. No rain fer so long meant food's bin harder to find, pretty much impossible to grow.

You ain't finished yer supper, Pa. Ain't you hungry?

Oh, I've et plenty, child. Here. Share the rest out between yuz.

He knew he warn't foolin us, but we all played along anyways.

Skinny as Pa is, he's a grown man. Too heavy to lift fer a scrappy little girl an me. We hafta heave him, inch by inch. Em slips an slides. She don't stop cryin. Pretty soon she's covered head to toe in red mud.

At last we git him on the cart. Pa's tall, so only the top half of him fits in. His legs trail out behind.

Where's Lugh? Emmi sobs. I want Lugh.

He ain't here, I says.

Wh-wh-where is he?

Gone, I says. Some men took him.

He's dead, she says. You jest don't wanna tell me. He's dead! Lugh's dead! He's-dead-he's-dead-he's-dead-he's-dead-he's—

Shut up! I says.

She starts to scream. She gasps an sobs an screams an screams an screams.

Emmi! I yell. Stop it!

But she cain't. She's gone. Outta control.

So I slap her.

An she stops.

She gasps with shock. Takes in great shudderin breaths till she calms down. She wipes her nose on her sleeve. Looks at me. There's a red mark on her cheek. I shouldn't of done that. I know I shouldn't. Lugh wouldn't of. She's too little to take a hit.

I'm sorry, I says. But you shouldn't of said that. Lugh ain't dead. Don't ever say he is. Now hold Pa's feet outta the mud. Use his bootlaces. It'll be easier.

She does it.

I turn an start pullin the cart behind me. It's hard goin in the rain an mud. Water runs into my eyes, my mouth, my ears. Mud coats my boots an I slide.

Em's hopeless like always. She keeps fallin over, but every time she does I stop an help her up an we keep goin. At least she ain't cryin no more. We reach the shanty. We shove an pull the cart with Pa on it inside.

The shanty walls is made from tires.

The home Pa built with his own hands is gonna be his funeral pyre. I bet he didn't ever think of that.

Emmi helps me turn our big old wooden table upside down an we drag Pa offa the cart an lay him on the table.

I go to the chest where we keep what clothes we got, which ain't much. When I lift the lid, the smell of dried sage rises up. I pull out Pa's thick winter tunic an toss it to Emmi.

Tear it into strips, I says.

I lift out Lugh's winter tunic. I bury my face in it an breathe in deep. But we put it away clean. It smells of clean cloth an sage. It don't smell of him.

I git on with tearin it into strips.

Once we're done, there's a good-size pile. I dig out the jug of rootmash whisky. Pa brewed it when times was better. We soak all the cloth strips in it. Then I set Em to stuffin 'em into the walls, into the cracks between the tires. I put the rest around Pa's body.

I start fillin my barksack with necessaries. Red gizmo knife, flint, medicine herbs, spare shirt.

The same men that killed Pa took Lugh, I says. I'm goin after 'em. I dunno where they took him. It might be a long ways from here. It might take me a while to find him. But I will. I'm gonna bring him back.

I put in a waterskin, nettlecord rope, an enough sourberry seed jerky an dried rootcakes to last us a few days. If we run out, I'll jest hafta hunt.

They got a head start an they're on four legs, not two, I says. I'm gonna hafta travel fast.

I collect Emmi's waterskin, her tunic an her dogskin cloak. I don't look at her when I says, I'm leavin you with Mercy by Crosscreek.

No, says Emmi.

I put her stuff in another barksack. Pa an Lugh told me to keep you safe, I says, an you'll be safe there. Mercy an Ma was friends. She helped when me an Lugh was born. She came when you was born too.

I know, says Em.

What we both know but don't say is that Mercy came too late. Emmi came early, Ma died an Mercy might as well of spared herself the trouble of a three day walk.

Mercy's a good woman, I says. Pa always said that if anythin was to ever happen to him, we should go to her. He told me an Lugh the way to Crosscreek. She might even have a kid fer you to play with.

I don't care, says Emmi. I'm comin with you.

You cain't, I says. I dunno where I'm goin or how long it'll take me. Besides, yer too little. You'll only hold me back.

Emmi crosses her arms an sets her chin in that stubborn

way she's got. Lugh's my brother too! she says. I got a right to look fer him, jest the same as you.

Don't give me no trouble, Emmi. I pick up the little peg doll Pa made her an throw it in the sack. It's fer the best. Once I find Lugh, I promise we'll come back an git you.

No you won't, she says. You hate me. You love Lugh an you hate me. I wish they'd took you instead!

Well they didn't, I says. Pa an Lugh left me in charge of you an I say yer goin to Mercy's. Let that be a end to it.

I shove Lugh's slingshot into my belt. Tuck Pa's knife into a sheath inside my boot. Sling my quiver an pistol crossbow on my back.

Hazy red light trickles through the small window. It lands across Pa's face.

I kneel beside him, take his hand in mine. Emmi kneels across from me an takes his other hand. He's still warm, she whispers.

After a little bit she says, You need to say the words now.

She's right. You always say special words to send a dead person on their way.

Pa said some fer Ma, before he lit her funeral pyre all them years ago, but I cain't remember what they was. Guess I was too young to take proper notice. Now it's his turn to have words said an I cain't think of nuthin.

Go on, says Emmi.

Then, Sorry, Pa, I says.

I didn't mean to say that, but my mouth moved an those're the words that come out. But I realize I am sorry. Truly.

I'm sorry yer dead, I says. I'm sorry you had it so hard here, specially the last while. Mostly I'm sorry you lost Ma when you loved her so much. I know you ain't had no joy since she went. Well . . . now you'll be happy. You'll be together agin. Two stars, side by side.

I'm goin after Lugh, I says. I'm gonna git him back, Pa. I won't rest till I find him. I promise.

I look at Em. D'you wanna . . . kiss him g'bye? I says.

She kisses him on the cheek, then I strike my flint an light the spills around his body.

Willem by Silverlake, I says, I set yer spirit free to return to its home among the stars.

The flames start to lick at the table.

G'bye, Pa, Emmi whispers. I'm gonna miss you.

We stand. I hand her the barksacks.

Go on outside, I says.

I light the spills set into the walls. I wait till the tires catch fire, till the flames start to run along the walls.

G'bye, Pa, I says.

I close the door behind me as I go.

✝   ✝   ✝

The rain stops. A hot southerly starts to blow. The afternoon sun blazes down.

Nero hangs in the air above us, ridin the thermals in lazy spirals. Jest like Lugh said he would, he fled the storm an saved hisself. If only we could of done the same.

It looks like any other day. It could be yesterday, last week, a month ago. But it ain't. This ain't any other day.

I never knew. Didn't know everythin could be fine one moment an then the next moment so bad that it 'ud be like the time before that moment was all a dream.

Or maybe this is the dream. A long an terrible dream about a storm an some men in black who killed Pa an took Lugh away. Maybe I'll wake up soon. I'll tell everybody about it an we'll shake our heads about how strange dreams can be.

I feel a dull throb in my right hand. I look at it. There's a cloth wrapped around it, all filthy an torn. I prod it. A sharp pain shoots along my arm. Feels real enough.

Somebody's sayin somethin.

Saba? Emmi's voice. Saba?

Huh?

What about Procter John?

I look down. His body lies sprawled on the ground, his face twisted with pain. Guess he didn't die right off.

I told you he's the right one. I should know. I bin keepin an eye on him all this time like you told me to.

Leave him fer the vultures, I says.

The smell of burnin tires on the wind. My scalp prickles. Smells real enough.

I heave my barksack over my shoulder. I start walkin. I don't look back. I ain't ever comin back to this place agin.

Dead lake. Dead land. Dead life.

THE TRACKWAY

THERE'S ONLY ONE NARROW TRACK. IT GOES INTO AN OUTTA Silverlake. Otherwise, it's all open country around here. Low scrub, boulders an the ruins of one or two Wrecker buildins.

The trackway runs northeast. It also happens that Crosscreek, where I'm gonna leave Emmi with Mercy, lies three days due northeast of here. Mind you, that's three days by Pa's reckonin. It won't be three days fer Em's short legs. An she's a fearful slow walker.

C'mon, Emmi, I says. Let's see you step lively.

I stride out. After ten steps or so, I check over my shoulder to make sure she's keepin up. She's stopped. She's standin in the middle of the trackway. She's got her arms folded over her skinny bird chest. Her barksack's dumped in the mud beside her.

C'mon! I yell. She shakes her head. I curse an turn back. I git to her an says, What?

We shouldn't go, she says. She lifts her stubborn little pointed chin. I know that look. She's set to cause ructions.

Why not? I says.

We need to stay here, she says. If Lugh comes back an we ain't here, he'll be worried.

He ain't comin back, I says.

He'll git away from the men, she says, I know he will. An

he'll come back an we won't be here an he won't know where to start to lookin fer us or anythin.

Listen, I says, you didn't see 'em. I did. Four men took him. Tied him hand an foot an put him on the back of a horse. He ain't gonna git away on his own. That's why I'm goin after him. By myself. I promised him I'd find him an that's what I'm gonna do.

After you find him, she says, we'll come back here. Right?

I can see by her face that she knows we ain't ever comin back, but she's gonna make me say it.

This place ain't fit to live in, I says. You know that. We'll find us a new place to live. A better one. Me an Lugh an . . . you.

Her eyes fill with tears. But this is where we live, she says. It's our home.

I shake my head. Not no more, it ain't. It cain't be.

After a moment, she says, Saba?

What? I says.

I got a bad feelin. I don't think we should go. I . . . I'm afeared.

I open my mouth to tell her not to be so stupid, but stop myself before the words come out. I'm in charge of her now an I don't want her diggin her heels in every time I ask her to do somethin. I try to think what Lugh 'ud do if he was here. He'd probly tease her, coax her.

Whaddya mean, afeared? I put on a face like I'm surprised. How can you be afeared with me in charge?

She gives a little smile. Ain't you afeared?

46

She says it almost like she's shy of me.

Me? I says. Naw. I ain't afeared of nuthin. I ain't afeared of nobody.

Really? she says.

Really, I says. I hesitate. Then I stick out my hand. She puts hers in it. C'mon, I says. Let's go.

✝   ✝   ✝

We ain't gone more'n half a league before we come across hoofprints in the dried mud. Five horses. The riders come this way with Lugh.

I kneel down an trace around the edges of a print. I feel dizzy from relief. I feared they might of headed straight across open country from Silverlake.

If they had of, I'd of lost a lotta time takin Emmi to Crosscreek an then comin back to Silverlake to try an pick up the trail.

The hoofprints lead straight ahead. Northeast. Same direction we're headed. Our first bit of luck.

C'mon, I says to Em. We gotta hurry.

I don't give her no quarter. I walk quick, my footsteps jerky. No time to lose.

She trots to keep up with me, her barksack thumpin aginst her back. Nero flies on ahead.

Lugh was here. He passed this way.

Lugh goes first, always first, an I follow on behind. I'll catch him up. I always do. Always have.

I'll find you. Wherever they take you, I swear I'll find you.

I walk faster.

†   †   †

Mid-afternoon. Second day on the road.

I hafta stop myself from screamin. From walkin fast. Runnin on ahead.

Emmi.

We couldn't be goin much slower an it's all her fault.

I wanna leave her by the side of the track an ferget she ever got born. I wish she'd disappear offa the face of th'earth. But I cain't wish that. I mustn't wish that. It's too wicked. She's my own flesh an blood, the same as Lugh.

Not the same as Lugh.

Nobody's the same as Lugh.

Never the same as Lugh.

We leave a thin stand of near-dead pine trees.

The hoofprints leave the trackway here. They head off due north.

Wait here, I says to Emmi.

I follow the prints till the hard baked ground turns to scrubby grass. The prints disappear. I shade my eyes. Stare out. There's a narrow belt of scrub grassland but after that I cain't see nuthin but wideness. Flatness. Desert. I ain't never bin here but I know what it is.

Sandsea.

A mean, death-dry place of winds an shiftin sand dunes. A hard land. A land of secrets.

Before Emmi, when Ma was still alive an everythin was happy, Pa used to tell Lugh an me stories about Wrecker times. Some of 'em was about Sandsea. He told us about whole settlements of people buried by wanderin dunes. Then, one day, the winds 'ud shift an the dune 'ud move on an all that 'ud be left was the shanties. No people. All gone. Not a trace of 'em left behind, not even bones. Only their dead souls, turned into sand spirits that wail in the night an cry fer their lost lives. Pa used to say he'd take us there an leave us if we warn't good.

I pile up some rocks. A cairn to mark the spot so's I can find it agin.

I walk back to the trackway.

Em sits in the dust, her head bowed. She's took her boots off.

We gotta keep movin, I says.

I look down. At her short, fine brown hair that grows in tufts. With her thin little neck an wisps of hair, Emmi looks more like a babby bird than a girl.

It's a wonder I didn't break her neck when I slapped her. Jest thinkin about it makes me feel sick, so I try not to. I know fer a fact that Em ain't never in her life bin slapped before I raised my hand to her. Lugh would never of done it, no matter what. Never. He'd be madder'n hell if he knew what I done.

I crouch down beside her. What's the matter? I says.

Then I see her heels. They're cut to a bloody pulp. She ain't used to walkin so far. They must hurt like nobody's business, but she ain't made a peep.

Why didn't you tell me? I says.

I didn't want you to yell at me, she says.

I look at her, her face so small an thin. I hear Lugh's voice in my head.

She's only nine, Saba. You might try bein nice to her fer a change.

You should of said somethin, I says. I wash her cuts an wrap her feet in clean strips of cloth. All right, I says, put yer arms around my neck.

I pick her up. I carry her as much as I can fer the rest of the day, but even a scrawny nine year old gits heavy. I'm carryin our packs too so I hafta put her down from time to time. She ends up havin to walk a fair bit.

She weeps quietly in the night.

My heart pinches at the sound. I reach out an touch her arm but she flings my hand off an turns away.

I hate you! she cries. I wish they'd killed you instead of Pa!

After that, I pull my cloak over my head so's I cain't hear her cryin.

We gotta keep on.

I gotta find Lugh.

† † †

Third day. Dawn.

I clean Emmi's feet agin an we set off. She takes two tiny steps an falls to the ground. She won't be doin no walkin today. I guess I ain't surprised. I pick her up an lay her down on a grassy patch in some shade.

I run my hands through my hair. Glare at the sky. I wanna scream or run around or . . . anythin to git rid of all the tightness inside of me. I kick the ground so hard I stub my toe. I curse mightily.

I'm sorry, Saba, Emmi whispers.

I try to smile, make it look like I don't care, but I cain't manage it. I turn my head away from her.

It ain't yer fault, I says. I'll sort somethin out.

I spend the rest of the mornin makin a dragger. I cut two of the springiest, strongest tree branches I can find. I lay 'em out on the ground an brace 'em crosswise with smaller branches to make it good an sturdy fer Em to lie on. I lash it all together with nettlecord rope. Then I make a yoke to go over my shoulders an pad it with our spare tunics.

51

It's ready by the middle of the afternoon. I tie Emmi an our packs onto it. I swaddle my hands in cloth. The right one's still sore from bein shot, so I wrap it in a clean bandage first. I don't want it gittin worse.

Then I start pullin. The dragger bumps an thumps over the ground, but Emmi don't complain or whimper or cry. She don't make a sound.

The sun beats down. It's merciless. Cruel. It makes me think cruel thoughts. Like:

Why couldn't they of killed Emmi, instead of Pa?

Why couldn't they of took Emmi, instead of Lugh?

Emmi ain't no use to nobody. Never was. Never will be.

She's slowin me down. Makin me lose time.

My brain whispers. My heart whispers. My bones whisper.

Leave her . . . leave her . . . walk away an leave her. What . . . to die? Don't even think about it . . . she don't matter . . . what matters is Lugh . . . go back to the cairn . . . head out across Sandsea . . . that's the way they went . . . you could be there in a couple of hours if you walked fast. . .

I give myself a shake. Shut my ears to the whisperin. I cain't leave Emmi. I gotta take her to Crosscreek to stay with Mercy.

Lugh said I had to keep her safe. When I find him, I gotta be able to tell him that she's okay. That I looked after her as good as him.

As I pull the dragger behind me, I wonder where he is. If he's afeared. If he misses me like I miss him.

My missin him makes my whole body ache. It's like . . . emptiness. Emptiness that's beside me, inside me an around me, all the places where Lugh used to be. I ain't never bin without him. Not fer a single moment from the day we was born. From before we was born.

If they touch him, if they hurt him, I'll kill 'em. Even if they don't, I might kill 'em anyways, as punishment fer takin him.

My shoulders ache. My hurt hand throbs. The sun beats down. I grit my teeth an make myself go faster.

Why don't Emmi cry? Why don't she whine?

I wish she would. Then I could yell at her.

Then I could hate her.

I push the mean thoughts away, deep inside to the darkest places of me, where nobody can see.

An Emmi don't cry. Not even once.

✝   ✝   ✝

Fifth day. Midnight.

We lie on the ground, in a hollow beside the trackway. We're wrapped in our dogskin cloaks. Emmi's tucked herself into one side of me. Nero's huddled on th'other side, fast to sleep, his head tucked unner his wing.

It's a warm spring night. A soft breeze lifts the hair on my forehead. In the distance, a wolfdog howls an another answers. They're a long ways off. Naught to worry about.

I stare up at the sky. At the thousands an millions of stars that crowd the night. I look fer the Great Bear. The Little Bear. The Dragon. The North Star.

I think about Pa. About what he told us. That our destiny, the story of our lives is written in the stars. An that he knew how to read 'em.

An then I think about what Lugh said.

Ain't you figgered it out yet? It's all in his head. There ain't nuthin written in the stars. There ain't no great plan. The world goes on. Our lives jest go on . . . in this gawdfersaken place. An that's it. Till the day we die.

I think of Pa layin out his stick circles an doin his spells an his chants, tryin to make the rain come. How he kept sayin he read it in the stars, that the stars said the rain was comin an how the rain never did come.

Well, not till after Pa was dead. Not till it was too late. That means eether Pa was readin the stars wrong or the stars was tellin him lies.

Or maybe the truth is this. That Pa couldn't read the stars becuz there ain't nuthin there to read. An all his spells an chants was jest him bein so desperate fer rain that he'd try any old thing, no matter how crazy.

I used to like lookin at the night sky. Liked to think how

one day Pa might teach me to read what the stars had to say. Now they jest look cold an far away.

I shiver.

I reckon Lugh's right. He always is.

There ain't nuthin written in the stars.

They're jest lights in the sky. To show you the way in the dark.

†　†　†

But.

But.

Pa knew about the men. Knew they'd come fer Lugh. Before I told him.

Are they here? Have they come?

They cain't be stopped, Saba. It's begun.

An he knew he was gonna die. Knew his story was about to end.

My time's nearly up. I dunno what happens after this.

If Pa couldn't read the stars, if the stars ain't got nuthin to say, how did he know all that?

How did he know?

CROSSCREEK

Sixth day. Late afternoon.

A breeze whispers by an, somewhere above my head, there's a flurry of dry clicks. I stop. I look up. Three deer-bones hung together, high in a tree.

I hear Pa's voice in my head.

After three days, the trackway'll take you through a deep pine forest. Keep yer eyes peeled. When you see the windchimes in the tree you know you reached Crosscreek.

Without the breeze, I would of missed 'em. I lick my parched lips. Emmi, I says. The windchimes. We're here.

I ain't never bin so glad to be anywhere in my life. Since yesterday noon, every waterhole an every streamlet along the way's eether bin dry or a deathwater covered in slimy yellow bloom. An we had our last meal yesterday mornin. We couldn't of gone on much longer.

Is this Crosscreek? says Emmi.

I set down the dragger fer the last time.

I close my eyes, stand there fer a moment. My body's so sore an stiff an bone-tired I wish I never had to move it agin.

I try to flex my fingers but they stay bent. They bin curled round the damn shafts so long they'll probly stay like this till the day I die. I never thought I'd be haulin Emmi an the packs fer three days. An Em's covered in bruises from head to toe, so she ain't ezzackly got off light.

I unstrap her from the dragger an help her to stand. I go to pick her up but she says, No. I'm gonna walk.

You sure? I says. She nods. I shoulder our barksacks. Shove the dragger deep into the bushes where it cain't be seen.

Leave the track. Follow the trail down the hill into the dell.

It ain't hardly what I call a trail. If you didn't know it was here, you'd never know it was. We weave our way through the trees. Pine needles soften our way, give off their warm scent as we crush 'em unnerfoot. Nero flits from branch to branch over our heads. He caws, all excited, tellin us to hurry.

The ground starts to slope down. It gits steeper. Then steeper still. The goin gits harder with the pine needles makin it all slippy. I take hold of Emmi's hand so she don't fall. We gotta slide on our bums some times an other times go down sidewise. We go on an on.

Then. Cookin smells tickle my nose. Meat. My mouth waters.

Is that stew? says Emmi.

I sure hope so, I says.

At last we're at the bottom of the hill. We step outta the forest into the open an we're in another world.

A shaggy haired pony grazes nearby in a patch of sweet green grass. He lifts his head to look at us fer a moment, then goes back to his meal.

We're in the dell that Pa told us about, at the bottom of a small river valley. Straight ahead of us, the land rises in a gentle slope. Two streams trickle down from the top. Near the bottom, they join to make one narrow little stream. Crosscreek. It winds an sparkles its way along the valley floor.

There's a flat bridge spans the creek an there, on the far bank, shaded by pine trees, sits a small wooden shack. Mercy's cabin. A red bench stands next to the open door. A cookin pot hangs over a fire.

There ain't no sound but the soft murmur of shallow water over stones. It's like the whole place is sleepin, quiet as a cat in the afternoon sun.

I ain't never seen such a place. Never even imagined there could be somewhere like it on this earth. Tears spring to my eyes. Pa never said it was like this. He never told us.

But he knew this place was here. He knew an he kept us by a dyin lake all these years, with food gittin scarcer an life gittin harder an all this only a few days' walk. I don't unnerstand. Why didn't he bring us here? I guess Lugh was right. Pa didn't care about us, didn't care about what happened to none of us.

I move like I'm in a dream, walkin slowly.

If Mercy ain't there, sit on the red bench by the door an listen to the creek while you wait. She won't be long. She ain't never far away.

I cross the bridge, drop the barksacks. I unlace my boots an kick 'em off. I walk into the creek. It's ankle deep. I kneel an scoop up some water. Clean. Cool. Beautiful. I drink. I splash it over my face, my neck, my head.

Then I lie down. I lie on my back an let the water flow around me.

I close my eyes.

†   †   †

It ain't every day I find somebody asleep in my creek, the voice says.

I open my eyes. A face hangin above me. The wrong way around. I blink. I feel slow. Stupid. Must of fell to sleep fer a second or two.

Are you upside down, I says, or is it me?

I guess that depends on your point of view.

A hairy dog face lunges at me. A long pink tongue slops at my face.

Hey! I says.

Tracker! Down, boy! A strong hand reaches out. I take it an it pulls me to my feet. As I stand, water pours offa my hair, my clothes.

It's a woman. Standin in the stream. Tall. Lean. Tanned. Lined face with shrewd brown eyes. Sharp cheekbones.

White hair cropped close to her head. Nine year ago, it was nut brown an shiny an down to her knees. A blue-eyed wolf-dog with one droopy ear leans aginst her side.

I nearly missed the windchimes, I says. You sure do make it hard to find you.

I like to keep the riff raff away, she says.

She touches a finger to my birthmoon tattoo.

Saba by Silverlake. Her mouth crooks up at one corner. You've grown some since I last saw you. I'm Mercy.

†   †   †

A bit more, Emmi? says Mercy.

Mmuh huh! Emmi shovels a last spoonful into her mouth that's already full. She holds her bowl out.

Didn't your pa ever teach you manners? says Mercy.

Emmi, I frown at her. Yer s'posed to say please.

Emmi chews, gulps, chews some more. Oh, she mumbles. Yes please. More please.

She eats like a jackal, I says. Pa let her run wild.

Child's on the skinny side of scrawny, says Mercy. An if you don't mind my sayin, you could do with a bit more meat on you too. Times tough at Silverlake?

I frown. No, I says.

63

You like a bit more to eat yourself?

I shove my empty bowl at her. She looks at me with one raised eyebrow.

Uh . . . yes please, I says.

We're sat outside to eat. Me an Mercy on the red bench, Emmi on the front step. Nero gobbled his lot down an now he's perched on the cabin roof, havin a good preen.

Bring your bowls, says Mercy. I ain't no servant.

She limps over to the cookin fire an Em an me follow behind with our bowls. She gives the pot a stir an ladles out seconds of the rabbit an root stew. I follow her back to the bench, stuffin mine down as I go. We sit an I nod at her foot.

What'd you do there? I says, my mouth full.

Broke my ankle, oh . . . over a year ago now. Had to set it myself of course an did a bugger of a job . . . well . . . as you can see.

How d'you manage by yerself?

She shrugs. I just do. Ain't got no choice.

Must be hard, I says. Yer pretty old.

She gives me a hard look. An you're pretty rude, she says. Anybody ever tell you that?

I feel myself flush red. Go all skin prickly.

I tell her all the time, says Emmi. But she don't pay no notice. Lugh's the nice one. You'd like him.

Shut yer trap, Em, I says. Look. We came here . . . we didn't jest come to tell you about Pa an Lugh.

I didn't think you did, says Mercy.

There's a basin of clean water between us. She pours in a tincture from a little brown glass bottle, dips a cloth in an starts cleanin my sore hand.

I'm goin after Lugh, I says. I'm gonna git him back. I aim to set off in the mornin. I'm gonna leave Emmi here with you.

I see, she says. Looks at me. Like she's waitin fer more.

Pa always said if anythin ever happened to him, we should come to you, I says.

Oh he did, did he? Mercy shakes her head. I don't know about that.... Tracker an me's set in our ways. We ain't used to company.

But you was Ma's friend, I says. Please, Mercy. Yer th'only one can help.

She don't answer fer a long moment. Then she sighs. She'll have to work for her keep, she says.

She'll work, I says.

An what does she have to say about it? says Mercy. Emmi?

Emmi don't say naught. She crouches over her bowl, her head down, eatin slowly. I know she's listenin.

Stop playin deaf, Emmi, I says. Mercy says are you happy to stay here an help her out while I go find Lugh?

Emmi lifts a blank face. Shrugs. She drops her head over her bowl agin.

I shake my head. She'll come round, I says.

I hope so, says Mercy.

She won't give you no trouble, I says. I promise.

† † †

What was our ma like? says Emmi.

Tracker's got his head laid in Mercy's lap. She rubs behind his ears an his eyes close in bliss. Nero dozes, huddled on my shoulder.

Of course, Mercy says, you never knew her. But Saba must remember.

Not so much, I says. Not no more. It's like . . . she's faded.

She laughed more'n anyone I ever met, says Mercy. There ain't a lot to laugh about in this life, but Allis always found somethin. I think that's why Willem, why your pa, loved her so.

Lugh's like that, I says. He takes after Ma. Pa never laughed after Ma died. Not that I can remember anyways.

No, says Mercy. I don't suppose he did.

We're quiet fer a bit. Then, It's my fault she's dead, says Emmi. She's bin drawin in the dirt with a stick an now she pushes at it hard. It snaps in half.

Mercy looks at me with her keen eyes. I look away.

Well, childbirth's a dangerous thing, says Mercy. An you

arrived a month early. I'll tell you somethin, sometimes I think it was my fault.

Yer fault? says Emmi, lookin surprised.

Yes, says Mercy. I was all set to come an help. It was planned. I was gonna be there two weeks before you was due an help with the birthin, just like I did with Saba an Lugh. Sometimes I think, if only I'd come earlier, if only I'd been there, maybe Allis would have lived. But you cain't think like that. If you do, you'll make yourself crazy. I did get there in time to help keep you alive, red little scrap that you were, an I comfort myself with that. With the thought that Allis might be gone, but her daughter lives. I see her in you.

You do? says Em, her eyes wide.

I most surely do. Except for the eyes, you favor your pa, but you're like her here. An here. Mercy touches her heart, then her head. I can see it. Would you like to know somethin else?

Yes, says Emmi.

Your ma wanted you so much, says Mercy. She couldn't of been happier when she found out you was comin . . . her an your pa.

I never knew that, whispers Em.

Well, says Mercy, now you do. An I know she'd be proud that you turned out so fine.

Emmi looks at me an then quickly looks down at the ground agin.

I always blamed Emmi fer the fact that Ma's dead. I never made no secret of it. Now, hearin what Mercy says, I start to think about the fact that nobody asks to be born into this world. An nobody can stop theirselves bein born. Not even Emmi.

Babies keep their own time, says Mercy. She takes Emmi's hand. It ain't no one's fault your ma died. There ain't no one to blame.

Pa said it was writ in the stars, says Emmi.

Oh child, says Mercy, there ain't no plan written in the sky. Some people just die too soon.

But Pa was a star reader, I says. He always told us how everythin was set in the stars the moment the world began. The story of everybody's life is right up there.

That's where Willem an me fell out, she says. Why we didn't all stick together when we left Hopetown. He looked to the sky for answers. I look at what's in front of me, what's around me, what's inside of me.

Lugh thinks it's all jest somethin Pa made up in his head, I says.

What do you think? she says.

Saba always thinks what Lugh tells her to, says Emmi.

I do not! I says.

Yes you do, she says.

Well, says Mercy, maybe it's time you started makin up your own mind about things. As far as I'm concerned, stars is just . . . stars.

She tips her head back. She stares at the sky so long, it's almost like she's up there with the stars an the moon an the planets, like she's fergot we're here. I clear my throat. She gives a start. Smiles at us.

Of course, she says, there's always a chance I could be wrong.

† † †

It took ages to git Emmi to lie down inside on Mercy's cot, even though she was pretty much to sleep on her feet. Mercy's laid on the red bench, her arms behind her head. Tracker's stretched out nearby.

I sit by the fire. Poke at the embers with the toe of my boot.

Why didn't Pa bring us here? I says. I keep my voice low, so's Emmi don't wake.

Mercy says, So things was bad at Silverlake.

Yeah, I says. An gittin worse all the time.

I asked him to come, she says. After Allis died. I might not be the most sociable person, but I'd never turn away a friend in need. There would of been room here for all of you. We could of rubbed along all right. But he wouldn't hear of it. Told me he didn't want my help.

I says, Lugh thinks he wouldn't leave Silverlake becuz of Ma.

Mercy sighs. That's partly true, she says. But there was more to it than that. He thought you'd be safe there. They both did.

Safe? I says. Safe from what?

Mercy says naught fer a moment, thinkin.

You know nuthin of the world, she says at last. It's a hard place. A dangerous place. Your ma an pa knew somethin of it. Enough to make em settle so far out of the way at Silverlake. Not many passersby. No neighbors. Like here at Crosscreek.

I think about how hidden away Mercy is here. No trail from the trackway, no way of knowin where to turn off if you didn't know about the windchimes high in the tree.

Are you . . . hidin from somebody, Mercy? I says.

I wouldn't say hidin, she says. More like . . . keepin out of the way.

I frown. Outta the way of what? Is that why Pa kept us at Silverlake? To keep us outta the way?

He meant to, says Mercy. It didn't turn out that way, though, did it?

Somethin in her voice, in the way she says it makes me go all still inside. I stand up, my fists clenched. D'you know somethin? I says. About who took Lugh?

I don't know, she says. I . . .

Tell me!

She glances at the cabin where Emmi lies sleepin. Let's walk, she says.

†   †   †

Tracker starts to git up. Mercy raises a hand. Stay boy, she says an he lays hisself back down with a sigh.

I follow her over the bridge an into the meadow. We keep to the creek bank an head on up the little valley. The moon lights us a silver path. The creek sparkles an murmurs over the stones. I breathe in the sharp, sweet air of the night.

Tell me what happened that day, Mercy says. Tell me everythin. Don't leave anythin out, no matter if you think it's important or not.

So I do. I tell her what happened that day. From Lugh an me goin to the landfill at dawn to Lugh shoutin at Pa an then the duststorm an the four horsemen showin up with Procter John.

Four of 'em, she says. Dressed how?

In long black robes, I says, with . . . like, heavy leather vests over top, an leather bands from their wrists to their elbows.

Body armor, she says. It sounds like the Tonton.

The . . . what? I says.

The Tonton, she says. They're . . . well . . . they're all kinds of things—couriers, spies, informers, bodyguards. Sometimes even executioners.

What? I says. I dunno what yer talkin about. How d'you know about these . . . Tonton?

Your ma an pa wasn't always at Silverlake, Saba. An I wasn't always here at Crosscreek. We came to know each other at a place called Hopetown.

I ain't never heard of it, I says.

It's a town, she says. If you're lucky, a week's hard walkin'll get you there. That's if you're lucky. You have to cross Sandsea an it don't welcome nobody.

Sandsea, I says. Pa used to tell us stories about it. The men . . . the Tonton . . . headed across there with Lugh. Their prints turned north off the trackway. D'you think they took him to Hopetown?

They might have done, she says. Hopetown's where the scum of the earth wash up. Every robber, every cheat, every lowlife who'd stab you for lookin at him the wrong way . . . they all find their way there eventually. It's run by bad people for their own ends. An they got the Tonton to keep all the scum in check. They control the place with violence an somethin called chaal.

That's them leafs Procter John used to chew, I says. Pa told us never to touch it.

He was right, she says. Chaal slows you down. Makes you

think you're smart when you ain't. Too much of it an you get all hopped up, go wild. Allis an Willem an me, we weren't there for long. We saw what the place was like an got outta there before it could suck us under. We got as far away as we could. We never wanted to hear of chaal or Hopetown again.

But why would the . . . Tonton take Lugh? I says.

Tell me more about that day, she says.

They came lookin fer him, I says. One of 'em said to Procter John, "Is this him? Is he the one born at midwinter?" Then they asked Lugh the same thing an they checked that he was eighteen. Procter John says to 'em, "I told you he was the right one." So . . . they knew all about Lugh. They came to find him.

Mercy don't say naught. Jest stares up at the night sky.

But how could they know about him? I says. An what's so important about him bein midwinter born? We're twins. Why didn't they take me too?

I don't know, she says. But let's think it through.

We're both quiet fer a bit. Then she says, Maybe they didn't want a girl. Maybe they wanted a boy. A boy born at midwinter eighteen year ago.

But why? I says. An how did they know where to find him? Like you said, Silverlake's nowhere. Besides you an us, nobody's ever bin there essept the rag man an Procter John. Pa told us so.

Your father lied, says Mercy.

Pa lied? I says.

Maybe that ain't fair, she says. Maybe lied's the wrong word. Maybe he just . . . didn't remember.

All right, I says. So?

You know I was there when your ma birthed you an Lugh.

Uh huh, I says.

Well . . . I wasn't th'only one.

Somebody else was there? Who?

A man, she says. A stranger. He stopped at Silverlake, two days before you was born. Didn't say much. Didn't say where he was from or where he was headed. An he sure didn't have nuthin. He was half-starved, with barely even a shirt on his back. Said his name was Trask, but who knows if that was true? Willem was wary of him, but he seemed harmless enough so they fed him an even gave him some of Willem's old clothes.

An he was there when we was born, I says.

Not you, she says. He'd left by then. You was born two hours after Lugh, remember. It was odd. There was Lugh, yellin an kickin to let us know he'd arrived in the world, an right away, Trask got all excited. He kept sayin a boy born at midwinter's a rare thing, a wonderful thing. An he went on repeatin it. Like it was important somehow. Then, when

I looked for him a little while later, he was gone. Didn't even say g'bye. Funny, but I'd forgot about him till now.

Why didn't Pa tell us? I says.

Maybe he forgot, she says, like me. It didn't seem terribly important. We thought he was just some crazy travelin man.

So d'you think Trask's one of the men who took Lugh? I says. One of the Tonton?

Oh no, he'd be too old. The Tonton are men in their prime. Trask must of had at least forty year on him an that was eighteen year ago.

He must of told somebody else about Lugh, I says.

It seems that way, she says. What about your neighbor?

Procter John? I frown. I got somethin dancin at the edges of my mind, somethin I cain't quite git hold of. Then, Now I remember! I says. He said somethin strange . . . he said to the men, I should know how old he is, I bin keepin a eye on him all this time like you told me to.

Mercy lets out a long breath. A spy, she says. The Tonton had him watchin over Lugh. Probly kept him in line with chaal an threats.

So Trask must of told the Tonton, I says. But I don't unnerstand why it had to be Lugh they took. Why they waited till he was eighteen.

I don't understand it myself, she says. But if you find that out, you may well find your brother.

†　†　†

Dawn's breakin as I step outside the cabin.

I wish you'd let me give you more, says Mercy. A bit of jerky an dried yam ain't gonna last you longer'n a few days.

Yer stores ain't ezzackly overflowin, I says. An, thanks to us, you got two mouths to feed now.

I'll take care of the child just fine, she says.

An I'll take care of myself, I says. I got plenty of water. As fer the rest—I pat my bow—I got this.

If you're sure, she says.

Don't worry.

Mercy puts her arm around Emmi. What say we walk Saba across the meadow? See her on her way?

Emmi shrugs. Picks at her peg doll's dress. If you like, she says.

I know I ain't Em's favorite person, leavin her here with Mercy, but at least she don't seem so hostile today. Any road, she'll git used to it soon enough. An she'll be safe here with Mercy an Tracker. Might even have a bit of fun fer once, ridin the pony an splashin around in the creek. A child oughta have a bit of fun.

They walk me across the bridge. Nero flies on ahead, chased by Tracker. The long meadow grass swishes aginst our legs.

I stop. I turn back. Take a last look at this peaceful green valley with its clear water an sweet air. My chest's gone all tight. Tears spring to my eyes. I cain't do it. I won't be able to find him. I cain't do it alone.

Saba? Mercy touches me gently on the arm.

I suck in a couple of deep breaths. I curse my own weakness. Swipe at my eyes. Lugh's countin on me. Only me.

They're gonna need you, Saba. Lugh an Emmi. An there'll be others too. Many others. Don't give in to fear. Be strong, like I know you are.

I ain't no quitter, Pa.

What is it, Saba? Emmi says.

I turn around. Nuthin, I says.

I got somethin to give you, says Mercy. Hold out your hand.

I do. She puts somethin in it an closes my fingers round it.

What is it? says Emmi.

I open my hand. A rosy pink stone nestles there. Smooth, shaped like a bird's egg, about the length of my thumb. It feels cool. Cold even. It's threaded on a leather thong to wear around the neck. I hold it up an the light gleams through it, milky an dull.

It's pretty, says Emmi.

It's a heartstone, says Mercy. She lifts it over my head. Your mother gave it to me, an now I'm givin it to you.

I touch it. A gift from my mother. I ain't never had nuthin that belonged to her.

What's a heartstone? says Emmi.

It lets you know when you've found your heart's desire, says Mercy.

How does it do that? Emmi frowns.

D'you feel how cold it is now? Even though it's next to Saba's skin?

Uh huh, she says, touchin it.

A normal stone 'ud warm up next to your body. Not this one. It stays cold until you get close to your heart's desire. Then the stone becomes warm. The closer you get to your heart's desire, the hotter the stone burns. An that's how you know.

I frown. I didn't think you'd believe in that kinda thing, I says.

I don't, says Mercy, not really, but your mother did. She said it showed her the way to Willem, to your father. So she gave it to me. Said she hoped it would show me my own heart's desire.

An did it? I says.

Well, says Mercy, I found this valley. I guess you could say it's my heart's desire.

But did the heartstone turn warm? I says.

Mercy don't answer fer a moment. Then she says, It's a long time ago now. I don't remember.

I look at her. I cain't tell if she's lyin or not.

Why're you givin it to Saba? says Emmi.

Allis always said you don't own a heartstone, says Mercy, you just become its keeper for a time. Once you have your heart's desire, you pass it on to someone else. Someone who needs its help.

I don't need no help, I says. I already know what my heart's desire is. It's to find Lugh an git him back.

I'm sure you're right, says Mercy. Anyways, whether you believe it or not, it's nice for you to have somethin that belonged to your mother. That meant somethin to her.

Thanks, I says. I mean, fer this an . . . well, everythin. I better git goin.

When you get to Hopetown, don't start askin questions, she says. You'll only draw attention to yourself an that means trouble. Be on your guard. Don't trust anybody.

I can take care of myself, I says.

An Saba . . . take care crossin Sandsea. It's one of the wild places. Listen to the winds. She hugs me fiercely. I wish you'd take my advice an travel by night.

I look at Em. She stares at the ground.

We'll be back before you know it, I says. Me an Lugh.

I reach out to mess her hair an she ducks away.

Well, I says. Best be on my way.

I pick up my barksack an start walkin. I ain't gone more'n ten paces before I hear, Saba!

Emmi runs up an flings her arms around my waist, clings on tight. Hurry back! she says.

You be a good girl fer Mercy, I says. I'm countin on you.

I step away.

Bye, Em, I says.

G'bye, Saba, she says.

When I reach the woods, the second I'm outta sight, I take the heartstone from around my neck an stuff it in my pocket.

I know what my heart's desire is.

I don't need no stone to tell me when I've found it.

SANDSEA

ANOTHER DAWN.

I bin travelin fast. Almost runnin at times. Since I left Crosscreek yesterday mornin, I bin so anxious to make up fer lost time that I kept goin all day an all through last night, only stoppin to sleep fer a couple hours. I don't feel tired. Not at all. I wish I never had to sleep agin. Not till I find Lugh anyways.

Here's my cairn. The marker I left to remind me where the hoofprints end. My heart lifts. Deep down inside, I was afeared it wouldn't be here. That I'd only dreamed I left it here to guide me.

The hoofprints is still here. The last trace of Lugh. If no rain comes to wash 'em away, it'll be a long time till the wind wears 'em down an they disappear. Maybe they'll still be here when I come back with him.

I dump my stuff on the ground—barksack, crossbow, quiver. Nero's bin flyin the last little while, swoopin an divin at me fer fun. Now he flaps down to have a rest on top of the gear.

I ease my shoulders while I uncap my waterskin an take a long swig. I pour some in my hands an wash the dust from my hot face. Wipe it dry with the ends of my sheema. I pour a little water in my eatin tin an put it on the ground fer Nero.

I look out across the wide open desert. Sandsea. It stretches ahead as far as I can see. No trees, no hills, nuthin but flat dry land fer days. The moment I step past this pile of rocks, I'm in a unknown world. Hopetown lies due north, at the foot of the Black Mountains accordin to Mercy. If I'm lucky, I'll be there in a week. A week, she said. If I'm lucky.

Before I know what it's up to, my hand slides into my pocket. It finds the heartstone an pulls it out. My fingers curl around its coolness, rub its smoothness.

My heart's desire. As if a bit of rock could tell me that. I shake my head. If Lugh was here, him an me 'ud laugh about it. I shove it deep in my pocket an swing my gear onto my back.

Let's go, I says to Nero.

I step past the cairn.

One step closer to Lugh.

I don't look back.

✝ ✝ ✝

It's a Wrecker settlement. Jest like the places in Pa's scare stories.

Settlements swallowed by wanderin sand dunes, great waves of sand that 'ud cover places in minutes. Then, months or sometimes years later, the sands 'ud move on, an the place 'ud still be there.

There's twelve metal shanties still standin here. Also a couple of rusty cars, a wind pointer an some other crappy lookin Wrecker junk piled up. A dry, mean, pinched kinda place. But it ain't none of it bin scavenged. If it had of, there'd be no doors or walls or anythin left on the shanties an they're all still here, jest bent an twisted, probly by the weight of the sand.

No scavengers means it ain't bin free of the sands fer long. Strange to think that if I'd passed here last week or yesterday or even a couple of hours ago, this might all still be buried outta sight. I could of walked right over it an never known.

I walk through slowly, Nero ridin on my shoulder. I keep a eye open. You always gotta keep a eye open. You never know when you'll come across somethin you can use. But I ain't inclined to take nuthin away from this place. It creeps me out.

There's a well. Water's probly bad, it mostly is in these old Wrecker wells, but in desertland you cain't afford not to check it out. I start to lift the rusted cover when I see the faint markins on it. Skull an crossbones. Deathwater. I drop the cover with a clatter. It sounds so loud in the silence it makes me jump. Nero flaps off in a panic.

Then I see 'em. Three rows of crosses stuck in the sand. The wood bleached silver by the sun, worn away, some to little stumps. The crosspiece of one hangs down, ready to fall.

A wily wind sweeps through, bent on makin mischief. It swirls sand around my feet, tosses it in my eyes an makes 'em sting. It moans, deep inside the well. Rattles at the doors of the shanties. Like somebody might open up an invite it in.

The loose crosspiece lifts on the wind. Drops silently to the ground. Blows away.

Deathwater. Shiftin sands.

Poor bastards.

Livin here.

Dyin here.

As I'm leavin the settlement, Nero swoops down at somethin on the ground. Starts to make the most almighty racket, shriekin an squawkin an flappin all over the place. I hurry over to see what's causin such a fuss.

What is it now, you crazy bird? I says.

He's got a little ring of smooth green glass in his beak. My heart stops.

Ohmigawd, I says. I drop to my knees beside him. Hold out my hand. He places the ring on it. Gently.

It's Lugh's. From the necklace I made him fer our birthday. It's still threaded onto a short piece of the leather thong, snapped at both ends. He must of yanked it from his neck when they warn't lookin.

Nero croaks.

I know, I says. He's leavin a trail fer us to follow.

I'll find you. Wherever they take you, I swear I'll find you.

You cain't, it's too dangerous. You gotta keep yerself safe. You an Emmi. Promise me you will.

He knows me. He knew I'd come after him.

We're on the right track, I says. I scoop Nero into my arms an kiss his head. He smells of dusty warm feathers. Yer the smartest bird ever lived. You know that, don't you?

He gives the little chuck chuck chuck that means he's pleased with hisself. Then he squirms fer me to let him go. Nero ain't much of a one fer huggin an such.

The wind starts howlin at me to move on, liftin up handfuls of desert an throwin it at my face.

Time to move, I says.

When I've gone half a league or so, I turn an look back.

The settlement's gone. Vanished.

Swallowed by the sands once more.

† † †

I see the tabletop plateau in the far distance around mid mornin. Dusty red rock, high an bare of trees. From the top of it, there should be a clear view in every direction. Maybe I'll even be able to see Hopetown an the Black Mountains from there.

Nero flies to the top of the plateau an down agin, tryin to hurry me along. He cain't ever believe how slow I am, how long it takes me to git places. I think he feels sorry fer me with my two legs.

I reach the plateau as the day starts to wane. I start to make my way to the top, weavin my way around rocks an over scree. Nero goes on ahead, hoppin from rock to rock nice an easy, then comin back to croak an caw at me to hurry along.

Show off, I says to him.

I pull myself the last bit an flop on my belly onto the top. I git my breath, then stand up. It's narrower than I thought it 'ud be, no more'n fifty paces across at the widest point.

I'm on th'other side in no time. I gasp.

As far as the eye can see, to the horizon an beyond, it's sand. Great crests of it, great sweeps of golden sand carved into waves an hills an peaks an valleys. Smooth on one side, ridged on th'other side. Vast. Endless.

No sign of any town. No sign of any mountains.

I cain't believe it. I thought I'd bin crossin Sandsea fer two days. But what I jest done was nuthin. That was only the beginnin. Here. Now. This is where the crossin starts.

My heart sinks into my boots. My belly clenches. I lick my dry lips.

Nero flutters down an lands on my shoulder.

It's big, I says. Whaddya think?

He croaks an bobs up an down.

No problem, eh? Easy fer you to say. I look out over Sandsea agin. It's too big, I says. Too damn big.

Don't give in to fear, Saba. Be strong, like I know you are.

I ain't no quitter, Pa.

If I'm careful, what water an food I got should last me another three days. After that, I got my bow an my wits.

Nero launches hisself over the edge of the plateau. He soars above the desert floor an caws, impatient fer me to git movin.

Okay, I says. I'm comin. You better be right about this.

An I start down.

✝   ✝   ✝

Dusk. I'll need to stop soon to make camp fer the night.

All of a sudden, the wind picks up. It comes outta nowhere, wailin an moanin. It plucks at the sand on the top of a nearby dune an flings it away. What was it Mercy said?

Take care crossin Sandsea. It's one of the wild places. Listen to the winds.

I take another step up the dune I'm climbin. I stop. Look around me. All around, the dunes is startin to shift, change shape.

Holy crap, I says. I wrap my sheema good an tight around my nose an mouth.

The wind's growin stronger. Bolder. It tugs at me, tries to pull me over. It wants me. Sand flies in my eyes, stings 'em. My cloak whips around my legs an snaps in the wind.

Nero! I yell. Nero! Where are you! The words git torn from my lips.

Nero swoops an dives, cawin frantically. I scream over the roar of the wind. Git outta here! I flap my hands at him. Go on! I'll be okay!

He disappears.

The world howls its rage around me. It's too big. I'm too small. The sand unner my feet starts to slide, starts to shift— like it don't want me on it no more.

Panic claws at my throat. My eyes is gritty. The sand's blindin me. It'll make me blind. Do somethin. Quick. I pull my sheema down over my eyes. Now I cain't see a thing.

What should I do? What do I do?

Feel the way. Go down. An git buried alive? Keep goin then, keep goin! An git swept away?

What should I do? What do I do?

The sand dune collapses unner me. An that's it. No choice. I'm swept away.

†   †   †

Dark.

Hot.

Cain't breathe. Oh gawd, I cain't breathe.

Weight. On my chest.

I'm movin. Slidin. Cain't stop. Cain't stop.

Cain't-breathe-must-breathe-must-breathe-cain't-breathe-cain't—

I'm out. I'm thrown outta the sand.

I fly through the air face first an thump down, land hard on the ground. I gasp. I breathe. I cough. I roll to my side an yank my sheema down. I cough an cough an take in great, deep gulps of air. I breathe it in, drink it in, I cain't git enough.

Then I grab my waterskin, rinse my mouth, spit out the sand.

After a bit, I start to calm down. I lie there, starin up at the pink dusky sky. I cain't believe I'm alive.

Then I realize. I'm lookin at the sky. I can see the sky. The first faint twinkle of stars. I ain't breathin in sand no more. The wind's gone. It must of left as quick as it came.

Slowly I stand, pull myself to my feet. I brush myself down, make sure I still got all my gear. Then I look.

I'm on a wide flat plain. The sand dunes is gone. Not a trace of 'em left. Like they was never there. Like I dreamed 'em.

An standin all around me is flyin machines.

† † †

Flyin machines. Flyers.

Hidden away. Sleepin unner the wanderin dunes of Sandsea fer who knows how long. Could of bin fer any amount of time—a day, a week, a year. Maybe even hunnerds of years. Maybe ever since they was left here by the Wreckers.

They're all laid out in neat rows on the sand. Like somebody planted 'em, thinkin they might grow.

They stretch out, on an on across the plain. So many rows, so many flyin machines that I couldn't even begin to count.

I walk in between 'em.

They're all sizes. Big, small an everythin in between. They stand quiet, patient, like they're waitin fer somethin.

They're all rusted, with their glass windows smashed an their tires slashed an their bodies cut up to be took away by salvagers. The holes in their sides gape open like wounds.

A flyin machine graveyard.

I know about flyers. I even seen parts of 'em before.

Once Pa brought home a curved metal sheet he picked outta the landfill that he said was most likely part of a flyer. He used it to mend our roof. But the funny thing was, not two days later a big hotwind blasted through Silverlake an that sheet jest lifted up an flew away. Like it couldn't wait to git outta there. The rest of the roof stayed put, jest that one bit went. Pa said that proved fer sure it was from a flyer.

I stand in front of one of the biggest ones. I stretch myself to my full height an go up on my toes, but I still cain't reach it.

Nero appears in the darkenin sky above me. He lands on my head, flappin his wings.

Hey Nero. I bring him down to sit on my hand. I rub his head as I walk among the sleepin metal giants. D'you think Lugh came this way? D'you think he seen these? He'd like to see a entire one close to, that's fer sure.

I come to a small one, more human-sized. I touch the metal with its faded paint. It feels cool. Buried in sand with no sun to warm its skin.

I put my hand on the door. If I'm respeckful, I cain't see how it 'ud do no harm.

Be good now, I says to Nero. Don't you go peckin at things.

The door creaks. Sand pours out as I pull it open an climb inside. I brush the seat clear, slide onto it an look out where the window used to be. I wonder what the world was like when this flyer was new made, so long ago. What it would of bin like to fly in one.

When Lugh an me was nippers, Pa told us all about how the Wreckers used to go up in the sky in their flyers. They'd soar an swoop all over the place, pretendin to be birds. Sometimes, he said, there'd be hunnerds of Wreckers all piled into one big one an they'd fly around together.

Me an Lugh thought that was the craziest thing we ever heard. We didn't believe him. An when we asked Pa why they did it, he said he didn't rightly know, they jest did, that's all.

We figgered fer definite he was tellin tall tales. But now I seen one fer myself . . . well, I dunno. Maybe it could be true.

The night's drawin in. There ain't no wind at all now. Not even a whisper. I feel so weary. My eyelids is so heavy, I cain't hardly keep 'em open. I slide down in the seat. Nero huddles on my chest an snugs hisself unner my chin. I might jest catch a little shut eye before I go on. Not fer long.

Jest a few minutes.

Jest a—

† † †

A sound.

I'm awake. Right away. Muscles tense. Ready to move.

Nero opens one eye. I hold a finger to my lips. He knows what that means.

There it is agin. Somethin movin. Outside. Then a snort. A horse. One that ain't sure of itself, one that's feelin a bit nervy.

I set Nero down on the floor. Then I roll outta my seat an crawl towards the back end of the flyer where there's a part of it missin. I slip outside. I land in a crouch on the ground, scramble to hide behind the back tires.

It's a bright clear night. The horse is gittin nearer. Its legs come into view. I cain't see the rider from where I'm at. The horse stops, jest in front of the flyer. I hold my breath. It snorts agin, shuffles its feet a bit. Then the rider clicks an it moves on.

A horse. Four legs, not two. Dependin on where Lugh is, where they've took him, I could be with him in days instead of weeks if I was travelin by horse. Looks like my lucky night. I slide Lugh's slingshot outta my belt. Pull a good-sized stone from my pocket.

I move silent as a cat, slippin between the flyers. My knees is shakin. My hands too. I tell myself I'm with Lugh, trackin a prairie chicken.

I check there's only one horse an rider, that they're headed away from me. Then I step out into the open, an take aim with the slingshot.

I wanna unhorse him, not kill him. I let fly. But my hands is too shaky. I hit him in the arm. He yells out.

I gotta have that horse.

I run at him. I leap at him, pull him offa the horse. He goes without a fight. I git him in a headlock an he starts screamin in a high screechy voice an kickin at my ankles.

An all the time I'm pullin an headlockin, I got all these thoughts runnin through my head. Like . . . what's a puny weed of a fella like this doin out here on his own . . . what a thin little voice . . . sounds more like a girl than a man . . . wait a minute, who does that voice remind me of? An then his hood falls back an—

Let go! she shrieks. Lemme go, you bastard!

Emmi? I says. I don't believe it. My heart jest about stops from shock. Emmi! I says. What the—?

I haul her up by one arm an grab her chin so's I can see her better. It's Emmi an no mistake. My blood boils over so fast I think the top of my head's gonna blow right off.

What're you doin here? I yell.

Saba? she says.

Who the hell else would it be?

I thought you was a sand spirit, from Pa's stories! She points at my face. Yer face is all white!

I brush at my cheek. Sand. I must be all coated with sand.

What're you tryin to do, kill me? That hurt! she says, rubbin at her arm where my shot hit her.

When I git finished with you, I says, you'll wish I had killed you. What the hell're you doin here?

I'm gonna help you find Lugh! She glares at me, with her stubborn chin. He's my brother too.

Gawdsblood, Emmi, I told you to—argh! I grab my hair with my hands. What've you done? You got no idea what yer doin!

Neether do you!

Don't you be pert with me! I grab the horse's rope bridle.

I know what the answer is but I still ask the question. Is this Mercy's horse?

Emmi folds her arms over her chest. Scrinches her mouth all tight.

I grit my teeth. Did. You. Steal. Mercy's. Horse. Answer me this second.

No! she says. No, I never! Stealin's wrong, I know that! I . . . borrowed it.

You borrowed it, I says. You said, Oh, by the way, Mercy, I'm jest goin after Saba, d'you mind if I borrow yer horse? An she said, Oh no, please, go right ahead! An don't you worry fer one second about my crippled old ankle an how th'only way I can git anywhere is on my damn horse. Is that it, Emmi? Is that how it went? Is that how you borrowed Mercy's gawdam horse?

No, I—oh, why don't you jest go to hell! She claps her hand over her mouth. Too late.

Gawdammit, Emmi, don't you swear! Don't you ever let me catch you swearin agin!

You swear all the time!

I do not!

You do too! Anyways, I'll swear if I want!

Oh no you won't! An you know what? If Mercy dies, it'll be yer fault.

Don't say that, she says.

Why not? It's the truth.

Yer the meanest person I ever met! I hate you!

You cain't hate me half as much as I hate you right now!

She starts to cry. I watch her, feelin all cold inside. I'm so damn mad at her, she can cry herself to death fer all I care. Then she chokes out, I was afeared you'd left me ferever. Jest like everybody else. Ma an Pa an Lugh. I know you don't love me, not like you love Lugh, but . . . please don't leave me, Saba. Please. Yer all I got.

My heart twists.

They're gonna need you, Saba. Lugh an Emmi.

I feel a heavy weight start to crush down on my chest. I try to push it off.

You cain't come with me, I says. It's too dangerous. You gotta go back to Crosscreek. But I ain't got time to take you. You'll hafta manage by yerself. You remember the way, don't you?

No, she says, crossin her arms over her chest.

Got enough water? I says.

She holds her waterskin upside down. Empty.

Food? I says.

I et it, she says.

Fer pity's sake, Em . . . what did you bring?

She pulls Fern from her pocket. The little peg doll that Pa made her.

I look at her. A doll, I says. You brought a doll.

I left in a hurry, she says.

I close my eyes. The weight thumps down on me. You, I says, are completely useless.

I am not! I found you, didn't I?

Stay here, I says. If you so much as move a finger, I'll kill you. An wipe yer damn nose.

She wipes it on her sleeve. Are you takin me with you? she says. To find Lugh?

What I'd like to do, I says, is leave you here fer the vultures to pick over.

I collect everythin from inside the flyer—Nero, my bark-sack an my weapons. I load the gear onto the horse an then I lift her on too.

Gawdam you, Emmi, I says. You always ruin everythin.

✝   ✝   ✝

I ain't spoke to Emmi fer two days. I ain't got naught to say to her. I'm still mad.

She tried to talk to me a bit at first but gave up when I didn't so much as grunt back. It don't seem to bother her too much. She talks to Nero an sings little songs to herself. Don't know what she's got to be so damn cheerful about.

We had some grub but not much. I pranged a jackrabbit with the slingshot a couple of days ago. Not too bad-tastin once it got roasted, specially seein how stringy it was. We managed on that till last night, but now our bellies twist, cryin out fer food.

I always save a little bit of whatever we got fer Nero, but mainly he's gotta hunt. He don't ever make a fuss, Nero, he jest gits on with it. An the sturdy little wild horse of Mercy's—name of Nudd—we're outta the sand dunes now into grass an dry scrub, an he seems to be findin enough to keep him goin. I might of known a creature of Mercy's 'ud know how to take care of itself.

Food might be scarce, but it ain't that I'm worried about most. It's water. Our supplies is low. We cain't seem to find no wet stuff anywhere on this mean hard plain. Even Nudd ain't bin able to sniff none out.

I've got us on strict rations an I'm collectin dew overnight, but with two of us an Nero an Nudd it ain't nearly enough.

In the far distance, I can see mountains. They look to be a day or two's walk from here, maybe a bit more. But it's hard to tell how far anythin is in the desert with the heat shimmer an all. I hope we'll be able to make it to there on what we got. We'll jest hafta, that's all. There's bound to be water in the mountains.

Meantime, the sun beats down. The wind blows steadily. It saps my strength. My mind.

I know we should do like Mercy said an travel by night, but I cain't stop.

I cain't rest. Not till I find Lugh.

We walk on.

† † †

Noon time.

I'm jest thinkin it's time to call a halt an take a break, when there's a dull thud behind me. Emmi's lyin on the ground. Nudd noses at her, whickers softly.

I trudge back. Stare down at her. My head feels so dull. Fer a long moment, I cain't think what I oughta do. Then . . . water. Emmi needs water.

I kneel, drag her into my arms an uncap my waterskin. I trickle a little into her mouth. She moans an turns her head away.

Emmi, I croak. You gotta drink. I tap her cheek. Emmi! C'mon!

I press the spout to her lips agin. Water dribbles down her chin. Then, all of a sudden, it's like she comes to life. She grabs the skin, tries to take a big swig but I pull it away. Water spills on the ground. The thirsty earth sucks it up.

Dammit, Em! I says. Now look what you done! She jest looks at me, dazed. Take tiny sips, I says. Or you'll git the cramp.

103

When I think she's had enough, when she starts to look a bit better, I give Nero a drink, then fill a tinny fer Nudd that he empties with two slurps of his big pink tongue.

I squeeze the skin to see what we got left. Git a sick feelin. Half a skin. That's it. I take the tiniest sip myself, then slip it back over my shoulder.

Emmi's sittin up. She looks at me, her blue eyes bright in her dusty face. An I wonder why I never noticed it before. Her eyes is jest like Lugh's.

Sorry, Saba, she says.

Ferget it, I says. It was time fer a break anyway.

✝   ✝   ✝

I'm jest liftin Emmi back onto Nudd so's we can git goin agin.

The wind flings sand into my eyes. I pull my sheema down to pertect 'em. Wind's pickin up agin, I says. We'll hafta watch it. I go to yank Em's sheema down too, but she stops my hand.

What's that? she says.

What's what? I says.

That. She points straight ahead. Over there.

I look. A plume of dust, bout a league away, is rollin towards us.

What is it? says Emmi. Another dust storm?

I shade my eyes an squint. I dunno, I says. It's too far away to tell yet an there's too much dust, I . . . hang on.

What? says Emmi.

Looks like a sail, I says, frownin.

You mean . . . a sail on a boat? Like the one Lugh made fer the skiff?

Yeah, I says. That kinda sail.

But boats go on water, she says. Not on land.

The dust clears fer a moment an I see what's comin at us. This one does, I says.

† † †

It's a boat all right. Well, more like a raft from the look of it. A flat wooden platform ridin high offa the ground on big tires. A hut in the middle, tucked right aginst the mast. A patchwork sail billows out, filled with the wind. It's headed this way.

They must of seen us by now. I look around. Nowhere to hide. Not a hummock, not even a rock. Flat in every direction.

I slip my crossbow offa my back. Hand the waterskin to Emmi.

All right, Em, I says. Listen to me an listen good. If I tell you to go, you go. No questions, no backchat, no tricks. You turn Nudd around an ride outta here. Let him have his head an he'll take you back to Mercy at Crosscreek. He knows his way home. An he'll know where to find water. If Nudd drinks it, that means it's safe fer you to drink. D'you unnerstand?

Yes, she says.

Good. Now promise me you'll do what I say.

She hesitates. I grab her hand, look straight into her eyes. Promise me on the life of Ma an Pa. When I tell you to go, you'll go.

I promise, she says.

I fit a arrow to my crossbow. My heart bangs aginst my ribs, my knees shake, my breath comes shallow an fast.

The landboat scuds along the plain towards us. It's movin fast. There's a person at the front. Leanin back, pullin hard on what looks to be a big wooden bar.

I take aim.

I can hear shoutin. As the boat races closer, I start to make out the words. Sail down! Let the sail down!

Suddenly, the top bit of the patchwork sail rips away, snatched by the wind. The rest of it collapses to the deck in a big heap.

The boat goes outta control. Anchor! yells the voice. Throw out the anchor!

† † †

Somethin goes flyin offa the back attached to a long rope. A big chunk of metal. Looks like a big fish hook. It hits the ground an skips along behind, throwin up clouds of dust.

But the boat keeps on comin. Look out! the voice screams. Take cover!

There's a terrible screech. One of the back tires comes free. It bounces high an goes spinnin off across the plain. The boat tips back an hits the ground with a almighty crack. It jack-knifes. Skids this way, that way, shriekin an blowin dust all over the place.

I'm still stood there, froze to the spot, my bow drawn.

Saba! Emmi yells. What're you doin?

I grab Nudd's rope an we dive outta the way. Nero flaps off in a panic.

The boat scrapes to a stop, right where we was standin.

There's silence fer a moment. Then there's a great groan an the boat tips forwards. Another silence. Then, I really must work on those emergency stops, says the voice.

† † †

There's a little old man. He's clingin to the mast like a lizard on a stump.

Don't say a word, I whisper to Em. I'll take care of this.

Good day to you! he cries. I . . . er . . . let me just get my—

He reaches into his coat.

Don't move! I yell. I run in front of the boat. I aim my bow right between his eyes. Hands up! I says.

Wait! he says. We come in peace! We mean you no harm!

Let go of that mast. I take two quick steps closer. Put yer hands up.

I assure you! We have nothing worth taking, my fearsome friend!

We? I says. Who else you got on there? Tell 'em to come out.

Did I say we? I meant I. I! No one here but me! A slip of the tongue, an error under duress!

I let fly with a arrow. It sticks in the mast jest above his head. He lets out a frightened squawk. Then he hollers, Miz Pinch! Miz Pinch!

A head struggles out from the heap of sail. A woman.

Emerge from your nest, my dove, he says. There's . . . er . . . this delightful young lady would like to meet you.

She might have gray hair, but she's a rawboned giant, the woman who shoves the sail aside an stands up. She's got a long head like a horse an pock-pitted skin, red an angry-lookin. She takes one look at me an says to him, Yer a idiot, Rooster.

I said hands up! I says.

They raise their hands above their heads. They gotta be the strangest pair I'll ever see. He only jest comes to her waist. He's got a fat round belly set on top of skinny little bird legs an he wears a cookin pot on his head fer a helmet. His tunic's cobbled together from the kinda rubbish you'd find in a landfill—cloth, slippy bags, shimmer discs an what have you. There's pieces of tire strapped around his knees.

That it? I says. Jest the two of yuz?

Yes! He bobs up an down, lookin like a silly quail. Yes, that's it! Please—I beg of you, my dear—please don't hurt us. You see, I have a weak heart and the slightest—

It's only a girl, you old fool! Miz Pinch kicks him in the ankle. Hard. He crumples in pain.

Yes, my heart's delight! he gasps. But, as you can see, she's a veritable warrior, armed and—

Keep yer hands up or I'll shoot agin! I yell.

They raise their hands. If thievin's yer game, the woman says, we ain't got nuthin worth takin.

I ain't no thief, I says. Who are you? What're you doin out here?

Rooster Pinch at your service, he says. Man of business and captain of the good ship Desert Swan. And may I present my lovely wife Miz Pinch, whom you've already—

Shut up, I says. I nod at the woman. You do the talkin.

We're pedlars, she says. On our way to Hopetown. We got blown off course.

Show me what yer peddlin, I says.

Well, what're you waitin fer? she says to him. Show her the trunk.

I . . . I'll have to put my hands down, he says.

Go on, I says. But no funny stuff.

He disappears inside the hut an comes out bum first, draggin a battered metal trunk behind him. He throws back the lid an starts liftin out bits of junk, holdin 'em up fer me to see—a couple of dirty glass bottles, pieces of bashed up Wrecker tech, a shovel, one squashed boot.

All right, I says, git back there with yer wife. Then, Emmi, I yell, git over here! She rides over on Nudd. Climb on an take a look inside that hut, I says. Check if they got any weapons.

She slides off Nudd's back, scrambles on board, scampers past 'em an ducks inside the scabby little hut. I keep my bow aimed at the pair of 'em.

He clears his throat. Lovely day, he says.

His wife clips him round the ear.

Emmi comes out agin.

All right? I says.

She nods. All clear, she says an jumps down to stand beside me.

You got water on board? I says.

Miz Pinch jerks her head an he goes scurryin into the hut agin. Comes out with a big plastic jug.

Take it, Em, I says. Fill the waterskins.

He hands it down to her an she hurries to do what I told her.

Now that I know they ain't got weapons, that they ain't

nuthin but a pair of shabby old pedlars, I ain't quite sure what the form is. Don't seem to be much point in shootin 'em. They stand there with their hands up, lookin at me.

Jest then, Nero decides to see what's all the fuss about. He drifts down an lands on Pinch's cookin pot helmet. Leans over an pecks him on the nose.

Ah! says Pinch, battin him away. Crow! Go on! Go away!

I lower my bow. All right, I guess yer okay. You can put yer hands down.

There you go, my treasure! Pinch says to his wife. I knew she was a good 'un!

Miz Pinch snorts an goes inside the hut.

That's what I call magnanimous! cries Pinch. That's what I call sporting! He slides down offa the Swan, grabs my hand an pumps it up an down. Well met, my gladiatorial friend! You have a merciful soul! A compassionate soul! A rare thing in these dark days, I assure you. Now . . . I know that such a model of justice wouldn't wish to hinder a man's efforts to remediate the cause of his most unfortunate . . . er . . . his most un—er . . . Dear me. I seem to have lost my train of thought.

You better fix that wheel, I says.

That's it! he says. Precisely!

Well, git on with it.

Pinch scurries off to fetch back the tire that bounced away. I go over to help Emmi finish fillin our waterskins. Then we drink till our thirst gits quenched an make sure Nudd an Nero git plenty too. The sounds an smells of cookin is startin to drift outta the little hut on the Desert Swan.

Emmi sniffs the air. That sure smells good, she whispers.

My belly's squeezed tight. My mouth waters. It's bin a long while since we et the last of that jackrabbit.

Pinch rolls up, pushin the tire in front of him. He's outta breath an the sweat pours offa him.

You wanna hand with that? I says.

✝   ✝   ✝

I help him prop up the boat. Then he gits his toolkit an we set to puttin the tire back on. Emmi sits crossleg a little ways off, drawin in the dirt with a stick.

You need tighter fixins on this, I says. Lemme see what you got in that kit.

He raises his hands to the sky. Not only merciful but a mechanic, he says.

While I pick through a glass jar of metal bits, he says, I'm afraid we intellectuals aren't very practical, my dear. I'm a constant trial to Miz Pinch, her cross to bear, but she never upbraids me for my failings, at least, not as much as I deserve.

You sure do talk peculiar, I says.

Ah! I knew you were a right 'un! he says. He wipes his hands on a kercheef, then reaches into a deep pocket in his coat an pulls somethin out. He holds it like it's a babby bird or a feather or the most precious thing in the world. It sure don't look like much. Two bits of brown leather wrapped around lots of thin little pieces of dried old leafs or somethin.

It's a book, he says. He gives me a look like I oughta be impressed.

You don't say, I says.

He folds back the top bit of leather. Then the first leaf. Then the second. They're covered all over with black squiggle marks.

Funny kinda leafs, I says. I reach out my finger to touch one.

Careful! Pinch brushes my hand away. It's paper. Pages made of paper. It's most ancient. Delicate. Rare. I found it locked away in a metal box.

I seen them squiggles before, I says to him. On landfill junk. I spit on the ground. That ain't nuthin special. Bloody Wrecker tech.

Oh no, it's good Wrecker tech. Noble even! From the very beginnings of time. Those squiggles, as you call them, are letters. Letters joined together make words. And words tell a story. Like this one.

He turns the pages over like he don't wanna disturb 'em.

It's the story of a great king, he says. His name was Lewis Ex Eye Vee. The Sun King of France.

France, I says. Is that around here?

No my dear, he says. It was a far away land, long long ago. Back in Wrecker times. The Sun King has been dead for many hundreds of years. Here, this is what he looked like.

He holds the book out to me. The lines an squiggles on the page curve into the drawin of a man.

He's got thick curly hair down past his shoulders an piled high on top. Animal skins thrown over one shoulder, trailin behind him onto the floor. Fancy shirt with frilly collar an cuffs. Short, puffy little britches that show his legs. High heeled shoes. Sword at his side. Walkin stick.

His people worshipped him, he says. They thought he was a god.

Well I never heard of him, I says. An he wouldn't of got far in them shoes. How'd you come to know all this?

There are some people—very few, mind you—who still have the knowledge of words and books. When I was a boy, he says, I was lucky enough to meet one such woman and she taught me to read.

So, the way you talk, I says, all them funny words. That's on account of . . . readin?

Yes, he says. Yes, I suppose it is.

Think I'll give it a miss then, I says.

Rooster! Rooster Pinch! Where're you at? It's Miz Pinch's screechy squawk.

Here, my angel! Pinch cries.

You better not be gabbin instead of workin!

I'm not, my angel! We're not! He takes the book an pops it back in his pocket.

We start in on the repairs. But it's like he cain't stop hisself talkin, cuz almost right away he says, She looks to be a smart little gal, your sister. Bright as a button. I can always tell.

She's a pain in the neck, I says. You got kids?

A son, he says. Then right away he says, The sun is fiercely hot today, don't you find? He mops at his head, lookin up at the sky. There's no other word for it but fierce. Most uncomfortable. We could certainly do with some cooler weather, but ah . . . sorry my dear, you were asking . . . ah yes, children. Sadly, my wife and I were never blessed.

He ducks his head down. Like he don't wanna meet my eyes.

Yer lyin, Rooster Pinch. Why would you lie about havin a kid?

We work in silence fer a bit. Then, like I don't give two hoots, I says, Where was it you said you was headed?

Hopetown, he says. My heart jumps into my throat. But, he says, as my good lady wife mentioned, the wind changed and the Swan was blown off course. We should have been heading due north.

Hopetown's due north of here? I says.

That's right, he says.

Well, if that don't beat all, I says. Hopetown's where we're headed too. We're jest on our way there.

He darts me a quick look. Well, well, he says. What an extraordinary coincidence. What a fortuitous meeting indeed. I don't suppose you'd like to . . . climb aboard and sail with us?

I believe we might like that very much, I says.

Then let us strike hands on it! He holds out a greasy paw an we shake hands. You've got yourself a ride, young lady.

✝   ✝   ✝

Why'd you tell him that? Emmi hisses.

I grab her arm an pull her away where we cain't be heard. Don't you listen to nuthin? I says. They're headed fer Hopetown. That's the place Mercy told us about, where they might of took Lugh. He might be there. An if he ain't, it's a good place to start. We can maybe ask around, find things out.

So we're gonna go with 'em? she says.

That's right, I says.

She folds her arms over her skinny chest, shakes her head. I don't like it, she says. An I don't like them. Not one bit.

It don't matter what you like, I says. I gotta find Lugh. An any way that helps me find him faster, I'm gonna take it.

You never listen to me, she says, her face all sulky. What about Nudd? We cain't jest leave him here.

He seems to know we're talkin about him. He lowers his head an butts it gently into her side.

We'll set his head fer home, I says. Mercy'll be glad to see him.

Do we hafta do it now? she says.

I nod.

G'bye, Nudd. She strokes his soft nose, kisses it. You stay outta trouble.

She stands back.

Go on home, Nudd, I says. Go home to Mercy. I give him a slap on the rump an he takes off across the plain, back the way we come.

It feels kinda funny, jest lettin him go like that, says Emmi.

Miz Pinch's voice comes from behind us. I jest about jump outta my skin. A pony like that ain't got a hope of outrunnin a wolfdog pack, she says.

Saba! says Emmi. Call him back!

It's all right, Em, I says. He'll be fine.

Suddenly, with her so close fer the first time, I realize how big Miz Pinch is. Over six foot, with broad shoulders, rough man-sized hands an strong lookin arms covered with dark hair.

Grub's up, she says.

† † †

We sit on deck to eat—me on a upturned bucket, Emmi on the floor an the Pinches on rickety wood chairs they pull outta the hut.

Miz Pinch digs into the cookin pot with a long wooden spoon an slops a hearty helpin into a battered tin basin.

Dried boar an sourberry, she says. She holds the basin out to me. That'll fill yer belly.

Pinch goes to grab it. She hauls off an whacks his hand with the spoon. Whacks him so hard he howls. She glares at him.

That ain't yers, she says.

An this one's fer you, girlie. She fills another eatin tin an hands it to Emmi, who digs right in.

My squeezed belly's so happy to be filled that I scarf down the lot double quick. When I'm finished, Miz Pinch hands me a chunk of flatbread. She gives a bit to Em too.

There you go, she says. Mop them bowls clean. Cain't go wastin good food. It's nice to see young 'uns with good appetites, ain't it, Rooster?

To share our modest portion with fellow travelers on the dusty road of life, he says. It's just the thing, my dear! That's what it's all about!

Git every last drop, she says, that's the way. All done?

Thanks, I says. I hand our bowls back. I yawn. Emmi rubs her eyes.

You girls feelin sleepy? says Miz Pinch.

My eyelids is feelin so heavy all of a sudden. I yawn agin.

Guess I . . . ain't used . . . to . . . all this walkin . . . , I says.

Saba, Emmi yawns. Why do I feel . . . so . . . tired . . . ?

She curls up on deck an right away, she's fast to sleep. Somethin ain't right here. I git to my feet. I stagger a little.

Whoa . . . I shake my head, try to wake myself. My head's so heavy, I cain't hardly hold it up.

The Pinches is watchin me, a sly look in their eyes.

Then I know. The food . . . , I says. You put somethin in . . . the food. I go to slide my bow offa my back but my fingers go all slack. My hand drops down. My knees buckle unner me. I fall to the deck.

Why'd you . . . do that fer? I says.

My eyelids flutter.

Once.

Twi—

✝   ✝   ✝

I'm lyin on somethin hard. Wood. My neck's stiff. My head's poundin. It hurts somethin fierce. I lick my dry lips. My shoulders ache. An my wrists. I groan.

I lift my head, force open heavy eyes. Rough wooden bunks, cookin pots hangin on the rickety walls. Where . . . cain't seem to remember . . . wait . . . the landboat . . . the

Desert Swan . . . Rooster Pinch . . . his wife. I must be inside the hut on the Desert Swan.

I go to move my arms but . . . I cain't. I give 'em a yank. Metal bites into my wrists.

My heart leaps. Starts to race. I'm wide awake.

I'm lyin on a bunk. I'm chained, wrists an ankles, to metal rings set into a girder. Emmi's on the next bunk, jest a few paces away. She's chained up too. This hut ain't the flimsy thing it looks to be. It's wood panels attached to a frame made from iron.

We're prisoners. A red hot wave of fury rushes through me. Fury an fear. Pinch! I roar, pullin at my chains. Pinch! Emmi! I says. Emmi! Wake up!

Slowly she lifts her head, eyes heavy an dull.

Wake up, Emmi! C'mon now! Emmi!

Her eyes widen when she sees me. She looks an sees her own wrists tied, sees her ankles. Her face twists with fear, she starts to breathe fast.

Saba! What's goin on? What're they gonna do to us?

Then I notice that the floor's rumblin. The pots on the wall swing an sway. The Swan's on the move.

Pinch! I scream. The hut door flies open. Miz Pinch steps inside an closes it behind her.

Well well, she says. Awake at last. Pleasant dreams, I hope.

Let us go! I yell. You got no right to do this!

Right ain't got nuthin to do with it, she says. In this world, you gotta take what you want. She shrugs. We want you.

Whaddya mean, you want me?

She lifts the lid on a water bucket an dips a battered tin cup in it. Yer young, she says, an strong. A natural-born fighter from the look of it. I knew it right off. You'll be perfect.

Perfect fer what? I says.

She straightens up. Look at me with her small dark eyes, cold as stones. Perfect, she says, fer cage fightin.

The little hairs on my arms stand on end. I shiver.

That's right, girlie, she says. You better be afeared. Cage fightin's mean. Nasty. An it's big business in Hopetown. You'll do well fer us.

I ain't doin nuthin fer you, I says.

You ain't gotta choice, she says.

You cain't make me do nuthin, I says.

Oh you'll do ezzackly what I tell you, she says.

I'll see you in hell first, I says. Let us go! Pinch! Help! Pinch!

Save yer breath, she says. He does what I tell him. She walks over with the cup of water. Bends down an holds my head up. Drink it, she says. Cain't have you goin thirsty. Cage fighters gotta be in prime condition.

I stare at her while I drink. I hold the water in my mouth, then I spit it in her face. She don't say naught. Jest stares at me a moment, the water runnin down her face.

You shouldn't of done that, she says.

She goes over to Emmi.

No! I yell. Don't touch her!

She slaps her across the face. Hard. Emmi cries out. She lifts her head an I see her lip's bin split open. Blood fills her mouth, trickles down her chin. She starts to cry.

Leave her alone! I yell. She's a child! She ain't done nuthin to you!

Miz Pinch comes over an kneels beside my bunk. Puts her face so close to mine that I can see every pock mark on her skin. So close I gag on her foul breath. It smells like meat left out in the sun. She smiles.

Every time you disobey me, she says, every time you try to git away, I'm gonna hit yer little sister. Hit her or . . . burn her. If I take the notion to, I might even break her arm. But I ain't gonna hit you. I ain't ever gonna hit you, my beauty.

She strokes a finger down my cheek. Her filthy nail scrapes aginst my skin.

An you know why? she says. Yer worth too much to me. Yer sister . . . she ain't worth nuthin. Not to me anyways. I guess we're gonna find out how much she's worth to you.

†   †   †

I feel it when the sails go down. The Swan gits slower an slower an at last it shudders to a halt. There's a clunk as the anchor hits the ground. We must be stoppin fer the night.

We bin watchin while Miz Pinch gutted an skinned a rock lizard an set it to stew on a bucket stove inside the hut, all the time hummin to herself. It's like we ain't even here.

I ain't opened my mouth since she said that about hurtin Emmi. I bin tryin to think of a plan. Tryin to think what Lugh would do if he was me. If he was here. An how much I wish it was him an me here together an not me an Em. It wouldn't be so bad then. I'd feel like maybe we had half a chance.

All right, Emmi? I whisper.

She nods, her eyes big in her thin little face. Her lip's swolled up where Miz Pinch hit her, the blood dried all dark an crusty. I cain't stand to think how I hit her too, back at the lake, an me her own flesh. She cried them first few moments after Miz Pinch whacked her, but she ain't made a peep since.

You was right about 'em, I says. I'm sorry. I should of listened to you.

That's okay, she says.

It ain't okay, I says. An it's my fault she hit you. I shouldn't of spit at her.

I'm glad you did, Emmi says.

That's the spirit, I says. I'll git us outta here, Em. I promise.

Quit yer gabbin! Miz Pinch yells at us. Then she yanks open the door an shrieks, Grub up!

Rooster Pinch slips inside the hut.

You lyin bastard! I says.

He's all shifty-eyed an hangdog an don't meet my eyes. Pretends he don't hear me. Smells capital, my dear! He rubs his hands together, all fake cheery, an sniffs the air. Sheer ambrosia!

Shut up, she says. Siddown.

They shovel it down. When he's finished, he swipes his finger inside his bowl an licks off the thin gravy. She nods our way.

You better feed 'em, she says.

Me, my dear? Oh! Do you think that's wise? You'd be much better at—

Her big hand shoots out an she clips him on the ear. He scurries to fetch a couple of tin basins an fills 'em with stew. He goes to Emmi first. He helps her to sit, scoops a spoonful an holds it out to her. She looks at me.

It's okay, I says. I smile at her an she gives me a little smile back.

She eats eagerly, hungrily, hardly stoppin to chew.

That's a good girl, says Pinch. That's the way. He looks over his shoulder. Miz Pinch's busy clearin up, hummin agin, not payin us no attention. He darts a look at me, whispers to both of us, It's best if you just do what she says, my dears. If you don't, believe me, it will go hard for you.

You gotta help us git away, I whisper. Please.

I can't. I don't dare. If you try to get away, she'll kill you. That's what she did to the last one. She sees everything. She—

Miz Pinch notices what he's up to. What's goin on over there? I hope you ain't talkin to them girls, Rooster.

No! Of course not! Wouldn't dream of it!

You better not be. An if I find out yer lyin to me, you know what'll happen, don't you? I'll give you the burn. How'd you like that?

I wouldn't, my treasure, he says.

Then git on with the feedin an be quick about it.

He hurries to finish with Emmi, then moves over to me. Whaddya mean, she killed the last one, I whisper. What last one?

He don't reply. I try to make him catch my eye, but he won't, he jest stares down at the bowl. His face is shiny with sweat an the spoon trembles in his hand. Fer the first time, I notice his hands an wrists is covered all over with ugly purple burn scars. Like somebody's gone at 'em with a hot poker.

So that's what she means when she says she'll give him the burn. That's what she does when he crosses her. He ain't gonna help us. He's too terrified.

We're on our own.

An I feel calm.

It seems crazy, seein how we're both chained hand an foot an there ain't a soul to help us, but I'm calm. Becuz now I see what I gotta do. An what I ain't gotta do, which is waste time thinkin that anybody's gonna help us. That somebody's gonna come along an rescue us. I cain't count on nobody but me.

So what I gotta do now is watch. An learn. An think. An plan. I'm gonna make sure we stay alive, Emmi an me. I'll do whatever it takes. I'll do what the hellhag tells me.

But I'll be watchin an waitin. An when the time comes, when it's the right moment to make a move, I'll be ready. I'll know what to do an I'll git us outta here.

Then we'll go find Lugh. I promised him I would. An I ain't no quitter. No matter what.

† † †

Miz Pinch comes towards me. She's got a knife. She reaches out an I cower back aginst the wall. She grabs the back of my neck in a tight grip. I feed you, water you an then I slit yer throat, she says. I know that's what yer thinkin. Huh. No such luck.

She grabs hold of my long braid an gives it a sharp twist, bringin my head down. I wince as pain shoots along my scalp. She saws at the top of the braid with her knife an pretty soon she's cut it off. She holds it up.

That's a fine tail of hair, she says. Should fetch a good price.

Then she brings over a basin of hot water, a bar of soap an a straight razor. Without sayin a word, she throws the water over my head, soakin me. She rubs the soap over my head. It runs down into my eyes, makes 'em sting an water. I don't make a peep. I look at Emmi, give her a little smile to tell her not to worry.

Then I stare straight ahead. Once she's got me soaped to her likin, she takes the razor an starts shavin off my hair. Clumps drop onto the floor with a wet plop.

You don't want hair fer the Cage, she says. A smart fighter shaves their head. You don't wanna give yer opponent nuthin to hang onto. Whatever you do, don't let 'em git hold of yer ears. They'll rip a ear offa yer head before you know it. Cage fightin ain't ezzackly what you'd call clean.

Jest then, I notice what she's got around her neck. My heartstone. The pink heartstone that my mother gave to Mercy. That Mercy gave to me. She must of gone through my stuff an took what she wanted.

I hiss in a breath. My heart leaps into my throat. I wanna rip it from around her neck. Claw her face to pieces fer darin to even touch it. I twist myself outta her grasp. Gimme that back! I says.

She jumps back, all startled. Then she sees what I'm lookin at. Stretches her mouth into a mean, thin lipped smile. Oh, she says, I see yer admirin my new necklace. I found it lyin around. Ain't it amazin how careless people is with their valuables?

I glare hate at her. Pull on my chains, my fists clenched.

Careful now, beauty, she says. She lifts the razor in her hand an looks over at Emmi.

I slump back.

She reaches out. Grabs my hair. Then she goes on shavin my head till I ain't gone none left. Till I'm completely bald.

✝ ✝ ✝

They set Emmi free an put her to work, scrubbin the floor, haulin water an washin the dishes an pots. All the dirty work they don't wanna do theirselves.

An jest to make sure I unnerstand the way things is, that she means what she says, Miz Pinch hits Em when she catches her speakin to me or when she don't move quick enough. Hits her over the head, pinches her on the arm. Once, she sticks out her foot an trips her while she's carryin a bucket of water an then she hits her when it spills.

Em jest picks herself up an keeps workin. She don't make a sound.

Neether do I. But my hands curl into fists an my nails dig into my palms so hard that they bleed.

We travel with the wind. Stoppin when it rests, movin when it blows. But it rests more'n it blows. I only git glimpses of daylight or moonlight when the Pinches come an go outta the cabin. I ain't got a clue how many days have passed an nor does Em. Feels like we've bin here ferever.

Emmi's face gits more pinched an pale. An she weeps silently at night.

They feed me all the best food. They want me to be strong.

I spend my time sittin on my bunk. I'm shackled hand an foot an chained to the wall fer good measure. Miz Pinch sets me free three times a day to stretch my arms an legs, but only inside the hut. While I do, she holds a knife to Emmi's throat.

But not jest any knife. My knife. The one I keep shoved down inside my boot sheath. The one she took offa me. Miz Pinch smiles, tauntin me, provokin me. Go on, that smile says, jest try it. Try it an see what happens. She'd like that. To hurt Em with my knife.

So I'm free but I cain't do a thing.

I don't let my face show what I'm thinkin. Don't let her see the hate that burns in my heart. The rage that gnaws at my gut. I keep my face blank.

I watch her. I watch him.

I wait fer the right moment.

If the wind blows us fair, tomorrow we'll be in Hopetown.

HOPETOWN

Rooster Pinch throws anchor on the Desert Swan jest outside Hopetown.

Miz Pinch unties me an jerks her head.

I follow her, shufflin onto deck in my ankle an wrist chains. I stand there, blinkin in the bright daylight. I feel dazed. I ain't bin outside the dark cramped hut since they snatched us. Must be five, six days ago now. I squint at the sun. High noon.

Hopetown spreads out in front of us, half a league away. It squats at the foot of a dusty hill an straggles up its slopes. I ain't never seen more'n one shanty at a time before. Heard tell of how Wreckers lived, all crammed close together in cities an towns, but never thought I'd see such a place.

An it never crossed my mind that if I did see such a place, it wouldn't be nuthin more'n a heap of ramshack shanties leanin one aginst th'other. It looks like the whole lot 'ud come tumblin down if you gave one a good kick.

What a fine sight! says Pinch. Nothing like the hurly burly of city life to gladden the heart!

There's commotion all around us. Folks rattle past the Swan in clouds of dust, in carts pulled by fierce-lookin wolf-dogs, on horseback, by mule an camel, on foot. They flow in an outta a big gate in the junk palisade that runs all around

133

Hopetown. I ain't never seen so many people before in my life. I look this way an that, tryin to take it all in.

Emmi's standin next to me. The Pinches ain't lookin. I lift my chained hands an she slips unnerneath. She wraps her arms around my waist an gives me a fierce hug. The Pinches keep her workin so hard, she's even scrawnier'n usual.

This is it, I says. Hopetown.

What's gonna happen now? she whispers.

I dunno, I says. We'll find out soon enough, I reckon. Whatever happens, keep yer eyes peeled fer Lugh.

Jest then, a familiar caw caw caw rings out. I look up. A big black bird circles, high above. I'd know that wingspan anywhere.

Nero! I says. He swoops down, buzzes jest over our heads, then soars on up agin. My heart soars with him. Tears spring to my eyes. He must of bin followin us the whole time, I says.

I knew he wouldn't leave us! says Em. I knew it!

You better move, I says. Quick, before she sees you.

I lift my hands an jest as she slips out agin, Miz Pinch turns around. She frowns. What's goin on? You know the rules!

She grabs Emmi. Raises her arm to backhand her. Jest then Pinch calls out, Miz Pinch! The chariot's here, my love!

She stops. Looks over her shoulder.

A scabby camel steps up beside the Swan. He's pullin a rusted out car behind him, hitched on with a harness. By the filthy look on his face, he ain't too pleased with how things've worked out fer him. He rolls his eyes an snaps his long yellow teeth at the legs of the little boy perched on his hump.

Miz Pinch turns back. I'll tend to you later, she hisses to Em. Right now, I got bigger business.

C'mon, missus, I ain't got all day, says the camel boy. Where to?

Miz Pinch yanks at my chains. I stumble forwards.

Take us to the Cage Master, she says.

✝   ✝   ✝

I peer outta the windows as we bump slowly through Hopetown on flat tires. It's so crowded with people we cain't hardly move. They press aginst the chariot, starin in at us. The camel boy leans down an cracks his whip at 'em, tryin to clear the way.

I look fer golden hair tied back in a long braid. Fer eyes blue as a summer sky.

Are you here, Lugh?

A man's back. Broad shoulders, gold hair—short, but they could of cut his hair by now—the right height. My heart skips a beat. Every muscle in my body goes tense.

Turn around, turn around, oh please turn around, let me see you.

He does. It ain't Lugh.

At that moment, a man leans through the window. He grabs my arm an starts to try an pull me out, chains an all.

135

I don't stop to think. I twist, I scrabble, I brace myself on the chariot, give myself a foothold.

Stop! Rooster Pinch beats at the man's head with his tattered umburella. Unhand her!

Saba! Emmi cries.

The red hot floods me. I bite down on his filthy hand. He yells out but hangs on. I bite harder. Deeper. I bite till I taste his blood. He shrieks an lets go. He falls back. Gits swallowed by the crowd.

That's it! shouts Pinch. Run, you villain! You coward! Ha! No one crosses Rooster Pinch!

Saba, says Emmi. Are y'okay?

I spit outta the window. Spit out the taste of him, the smell of him, the feel of him. I sit back in my seat. I wipe my mouth with my chained hands. I'm fine, I says.

I look over at Miz Pinch. She ain't moved through the whole thing. She's jest sat there, starin at me.

An there's a little smile on her face.

† † †

The camel boy parks the chariot in front of a long low stone buildin on the edge of Hopetown. It's a proper built place, not a Wrecker-junk shanty like the rest.

You bring the child an remember, keep yer mouth shut, says Miz Pinch to Rooster as we git out. I'll deal with the Cage Master.

She grabs my hand chains an hauls me along behind her. Pinch brings Emmi by the hand. Two big mean-lookin men step in front of the door as we come up to it. My heart skips a beat. They're dressed in long black tunics with leather body armor over top. Jest like the men who took Lugh. They must be Tonton, like Mercy told me about.

Cage Master ain't in, says one.

He'll be in fer me, says Miz Pinch. Tell him Miz Pinch is here. Say I got somethin special fer him.

They look at us with hard eyes. They got merciless faces.

Didn't you hear me? the Tonton says. I said, he ain't in.

You'll tell him I'm here if you know what's good fer you, says Miz Pinch.

One of 'em jerks his head an th'other one opens the door an disappears inside. He's back soon.

You can go in, he says. But you better be quick.

We all go in.

The Cage Master sits behind a big stone table in a white room. In the wall behind the table, there's a big wooden door. A dull roar, the muffled sound of many voices, comes from behind it.

There's partly et food spread out all over the table in a big mess—flatbread an platters of roast meat an boiled pigeon eggs an jugs of grog. The Cage Master hardly even looks up when we come in, he's so busy stuffin it all into his mouth. He's got a fat, round, pink face with three chins an a few long hanks of hair plastered flat to his skull. There's a red napkin tied around his neck.

Puffed up, greedy toad. I ain't afeared of you.

He picks up a roasted sparrow an crams the whole thing in his mouth. Well, what is it? he says. I'm a busy man, Miz Pinch. I ain't in the mood fer no time wasters.

Miz Pinch goes still. Like a rattlesnake about to strike. Them Tonton guards of yers is all chaaled up, Cage Master, she says. You better hope that my—that . . . certain people don't find out that yer lettin standards slip.

His face goes pale. He pulls the napkin from his neck an wipes his greasy mouth an fat greasy fingers on it. But . . . my guards're clean, he says, I swear they are!

It don't look that way to me, says Miz Pinch. Ain't that right, Rooster?

Yes my dear, he says. Whatever you say, my dove.

I look at Miz Pinch, then the Cage Master. They're starin at each other. The Tonton warn't chewin on no chaal leaf. She don't like the way he talked to her an she'll settle the score by makin trouble fer him.

Well, what're you waitin fer? says Miz Pinch. You better see to it.

Yes, he says. Yes. He hesitates, still chewin. Then, he heaves hisself to his feet an waddles around the table.

DeMalo! he bellows. DeMalo!

The door behind the table opens a crack. The noise outside spills in, a deafenin roar, as a man slips through. The sound fades as he closes the door behind him.

He's a Tonton. Tall, like they all seem to be, an robed head to foot in black. But this one wears metal body armor over his robes where the rest wear leather. A shiny breastplate an armbands from his wrists to his elbows. Long dark hair tied back. A watchful face. A strong face, with broad cheekbones. You don't call men beautiful, I know that. But all the same, that's what he is.

He says nuthin. Waits.

The Cage Master, so cocky jest a moment ago, shrinks. He looks off to the side of DeMalo when he says, Uh . . . this . . . uh Miz Pinch seems to think there's a problem with the guards on the door. Of course I uh . . . assured her that we run a tight ship here but uh . . . I'd be ah . . . most . . . ah . . .

DeMalo don't show that he's even listenin. He moves towards the main door, silent as a cat. As he goes past us, he pauses. Right in front of me.

He raises his head. His eyes meet mine. They're deep set. Dark, almost black. Full of shadows.

Time shrieks to a halt. I cain't move. Cain't breathe. Cain't take my eyes from his. I don't want to.

Lookin deep inside of me.

Findin my darkest thoughts, my worst fears.

I know you, a voice whispers. *I know you.*

Cold starts to creep through my blood. I shiver. It runs through my whole body, from my toes to my head. He feels it. Sees it. There's a slight flicker in his eyes. Then he moves, slips through the door an he's gone.

It only lasted a heartbeat. Him an me, locked inside a heartbeat.

Nobody says nuthin fer a long moment. Nobody moves. It's like we all felt the same thing. Like we all stopped breathin.

What jest happened here? Who is he? They're all afeared of him.

Then the Cage Master lunges at the table, pours hisself a cup of grog an drinks it dry. He slumps into his chair, moppin at his forehead with his napkin.

So, says Miz Pinch, we unnerstand each other, I think.

Yes, he says. Of course. Now, you've brought somethin to show me. Yer latest acquisition, I take it. He looks me over with his greedy little eyes. So, you think she'll be good in the Cage.

I don't think, Miz Pinch says, I know. This one's very rare. Very fine.

Not like that last one you brought me then, he says. She was a disappointment. Didn't cooperate at all. I was startin to think that maybe yer judgement ain't what it used to be, ha ha!

Miz Pinch's neck flushes a dull red. Her hands clench into fists. Mind what you say, Cage Master, she says.

I . . . I meant no disresspeck, Miz Pinch. You know me, I didn't mean to—

Jest remember who yer talkin to, she says. Who I am. I got influence! Anyways, I dealt with that girl. She got what she deserved.

That's right! That's the way! Yer one in a million! Well go on, he says, let's take a good look at this prize of yers.

Step up, she says to me. She goes to give me a push between the shoulders but I shrug her off.

Don't give in to fear, Saba. Be strong, like I know you are.

I take my time walkin up to the table. My ankle chains clank on the stone floor. I hook a chair with my foot, pull it over an sit down.

I lift my chained hands, help myself to one of the roasted sparrows an bite the head off. Then I pour a cup of grog an drink it down, starin at him the whole time. I put the empty cup upside down on the table.

He narrows his eyes. Well, he says, she's bold enough, I'll grant you that. Stand up girl, let's see you proper.

I look him up an down. I curl my lip.

He's around the table in a flash. He grabs my arm an hauls me to my feet. Who'd think a fat man could move so fast? An he's much stronger'n I thought he'd be. He pulls me tight aginst him.

Be very careful, he whispers in my ear. I'm in charge here. I don't care who you are or where you come from. In

Hopetown my word is law. Unless I say so . . . yer nuthin. Less than nuthin. The dirt under my feet's more use to me than you are. Do you understand?

I nod.

Good, he says. He licks my ear slowly. Then he steps away. My stummick turns over. I feel the blood rush to my face. I wanna scrub at my ear, chuck up, run from the room, but I cain't. I don't. I jest stare straight ahead.

She's strong, says Miz Pinch. An smart too.

Strong, smart an bold. The Cage Master struts around me, lookin me up an down. Well, she looks impressive. You might just have somethin here.

I told you, she says.

The Cage Master stares at me. Then he says, The question is, can she fight?

Only one way to find that out, says Miz Pinch.

Quite right, he says. An there ain't no time like the present. Come.

The Cage Master walks to the door that DeMalo came through an throws it wide open. The roar that we heard before spills into the room an fills the air. He steps outside. We follow him.

We're standin on a platform, lookin down on a great crowd of people.

Welcome to the Colosseum, he says.

I try to take it all in. The Cage Master's house sits on the top of a hill. It sweeps down an away from the house. Down below us, cut into the hillside, there's rows an rows of benches with three clear paths that cut through 'em from top to bottom.

The benches is crammed full of people. Everybody's shoutin an some of 'em's leapin around an pointin an shakin their fists. An they're all lookin at one thing.

A cage. At the bottom of the hill in a open space stands a big metal cage.

Inside there's two men fightin. From the roar of the crowd, from the smell of the excitement in the Colosseum, it looks like it's buildin up to a big finish.

The fighters both barefoot, bare-armed, bare-legged. They wear short tunics. No weapons. They punch, wrestle, kick at each other, scramble up the sides of the cage an throw theirselves off to land on their opponent.

One of 'em's gittin tired. Blood's pourin outta his nose an he's startin to stagger, throw wild punches.

Looks like the end fer Artashir, says the Cage Master.

Artashir's opponent backs him into a corner, picks him up by the throat with both hands an holds him there, slammin him aginst the cage bars. Artashir goes limp. The guy lets him go an he slithers to the floor.

The winner holds his hands over his head, pumps his fists in the air an the crowd goes crazy. They're all pointin at the Cage, screamin an jumpin around. Some of 'em's even fightin with each other an guards wade in to break it up. Their eyes look wild.

Artashir pulls hisself slowly to his feet. He stands there, swayin slightly. The crowd boos. Then they turn to face our platform an start to chant, Gauntlet! Gauntlet! Gauntlet!

Artashir looks up at the Cage Master. The Cage Master stares down at him.

I usually look forwards to this bit, he says. But there's somethin about this one. . . . His will to live seems to be stronger 'n most. I s'pose that's why he's lasted so long. He's certainly been good for business. Well, no point gettin sentimental. He's lost his last two fights an this one makes three. Rules is rules.

He tugs the red napkin from around his neck an, holdin it in his right hand, raises it above his head. The crowd's screamin even louder by now.

The Cage Master sighs. Oh let's get on with it, he says. Then he brings down his arm.

Two burly cagekeepers open the cage door an pull out Artashir. The crowd all rushes towards the path that runs up the middle of the Colosseum, climbin over each other, punchin an kickin to get right next to it.

Armed guards haul people outta the way, push 'em back so the path stays clear.

They live fer this, says the Cage Master. They're worse than animals. That's what too much chaal does to you. Fools.

Then everybody starts to stomp their feet on the ground. The whole place shakes, even the platform we're standin on. The stompin gits faster and faster.

The keepers push Artashir forwards. He looks around the Colosseum. He drags in deep breaths through his nose, his head held high. Then his face changes. Hardens. Like he's made a decision. He stares up at the Cage Master an spits on the ground.

The Cage Master gives a little laugh.

Then Artashir throws back his head an roars. Bellows like a wild beast that's bin hunted down, that's cornered but that's gonna go down fightin.

He starts to run. He sprints up the center path. Hands reach out, hit him, grab at his tunic, tryin to pull him down. He throws a punch an gits hisself free. Manages to stagger on a few steps more. But the crowd surges forwards onto the path, howlin like wolves at a kill, an bodies close over him. Waves pullin down a drownin man. Artashir disappears.

My stummick heaves.

It's a shame when a good fighter goes down to the gauntlet, the Cage Master says. He looks at me. He reaches out a clammy hand an strokes it down my cheek. Now it's yer turn, he says.

† † †

The girl's smaller'n me.

She comes at me hard, right from the off. She moves so fast I cain't even see her fists. The first punch to my face. Then my ribs. An I jest stand there. Like I'm asleep.

But then the red hot kicks in an at last I unnerstand what it is. It's like animals. A animal will do anythin to live. Even chew off its own leg if it's caught in a trap. That's the red hot. An I'm gonna hafta learn to use it if I wanna survive in the Cage.

The girl's tough. And she fights hard. She fights mean. She lost her last two fights. This is her last chance. So she's got the red hot in her too.

But mine is stronger than hers.

I watch what she does.

I learn fast.

She gives me a helluva beatin before I learn enough. Then I git lucky. I go at her with a flyin kick to the stummick that slams her hard aginst the bars an that's it. She don't git up till the keeper pulls her to her feet.

An it's over. The end.

The end fer her. The beginnin fer me.

They don't tell me her name. There's a little pink birth-mark on her face. It looks like a butterfly.

Like the Cage Master says, it's a shame when a good fighter goes down to the gauntlet.

But one of us had to.

An it sure as hell warn't gonna be me.

✝   ✝   ✝

The Pinches is outside on deck. They're celebratin their good fortune with a jug of squonk an a roast pigeon. Tonight's our last night on the Desert Swan. Tomorrow they move into a place in town. The Pinches an Em, that is. I'm gonna be moved to the cellblock where they keep the cage fighters.

I lie on my bunk. I'm chained, hand an foot, like usual. Em sits beside me. She's got a cloth dipped in cranesbill juice an dabs it, real gentle, on the cut near my eye.

I ain't hurtin you too much, am I? she says.

I know my body's sore. It must be. But I feel the hurt from a long ways away, like in a dream. Like I ain't inside my body no more. Like I'm floatin around somewhere outside it. I'm sorry, I whisper to Em.

Sorry fer what? she says.

You shouldn't of had to see that, I says. Her an the Pinches stood with the Cage Master on his balcony. She saw everythin from start to finish.

147

I was so afeared, she says. She would of killed you if she could.

I ain't gonna let nobody kill me, I says. I'm gonna live. I'm gonna live an I'm gonna git us outta here an we're gonna find Lugh. I promised him I would an I . . . oh Emmi . . . Emmi, what're we gonna do? What am I gonna do?

An that's it. I'm undone. The tears trickle at first. She tries to wipe 'em away, but they start comin too fast.

Shhh . . . She strokes my face. Shhh . . . don't let 'em hear you, she says. Don't ever let 'em hear you cry.

She gives me the cloth to stuff aginst my mouth.

She lays down beside me on the bunk. She puts her skinny little girl arms around me an holds me tight. It's all right, Saba, she says. Everythin's gonna be okay.

I double up in pain. I howl into the cloth, my whole body shakin.

I weep fer the girl with the butterfly on her cheek.

I weep fer Emmi. Fer Pa. Fer Lugh. Fer me.

Fer what we used to be.

Fer what got took from us.

Fer what's lost to us ferever.

HOPETOWN

ONE MONTH LATER

They call me the Angel of Death.

That's becuz I ain't never lost a fight. Every time they take me to the Cage, I let the red hot take me over an it fights till it wins.

If it's the third time unlucky fer the girl that's jest bin beat, I turn my back so's I don't hafta see her run the gauntlet. I cain't help hearin, though. The bayin of the chaal-crazy crowd, like a pack closin in on their kill.

I close my mind off. Don't let myself think about it. I gotta stay alive. Gotta git outta here an find Lugh. He's still out there somewhere, waitin fer me to come. I know it. They could be keepin him right here in Hopetown.

Hopetown. It's a cesspit, jest like Mercy said. Every scurfy villain that ever crawled outta a dunghill seems to find their way here.

An the Tonton. They're everywhere, also like Mercy told me. They're personal bodyguards to the Cage Master, who watches the fights from the comfort of his balcony. They control the Gate, checkin who comes into an outta Hopetown. They're in the watchtowers, one at each corner of the palisade surroundin the city. They're in charge of the armed guards who control the Colosseum crowds an patrol the streets. They're in charge of the scum who guard us here in the cellblocks—one block fer the men fighters an one fer the women—an supervise us in the exercise yards.

An the Tonton in charge over all of 'em is DeMalo. They say he answers to the Cage Master, but from what I seen that first day, DeMalo don't answer to nobody but hisself. From time to time, he stands on the Cage Master's balcony while a fight's on. I ain't never seen him close up agin. An I hope I never do.

But all the guards an the watchtowers an the locked cells an the chains that bind me . . . none of that's stopped me tryin to git away.

The first time, I waited till it was night, then I picked the lock of my cell with a rusty nail I found in a corner of the exercise yard. I got caught tryin to lift the keys from the guard's belt while he was forty winkin it.

The second time, I was on the way back from the Colosseum when I punched my guard in the face an made a run fer it.

Both times, they shoved me into the Cooler to try an break my spirit. That's what they always do with troublemakers. But a few hours locked in a metal box unnerground ain't gonna stop me tryin to git outta this place an they know it.

That's why they started chainin me to my cot all the time I'm in my cell. That's why they keep me in a locked transport cage on my way to an from the Colosseum to fight. An that's why they search me before they lock me back in my cell.

But they don't ever hurt me. Don't ever lay even a finger on me. I don't fight more'n twice a week. The Angel of Death's a big draw fer the crowds. I'm the best thing that's happened to Hopetown in a long time. They wanna make sure it lasts.

I dunno what kinda deal the Pinches made with the Cage Master, but whatever it is, they must be doin fine by it. Sometimes I see her, Miz Pinch, on the Cage Master's balcony, watchin me fight, but other'n that, I ain't had no more to do with any of 'em.

I also ain't seen Emmi. I hate not knowin if she's okay or not, but I ain't got no way of sendin a message to her. All I can do is hope that she'll find a way of sendin one to me. An that she's somehow keepin outta the way of Miz Pinch's fist.

I'm well fed. I got my own cell an a cot with a blanket. Th'other girl fighters is all kept in one big cell together an hafta to bunk down on the cold ground at night. They don't git no special treatment.

Even the watch captain, Mad Dog, keeps his distance from me. He's called Mad Dog on account of the times when he's so hopped up on chaal there's no tellin what he might do. An he does plenty. To the guards, to th'other fighters. But not to me. He don't dare touch me.

So I eat what they give me, fight when they make me, an look fer my chance to git away. I'll take any chance at all. A guard lookin th'other way. A door left open at the right time. Anythin. They can slam me in the Cooler all they like. I only gotta git lucky once.

In the still of night, I sit or pace my cell. I don't sleep more'n a hour or two at a time. An that's because the moment I shut my eyes, the darkness comes fer me. It slithers outta its hidin place to wrap me in its cold cold arms. It slides into my blood, my bones, my soul. It squeezes out all hope.

If I let it in, I'll never git outta here. I'll stay an fight in the Cage till I start to lose. I'll stay till I die in the gauntlet.

I'm afeared that, in the end, the darkness will turn out to be stronger'n the red hot.

The moment I shut my eyes, it comes.

The darkness comes.

The darkness an the dreams.

† † †

I'm in the Colosseum.

It's silent. Empty. Dark. The dead time of night.

I'm in the Cage, my feet bare, my clothes in rags. I rattle at the door, but it's locked. I'm trapped inside.

I feel a pricklin at the back of my neck. Slowly I turn.

They all stand there. Every girl I ever fought. Every girl I beat an sent to the gauntlet. Locked into the Cage with me. They ain't nuthin but shadows, their faces in darkness, but I know them. Each an every one. The color of her eyes, the shape of her nose, how the fear smells on her skin.

They start movin, glidin towards me on silent feet.

Fergive me. I whisper it, say it, scream it—fergive me fergive me fergive me—but no sound comes outta my throat.

They're on top of me now. They surround me. They pull me down.

✝   ✝   ✝

Thick darkness, like a blanket.

Voices. Whisperin. Mutterin. Sighin. But far away, so's I cain't make out the words. Then, Saba! Saba, help me!

Lugh's voice. But when he was small. Emmi's age.

Lugh! I call. I'm here! I'm tryin to find you! Where are you?

I dunno! Hurry, Saba! It's so dark. I . . . I'm frightened. He starts to cry.

It's okay, Lugh! I call. I'm gonna find you! Keep talkin so I can find you!

I cain't! I cain't! Saba! They're comin!

He screams.

Lugh! I yell. Lugh!

Silence.

Then the voices agin. Closer now so I can hear what they're sayin.

Too late . . . too late . . . too late . . .

No, I whimper. No! Please! Lugh! I'm here! I'm comin!

I drag myself outta the dream. I'm soaked with sweat. I sit up, my heart poundin.

I wait. It always takes a couple of minutes fer me to come to, to git my breath back. My blanket's all twisted an tangled with the chain on my right ankle.

Every night I dream of Lugh. I never see him. Only hear him. Sometimes he's frightened an callin fer me, like tonight. Other times he's angry, shoutin.

Gawdam you, Saba, where are you? What's takin you so long?

But the worst dream is the one where he says my own words back to me.

I'll find you. Wherever they take you, I swear I'll find you.

Over an over, never endin until I wake up an it stops.

Some nights I fall back to sleep after the dreams, other nights I lie awake an wait fer the dawn to creep into the cell-block. I roll my blanket unner my head, lie back an wait to see what it's gonna be tonight.

Was it a bad 'un this time? A whisper from the cell next to mine. The one where they keep all th'other female fighters locked up together.

I don't say nuthin. I don't like to talk to them I fight or them I'm gonna hafta fight. An none of 'em talk to the Angel of Death. They're afeared of me. I reckon it's better that way. I know most of their voices though an I don't recognize this one, so she must be new. A low, soft voice. Nice.

I heard you last night too, she says. An the night before. Ever since I came.

Now I know. They brought in a girl three nights ago. Tall an thin. A bit sickly lookin. A few years older'n me, maybe twenny. She lost her first fight today.

If she hears me, that means the rest of 'em can hear me too. It's dangerous to let yer enemy see weakness. Weakness can git you killed. Then, it's like she sees inside my head. She says, It's okay. Nobody else knows. Jest me. I don't sleep much.

I hear her shuffle closer to the bars. I cain't see her, not even her shape in the dark. The cellblock ain't got no windows. It's lit by torches durin the day an when night comes, it's black as black.

You lost today, I says. I heard 'em talkin. They say you didn't even try.

I ain't no fighter, she says, not like you. The sooner I lose, the sooner it's all over.

You wanna die? I says.

I wanna be free, she says. I ain't never bin free. Not my whole life. She's quiet fer a moment or two. Then she says, D'you mind that they call you the Angel of Death?

No.

The other girls're afeared of you. They know that if they fight you, it's the end.

I don't say nuthin.

My name's Helen, she says.

I'm Saba, I says.

Saba. That's a nice name.

I pull my blanket around me an lie down.

G'night, Saba, she says. Sweet dreams.

G'night, Helen, I says.

An I sleep.

† † †

Emmi's figgered out how to git herself into the cellblock to see me. She's started to come in with the water carriers. They're the grubby kids who turn up first thing every mornin jest before dawn. They come with their buckets of fresh water an empty 'em into the troughs that run along the edge of the cells. Emmi slips out to see me an is back at work with her morning chores before the Pinches wake up.

It's Emmi who whispers to me what's goin on in Hopetown, who tells me how the place works an where everythin is.

She's tougher'n she used to be, that's fer sure. You wouldn't know her to be the same girl as left Silverlake that day. A couple of times she's come in with a cut lip or bruise on her arm that made my fists clench, but fer the most part she manages to stay outta Miz Pinch's way.

Emmi. On her own in a hellhole like this. Somehow managin to fend fer herself. Who'd of thought it?

†   †   †

It's bin four nights since Helen first spoke to me. Her an me talk a little bit every night now. I ain't never bin much of a talker essept with Lugh, an since I bin in this place I'm outta the habit of it even more.

But I like Helen. She's about th'only person I met fer a long time who ain't crazy. An she ain't afeared of me. Says she won't live long enough to meet me in the Cage, so what's the point, we might as well be friends.

We always wait till th'other girls fall to sleep an the cell-block guards do their last check. They sit outside till their relief comes on at daybreak, so we're safe once we hear the door slam shut an the bar slot into place.

Then I slide offa my cot. My leg chain's long enough fer me to sit next to her on the cold floor, with the cage bars between us. The warmth of her body puts me in mind of how Lugh an me used to sit, back to back, an how I could feel his heartbeat in my body, feel his breathin.

Helen lost her second fight today. She ain't told me herself but I heard th'others talkin. We both know she ain't got much time left.

Now she says to me, tell me what happened to yer brother.

So I do. I tell her what happened the day the Tonton came

161

an killed Pa an took Lugh away. It's such a relief to talk about him, after him jest bein inside my head fer so long. When I git to the bit where they asked about Lugh bein born at midwinter, I feel her go still.

Wait a minute, she says. Midwinter. D'you remember what they said? Their ezzack words, I mean.

I don't even hafta think before I answer her. The words is burned into my brain. I says, The guy says to Procter John, is this him? Golden Boy here? Is he the one born at midwinter? An Procter John says yes an then the Tonton, he asks Lugh how old he is. Lugh says eighteen an then he asks him agin, was you born at midwinter. Lugh says yes, an that's when they took him.

It's like they came lookin fer him, says Helen. Like they knew they'd find him at Silverlake.

I'm surprised she says it, jest like that. That's it, I says. That's it ezzackly.

Was there anythin else? she says.

No, that's about it. Oh, of course. Mercy says there was a stranger there when Lugh got born, a man.

A man. Who was he? D'you know his name?

Yeah. Trask. Mercy said he called hisself Trask. Said he got all excited when Lugh came, said how he went on an on about how a boy born at midwinter was a wonderful thing. He kept sayin it over an over an nobody knew why an then he jest . . . disappeared. They never seen him agin.

No, says Helen. I don't s'pose they did.

My heart slams aginst my ribs. I grab at her through the cage bars. Find her hand an hold it tight in both of mine.

Helen, what is it? You know somethin. Tell me.

I don't want to, she says.

Jest say it, I says. Say it quick.

All right, she says. Saba, John Trask was my father.

† † †

I wish I could see her face. Look in her eyes an know if she's tellin the truth. I squeeze her hand hard.

Don't lie to me, I says.

I wouldn't, she says, I swear it's the truth. Saba, yer brother is in great danger. It was the Tonton who took him all right.

Is he here in Hopetown?

I don't think so, she says. No. I think they took him to a place called Freedom Fields.

Where is it? I says.

North of here, she says. Deep in the Black Mountains. It's hard to git to. Hidden away.

Freedom Fields, I says. Lugh's at Freedom Fields. What else d'you know?

Listen, Saba, she says, if he's at Freedom Fields, that means the King's got him.

The King? I says. I ain't never heard of him.

Hopetown belongs to him, she says. Hopetown an all the land around, as far as you care to go. DeMalo's his man. His second in command.

What about the Cage Master?

He does what they tell him, she says. There's the King, there's DeMalo an there's the Tonton who're like his . . . his personal army. That's who you gotta be afraid of.

What else? I says. I need to know everythin.

The King ain't right in the head. None of 'em are. They believe strange things. Mad things. My father believed 'em too.

Yer father, I says. John Trask.

Yes. He was one of 'em. A Tonton, a spy fer the King. He's dead now, but he was definitely the one at Silverlake that day. I was only little but I remember him comin back to Freedom Fields an how excited they all got when he said he'd found the one, he'd found the boy.

Found what boy? I says.

She's silent.

Helen! I says.

I don't wanna tell you, she whispers.

You've gotta, I says. Please, Helen. Go on.

He said he'd found the boy, she says. The boy born to be killed at midsummer. Killed so the King will live.

My stummick twists. My breath tightens. I . . . I don't . . . unnerstand, I says. What d'you mean . . . kill him so the King will live? What're you talkin about?

She starts to talk fast. Low, so's we don't disturb nobody. It's all about chaal, Saba. You seen this place. Everyone here's chewin it or smokin it. Mad Dog, the cellblock guards, everybody who comes to see us fight. An one person controls the chaal. He grows it, harvests it, an supplies it.

The King, I says.

That's becuz there's only one place with the right conditions to grow it. You need the right kinda earth, the right light, the right amount of rain.

Freedom Fields, I says. In the Black Mountains.

The Tonton round people up, take 'em to Freedom Fields as slaves an force 'em to work in the fields.

An they control 'em with chaal, I says.

Now yer gittin the idea, she says.

So the man who controls the chaal, controls everythin an everybody. He's all powerful, I says.

That's the King, she says.

But . . . I still don't unnerstand, I says. What's all this gotta do with Lugh?

Every six years, on midsummer's eve, they sacrifice a boy.

They kill him. An that boy cain't jest be any boy. He's gotta be eighteen year old an born at midwinter.

The little hairs stand up on the back of my neck. Lugh, I says.

The King believes that when the boy dies, that boy's spirit, his strength moves into him, it moves into the King. An his power's renewed fer another six years.

But that's . . . crazy, I says.

I told you, she says, the King's wrong in the head. But he believes it. An becuz he believes it, the rest of 'em do. It's the chaal, Saba. Jest enough of it makes people dull-witted an slow an easy to control. Too much of it an they're outta control, like the crowds in the Colosseum when a fighter runs the gauntlet. Like Mad Dog. Once they start on it, they cain't stop. They don't wanna stop.

But sacrifice, I says. I don't believe it.

I know how it sounds, but it's true. I seen it myself. This midsummer's eve it's six years since the last sacrifice. Yer brother's eighteen. He was born at midwinter. It's his turn.

An they knew about Lugh becuz of yer father, I says.

Yes. Like I said, he told 'em about Lugh. After that, they kept watch on him over the years to make sure he didn't come to no harm.

Our neighbor, I says. Procter John. That's what he meant when he said, I bin keepin a eye on him all this time.

Don't blame him, Saba, they would of forced him to do it.

But why didn't they take Lugh when he was born? I says. Or later on? Why wait till now?

Becuz they need the boy to have a strong spirit. An lettin him live with his family, livin in freedom, keeps his spirit strong.

Lugh's strong as they come, I whisper.

The stronger he is when he dies, the stronger the King will be. Listen Saba, she says, it's less'n a month to midsummer's eve. If you wanna save yer brother, you gotta find a way of gittin outta here soon. You gotta—

The cellblock door flies open an Mad Dog, the watch captain, comes in. He's twirlin a long thick stick in his hands. He's outta his head on chaal, all jittery an bright-eyed, laughin to hisself. The guards light his way with torches.

How's my girls tonight? says Mad Dog.

The fighters in the main cell wake up right away. They're on their feet, scuttlin into the shadows so's he cain't see 'em to pick on. I was back on my cot the moment the door flew open.

He runs the stick along the cell bars.

Wake up, he says. Daddy wants to play.

Helen, I says, move!

She's froze with fear, still crouched down by the cell bars where we was talkin.

Mad Dog spots her.

What're you doin there? He pushes his stick through the bars an pokes at her. Come on out, you rat! She shrinks away.

Leave her alone, I says.

Oooh, he says. He moves along to my cell an leers at me. If it ain't the Angel of Death.

I stare at him. Let him see how much I hate him.

You think yer somethin, don't you? he says. I tell you, if it was up to Mad Dog, you'd be outside right now gittin a beatin you'd never ferget. That day will come. An when it does, you'll be beggin me fer mercy. But not now. Yer the star attraction in Hopetown these days an Mad Dog don't wanna git into trouble. But I'm bored. I wanna bit of fun.

He points at Helen. Bring out the rat, he says.

He jerks his head an the guards unlock the main cage, push their way in through the girls. They twist Helen's arm behind her back an haul her out.

Helen! I says. Wait! Leave her alone!

Mad Dog drags one of the guard's chairs into the middle of the cellblock an sits on it backwards. His eyes spark with excitement an he's startin to twitch. His fingers, his shoulders, his feet. That means trouble.

Let's see, he says. How's about you sing me a song?

I dunno no songs, says Helen in a low voice.

She don't know no songs. Mad Dog looks all around, like he's surprised. Well, can you dance? Do me a little dance . . . rat. Go on, what're you waitin fer? Dance.

Helen don't move.

I said, dance!

Leave her alone! I says.

Shut up, jest shut up! Gawdammit, he yells, do I hafta do everythin myself?

He throws his chair aginst the wall an it smashes into bits. Then Mad Dog starts dancin. He twirls his stick, throws it in the air, dances around it.

See? he says. Look how easy it is! I'm dancin! Let's everybody dance! C'mon!

Helen's stood there, her arms clamped to her sides, starin at him.

Suddenly he stops. What're you starin at, rat? I said . . . what're you starin at? He screams it at the top of his voice, the veins in his neck poppin out. He grabs her by the arm an starts draggin her towards the door. She cries out.

Helen! I scream. Let her go, you bastard! I leap at the cell door, fergettin I'm chained to the cot an the cot's fixed to the floor. I land face down but scramble up right away.

Mad Dog shoves Helen at the two cellblock guards. Take her outside, he says. They take her by the arms an hustle her outta the door.

Helen! I says. No! Helen!

Mad Dog's unlockin the door of my cell. I scrabble back onto my cot, into the corner, an kick at him as he unchains me from the cot. He grabs my arm, yanks me to my feet an outta my cell. He pulls up the metal trapdoor in the floor of the cellblock an shoves me down inside.

Sweet dreams, Angel, he says. Then he spits on me. He slams the door shut an I'm in the Cooler. In the darker than dark. The blacker than black.

I know I'll never see Helen agin.

† † †

The girls in the cellblock stay silent. They don't do much talkin to each other an sure as hell they don't talk to me. They blame me fer Helen bein dead.

They ain't wrong at that. I blame myself. If she hadn't of bin talkin to me, if I hadn't needed to know about Lugh so bad, we would of bin more careful. Not talked so long. We would of heard the guards an Mad Dog comin. If we had, Helen might still be alive.

But not fer long. That's the truth of it. Helen's time was runnin out. Everybody knew it. She knew it. She was only waitin to lose her third fight. She was only waitin to die in the gauntlet.

I seen what's left of a person after they run the gauntlet. At least she got spared that.

She's free now. Like she wanted to be. But she lies heavy on my heart.

When I ain't thinkin about Helen, I'm thinkin of how

I'm gonna find a way outta here. Midsummer eve, she told me. I gotta git to a place called Freedom Fields in the Black Mountains by midsummer eve. Jest over three weeks from now.

So I watch. An I wait.

My chance is gonna come soon. I know it will. It must come.

It must.

† † †

I stand in the middle of the Cage. Stare out at the crowd. They jump to their feet an roar fer me. I'm the biggest draw they ever had in Hopetown. They pack in when I'm fightin.

I look up through the top bars. Nero's there, like always. Perched on top of the light tower that stands right next to the Cage. It ain't carried light since Wrecker days, of course. Now all it carries is the people who clamber up to watch the fights from there. The light tower's the cheapest seats there is.

Essept nobody sits there when I'm fightin. Not with Nero perched on top. Everybody's skeered of him. They all believe that crows bring death. Defeat. Destruction. They believe I git my powers from him.

I like to look up an see him there. He always stays till I win an then he flies off. He's done it since my first fight.

But my power ain't down to Nero. It's down to the red hot. That's what keeps me winnin.

There's a girl in the front row today. Tall, gold skinned, with a proud nose.

She ain't like most what comes to the Colosseum. Other people might not take no notice, but the moment I see her, I know her right off fer a warrior. She's got a look about her. She takes things in with quick eyes, things that other people'd jest pass over without noticin.

An she don't take leaf from the chaal man when he offers it. Not like everybody else who comes to the fights. Neether do the three girls with her take any.

In fact, they jostle him so's his basket tips out an then they scuff all the chaal leaf unner their feet so they git all crushed an filthy. When a armed guard comes over to see what's goin on, they pretend it warn't nuthin to do with 'em.

She sees me lookin at her, watchin what they're doin. Raises one eyebrow as if to say, what's it to you anyways?

The cage door opens an my opponent enters to boos an jeers. She's a tough-lookin, brown-skinned girl, name of Epona. She only arrived a couple of days ago. I ain't never fought her before but the word is she fights dirty. The Cage allows pretty much anythin—hits, kicks, stranglin, twistin legs an arms—but not bitin or gougin. I heard she'll try both if the cagekeepers ain't got a clear view an she gits the chance. I'll hafta watch her.

I put the girl in the front row outta my mind. I put everythin outta my mind. I clear it so the red hot can take over. That's the way it's gotta be if I wanna survive.

The keeper sounds the gong an we're off.

✝ ✝ ✝

Epona gits me in a stranglehold on the ground. While I'm strugglin to git free, I look up an there she is, the girl in the front row, starin right at me. Our eyes meet.

She's tryin to tell me somethin. But what? What is it?

My concentration slips. Epona's got advantage. She shuffles us around, outta sight of the keeper, an bites me on the hand.

I roar with anger. The red hot kicks in an I'm back in the fight, full strength. I throw Epona offa me. I git her on the ground in a leg an arm twist. She moans. I twist harder. Then even harder.

Quit! she yells. Quit!

Epona's first loss. She glares hate at me as they take her from the Cage.

I look at the front row. The girl an her friends is gone.

Damn her. She nearly made me lose my fight.

✝ ✝ ✝

I'm in my transport cage on the back of the mulecart, bein driven back through Hopetown to the cellblock. Two armed guards sit up front an, like always, crowds surround the cart. Everyone wants to see the Angel of Death close up. The brave ones reach in through the bars an try to touch me so's they can brag to their friends later. I snap my teeth at 'em an they shrink away, shriekin with excitement.

The warrior girl pushes through till she's close beside the cage. She's about my height. She's got golden skin with tiny freckles sprinkled all over. She's huddled inside her cloak, but I can see she's got curly hair the color of dark copper an eyes green as forest moss. She's the most beautiful girl I ever seen.

You nearly made me lose that fight, I says.

I'm sorry you didn't, she says. That's my girl you beat.

Epona? I says. Whaddya mean, yer girl? Who are you?

I'm Maev, she says, walkin alongside. We're the Free Hawks.

I look closer at who's walkin beside the cart. Three tough-lookin girls, the ones who was sittin beside her in the Colosseum.

Look around, says Maev.

I scan the crowd through the bars of my cage. Another girl in a robe. She moves it slightly so I can see the crossbow at her side. So they're smart enough to smuggle weapons past the Gate guards of Hopetown. As I look over the crowd, another girl nods at me.

So Epona's a Free Hawk too, I says.

She is, says Maev. An we're gonna git her outta here.

My heart skips a beat. How? I says.

I'm workin on it, she says. Security's pretty tight here. But in the meantime, I'd appreciate it if you didn't git my fighter killed.

The Free Hawks is fighters, I says.

Warriors, she says, like you. An occasional highway robbers.

An you don't want Epona to lose, I says.

That's right, she says.

Well I don't wanna lose eether, I says. Losers go down to the gauntlet.

That's true, says Maev.

Maybe we can help each other, I says.

My thoughts ezzackly, she says.

Our eyes meet. How do I know I can trust you? I says.

She gives the nod to two girls standin next to one of the armed street guards. They move in on him. Suddenly a surprised look crosses his face. He starts to slump to the ground. They catch him an drag him back into a dark doorway. They step out agin an disappear into the crowd.

You better not try that too often, I says. Where're you stayin?

We're holed up in the northeast sector, she says. There's a empty shanty in a place called Spanish Alley.

I'll git word to you, I says. I'll send my sister. Her name's Emmi.

I'll be waitin, she says.

Then she's gone.

† † †

I ain't seen Emmi fer a good few days now. Not since Helen told me about Lugh. Not since I spoke to Maev.

Every mornin, when the water carriers show up jest before dawn, I peer through the gloom of the cellblock to see if she's with 'em. I started to ask one of 'em, a skinny little boy with skeered eyes, if he'd seen her, but he ran off the moment I opened my mouth to talk.

I'm startin to git worried. I need to see her. Make sure she's all right. An I need to talk to her about Lugh. About Maev an the Free Hawks. About my plan.

The cellblock door opens. The weak light of dawn trickles in. The guards light the wall torches as the water carriers shuffle in an start emptyin their buckets into the troughs.

This time Emmi's with 'em. I let out my breath in relief as she makes her way over to my cell, carryin her heavy bucket carefully so's it don't slop too much.

Nobody's lookin our way. I go over to the trough, kneel down an start scoopin up water, splashin it over my face, neck an hands while she pours it out slowly from her bucket.

Where you bin all this time? I was gittin worried, I says.

I couldn't git away, says Emmi. Miz Pinch had bad tooth-ache the past few days. She warn't sleepin like usual. It's back to normal now.

Are y'all right?

I'm fine. You look awful.

I ain't bin sleepin much eether, I says. Listen, Em, I found out where they took Lugh. It's a place called Freedom Fields. An I met somebody who's gonna help us git outta here.

Her eyes widen. Really? Who?

Her name's Maev, I says. I'm gonna need you to git a message to her.

Okay, she says. Where do I find her?

She's stayin in a empty shanty in Spanish Alley, I says. Northeast sector. D'you know it?

Yeah, I think so, she says.

Good, I says. All right, here's what you need to—

Hey! Hey you! Girl! A guard's lookin our way, frownin.

I better go, says Emmi.

Come back tomorrow fer the message, I says, it's important.

I'll be here. Oh! she says. I nearly fergot!

She pulls somethin outta her pocket an hands it to me. A smooth pink stone. My heartstone that Miz Pinch stole from me.

She flashes me a big grin. I took it when she warn't lookin, she says.

Thanks, Em, I says. I shove it down inside my vest, next to my heart.

Girl! What's takin so long over there? The guard starts to head over to us.

See you tomorrow, Saba. Emmi picks up her bucket, ducks her head down an scuttles past the guard an outta the door.

† † †

The cellblock guards lead me, chained at wrist an ankle, into the female fighters' exercise yard. Everybody's here, they always are fer the evenin session.

I need to speak to Epona. Tell her about my plan. I take a quick look around. There she is, with a group of girls.

The Angel of Death don't talk to nobody. That's how I like it. So I cain't jest walk over to her, it 'ud draw too much attention. I'll hafta be careful about how I do this.

She looks my way an I catch her eye. Jerk my head a little bit, to tell her to come over, I wanna talk. Her eyes widen, but she gives me a nod. She's smart. She'll wait fer the right moment.

I stand while the guards unchain me so's I can move about. The male fighters is in the exercise yard next to ours. Now they start up like they always do when they see me. They come crowdin up to the chainlink fence, makin kissin noises an callin out, Help! It's the Angel of Death! Save me!

I used to glare at 'em, but it set 'em off even more. Now I jest ignore 'em.

There's one, though, who don't come to the fence. He leans in the corner of the men's yard, one leg crossed over th'other, cleanin his fingernails with a bit of twig like he ain't got a care in the world.

I ain't seen him before. He ain't battered up like the rest of 'em, so he must be new. He ain't even had his head shaved yet.

Jest then, like he feels me watchin him, he stops what he's doin. He lifts his head. Our eyes meet. He tosses the twig away, saunters up to the fence an hooks his hands into the chainlink.

He don't say a word. He jest runs his eyes slowly over my body, right down to my feet, then up agin. Th'other men whistle an jeer. I feel heat rushin through me. Feel it strain my chest, my neck, my cheeks. I know I must be bright red. Then he smiles. A lopsided, crook of a smile.

My fists clench. Cocky bastard. Who does he think he is?

So I do the same to him. I cross my arms over my chest an look him up an down. Brown hair to his shoulders. Silver gray eyes in a tanned face. High cheekbones, a shadow of beard. Crooked nose, like it's bin broke. Lean but strong lookin. Like he knows how to take care of hisself.

Our eyes meet agin.

Like what you see, Angel? he says.

I step to the fence. Hook my hands into the links, next to his. I lean in close. He's got tiny white lines around his eyes from squintin. Or maybe smilin. He smells of warm dust an sage.

You ain't my type, I says.

As I turn on my heel an walk away, one of the men calls out, She sure told you, Jack!

I hear him laugh.

His name's Jack.

Heat burns into me. Crawls over my skin. A trickle of sweat runs down my chest. I pull out the heartstone tucked safe inside my vest. It's warm. No. Hot.

That's strange. I look at the sky. The sun's dyin in the west. The day should be coolin down.

But it feels like high noon. White hot.

† † †

Epona makes her way slowly in my direction. She does it so's you wouldn't notice unless you was lookin out fer it. At last she stops a little ways off from me. She squats down an starts tracin in the dirt with her finger.

I start with my usual exercises. Stretches first. Arms an then legs.

I talked to Maev, I says. I speak in a low voice, don't look at her direct.

I saw her at the fight today, she says.

Looks like we'll be workin together to git outta here, I says.

Suits me, she says. What's the plan?

How many Hawks is there? I says.

Forty some odd, she says.

Can Maev git 'em all here? I says.

Yeah, she says. But they won't all git through the Gate past the guards. That many girls 'ud make the Tonton suspicious, even if they came in smaller groups.

Maybe they wouldn't git suspicious if there was a lotta other people tryin to git in at the same time, I says.

Go on, she says.

I'm in the Cage agin in two days, I says. I'm due to fight you. I plan to lose that fight. When people hear the Angel of Death's on a losin streak, they'll pack the place out. The Tonton won't be able to keep track of who's comin an who's goin. They'll pull most of the guards away from the cellblocks to help keep the crowds unner control.

She grins. A quick flash of white teeth, a dimple in her cheek. A completely different girl. I like the way you think, she says.

I'm gonna lose aginst you three times, I says. Then I'm gonna run the gauntlet.

She gives a low whistle.

Oh, I got no intention of dyin, I says. That's where the Hawks come in. When I start to run that gauntlet, th'only people on eether side's gonna be Free Hawks. They'll pull me down all right, but only to help me disappear.

I git it, says Epona. It'll take a little while fer everybody to figger out yer gone but when they do . . . all hell's gonna break loose. That crowd ain't gonna like bein cheated of the Angel's blood.

An while that's goin on, I says, you'll be escapin from the Cage an . . .

She looks around the yard, at the rest of the fighters.

. . . the Hawks'll be settin all of these free, she says. Then we'll burn Hopetown to the ground. You'll help us, won't you? You know this place an the guards better'n anybody.

Of course I will, I says. I look her straight in the eye.

Lugh always says it's the best thing to do when yer tellin a lie.

† † †

Emmi manages to find Maev in Spanish Alley an tell her about my plan.

Maev thinks it'll work fine. She's already sent fer the rest of the Hawks an, over the next few days, they'll all be gittin ready.

She sent word back with Emmi that once they smuggle me through the gauntlet, we'll head straight fer the cellblocks where I'll help 'em set all the fighters free. After we set fires goin all over town, we'll make our way to the northeast corner, well away from the Gate. Everybody else'll be leavin the burnin town that way. Not us. The Hawks is makin a hole in the palisade fer us to escape through. One of the Hawks'll bring Emmi there.

So that's it.

Well . . . not quite. I'm fine with everythin up to the point where the Hawks smuggle me through the gauntlet. After that, I got other plans fer me an Em.

† † †

I lose to Epona.

I make it look good. Real good. I let my right foot slip an Epona's on me like a jackal on a corpse. She gits me in a strong headlock. I push back the red hot that tells me to fight back.

In the blue skies above the Colosseum, Nero swoops an screams with fear. I wish I could tell him why I'm doin what I'm doin, but I cain't.

At first, the crowd cain't hardly believe it. You can see it in their faces. Not the Angel of Death. She's unbeaten. Unbroken. Unstoppable.

But then they git the whiff of blood, my blood, an they howl fer more. In the end, they don't care whose blood it is.

Maev's in the front row. As I lie on the ground, our eyes meet. She nods. That's one fight down. Two more to go.

✝   ✝   ✝

I ain't bin back in the cellblock more'n a few minutes when the door slams open.

There's a shout. Make way fer the King! Make way!

My innards lurch. My mouth goes dry. I go over to the door of my cell. Press myself aginst the bars so's I can see better.

Twelve Tonton with torches run in, pushin the cellblock guards outta the way. They line theirselves up along the length of the cellblock. They lift their torches to light a path.

A man steps through the door.

I don't believe it. It's the man from Rooster Pinch's book. He stands in the doorway with his walkin stick. Jest like the picture in the book. Thick black curly hair down past his shoulders an piled high on top. Animal skins thrown over one shoulder, trailin behind him onto the floor. Fancy shirt with frilly collar an cuffs. Short, puffy little britches that show his legs. White stockins. High heeled shoes. Sword at his side.

His face is painted white. His mouth's painted red, like one of the Hopetown whores.

What was it Rooster called him? Lewis Ex Eye Vee. The Sun King of France. Dead fer hunnerds of years, he said. So it cain't really be him. It's somebody who looks like him.

He starts to walk down the cellblock, head high. He takes tiny steps, like his shoes is too tight. He's holdin a white lace keercheef to his nose.

The fighters in the big cage next to me, they're all doin like I am, crowdin up to the bars of their cell to git a good look at him.

The Tonton bow their heads. Your Majesty, each one murmurs as he goes past.

A man follows a little ways behind him. It's DeMalo. My heart clutches. No. Please. Not him. Right away, my body goes all tight.

After DeMalo, comes Miz Pinch. What the hell's she doin here?

Suddenly I realize. They're comin straight down the cellblock. Straight towards me. I scramble back onto my cot. Push myself into the corner. Feel the cold stone of the wall through my thin tunic.

The King's here. The one who's got Lugh. Maybe he's here to take me. Maybe they caught Maev. Somehow found out our plan.

Don't say a word. Don't give nuthin away. Don't look at DeMalo.

The King stops in front of my cell. DeMalo stands jest behind him, in the shadows. My heart's bangin in my chest so loud, they must be able to hear it.

Miz Pinch rushes past DeMalo. She grabs hold of my cell bars an shakes 'em. I know she wishes she was shakin my neck.

What was that? she shrieks. What d'you call that?

I says naught. Keep my head down.

You threw that fight! she spits. You might be able to fool them chaaled-up morons, but you don't fool me. You threw it an I wanna know why.

Calm yourself, woman. The King's got a voice like a mouth full of damp earth.

A shudder ripples along my spine.

But I know her, son, says Miz Pinch. Vicar, I know this one! She's the—

His arms fly up. He smashes her in the face with his walkin stick.

She cries out. She stumbles, grabs onto the cell bars to keep from fallin. She crouches on the ground. Her lip's split open. She looks old. Frightened.

I cain't hardly believe it. Miz Pinch, the mother of this man.

The mother of the King. Vicar Pinch. But it all makes sense. The picture in Rooster's book. The way Vicar Pinch looks. Why Rooster Pinch lied when I asked him if he had any kids.

How do you address your King? says Vicar Pinch.

She don't speak. Jest cowers there.

Then he screams it, spit flyin from his mouth. How do you address your King?

Yer . . . Yer Majesty, she says. I address my King as Yer Majesty.

If you forget again, he says, he will have you killed. Do you understand?

She nods her head, grabs a corner of his robe an kisses it. Yes, she whispers. All I wanna do is please . . . Yer Majesty. It's all I ever wanted.

He kicks her hand away. Do not dare to touch your King! he says. Now. What were you saying about this girl?

Yer Majesty, I only said that . . . that I know her, Yer Majesty. She ain't like the rest. Her spirit's too strong to let her be beat. She lost today because she wanted to lose. She's a sly one. She's up to somethin.

Miz Pinch glares hate at me.

Enough! He waves his keercheef an she scuttles off into a dark corner of the cellblock. The King will speak to her, says Vicar Pinch. This . . . Angel of Death.

DeMalo steps up to the cell. Come here, girl, he says. His Majesty wishes to speak to you.

It's the first time I've heard his voice. It's deep. Dark. Jest what I'd especk it to sound like.

Come, he says.

I git to my feet, real slow. I take a couple of steps. Stop.

Closer, he says.

I move. Then I'm right next to the cell bars. Right next to him. I don't look up. But I feel him. The warmth of him. The cold of him.

Saba, I think I hear him whisper.

A strange weakness grips me. I sway towards him. Grab at the bars to stop myself.

Then he's turnin away, he's bowin to the King, he's movin back into the shadows. Did he say my name? No . . . I must of imagined it.

Now Pinch steps up to my cell. His hands shoot out. Grab me through the bars. Grab me by the neck. His fingers is strong. They press on my windpipe. Jest enough to make it hard to breathe.

Is the woman right? he says. Did you deliberately lose that fight?

No! I says. I didn't! I wouldn't!

His fingers tighten. I grab his wrists. Struggle to git free. He's too strong. I drag in air through my nose, frantic. He stinks like nuthin I ever smelled before. Sour, sweet, rotten . . . all at the same time.

Your King has made a long and arduous journey to see

you fight, he says. The miraculous warrior they're all talking about, the Angel of Death. He would be vastly displeased to find that he was being deceived.

I ain't deceivin!

Last chance! Are you lying!

No! I gasp. Losin means death! Everybody knows that!

Indeed, he says. Why would you lose on purpose? Why would anyone? It makes no sense.

Suddenly he lets go. I fall to the ground, gaspin, holdin my throat where he pressed on it.

You're imagining things, woman, he says to Miz Pinch. You've had a good run. She's made you a small fortune. You'll just have to find yourself another fighter once this one's run the gauntlet.

I'm sure yer right, Yer Majesty, she says. Yer always right, you always know best. I shouldn't of bothered you. I'm sorry fer wastin yer time, Yer Majesty.

Miz Pinch, a cowed dog at her master's heels.

Slowly I git to my feet.

Wait!

Pinch grabs my wrist. Hauls me aginst the cell bars. He presses a cold finger on my cheekbone. Right on my birth-moon tattoo. He hisses in a breath.

What's this? he says.

It's a . . . tattoo, I says.

The King can see that. Where did you get it?

I think fast.

Where I come from, everybody's got 'em, I says.

And where's that? he says.

Out east, I says.

East, he says. I see.

He stares at me a long moment. His small, dead eyes so much like his mother's. He lets me go. He steps back an holds the kercheef to his nose agin.

DeMalo, he says, the King will remove from this pestilent hole.

Majesty, says DeMalo an bows his head.

But not before I see it. The slight twitch of his lips. A flicker of somethin across his face.

He despises Vicar Pinch.

The Tonton bow the King out like they bowed him in. When they reach the cellblock door, DeMalo lets Pinch an his mother go through first.

Then he turns back to look at me.

My breath catches in my throat. I drop my head. I mustn't meet his eyes. I don't dare. Not even in the gloom of the cellblock.

I feel it when he leaves.

Somethin . . . lets go of me.

An I can breathe agin.

☦   ☦   ☦

The word's out.

The Angel of Death's goin down.

Hopetown's packed. The scum crawl out from whatever rock they live unner to be there, to bet on the next two fights. The Cage Master's only takin primo Wrecker junk as bets—coins, glass beads, gold rings, silver chains . . . they bring what they got to him an he decides what it's worth, if anythin.

Looks like the prospect of my death's worth plenty. To him. To Miz Pinch. An to anybody in Hopetown with a flea-infested bed goin spare. Em tells me they're rentin beds out by the hour, not the night.

Right now the Cage Master's givin even odds on me or Epona to win.

He ain't bin to see me since that first day. When he told me he didn't care if I lived or died. It's true. We're all the same to him. We're all the same to all of 'em who come to see us fight.

While I'm waitin to go into the Cage, I look up to the Cage Master's balcony. He's there, along with DeMalo an the King.

The King leans on the railin, starin down at me. He's dressed all in red today.

My birthmoon tatoo bothered him, that's fer certain. It makes me believe that Helen's right, that he's holdin Lugh prisoner at Freedom Fields. He must of noticed Lugh's tatoo.

I can only hope that he bought my story about how I came by mine.

I lose my fight, of course. That's two fights down. One to go.

Tomorrow's the day.

✝   ✝   ✝

It's him. Jack. Legs crossed at the ankle, arms crossed over his chest, leanin aginst a wall in a corner of the male fighters' exercise yard. Starin at me.

When he sees me lookin at him, he pushes off from the wall an wanders over to the fence. Without my tellin 'em to, my feet start movin an all of a sudden I'm standin in front of him. His long hair's gone now. Shaved off, like the rest of us.

Angel, angel, he says. He's smilin an shakin his head. What're you up to?

I dunno what yer talkin about, I says.

You don't lose fights, he says. Not unless you want to, that is.

His silvery eyes flick over to where Epona's standin, talkin to some of th'other girls.

I saw you talkin to yer friend th'other day, he says. Looked like a mighty innerestin conversation.

I dunno what you mean, I says. Heat's startin to crawl all over my chest. The heartstone feels warm aginst my skin.

The same thing that happened the last time I talked to him. I frown.

He shrugs. All right, he says. Don't tell me. I'll find out eventually.

You won't find out nuthin, I says. Cuz there ain't nuthin to find out.

Suddenly he's got hold of my wrist. I didn't even see him move. A tingle shoots up my arm. Like when Lugh an me was nearly hit by the lightnin that day.

The smile's gone. His face looks dead serious. Looks to me like yer playin a dangerous game, he says.

Why should you care what I do?

We stare at each other a long moment. Then, No reason, he says. Jest . . . be careful, Angel. That's all. He lets go of my wrist slowly. Almost like he don't want to.

As I move away from him, the heartstone starts to cool down.

†   †   †

Darkness. Hard to see. Smoke fills the air. Burns my throat, my nostrils, stings my eyes.

Where are you? I scream.

No answer. Hungry flames lick at wood. Embers pop an hiss.

I hafta find him. Cain't leave him here.

The sound of a heartbeat. My heartbeat. Over an over. So loud. It fills my brain, my head. I cover my ears with my hands. Panic grips me. I turn in circles, blind.

Where are you? I shout. Where are you?

Another voice now. Whisperin. Mercy's voice.

The heartstone lets you know . . . the heartstone . . . heartstone . . . hurry, Saba. . .

Bright sun. Exercise yard. Epona smiles. We're gonna burn Hopetown to the ground, she says.

I gotta find him. Before it's too late.

Too late . . . too late . . . too late . . .

I wake, mutterin to myself. I'm soaked with sweat, my blanket twisted around my legs, my heart poundin in my chest.

That was a new one. I ain't dreamed of fire before. An it warn't Lugh I was searchin fer so frantic. I dunno who it was.

I do what I always do to chase the nightmares away. I sit on my cot, hug my knees to my chest an close my eyes.

I think of water. Clean, clear water. A lake. I dive in. It washes over me, around me. My tired body, my tattered soul, my heavy heart. As I swim, it washes me clean.

An so I make it through to another dawn.

† † †

The keeper opens the door. I step into the Cage fer the last time. My hands an legs feel far away, like they don't belong to me. My stummick's clenched into knots. My mouth's dry.

I cain't hear myself think fer the noise of the crowd. Them that couldn't squeeze into the Colosseum fill the streets an sit on rooftops. Even if they cain't see what's goin on, they can hear the shouts an roars. One way or another, they all wanna be part of the Angel's end. Of my end.

The chaal vendors is doin a roarin trade, strugglin through the crowds with big baskets of the dark green leaf balanced on their heads. They wanna git everybody hopped up fer the big finish.

The Cage Master's on his balcony, all crammed with people dressed in their finest. I can see the Pinches there—Rooster an Miz Pinch pushed into a corner. Vicar Pinch, the King, is the center of attention. He sits on a fancy golden chair an everybody dances around him, offerin him cups of this an plates of that. He waves 'em all away with his lace kercheef an stares down at the Colosseum.

DeMalo stands nearby.

I hope Emmi's safe. The Free Hawks said they'd look after her, but I won't be happy till I see her fer myself.

I stare at the center aisle. It runs from the bottom of the Colosseum right to the top in a straight line.

The gauntlet run.

Maev's in the front row on the center aisle. Right next

to the gauntlet run. She gives me the tiniest nod. She looks behind her an then looks back at me.

Fer the first ten rows or so, there's tough-lookin girls packed in at the ends of the rows, also right next to the gauntlet run.

I see a man try to push one of 'em outta the way. Tryin to steal her place along the gauntlet, to git closer to where the action's gonna be. The girl don't even look as she chops him in the throat with her elbow.

The Free Hawks is here. Jest like Maev promised.

Nero sits on the light tower that stands right next to the Cage. He cries out, over an over agin. He's beside hisself with fear, I can tell. All of a sudden, he swoops down, lands on the Cage an slips in through the bars. He ain't never done that the whole time I bin fightin.

He flutters down to sit on my shoulder. The whole place goes quiet. Even though I'm on a losin streak, they still believe I git my powers from him. Even fer this, my last fight, they ain't bin able to sell the cheap seats on the light tower becuz he's there.

He hops onto my hand. I rub his beak, scratch his head. He purrs in that way crows have, jest like a cat. I didn't know how much I bin missin him till right now.

Okay, I whisper to him, good boy Nero. He leans his head to one side. Looks straight at me with his bright black eyes. It's okay, I says. I'm gonna be okay.

He gives a croak. He knows what okay means. He unnerstands.

I lift my hand an he flies outta the Cage. Lands on his usual
perch on the light tower. The crowd murmurs, mutters, shifts
in their seats.

The Cage door creaks open agin an Epona walks in.

My heart's bangin aginst my ribs. The blood pounds in
my ears.

We face up. Eye to eye. Crouch down. The keeper sounds
the gong.

My last fight begins.

† † †

I let Epona set the pace. Let her chase me round the Cage,
corner me, hurt me.

But then the red hot kicks in. I try to shove it down, push
it away, but it rips through me. Takes me over. The red hot
don't know Maev. It don't know she's got a plan. It don't trust
her. Becuz the red hot don't know plans or people or trust. It
only knows one thing. Survival.

An I cain't keep it down. It's wild. Cornered. It starts to
fight Epona. It fights fer my life.

What're you doin? she says, her eyes wide. Epona's

strong. She's smart. She pushes me to the edge. But I push right back. I got more to lose than her, with the gauntlet in my sights.

We fight till we're both bloodied, battered, exhausted.

At last she makes a mistake. I git her by the throat. I push her aginst the bars. The crowd goes crazy. They leap to their feet. Outta the corner of my eye, I see Maev. By her face, I know she cain't believe what she's seein. She waves her arms at me. Her mouth moves. Sayin somethin I cain't hear.

But it's the red hot that fills my ears now. Roars at me to squeeze Epona's neck. My hands tighten. Wait! No! No! I grit my teeth, think of smotherin the red hot with blackness, holdin it down in deep black water till it cain't breathe. There's somethin . . . I know I gotta do somethin or . . . remember somethin but I . . . cain't git hold of it, cain't . . .

Lugh. Lugh. I nearly fergot him. How could I?

I'll find you. Wherever they take you, I'll find you. I swear.

I raise my head. The roar of the red hot starts to fade. Then it's gone an I come back to myself.

The need, deep inside me, fer my heart to keep on beatin, fer my lungs to keep on breathin, that powerful need nearly took me over.

Lugh's waitin fer me. Countin on me. Maev. The plan. It's my only hope of gittin outta here. What was I thinkin of?

I let go. Epona falls into my arms. I hold her as she gasps fer breath.

I'm sorry, I says. Sorry. Then I step back. Hold my arms out wide.

Epona lifts her head, holds her hand to her neck. She looks at me, her face confused.

I nod. Go ahead, I says. Do it.

Then she does. She takes me down.

†   †   †

The two cagekeepers haul me to my feet an take me by the arms. Before I know it I'm walkin outta the Cage an standin in front of the crowd.

They're off their heads with rage. They know damn well I took a fall. They hate bein cheated. They boo an bay fer my blood like a pack of wolves. Them that stands near to the gauntlet run, climb an punch an push to git the best place. They all want their chance to be in on the kill.

The red hot's gone. My stummick's in knots. My knees is shakin. I drag in deep breaths, try to git air into my lungs. I thought I felt terror before, but never like this. Never like this.

I look at Maev in the front row. At the Free Hawks, standin at the start of the gauntlet. They look confident. Strong. Hard. Maev's eyes burn into mine.

I've put my life in her hands. Lugh's life. Emmi's. What was

I thinkin of, trustin a stranger? Even if she can be trusted, what if she cain't pull it off? What if the Free Hawks ain't the warriors she says they are an she's jest a girl who talks it up an acts tough?

I look over at the Cage Master's balcony. Everybody in the Colosseum turns to face it. The whole place falls quiet.

Vicar Pinch stands. Takes the red kercheef from the Cage Master. Raises his arm.

I don't dare breathe. When his arm falls, I gotta run. My legs feel like water. Too weak to move.

At that moment, Pinch turns to the Cage Master. Leans in an whispers somethin in his ear. As the Cage Master listens, a little smile comes over his face. He moves to the edge of the balcony. Holds up both his arms.

Ladies and gentlement! he cries. This ain't no ordinary warrior! This ain't no ordinary death! On such a historical occasion, your King demands a clear view of proceedings. Therefore! He decrees that the gauntlet will be run . . . here!

An he throws open his arms. Opens 'em out to the aisle that runs from the Cage to right below his balcony.

Pinch has changed the gauntlet run. He's moved it.

My whole body starts shakin. Sick rises in my throat.

The crowd busts out talkin, yellin, protestin. The gauntlet's always run in the same place, always without fail. People bid more to stand by it an be in on the action. They start to face up to the Tonton an the guards, pushin an shovin at 'em.

No! shouts Epona from inside the Cage. She launches herself at the bars, screamin, No, no, no!

Vicar Pinch smiles.

I look at Maev. Her head moves this way an that—lookin at the Free Hawks, at me, at the new gauntlet run where people's already crowdin in. I can see from her face that she's frantic, tryin to think what to do. But it's too late fer a new plan, too late fer the Hawks to move to the new spot. Anyways, the guards an the Tonton's already in place at the top an bottom of the run to stop people pushin in.

The cagekeepers take me by the arms an drag me over to stand in front of the new run.

So.

After all I bin through, it comes down to this.

Me. Alone. No Maev. No Hawks. No plan.

If I don't think of somethin quick, I'm gonna die in the gauntlet.

Nero calls. Over an over, urgent like I never heard him before.

He's perched on top of the Cage. As soon as he sees me look up, he calls agin an flaps over to land on the light tower. Back to the Cage. Then back to the light tower.

Not so alone after all.

It's a long jump. Maybe six foot.

But I ain't got no choice.

Pinch raises his arm agin. The red kercheef goes down.

Suddenly, I make my legs collapse. I take the cagekeepers by surprise. They lose their grip. I slip free. I run. I spring at the Cage an grab the bars. I start to shin up the outside of it, fast as I can go. My bare toes give me good grip.

One of the keepers leaps. Grabs my foot. Pulls. I'm hangin on with one arm. I kick out. Hit him in the face with my heel. His nose crunches. Blood spurts. He cries out, lets go, falls to the ground. I keep goin. Don't look back.

I pull myself onto the top of the Cage. Stand up, run across the top.

Careful! Careful don't fall through!

Down below me, inside the Cage, Epona takes a runnin leap at the keeper who's still there with her. Outta the corner of my eye, I see him go flyin. Good girl.

I'm nearly at the edge closest to the light tower. I pause. Glance back. Tonton an guards is swarmin up the Cage now, after me. One's jest about to pull hisself onto the top.

I eye up the gap between the Cage an the light tower. I take two steps back. I run. I leap offa the Cage an launch myself into the air.

I throw my hands up. Fingers scrabble. There! I grab warm metal. My body slams into the tower. A jolt through my arms, my shoulders. Jest made it. I pull myself up. Start to climb. Climb higher. Scramble through to th'other side of the tower. The Hopetown side. Down below me, shanty roofs, all crammed in tight together. People who's on the rooftops to hear the fight better stare up at me, their mouths hangin open.

I jump offa the tower. People dive outta the way as I land on the nearest shanty roof. It's crude, made of some flimsy wood. I go right through the roof an land on a table inside. It collapses unnerneath me.

I'm dazed fer a second. I look up through the hole in the roof. Surprised faces look down at me. I leap to my feet an head outta the door. I grab a cloak from a hook on my way out an throw it over me. I need a pair of boots, but no time to stop an look now.

Hidden inside the cloak, I quickly lose myself in the crowds fillin the streets. I keep to the edges, move in an outta doorways.

I can hear the commotion back in the Colosseum. It's startin to spread to the streets.

My heart's beatin like mad. An I'm jest noticin that my elbow an ribs hurt like nobody's business. I must of banged myself up a bit when I landed on the table. Not to mention the poundin I took from Epona.

Well, I sure gave Maev the diversion she wanted.

Now to steal a couple of horses an meet up with Emmi.

She knows the plan. While the Hawks is lettin out the fighters an settin Hopetown on fire, her an me's gonna meet at the northeast corner. There's probly gonna be a Hawk with Em. I'll hafta git her outta the way. But once that's done, we should be free an clear. We'll leave through the hole that the Hawks've made in the palisade wall an head north, deep into the Black Mountains where we'll find Freedom Fields, jest like Helen said.

Where we'll find Lugh.

Jest then, somebody grabs me.

✝ ✝ ✝

Strong arms yank me into a stinkin alley. I throw wild punches. I twist an turn, tryin to free myself.

Wait! Stop, you idiot! a voice yells. I'm a Hawk!

I stop fer a second, pantin. The person pushes back their hood. It's a girl I ain't seen before. Six foot tall, light brown hair, hard eyes. Strong lookin.

I'm Ash, she says.

Oh, I says. Right.

Didn't have you down as the nervous type. She reaches unner her cloak an throws me a crossbow an a quiver. Right. This way.

I hesitate.

C'mon, she says.

I'm exhausted. Sore. In no shape to fight her. I'll play along now. Ditch her the first chance I git.

The alley's short. It ends in a high metal wall, battered an bent.

You go first, I says.

No, she says. You go.

I sling the bow an quiver on my back an launch myself at the wall. I grab the top an pull myself up. Nobody in sight. I drop down on th'other side an Ash is right there behind me.

We race along a narrow street with shanties crowded up close together, turn right, left, then right agin. White rays of light slice through the darkness. I got no idea where we are.

There's the sound of runnin feet. Voices. Shoutin. To our left.

Fan out! somebody calls. Cover all the streets!

This way! Ash dives into a ramshackle stone buildin. I'm right behind. She runs to the corner an lifts a wooden hatch in the earth floor.

Follow me, she says. Close the hatch behind you.

I wait fer a split second. Then I turn to run.

She grabs my arm an twists it behind my back. She's strong. Real strong. Oh no, you don't, she says.

Let me go, I says. I gotta find my brother. I try to twist outta her grasp, but she's got me in a strong grip.

I see, she says. The Hawks help you out, risk our lives fer you an yer sister an you cheat us.

You couldn't of done nuthin without me. I glare at her. I could of killed Epona, you know.

The Hawks help you, she says, you help the Hawks. Then yer free to go after yer brother. That's the deal you made with Maev.

She yanks harder on my arm. I cry out. You don't need me, I says. There's enough of you.

So you'll leave all them fighters, she says, the ones stole by slavers jest like you an yer sister was, you'll leave 'em in this place. That's the kinda person you are. Somebody who don't keep their word. Somebody who lets people down.

No, I says. No, I ain't like that.

She waits.

All right, I says. All right, I'll keep my word. I promise I will.

She lets me go. I straighten up, easin my sore arm. I'm sorry, I says.

We look at each other a moment. Then she smiles. Her eyes don't look so hard after all. She lifts the wooden hatch. After you, she says.

I swing myself down into the hole, set my feet on a rickety ladder I find there an start down it. Ash follows me an closes the hatch behind her.

It's black. I cain't see a thing. The cool earth smell of bein unnerground fills my nose. I feel my way to the bottom, ten rungs. Ash jumps down beside me an lights a torch.

Where're we goin? I says.

You'll see, she says. This way.

We crouch over an head down a low tunnel. Pretty soon, we reach the end. The tunnel ends in a brick wall. There's weapons piled up along with a crowbar an some glass bottles filled with what looks like water an rags stuffed in their tops.

Hold this. Ash hands me the lit torch. Keep it well away from them bottles. She picks up the crowbar, sticks it in between the bricks an starts workin one free.

What is this? I says. Are we breakin in somewhere?

I sure hope so, she says. Otherwise we've jest spent the last three days clearin out this tunnel for no good reason. We're talkin in whispers. The first brick's free. Take it, will you?

While I pull the brick free an put it on the ground, she starts on the next one. So this was already here, I says. How did you know about it? Where does it lead to? The second brick's loose. I take it away.

There was a big escape from this place about ten year ago, she says. The fighters dug theirselves out. One tunnel from the men's cellblock an one tunnel from the women's cellblock. They filled in the tunnels afterwards. If they'd bin smart, they would of collapsed 'em.

Third brick done. So we're breakin into the cellblock, I says. My cellblock?

That's the idea, she says.

An yer gonna tell me that there's a good reason why we ain't jest takin out the guards an cuttin through the fence to let 'em out? I says.

There's a full guard shift on duty, she says. They must of bin nervous that the fighters 'ud try somethin unner cover of all the activity in town. You should always have a Plan B.

I'll remember that, I says.

Shhh, says Ash as I take away the fourth brick. She blows out the torch. She nods at the hole an we look through.

We're lookin straight into the female fighters' cellblock. In fact, we're lookin down into my cell.

† † †

My cot's directly below us. My cell door stands open. The girls in the big main cell's all mainly sittin or lyin down on the floor. They ain't got no cots, not even blankets. At the far end on eether side of the main door, there's two cellblock guards sittin on chairs.

We can work the last few bricks free with our hands. We're silent, quick about it. When we got a hole big enough fer us to slip through, she takes a blowpipe outta her belt an slides a dart into it.

Jest then, one of the girls in the main cell sees us. Her eyes go wide. I shake my head. She gives a little nod.

Ash lifts the pipe to her lips. Takes in a big breath. Blows.

It's a hit. The guard to the left of the door cries out. He

slaps a hand to his neck an falls offa his chair. Th'other guard jumps to his feet, but Ash sends another dart flyin. He don't make a sound. Jest crumples to the ground.

Very neat, I says.

Let's go, she says.

She slides through the hole an jumps down. While she gits the key ring from the guard's belt an unlocks the main cell to let the girls out, I toss the weapons down onto my cot. Bows, quivers full of arrows, slingshots, bolt shooters.

Help yerself to weapons, girls! Ash says. Then wait fer us by the door. They come runnin into my cell an in a minute or two they've scooped up all the ammo.

Now, says Ash. We're gonna take four of the bottles an leave the rest there. Be careful.

I hand the rag-stuffed bottles down to her an she sets 'em gentle on the ground. Then I jump down outta the hole. Strange to be back in my cell like this.

Ash takes two of the bottles an I take two. Th'others should be lettin the men out, she whispers. She cricks open the main door of the cellblock. She waits fer a moment, then she slips outside an starts up the outside steps, real slow an careful.

She comes runnin back down an throws the door wide open. Git outta here! she says.

The girls don't wait to be told a second time. They go runnin past her an don't look back. When they're all gone, when the cellblock's clear, Ash grabs a lit torch from a wall sconce an says, Let's git this party started.

I follow her out the door an up the stairs into the exercise yard. She holds up one of her bottles. She grins a wicked grin. Wreckers called these cocktails, she says. Two should do the trick. Throw it, then run like hell.

I hold one of my bottles out.

My pleasure, she says. She touches the torch to the rag an it catches light right away. Quickly she lights her bottle. We toss 'em down the stairs. Then we run like stink. Two seconds later, there's a huge bang. The ground shakes unner our feet.

We stop, turn an look behind us. Flames come shootin up the stairs, outta the cellblock.

Wait'll them flames hit the bottles in the tunnel, she says. Then we'll really see some action.

The female fighters is jumpin up an down, shoutin an huggin each other an cheerin. They pound Ash an me on the back. We look around. There's Free Hawks everywhere an dead guards lyin on the ground. The male fighters is all streamin outta their cellblock now.

There's about six Hawks climbin all over the fence around the compound, snippin at it with wire cutters an rollin it back so's everyone can git out. Other Hawks stand near a weapons pile an throw bows an spears an slingshots to whoever's runnin past.

I can see flames shootin up all over Hopetown. Maev warn't foolin when she said she was gonna wipe it offa the face of the earth.

I'm lookin fer one person but I cain't see him nowhere. Silver gray eyes an a crooked smile.

I grab one of the men runnin past. Where's—? He pushes me off.

I grab another. I'm lookin fer Jack, I says. He's a new fighter. They brought him in a few days ago. Gray eyes, came in with long hair, down to his shoulders.

I know, he says. He jerks his head back to the men's cellblock. Try the Cooler. They threw him in there yesterday.

My heart leaps into my throat. The Cooler. Jest like in the female cellblock, the men's block has a metal punishment box sunk into the floor. I grab the man by the shoulders. He ain't still in there? I says.

Well I didn't let him out, he says an runs off.

Ash! I yell, lookin all around me to see where she is. Ash! There's somebody trapped in. . .

Then I see her.

She's lightin another cocktail.

Aimin it at the door of the men's cellblock.

✝ ✝ ✝

Ash! I scream. No! Don't!

I start to run towards her. But I cain't go fast enough. It's like the whole world slows down to a crawl.

Ash pulls her arm back. She throws the lit bottle down the steps of the men's cellblock. She turns, runs towards me. She holds up her arms in victory, a big grin on her face.

Aaaaash! I yell. The ground shakes, the flames come shootin up the stairs. I grab her arm. There's somebody in there, I says. He's locked in the Cooler.

Her eyes go wide. It's too late, she says.

No, I says. It cain't be. I start to run, pullin her along behind me.

Jest then, there's the most almighty blast. We're sent flyin into the air. I land hard on the ground. I lift my head. A great plume of black smoke billows into the sky. Ash scrambles to her feet, gives me a hand up.

That must of bin the bottles in the tunnel! she says. The whole town's burnin! You cain't go in there, Saba! It ain't safe!

I cain't leave him there, I says. Where's the keys?

That was Ruby's job. Ash looks around. She sticks her fingers in her mouth, gives a sharp whistle. A short girl by the weapons pile lifts her head.

Ruby, Ash yells. I need the keys!

Ruby runs over an tosses 'em at us. I catch 'em one-handed an start to go. Ash grabs my arm. It's too dangerous, she says.

Let go, I says.

She swears. Who is this guy? What's he to you anyways?

Jack, I says. His name's Jack.

She lets go an I'm runnin towards the burnin cellblock.

Saba! Ash screams. Come back! You got no boots on!

I don't stop.

✝   ✝   ✝

Smoke pours outta the door of the men's cellblock. I wrap my cloak around my head to cover my mouth an nose. Then I plunge inside.

Darkness. Hard to see. Smoke fills the air. Burns my throat, my nostrils, stings my eyes.

It's ezzackly the way it was in my dream. The fire dream. I'm here. It's happenin.

Jack! I shout. Jack! Where are you?

No answer. Hungry flames lick at the wood beams in the walls an ceilin. Embers pop an hiss.

He's in the Cooler. The guy said so. But where is it? I know it's sunk into the floor, but how far along the cellblock? Halfways? At the far end? It could be anywhere. He'll be cooked to death in that metal box if I don't git him out.

I move ahead real careful, feelin my way with my hands an bare feet. I keep my eyes closed aginst the smoke. I ain't never bin in here before, but I'm hopin the layout's the same as in our cellblock. A ember lands on my cloak, hisses greedily as it burns a hole. I rub it out.

Jack! I shout agin. Jack! Where are you?

No reply. I go forwards. Call out agin. Take another couple of steps. Then another.

The sound of a heartbeat. My heartbeat. Over an over. So loud. It fills my brain, my head.

He must be in here. But what if he ain't? What if that guy was wrong? What if somebody else told the Hawks he was in the Cooler an they found him an let him out? If they did, he'll be long gone. I curse myself fer not askin Ruby.

I cough. The smoke's burnin my throat. It's gittin hard to breathe. He ain't here. If he was, he would of heard me an shouted out. I need to git outta here. I cough agin. My breath comes short an shallow.

Panic grips me. I turn in circles, blind.

Jest like in the dream.

I'm bathed in sweat. It's so hot in here. I'm startin to feel funny, kinda dizzy. I need air. Gotta git outta here an find the door. I should go back to the door.

Another voice. Whisperin. Mercy's voice.

The heartstone lets you know . . . the heartstone . . . heartstone . . . hurry, Saba . . .

Heartstone. My hand fumbles unner my cloak. There it is. An it's warm. Strange. It's always cool. Even on the hottest day, next to my skin, it stays cool. It was only warm twice. An both times, I was standin in front of him. Warm heartstone means . . . it means somethin, Mercy said so but I cain't . . . remember . . . cain't . . . think . . .

The heartstone . . . lets you know . . .

My fingers clutch it tightly. One last time. I'll shout fer him one . . . last time. I take a couple of steps forwards. I feel the heartstone git warmer.

Jack! Jack! Where are you? I call out.

I wait.

Nuthin.

I turn to go.

Then.

I hear it.

Poundin.

A faint voice.

He's here.

† † †

Strength floods through me. I stumble ahead, my eyes streamin, squintin through the smoke. My toe hits the edge of somethin. The trapdoor to the Cooler? I fall to my knees. Feel around. I touch hot metal. Yes! The door. I wrap my hand in my cloak an pound on it to let him know I'm here. He pounds back.

Jack! I yell. Hang on! I'm gonna git you outta there!

Keys. Quick. I feel the keys on the ring in my hand. My heart stops. There's gotta be ten keys on here. All the same size.

Jack! I yell. I got the keys! I jest gotta find the right one!

He thumps to let me know he heard. I run my hand over the trapdoor. There it is. The keyhole. Try the first key. Gotta work fast. Faster. Too fast. Fingers clumsy. The key slips an slides past the keyhole.

Fer each key I try, I hold the fingers of my other hand aginst the keyhole to guide it in. Then I snatch it away as soon as I know the key ain't the right one. I grit my teeth.

My hands is slippery with sweat. It's runnin down my face, into my eyes. My heart's poundin. Time's runnin out. Once the roof timbers burn through, this ceilin's gonna come down an that'll be it.

Hurry, hurry, hurry, I mutter.

The second to last key slips in. I turn it. Leap to my feet. The second I touch the handle of the trapdoor to pull it up, I snatch my hand away, cursin. The metal's hot. I throw my cloak over my hand, grab the handle an haul the door open.

I reach down in the darkness. His hand shoots up, grabs mine with a strong grip. I lean back an help him climb out. He's coughin. I pull my cloak over both of us.

This way! I says. We head towards the door of the cellblock. To the outside an fresh air.

The groan of creakin timbers splits the air. The roof! I says. It's gonna go! Another groan an, then, at the door end of the cellblock, the roof collapses with the most almighty crash. Dust an dirt mix with the smoke an billow towards us.

We're trapped! he says.

Go back! I says.

We turn around, head back the way we jest come.

Think, Saba, think. You an Ash went in through the tunnel. How did Ruby git in here? The same way?

A tunnel! I yell. I think there's a tunnel in the wall at the end!

We feel our way to the back wall of the cellblock. Run our hands up an down an along the bricks, searchin fer a hole.

There ain't nuthin here! he says.

There's gotta be! I drop to my knees, my fingers fumblin, feelin all along the bottom of the wall, down near the ground, then over to the corner an—

Here! I says. C'mon! I git down on my belly an start crawlin through it. He's right behind me. The tunnel's filled with smoke. I go as fast as I can go. There ain't no sound but our shallow breathin, our gasps fer air. Then the tunnel starts to widen, the ceilin's higher an we can crouch an run along. The smoke starts to thin out.

I can see light ahead! I says.

Then we're at the end of the tunnel. A rusted metal ladder. A pale golden light beams down. I scramble up the ladder. He's right behind me.

There's sackin laid over the hole at the top. I push it up, real careful. Bits of straw drift down. I peer out. Straw all around. I lift the sackin a bit more.

The tunnel comes up into a fenced yard between two shanties. Straw on the ground, three pigs snufflin in the corner. Besides them, nobody in sight.

In the distance, screams an shouts fill the air. The smell of smoke's strong.

It's safe, I says. Let's go.

✝   ✝   ✝

We climb out, vault over the fence, run along a little alley an peer around the corner.

Looks like Maev an the Hawks've done theirselves proud. Smoke's billowin high into the air. A hotwind's sprung up to help spread the fire through the town from the direction of the cellblocks. It catches up sparks an bits of burnin wood an blows 'em onto rooftops an inside the flimsy buildins.

People hurry through the streets, headed fer the main gate, all loaded down with what valuables they can carry. They're pullin bulgin samsonites behind 'em, clutchin lumpy bundles to their chests an pushin handcarts loaded up so high they cain't see over 'em.

Follow me, says Jack. He dives into the crowd an I follow him as he dodges in an out among all the people. There's a little kid wailin with fright, red-faced, as he's hauled along by the hand.

The Angel of Death's a bit too well-known here, says Jack. His hand shoots out an next thing I know, he's nicked a hat offa some man's head an crammed it down on mine. That'll help, he says.

I gotta find Ash, I says, scannin the crowd. An the rest of the Hawks. They got my sister.

I always wanted a sister, he says. So this is the Hawks' doin. Very nice.

You know 'em? I says, still lookin fer anybody I can recognize.

I heard of 'em, he says. I travel a fair bit in my line of work. C'mon, this way! He grabs my hand an heads down a alley to the right. At the end we turn left, then right agin. There ain't nobody left in this part of town at all. It's all quiet. Jest the faint sound of shoutin in the distance.

He checks inside a shanty. Nobody home, he says an pulls me after him through the door.

He dumps a pile of clothes on the table.

Where'd you git all that? I says.

Lesson number one, he says. Best place to steal anythin is in a crowd. Specially a crowd in a hurry to be somewhere else.

He pulls off his shirt. When I see his bare chest I git a jolt, deep in my gut. Three long scars—pink, twisted, puckered—run from his right shoulder all the ways down to his left hip. Claw marks. I ain't never seen the kinda beast that'ud leave marks like that.

He pulls the new shirt over his head. Starts to undo the top button of his britches.

What're you doin? I says.

What does it look like I'm doin? If yer the shy type, I'd advise you to turn around.

Oh! I turn my back on him quick.

Lesson number two, he says. Even if yer in a hurry, go fer the best boots you can find. Don't compromise on quality. Here, these should fit you. He tosses me a pair of boots. Well go on, he says, try 'em fer size.

I sit on the ground an pull 'em on. Jump to my feet an give 'em a stamp. They fit, I says. That's amazin.

I got a good eye, he says. Right, that's me done. You can turn around now.

I do. We stare at each other. His face is streaked with soot an ash. His teeth flash white in the gloom. You know my name, he says. What's yers? Yer real name, I mean.

Saba, I says.

Saba, he says. I like it.

I gotta git movin, I says. My sister'll be waitin with the Hawks an—

Before I know what he's up to, he grabs my hand.

Hey! I try to pull it away but he holds it even tighter.

Saba, he says, I dunno what happy star sent you lookin fer me but I'm mighty thankful it did. If you hadn't of turned up, I'd be dead by now.

Then he brings my hand to his lips an kisses the back of it. While he's doin it, he looks straight at me with his silver moonlight eyes. I can smell the smoke on his skin. That an dried sweat an—faint, like a whisper—sage.

Thank you, he says.

Heat washes over my chest an up my neck. Rushes into my face. I snatch my hand away, shove it unner my armpit an glare at him. What'd you do that fer? I says.

I was thankin you, he says. I was bein polite.

I ain't never seen polite like that before, I scowl.

Oh that ain't nuthin, he says. I can be a lot more polite than that. He grins. A cocky, jimswagger grin like he's king of the world. Then he bends down to pick up a crossbow an quiver that he must of took at the same time as the clothes.

I need to find my sister, I says. She should be with the Hawks.

Always good to have a plan, says Jack. Where you meetin her?

At the gate in the northeast corner, I says.

There ain't no gate there, he says.

There will be by the time I git there, I says. Nice to meet you, Jack. I turn to go.

Wait! he grabs my arm. I ain't in no particular hurry, he says. I'll tag along. Make sure you find 'em.

† † †

I duck down the side streets an alleyways, headed fer the north-east corner of Hopetown at top speed. Jack's right beside me.

We swerve an leap as bits of burnin buildin crash to the ground. Roof timbers, a door. The metal shanties twist an buckle an groan in the heat.

Ever heard of the rule of three? he shouts as we run.

No!

If you save somebody's life three times, their life belongs to you. You saved my life today, that makes once. Save it twice more an I'm all yers.

I'll jest hafta make sure that don't happen, I says.

We shoot out onto open ground an there they are. Emmi, Maev, Ash an a bunch more Free Hawks waitin fer us with horses. They've cut out a big section of the tall palisade fence big enough fer us to git through. A back gate, jest like Maev said.

Jack grabs both my arms. Turns me to face him. It'll happen if it's meant to happen, he says. It's all written in the stars. It's all fate.

I don't believe in the stars, I says. Not no more.

We'll see about that. G'bye Angel. Before I know what he's up to, he pulls me to him, gives me a quick hard kiss an then he's off an runnin back the way we jest come.

I hold my hand to my tinglin lips an stare after him.

✝   ✝   ✝

Saba! Emmi runs to me an I sweep her up. She throws her skinny little girl arms around my neck.

You all right? I says. She nods. Buries her face in my neck an squeezes so tight she jest about chokes me.

Where's Nero? I says.

I dunno, she says. I ain't seen him fer ages.

Saba! yells Ash. C'mon! We're outta here!

They're all climbin onto their horses. Maev's holdin the bridle of a fine chestnut stallion with a broad chest. His name's Hermes, she says to me. He's fast.

I swing myself onto his back. Then I lean down an pull Emmi up to sit in front of me.

I see you found yer friend all right, says Maev. She hands

me a pistol crossbow an a quiver. Leather armbands. Gives me a sly little smile.

Yeah, I says. I feel my face flushin hot. I busy myself strappin on the armbands an slippin the bow over my head. Sorry, I says, I didn't mean fer it to take so long. Listen Maev, thanks fer—

You can thank me later, she says, cuttin in. Let's git outta this hellhole first. Heeya! She heels her horse in the flanks. Heeya!

Hold tight, Em, I says.

We stream through the gap in the palisade at a gallop an head north. Maev rides on my right side. Somebody pulls up on my left. It's Epona. She shoots me a grin, her eyes sparkin.

Glad to see you made it, I says.

Likewise, she says. That was a nasty moment. Who'd of thought they'd change the gauntlet run?

Once we're well away from Hopetown, we pull up the horses an look back. Streams of people pour outta the burnin town through the Gate. They're all headed south. Nobody's comin this way, nobody's followin us. The sky's filled with great clouds of gray smoke.

The Hawks break into cheers an pound each other on the back.

We did it, I says. I reach over an grab Maev's hand. You got us all out. I gotta tell you, I didn't think you could do it.

I know you didn't, she says. But yer gittin out alive warn't nuthin to do with me in the end. She tilts her head back an looks above us. You need to thank that crow of yers, she says.

Nero swoops down over our heads, cawin an callin out in his hoarse voice.

I will, I says. I wave a arm at him.

He does one last swoop down then soars up high. He likes a good view.

I ain't never seen a creature like that before, she says. He's so smart, he's—

More like a person than a bird? I says.

Yeah, she says. That's it.

Whatever you do, I says, don't tell him that. I'll never hear the end of it.

† † †

We head due north, in the direction of the mountains that cut across the plain. They look to be a good five or six leagues off.

Is that the Black Mountains? I says to Maev.

That's jest the beginnin of 'em, she says. Foothills, I guess you'd call 'em.

My brother's in a place called Freedom Fields, I says. Deep in the Black Mountains. D'you know it?

She shakes her head. Never heard of it, she says.

My heart sinks.

Come with us, she says. To our summer camp at Darktrees.

It's half a day's ride from here. Once we git there, you can rest up. We'll git you kitted out, help you make plans to find yer brother.

I ain't got time to rest, I says. I gotta git there before midsummer.

She looks at me. That's less than two weeks from now, she says.

I know, I says. I'd be glad of some clothes an food if you got any to spare.

I think we can help with that, says Maev.

An I'd like to leave Emmi with yuz, I says. Emmi looks up at me. She's bin ridin in front of me the whole time, not sayin a word. She looks away quick.

Jest till I git back with Lugh, I says. I got no idea what's at Freedom Fields or what I'm gonna hafta do to git there. I need Emmi to be safe.

We'll take care of her, says Maev. Whaddya say, Emmi?

Okay, she says.

Ash gallops past. Hey Maev! she shouts, jerkin her head back towards Hopetown. We got company! She rides on ahead to catch up with th'other Free Hawks.

Maev an me turn to look over our shoulders.

Holy hell on earth, says Maev. What's that?

✝ ✝ ✝

A cloud of dust's comin at us from Hopetown way. It's movin fast.

That ain't no horse, says Maev. Not travelin that fast. Let's git the lead out.

In the pit of my stummick, I know what's inside that cloud of dust. The wind's picked up. Perfect conditions fer a landboat.

Hang on, Em! Heeya! I yell. Heeya! I dig my heels into Hermes' sides. A quiver of excitement ripples through him. It's like he's jest bin waitin fer me to give the word. He stretches his neck out. Then he shoots off like a arrow from a bow, his hooves thunderin on the dry ground.

I look behind. The dust cloud's gainin on us.

Whatever it is, it's movin too fast! shouts Maev. We got no chance of outrunnin it!

Up ahead, Ash has caught up with th'other Free Hawks. Told 'em what's goin on. They all turn in a wide arc an start racin back to join us.

I look back agin. The dustcloud's even closer. Now I can see what's makin it. An it's jest like I thought. It's the Desert Swan. With this fierce wind behind it, the sails is billowin.

Maev whistles. Friends of yers? she says.

No, I says. Not friends. Not at all.

Emmi looks up at me with big eyes. It's the Pinches, she says.

They're after me, I says to Maev.

Right, she says.

The Hawks thunder up.

Keep Saba an Emmi in the middle! yells Maev. They move to surround us, takin up positions to the front, the sides an the rear. Nero flies jest overhead. We're still headin fer the mountains, with the horses at full stretch. Epona's ridin right beside us.

Don't be frightened, Em, I says. I ain't gonna let 'em hurt you.

I ain't afeared of them! she says. From her quavery little voice, I can tell she's terrified. I give her a squeeze.

They'll hafta git through me first, Epona calls over, with a smile. I don't take kindly to people who try to do that.

Jest then, the Free Hawks at the back of the pack start yellin. We look back. The landboat's comin at us, full speed.

They're gonna run us down! I yell.

Break out! says Maev. Break out!

The pack breaks apart an behind us the Hawks scatter in all directions.

Epona! I yell. I pull on the reins, start to slow Hermes down. Take Emmi!

Right away, she pulls in tight beside me. I wrap a arm around Emmi's waist an swing her over to sit in front of Epona.

Take her to Darktrees! I says. I'll meet you there!

Epona nods an they race off towards the mountains with a few of the Hawks.

I rein in Hermes. He rears an squeals an dances. Maev

turns her horse too. This is my fight, I says to her. You done enough already. Leave me to it.

Not on yer life, she says. Then, Ash! she yells. With me! The rest of yuz, go!

The three of us wheel our horses around, give 'em the heel an head straight towards the Desert Swan at a full gallop.

Keep in tight! Maev says. We pull up close together, ridin so's our knees almost touch. Maev on my right, Ash on my left.

Bows! Maev yells. We pull our crossbows round an load 'em up.

Vicar Pinch clings to the mast. His robes billow behind him. Rooster works the sails. The Cage Master steers. Miz Pinch is tied to the front railin, beside the Cage Master. She's aimin a crossbow at us. She shoots.

The arrow comes straight at Ash.

She's lookin away, yellin somethin at Maev. I fling my arm in front of her head. She turns, startled. Th'arrow pierces my armband, sticks in the thick leather pad. I yank it out.

That would of had me! Ash says. Thanks, I owe you.

Ready, aim, fire! yells Maev. We let fly with our arrows.

Miz Pinch ducks. But the Cage Master's too slow. Two of our arrows catch him direct in the chest. He cries out, lets go the steerin bar an goes tumblin over the railin. He falls unnerneath the Swan. As the wheels hit him, the landboat fishtails wildly. The right back wheel snaps off. The one I helped Rooster fix. I guess we didn't fix it too good. It goes bouncin an rollin off.

The Desert Swan's outta control. Jackknifin all over the place.

Look out! shouts Maev.

Her, me an Ash scatter outta the way.

Rooster works the sail ropes madly. The Swan tips. It rolls. Once, twice, three times, four. Real quick. Like a tumbleweed. Miz Pinch gits thrown out. She flies through the air an lands hard. She don't move. The landboat skids across the ground, upside down, throwin up a great dustcloud. It comes to a stop an it's all quiet.

Me, Maev an Ash ride over. Maev goes to git down, but I says, No, let me do it.

I dismount an crouch to peer unnerneath the Swan.

Rooster dangles head down. Trapped by the steel beams of the crushed hut. His eyes an mouth is wide open. He looks surprised. Vicar Pinch lies on the ground, his curly long hair in a heap beside him. He's completely bald, with ugly lookin open sores all over his head. Blood covers his face. His right leg splays out at a strange angle.

I wait fer a moment, my heart bangin in my chest. Silence. Neether of 'em moves. Neether of 'em's breathin.

They're dead, I says. The King's dead! That means that Lugh's safe. They won't have no reason to kill him now.

Good, says Maev.

Then I ride over to Miz Pinch. Looks like her neck broke when she hit the ground. She lies on her back. Her open eyes stare up at the sky. They're full of fury, even in death.

I dismount. Stare down at her. I fit a arrow to my bow. Take aim. This is fer Emmi, I says. Then I shoot her in the heart.

Nero flaps down an lands on her chest. He spreads his wings an caws. Plucks at her shirt with his beak. Pecks at her hand.

That's enough, Nero, I says. Let's go.

He flies onto my shoulder. I pull Hermes round an turn his head towards the mountains.

The mountains an Lugh.

†   †   †

We ain't gone more'n a league.

We're pickin our way over a big rocky outcrop when Ash glances over her shoulder. Here they come, she says. She wheels her horse around an me an Maev follow her to the edge of the outcrop. From here, we can see over the plain back to the fires an smoke of Hopetown.

We can also see the Desert Swan. An the little group of Tonton riders, maybe ten in all, headed towards it.

Better not hang around, says Maev.

Not when you got a brother to find, Ash says to me.

DARKTREES

Jest before midnight, we ride into the Free Hawk summer camp at Darktrees.

Nero flies on ahead to tell 'em we're comin. Emmi runs up the moment we ride into view an runs an skips along beside the horses.

Saba! Yer here!

You should be asleep, I says.

What took you so long?

We got here soon as we could, I says.

I swing myself down offa Hermes' back. She leaps at me, wrappin her arms an legs around my waist an neck.

Are they dead? she whispers. Did you kill 'em?

You don't need to worry about 'em no more, I says. How'm I s'posed to do anythin with you hangin on like a leech?

I give her backside a swat an she slides down. She follows at my heels while I rub Hermes down, water him an send him off into the trees to join th'other Hawk horses an ponies to graze on the scrubby grass in the forest clearins.

She chatters on, about Epona an how we're gonna sleep in the same bunkhouse as Maev, but all the time she keeps hold of the edge of my tunic an sticks close.

I turn an jest about trip over her. I kneel down an take her hands. They're tremblin.

Hey, hey, Emmi, I says. It's okay. I'm here.

No you ain't, she says. Yer leavin to find Lugh. An it could be dangerous. You said so yerself.

I'll be fine, I says. I'll be back before you know it. An I'll be bringin Lugh with me.

Yer sure I cain't come with you?

I'm sure, I says. I promised Pa an Lugh I'd keep you safe. I ain't done a very good job so far.

You done okay, she says.

Hey, I says. I dunno about you, but I'm startin to feel mighty tired. Why don't you show me that bunkhouse you was talkin about?

Okay. Hey . . . Saba?

Uh huh?

Would it . . . would you give me a pickaback ride to the bunkhouse? She says it shy-like, not lookin at me but at the ground where her boot's tracin a line in the dirt.

I ain't never let Em ride pickaback on me in our whole lives. Lugh was the one who played with her like that. He'd grab her by the hands an swing her around till they both fell dizzy on the ground. Or she'd jump on his back an he'd gallop around an leap while she squealed with delight. I never used to like it when he spent time with her. Or anybody else fer that matter. I always wanted him all to myself.

I look down at her. At the back of her neck, scrawny an grubby. She always was small fer her age.

She's only nine, Saba. You might try bein nice to her fer a change.

A pickaback? I says. I thought you'd never ask.

†   †   †

Human sacrifice. Maev frowns. That's . . . crazy.

Her an me's sittin on a log in the cool mornin shadows of the clearin where the Free Hawks camp is. I check to make sure Emmi ain't in earshot. She don't know none of this an I don't want her overhearin. But she's over by the bunkhouse with Nero. They're playin some countin game with twigs laid out on the ground. Nero loves to count things.

I know, I says. But that's what Helen said.

An you believe her, says Maev.

I do, I says.

An she says it was the Tonton took Lugh to this place . . . Freedom Fields.

Deep in the Black Mountains, I says. That's what she said.

I wonder what goes on there, says Maev.

Helen got killed before she could tell me everythin. But from what she said, it's all to do with chaal.

Everythin's to do with chaal, she says. An the Tonton's right in the middle of it.

We're silent fer a minute, then I says, You know, Maev,

when Vicar Pinch saw my birthmoon tattoo, he looked like he'd seen a ghost.

Whaddya mean?

What I mean is, I don't think it was the first time he seen it.

Where'd you git it anyways? says Maev. I ain't never seen one before.

It was my pa, I says. He tattooed me an Lugh. Midwinter twins.

You think that's where he seen it? On Lugh?

I'm certain of it. What else could it be?

Well, Pinch is dead now, so it don't matter. They won't be goin ahead with, you know . . . the sacrifice.

We cain't be sure of that. An when they find out what happened to their King, they might be so mad they do somethin to him anyways. He won't be safe till he's outta there. I gotta git goin.

I stand up.

Oh no. She stands too, puts a hand on my arm. You ain't in a fit state. Look at you. You need to rest an eat. We need to see to them bruises. Epona worked you over good in the Cage.

It don't matter, I says.

Yes it does. You don't know what you got ahead of you. You gotta be strong.

Leave me alone, I says. But I know she's right. I'm dog-tired an I ache all over my body.

C'mon, Saba, she says. I ain't yer enemy, I'm yer friend.

My friend, I says.

That's right. Yer like me. Yer a survivor.

I'm jest stubborn, I says.

I'm sorry to hafta say this, she says, but bein friends an all, it gives me the right to say . . . when was the last time you had a wash?

I realize I cain't remember. I dunno, I says. A while back, I guess.

A long while back, I'd say, she says. She pushes past me, heads down the path further into the woods. I got a surprise fer you, she says. This way.

✝   ✝   ✝

We step outta the darkness of the forest into the shock of bright sunlight. We're standin on a narrow shelf of bare rock that juts out into thin air. Straight across from us, water roars outta the side of a mountain. It rushes an tumbles down the rocks till it plunges into a deep pool below, where the sunlight dances an sparkles.

Maev disappears over the side of the rock.

I stare at the waterfall. It's beautiful. Clean. Pure.

Are you comin or not? Maev hollers. Her voice echoes offa the canyon walls.

I follow behind as she picks her way over the rocks to the bottom. I ain't bin swimmin fer such a long time. Me an Lugh used to swim in Silverlake all the time when we was little. Back before the lake dried up an everythin went wrong.

I'll take one dive into that cool water. Jest one. It'll help clear my head. Then I'll be able to think.

Maev jumps down onto a big flat rock at the side of the pool. She shimmies outta her clothes quick an then she's naked as the day she was born. Golden freckled skin, long strong legs, a tangled mane of copper hair. She takes a runnin leap, her legs an arms flyin, an disappears unner the water. She breaks the surface, a big grin on her face.

It's fantastic! she yells.

I realize I ain't never seen Maev smile before. She looks young. Like a kid.

Maev kitted me out this mornin, everythin from shirt to skivvies. At first, I didn't wanna take their stuff, but she said the Free Hawks is by way of bein highway robbers an that's where it all comes from. When she told me that, I should of said no thanks. I know that stealin things is bad. But my clothes was nuthin but dirty rags an my ideas about what's right an wrong ain't so fine as they used to be.

I take off my stolen clothes an fold 'em in a neat pile on the warm rock. Then I dive in.

The icy cold water shocks my eyes wide open, slams into my heart. I shoot to the surface, gaspin. Maev's laughin her head off.

You rat! I yell. It's freezin cold!

It'll do you good!

I duck myself, over an over, in the sparklin cleanness till the filth of Hopetown's washed from my body. I pull a handful of needles from a low hangin pine tree an rub 'em over my skin. Then Maev starts to chase me around an we splash an dunk each other.

After a bit, I realize I ain't thought about Lugh fer the past few minutes. Not even once.

Right away, I turn an swim back to the rock. Maev follows. I pull myself out an gather my clothes.

What's the matter? Maev climbs out.

I ain't got time fer this, I says. I cain't stop till I find Lugh. I promised him.

Oh, not this agin! She grabs the clothes from me. What, you promised him you wouldn't wash? Or eat? Or sleep? Don't be stupid.

Gimme them clothes, I says.

She holds 'em away. No, she says. It was a wash an a swim. It ain't like you was dancin an singin. Now siddown an jest be quiet fer three minutes while we dry off.

No. Gimme my clothes, Maev.

Gawdammit you stubborn mule . . . siddown! She roars it at me. She grabs my arm an pushes me down. I'm so surprised, I don't even try to git up. She drops the clothes an sets herself down beside me, holdin tight to

241

my wrist. Now, she says, we'll jest sit here fer a bit an be quiet.

Maev—

Shhh!

I jest—

She holds a finger to her mouth. She lays back, closes her eyes an raises her face to the sun. I lie beside her, starin at the sky. After a bit, I'm feelin warm, a little drowsy. My eyelids is heavy. They start to close.

I don't unnerstand it, I says.

Unnerstand what? she says.

I cain't believe you never heard of Freedom Fields. This is yer territory. You must of bin all over the Black Mountains.

Not all over, she says. Hawk Territory ends a day's ride north of here. You don't keep what you cain't defend an there's only forty of us.

But you meet people, I says. You must talk to 'em when yer . . . you know . . . robbin 'em.

We don't ezzackly stop to chat, she says.

Even so, I says, I cain't believe you never heard anythin about it, ever, not even the slightest hint.

Well believe it, she says. Cuz I'm tellin you, I ain't never heard of Freedom Fields.

A man's voice comes from behind us. Deep. Husky. That's because they don't want you to know about it, he says.

Neether of us stop to think. We roll offa the rock an into the water. Maev races away, but somethin stops me followin her.

A familiar heat's crawlin over my skin. Shudderin up my spine. It's the heartstone. It's hot an no matter that the water's freezin. I bob to the surface.

Jack, I says.

He stands there, his arms crossed over his chest, his hat down low over his eyes. He smiles his lopsided smile. My stupid stummick does a flip.

Fancy meetin you here, he says.

Maev's head pops up over by the waterfall. What're you doin? she yells at me. Are you crazy?

It's okay, Maev, I says. This is Jack.

Jack? she calls. Who's . . . oh . . . Jack!

I flush even redder. Maev knows I went into the burnin cellblock to git him out. Ash told her about it.

Are y'all right, Saba? says Jack. You look kinda warm.

Too much sun on my head, I mutter. I swim back to the rock. Maev joins me. We hang onto the edge an look up at him.

Jack nudges our pile of clothes with his foot. Grins. Well, ain't this a innerestin sitchation? he says. Two girls naked in the water an me with all their clothes.

Turn around or I'll rip yer heart out, says Maev.

Bloodthirsty, says Jack. I like that in a woman.

Turn around!

Ain't it a bit late fer that? he says. I mean, I already seen all there is to see.

But he turns his back while we scramble outta the water an into our clothes.

What're you doin here, Jack? I says.

How'd you git past the Hawks? says Maev.

He shrugs. I asked where I could find you. Ash said to try here.

You got past Ash? says Maev.

Uh huh, he says. She took a bit of . . . persuadin but in the end she came round. Nice girl.

Nice girl? says Maev. Are you sure it was Ash you met?

Listen, he says, I know it ain't my business, but you might wanna have a word, tighten up yer security.

Yer right, she snaps, it ain't yer business. See you back at camp, she says to me. She brushes past him an disappears into the forest.

He turns around as I'm pullin on my boots. She likes me, he says. I can always tell.

D'you rile somebody every time you open yer mouth? I says.

Pretty much, he says.

You didn't answer my question. What're you doin here, Jack? I frown. Are you followin me?

My my, he says, you do have a high opinion of yer charms.
No, I jest . . . happened to be passin by is all, an I remembered
you sayin somethin about hookin up with the Free Hawks. I
jest wanted to make sure you got here okay an . . . all that. So.
Is . . . everythin okay?

Uh huh, I says.

You found yer sister okay?

Yup.

Good. That's good. Did I mention I always wanted a sister?

Yup.

He folds his arms over his chest. Smiles at me. I stare at
him. Finally he says, I know the way to Freedom Fields. I can
take you there.

Every bit of my body tightens with excitement when he
says it. But right away there's somethin nigglin at me, so I
says, It's mighty strange, Jack, you jest happenin to turn up
here an you jest happenin to know the way to Freedom Fields.

I told you before, he says. It's fate.

An I told you I don't believe in fate, I says. How do I know
I can trust you?

You can trust me, he says.

You would say that. How do I know you ain't lyin?

You don't. But I ain't.

I feel the blood rush to my head. I throw up my arms
an yell, You are the most infuriatin person I ever met in my
whole life! Talkin to you's like talkin to a eel!

He gives me that crooked, cocky smile.

An don't look so pleased with yerself, I says. It ain't a compliment.

So, he says, d'you want a guide or not?

Tell me, Jack, I says. What's in it fer you?

Instead of answerin my question, he takes a step closer to me an says, Why'd you come after me?

What?

Why'd you come after me? he says. Back at Hopetown. That cellblock was on fire. You'd hafta be crazy to go in there. But you did. You risked yer life to save mine an you didn't even know me.

The heartstone's almost burnin a hole right through my skin. I sure ain't gonna tell him that sorry yarn Mercy spun me, about it turnin warm when you stand in front of yer heart's desire. You wouldn't think a grown woman could be so silly.

I cross my arms over my poundin heart an stare down at my feet. I dunno why, I says, I jest did.

An I dunno why I'm here, he says. I jest am. I mean, it ain't like I don't have better things to do. I got people to see. I got . . . business interests.

Then go, I says. I didn't ask you to come after me. I can manage perfectly fine on my own. I don't need yer help. Go on, git outta here.

Ain't you bin listenin? He grabs my arm. I cain't!

We glare at each other. The space between us feels heavy somehow. It presses aginst me, makes it hard to breathe. Finally I says, So, are you gonna take me to Freedom Fields or not?

He runs a hand over his head. I must be crazy to even think about it, he mutters. Yes. I am. But first . . . I need to cool down.

He pulls off his boots an yanks his shirt over his head.

I stare at his chest. I cain't seem to make my eyes move away. When I seen him without his shirt before, back at Hopetown, all I noticed was the scars. But now all I can see is how lean an strong he is. With wide shoulders an arms roped with muscle. He ain't got no hair on his chest, not like Pa an Lugh. My fingers itch to touch it. Find out if his skin feels as smooth as it looks.

Be careful, Angel, he says. When you stare at a man like that, he's likely to git any number of . . . innerestin ideas.

I don't move.

He reaches fer the fastenin of his britches. Raises one eyebrow. You got three seconds, he says, then they're comin down. He starts to count. One . . . two. . .

I turn an run.

I can still hear him laughin when I'm halfways back to camp.

† † †

Maev sits crosslegged on her cot in the bunkhouse, watchin me pack the gear she's gived me. She tosses a pebble from one hand to th'other.

Whaddya know about this Jack character anyways? she says. It don't feel right, him showin up outta the blue like this.

I know as much about him as I know about you, I says. Not much.

She chews on her bottom lip. I don't trust him, she says. D'you?

He says he knows the way to Freedom Fields, I says. If I'm gonna find Lugh, I gotta trust him. Jest like I trusted you to help me git outta Hopetown. I didn't know you but I . . .

Took a leap of faith? says Maev.

Yeah, I says, that's it. A leap of faith. An you turned out okay.

Yeah, well . . . Maev mutters. She don't look at me when she says, I'd send a couple of Hawks with you, but I got a territory dispute with some chancers on the western road to sort out.

I git the feelin she ain't bein entirely truthful but I says, You don't owe me nuthin.

There's jest . . . somethin about him, she frowns. He's got secrets. An he's, uh . . .

Arrogant? I says.

Oh yeah.

Annoyin?

Definitely.

Slippery?

As a snake, she says. She watches me fer a bit, then she seems to throw off whatever it is that's botherin her. She gives me a sly little smile an says, He's good lookin, I'll say that much.

Is he? I feel my cheeks go hot. I shrug, don't look at her. Cain't say I noticed, I says.

He's got nice eyes.

Too close together.

Nice smile.

Too many teeth, I says. Anyways, he ain't my type.

She throws the pebble at me, laughin. Yer type! Don't you kid yerself, he's jest yer type. The trouble type, that is.

I already got enough trouble with findin Lugh, I says. I don't need no more.

You sure of that? she says. You look a bit . . . warm whenever he's around.

It's ever since that damn fire, I mutter. All that heat must of got in my blood or somethin.

Or somethin, she says.

I finish packin. I tighten the drawstring of my pack. Thanks fer keepin Emmi, I says. Lugh an me'll come back fer her soon as we can. Maev?

Uh huh?

If . . . if anythin was to happen . . . if fer some reason I don't come back—

Oh no, Saba, don't—

If anythin happens to me, promise you'll take care of Emmi. Raise her up proper. Please. I gotta know she'll be okay.

Maev looks at me a long moment. Then, All right, she says. I promise.

Thanks, I says. She don't like to wash. Make sure she does. I heave my pack over my shoulder. Better go load the horses, I says.

She touches my arm, stops me as I pass. Listen, she says, if you ever git the itch to join up with a bunch of thieves an no-goods, we'd be glad to see you back here any time. You'd make a damn fine Free Hawk.

† † †

Jack slings saddlebags over his horse's back. On his way outta Hopetown, he managed to steal hisself a big white stallion— he calls him Ajax—that turns out to have a bad temper an a bite to go with it.

He looks over to where Emmi's drawin circles with a stick in the dirt. Her head droops down like a wilted wildflower. Are you really gonna leave her behind? he says.

Of course, I says. I slip the nettlecord bridle over Hermes'

250

head, fix the bit in his mouth. She's jest a child. It's too dangerous. Anyways, she'd only slow us down.

Jack knows why I gotta git to Freedom Fields before midsummer eve, how important it is. Last night I told him everythin I know, everythin that Helen told me before she died. He listened but didn't say nuthin, jest grunted a couple of times.

Lugh ain't jest yer brother, he's Emmi's too, he says. Don't you think she's got as much right to go as you?

No I don't, I snap. An mind yer own business. Maev said she'd look after her an that's the way it's gonna be.

If you say so.

I do.

Jack sticks his fingers in his mouth an whistles. Emmi's head shoots up. He motions her over an she comes runnin.

Yer sister don't want you to come with us, he says. She says you'll slow us down.

Jack! I says.

I wouldn't slow you down! says Emmi. I'm a good rider. I rode on Nudd all the way from Mercy's all by myself an then I rode him all the way across the desert to find Saba. We nearly skeered her to death.

Is that right? Jack lifts a eyebrow at me.

It ain't jest that, I says to Emmi. Things could git dangerous. I don't want nuthin to happen to you.

I can take care of myself, says Emmi. I can fight.

No you cain't, I says.

Can too!

Here. Jack unhooks his slingshot from his belt. See that shimmy? He points at one of the shimmer discs the Hawks got hangin from a tree to keep the rooks from roostin. Let's see if you can hit it right in the middle.

C'mon, Jack, I says, this is a complete waste of time. She ain't never shot nuthin in her life.

Ignore her, he says to Em. He hands her his shooter. You give it a try.

It's okay. Emmi untucks a slingshot from the back of her britches. I got my own.

Since when did you carry a shooter around? I says. Hey, wait a minute . . . that's mine.

No it ain't, says Em. It belongs to Lugh.

All right. But I thought the Pinches bartered all our gear at Hopetown.

They didn't take this, says Em. I snuck it when they warn't lookin an kept it in my secret hidin place. I'm keepin it fer Lugh. I'm gonna give it to him when I see him.

Well, if that ain't a nice sisterly thing to do, says Jack. That's real thoughtful of you, Emmi. Now, go on. Let's see you try an hit that target.

She lifts the slingshot, aims an shoots. She hits the shimmy dead center.

She beams.

I don't believe it. Em lined that shot up an took it like she's bin shootin every day of her life.

She's got a good eye, Jack says to me. Close yer mouth, you'll catch flies.

Where'd you learn to do that? I says.

She shrugs. I watched you an Lugh. Then I practiced an practiced till I got it right.

I didn't know that, I says. Why didn't you tell me?

You never liked it when I talked to you, she says. You always told me to shut up an go away.

I never! I says. But I feel my cheeks go all hot becuz we both know it's true. It sounds so awful when she says it like that, that I never had no time fer her, but she's right. I didn't. Not when I had Lugh. When we're together he's all I need. An that's bin the way of it since the day we was born.

So let's see, says Jack, she can ride, she can shoot an she's got guts. Did I leave anythin out?

What you left out is, she's nine year old, I says.

He's my brother jest the same as he is yers, says Emmi.

Good point, says Jack. An she was sisterly enough to save his slingshot.

They look at me.

No, I says, glarin at 'em. No, no, no!

They don't say nuthin. Jest keep lookin at me.

Don't look at me like that! I sigh. Aw hell. All right, you can come. But you gotta do what I say an you better not gimme cause to regret this cuz if you do, Emmi, there'll be trouble an no mistake.

I'm talkin to myself. The second she hears the word "come," Emmi starts whoopin an her an Jack's shakin hands an then she's huggin me an lookin at me with shinin eyes. I ain't never seen her so happy an excited.

I won't let you down! She skips an jumps her way to the bunkhouse, callin as she goes, Epona! Hey Epona! Guess what?

I point at Jack. If anythin happens to her, I says, I'll know who to blame.

He grabs my hand. His eyes is hard as stone, cold as a gray winter sky. His hand's warm. His skin's rough. A tingle runs up my arm. You don't fool me, he says.

Is that right?

Yeah, he says. I see it in yer eyes. All you care about's yer precious brother.

That ain't true, I says.

If it'd bin Emmi they took, he says, Emmi an not Lugh . . . would you of gone after her?

I take in a breath to say of course I would but the look on his face stops me. There ain't no point in lyin when he already knows the truth.

He leaves go of me an steps back. I thought so, he says. Yer sister'll be safer with me than she could ever be with you. You jest ride along on yer high horse an leave her to me.

Gimme yer hand. Maev says it in a low voice, so's nobody else can hear. She slips a gold ring onto the middle finger of my right hand. If you ever need me, she says, if you need the Hawks, send Nero with this an we'll come. Wherever, whenever . . . you send this ring an we'll be there.

She steps back.

My heart swells in my chest. From Hermes' back, I look down. She smiles at me.

You got us outta Hopetown, I says. Saved our lives. You gave us clothes an food an horses . . . the chance to find Lugh. I . . . we owe you so much, I don't see how I can ever repay you, but once we—

Friends don't owe, she says. Friends don't repay. Go well. I hope you find yer brother.

G'bye! Emmi leans down an hugs Epona around the neck.

You do what Saba an Jack tell you, says Epona.

Keep 'em safe, Jack, says Maev. If you don't, we'll hunt you to the ends of the earth. An when we find you, we'll rip out yer guts an feed 'em to the jackals while you watch.

I'll bear that in mind, says Jack.

Nero circles above. He caws, impatient to git goin. I look up. Time to go, I says. I click my tongue at Hermes an we start to move out. Jack leadin the way on Ajax, Emmi in the middle on a pony called Joy, an me bringin up the rear, with our packs an saddlebags an waterskins filled thanks to the Free Hawks.

They're all gathered to see us off. Now they start shoutin. G'bye, good luck, don't ferget about us, see you soon, an all that kinda thing.

I take one last look. At Ash, Epona an the rest, smilin an wavin.

But not Maev. Not smilin. Not wavin. Jest standin there.

Lookin like she don't especk to ever see us agin.

THE BLACK
MOUNTAINS

WE BIN TRAVELIN ALL DAY. I HAFTA GIVE IT TO JACK, HE sets a good pace. Fast enough fer my hands not to git itchy on the reins but not so fast that Emmi cain't keep up on her pony.

Jack says we're still in the foothills of the Black Mountains. Says we won't reach the mountains proper fer a couple of days yet. We climb steadily, windin our way through forests of evergreens an across dry open valleys covered with scrub.

Nero's pleased to have me back after bein apart fer so long while we was in Hopetown. I feel the same. Mainly he's happy to jest ride on my shoulder, makin conversation an remarkin on the scenery as we go along. From time to time he'll disappear fer a bit on some crow business.

He's bin missin since mid-afternoon an I'm jest startin to wonder where he's got to when he appears outta nowhere. But instead of comin to me, he flutters down to land on Jack's head. Then he leans over an starts to nibble lovinly on his ear.

I cain't believe my eyes.

Nero! I yell. Leave Jack alone!

He shoots over to me so fast he's jest a blur. Lands on my shoulder an hunches there, not lookin at me. I never knew a crow could look guilty, but he does all right.

Jack looks back an smiles. Don't call him off on my account, he says.

Bloody Jack. What is it with him? What is it about him that he seems to charm everybody an everythin that crosses his path? Ash an pretty well every other Free Hawk, my sister an now my damn crow. I swear, if there was a rock in his path that he couldn't be bothered steppin over, all he'd hafta do was give it one look an it'd roll outta the way.

Not me though. I don't roll outta the way fer nobody. Not even him. Especially not fer him.

✝ ✝ ✝

As dusk starts to fall, we sets up camp in a stand of pine beside a little trickle of a creek. The layers of dead needles feel soft an springy unner my feet. The sharp sweetness of warm pine fills the air.

Jack closes his eyes an takes in a deep breath.

We'll have sweet-smellin beds tonight, Emmi, he says.

I'm gonna make 'em real good, Jack, she says. You see if I don't.

I collect wood an git a fire goin while Jack sorts out the rest of our gear. Emmi bustles around, unloadin the bedrolls from the horses an settin 'em out beside each other. She chats away to herself an I let it roll over me, like usual.

I'll sleep here, she says. An Jack'll be . . . here . . . an then Saba can go . . . here. Right between me an Jack.

My head shoots up. What? I says. Oh no! I go over an grab my bedroll. You go in between Jack an me. That 'ud be better, don't you think? That way, uh . . . you can talk to both of us. How about that?

But Jack put me in charge! Emmi puts her hands on her hips. He unloads the horses, you do the fire an I set out the bedrolls! Ain't that right, Jack?

I thought it was, says Jack. But I guess yer sister don't think yer up to the job, Emmi.

They both look at me. Emmi's got her face all scrinched tight. She does that when she's upset an tryin not to let her chin wobble. Jack's face is blank, like he don't give a hoot one way or th'other. I don't trust him fer a second. He knows I don't wanna lie next to him, but I cain't tell Em that. As far as she's concerned, I'm jest bein mean to her like usual an not givin her a chance. He's got me this time.

That ain't true, I says. I hand my bedroll back to Em. Sorry, Em. Of course it's yer job. I'll leave it to you.

While she's busy puttin her arrangements to rights agin, I go over to where Jack's unloadin Ajax an Hermes.

I know what yer up to, I says. An it ain't gonna work.

Is that right? He don't look at me, but keeps on pilin the saddlebags an other gear. Fer future reference, he says, I'd be grateful if you'd tell me what it is I'm supposed to be up to that ain't gonna work. That way I won't bother gittin up to it agin.

I frown. There you go agin, doin that eel thing, I says. What yer up to, Jack, is . . . is tryin to make me look like a fool all the time!

Oh, is that what I'm up to?

You know damn well it is!

Then I apologize, he says. Most sincerely.

He smiles. A pleasant smile. Not cocky or arrogant. I dunno what to make of it.

Well . . . , I says, all right then. Jest mind you don't do it agin.

I promise, he says, the next time you look like a fool, it'll be all yer own doin. He winks at me as he picks up the saddle-bags. Fire needs tendin, he says.

I stand there fer a moment. He jest got me agin, the bastard.

But I feel a little smile sneak over my face.

† † †

Night, Saba, says Emmi. Night, Jack.

She rolls over onto her side, facin away from me, an soon she's fast to sleep. Nero's set on his roost in a tree nearby.

I stare at the night sky. It's high an light an clouds scud

across the face of the moon. I clutch my blanket around me tight, lie stiff as a board. I'm so aware of Jack lyin next to me. The warmth of him, the sound of his breathin, the slight rise an fall of his chest I can see outta the corner of my eye.

There's a rustle as he moves. I look an he's facin me, propped up on one elbow. The dyin fire catches on his cheekbones, shadows his eyes. My stummick jumps. Shivers. I look away.

He reaches out an touches the heartstone, lyin in the hollow of my neck. Draws his hand away quick.

It's hot, he says.

I know, I says. I pull it over my head an shove it down in my bedroll. Stupid thing, I says. Dunno why I wear it.

After a bit he says, Tell me about yer brother.

We're twins, I says.

Ah, he says. I figgered he must be somethin special fer you to go through so much to find him. What's he like?

I think. It's always the same when somebody asks me about Lugh. Mercy, Helen, Maev . . . even Emmi. I wanna talk about him an at the same time I don't. I feel like, if I do talk about him I'm givin away little bits of him that I wanna keep to myself.

Our ma died birthin Emmi, I says. An after that, Pa . . . well, he warn't ever the same. He didn't seem to care about nuthin no more. Not us or . . . not anythin . . . not really. If it hadn't of bin fer Lugh keepin food on the table an a roof over our heads, I believe we would of all died. Lugh an me was only

nine year when Ma died, same as Emmi is now. So he ain't
afeared of takin things on. Never has bin.

But what's he like? says Jack.

He's . . . well, he's funny, I says, an kind an . . . he's real
smart. I guess he paid attention to what Pa told him. Not like
me. He knows . . . everythin. He can fix anythin, he knows the
land an creatures an . . . me. He's th'only person in the world
who really knows me.

DeMalo. Dark eyes, almost black, meet mine.

*Lookin deep inside of me. Findin my darkest thoughts, my worst
fears.*

He sounds too good to be true, says Jack.

His voice seems to come from a long ways away.

What'd you say? I says.

I said . . . that Lugh sounds too good to be true.

You got no right to say that. You don't know nuthin about
him.

I says it real quick, to block out the thought of how Lugh's
bin changin over the past year or so. How he was that last
day. How he said he couldn't wait to leave Silverlake an the
look on his face when he called Pa a foolish old man livin in
a dream world. I hate that Pa died with them bein the last
words spoke between 'em.

Hey, says Jack, I'm sorry, it was a stupid thing to say. I'm
sorry. So, if yer twins he must look the same as you?

I turn on my side to face him.

No, I says. He's beautiful. Like Ma was. Gold hair like the sun. Long, in a braid right down to his waist.

Yer hair's startin to grow back, he says. It's dark.

Black, I says. Like my pa's. It used to be nice. Thick an long an . . . I must look real stupid.

No, he says.

When Ma was alive, she used to say, yer the night-time, Saba, Lugh's the day. I'm the one who always takes things too serious. Lugh's the one who smiles, makes you laugh. He's a good person, Lugh. He's everythin I ain't.

Is that what you believe? That you ain't a good person? That you ain't beautiful?

I don't say nuthin.

You must miss him, he says.

I never knew that missin somebody could hurt, I says. But it does. Deep inside. Like it's in my bones. We ain't never bin apart till now. Never. I dunno how to be without him. It's like . . . I ain't nuthin.

Don't say that, he says. Don't ever say that. You are some-thin, Saba. Somethin good an strong an true. With him or without him.

He reaches over an brushes my tears away with his thumb. I didn't even know I was cryin. A warm path trails behind his touch.

The clouds clear fer a moment an I dive into his strange sil-very eyes. They're like a moonlit lake. We lie there fer a good long time, jest starin at each other in the soft, piney night. At last he says, We'll find him. I promise. Now try an git some sleep. I'll take first watch.

Wake me when it's my turn, I says.

I will, he says.

G'night, Jack.

G'night.

He sits, his back propped aginst a tree.

Jack? I whisper.

What?

Thank you.

Sweet dreams, Saba.

But I don't sleep fer ages.

Somethin good an strong an true. That's what he said. Nobody ever used such words about me before. I wonder if he really means 'em.

The Jack I seen up till now, that Jack's all charm an quick words an easy smiles. But the way he is tonight, the way he was while we was talkin, I warn't espektin that. It put me in mind of Mercy. I felt this . . . stillness, I guess you'd call it . . . at the heart of him. That's the same feelin I got from her. Stillness, like calm water.

I dunno what to make of it. It don't seem to fit. An jest when I thought I had him all figgered out too.

But the thing is, I think I might be . . . startin to trust him. I know Maev thinks he's hidin somethin, that he's got secrets.

An she could be right. She's seen a lot more of the world than me, met a lot more people. Emmi seems to like him jest fine, but what does she know? She's jest a little kid.

I dunno if I'm right to trust him.

I stare up. The gray clouds brush over the black of the night sky.

I wish Lugh was here. He'd tell me. He'd know.

† † †

It's the middle of the day. We're still in the foothills, dry an dusty, but the land's gittin hillier, rockier, with more'n more tree cover as we go along.

Jack's bin ridin a little ways ahead of us all mornin. I'm glad not to hafta say much to him. I'm wishin I hadn't of said so much to him last night. I ain't quite sure why I did. I shouldn't of let him fool me into sleepin next to him.

Emmi's ridin beside me an Nero's hitchin a ride on Hermes' rump. Emmi starts lookin behind us, over her shoulder.

What is it? I says.

She frowns. Nuthin, she says. But as we go on, she keeps lookin back. I can tell she ain't easy. That she's got somethin on her mind. Finally, I cain't take it no more. I reach over an grab Joy's reins. Bring her to a halt.

Yer drivin me crazy, Em, I says. Tell me what it is.

Jack turns Ajax around an rides back to join us. What's goin on? he says. What is it, Emmi?

She chews on her bottom lip. Looks all uneasy.

Emmi, I says. Spit it out or I'll shake it outta you.

I . . . I think somebody's followin us, she says at last.

What? I says.

Where? says Jack. He reaches into his saddlebag an pulls somethin out.

South, says Emmi pointin back the way we come from.

Jack holds the thing to his eyes. It's made of black plastic. He looks through the narrow end an now I see there's two big circles of glass at th'other, wider, end. He twirls a little knob in the middle.

What the hell's that? I says.

It's a long-looker, says Jack. Lets you see things far off in the distance.

Wrecker tech! I says.

As a matter of fact, it's mighty useful, he says. Picked it up back in Hopetown. It's amazin what people leave lyin around. You don't come across these very often an them you do find ain't usually in one piece.

He takes a good long gander, sweepin it right across the horizon.

I cain't see nuthin untoward, Em, he says. Here, Saba, you wanna take a look?

He hands it over an I hold it to my eyes. All of a sudden, the little copse that we passed through a half hour back rushes right up close to me. I can see every leaf on every branch on every tree.

Whoa! I give Jack a big smile. That's amazin!

He stares at me, a funny look on his face. That's the first time I ever seen you smile, he says.

I scowl at him. Whaddya mean? I says. I smile all the time.

No you don't, Emmi pipes up. You used to, when Lugh was around, but ever since he went, you bin all mean an cross an horrible an—

All right, I says, that's enough.

I was only sayin—

Well, don't!

I lift the long-looker to my eyes agin an make a good check of everywhere I can see.

Nuthin, I says at last. There ain't nobody followin us. Next time you imagine you see somethin, Emmi, do us all a favor an keep it to yerself.

She pinches her lips together tight, wheels Joy around an pushes past me, her chin in the air.

Jack opens his mouth to say somethin, an I point my finger at him.

Don't even think of it, I says. She's my sister an I'll talk to her any way I want.

He turns Ajax an walks him past me.

She's nine years old, he says. Give her a break.

Nero caws at me. Like he's repeatin what Jack jest said. I stare at Jack's back. How strange. Almost the ezzack same words Lugh said me, that last day when we was fixin the roof.

She's only nine, Saba. You might try bein nice to her fer a change.

Lugh. Jack. Emmi. I frown. It's makin my head hurt.

I'll think about it later.

† † †

Jack's hand on my arm wakes me. It must be my turn on watch. He took the first half of the night an I'll take us through till dawn. Right away, I'm wide awake, sittin up. His eyes gleam in the darkness.

You let the fire go out, I whisper.

No, I put it out, he whispers back.

What'd you do that—

Emmi was right, he says.

What?

There's a light on the ridge.

My heart starts thumpin. I slide outta my bedroll. Show me, I says.

Tonight we're camped on a hill at the foot of a light tower. There's a line of 'em, marchin across a wide mountain plateau towards the ruins of a big Wrecker city, about three leagues due north of here. You can see the rusted iron skellentons of the tall buildins in the distance. Skyscrapers, they used to call 'em.

Jack scrambles up the leg of the light tower an I follow him. We go high enough to git a good view an then he hands me the long-looker.

There, he says. He points south, back the way we come from.

I look through it. Light. Faint. Flickerin on the ridge that we came over this mornin . . . no, yesterday mornin now.

A campfire, I says.

They lit it jest after midnight, he says. I bin watchin an it ain't moved since.

They must be camped fer the night, I says.

Maybe, he says.

We cain't be th'only people travelin through here, I says. It's probly fine.

Jest then, the light goes out. Then another one appears. But this one's movin. It bobs over the ridge an starts down. It's headed this way.

That don't look fine to me, says Jack.

Let's wake Emmi an git outta here, I says.

Good plan, he says.

✝   ✝   ✝

We ride into the dead city jest as the sun's startin to rise up.

Sometimes Pa used to tell us about the big Wrecker cities that sprawled over leagues an leagues. Lugh an me always thought he was tellin us tall tales, but it looks like he was right. The remains of a vast city, spread out across this plateau in the mountains.

A long straight trackway, a old road covered now in grass an low shrubs, lies ahead of us as far as the eye can see. The rusted iron skellentons of skyscrapers, the ones that we seen in the distance, line both sides of the road. Other roads lead off from the main one, like branches on a tree.

You can see where there was buildins, way back when. Now they're nuthin but bumps an grass-covered hills. They fell down long ago, bit by bit, an ever since then the earth, the plants an the winds, they bin quietly movin an shiftin to cover what's left. To hide it away. Bury the past.

There ain't no sound but the wind. It moans around corners. Sighs as it brushes past us, whisperin the long-forgotten secrets of this place. Listen to the wind, Mercy told me. If only we could unnerstand what it's sayin. Maybe it's tellin us how many people lie buried unner our feet an how they came to die. Could of bin plague or hunger or thirst or wars. Or maybe all of 'em all at once. The Wreckers did it all.

Now there ain't nuthin livin here but cats. An where there's cats, there's mice. One runs in front of Hermes, but he's too smart to be bothered. The cats don't give us a second glance as they slink along on their business. Nero dives at 'em fer fun, fallin silent outta the sky an sendin 'em racin off in a panic.

We pull up the horses an swing ourselves off.

The second I hit the ground, it shifts. I don't even have time to shout out before my right leg's disappeared up the knee.

Emmi giggles.

I fergot to mention, says Jack. If the ground dips, go around it. In this kinda place, a dip usually means there's a hole.

He watches, arms folded, as I pull myself out.

Thanks, I says. I'll try to remember that.

We better check where our friends are, he says. He hands the long-looker to Emmi. You wanna shin up an take a look?

She nods. She ain't said nuthin to me since we shook her awake to tell her about the lights an strike camp. I'll take her aside later when Jack ain't nearby, tell her I'm sorry I didn't believe her when she said we was bein followed. I guess even Emmi can be right sometimes.

She scampers up a big hill nearby an climbs the metal tower stickin outta the top of it. She wraps one arm around a girder an holds the long-looker to her eyes.

I can see 'em! she shouts, all excited.

How far away? calls Jack.

Uh . . .

She cain't tell distance, I says.

I can so! Two leagues, she says.

How many are there? says Jack.

Four! No, wait! Uh . . . I cain't see very good!

Try twistin the knob in the middle, Jack calls.

She lets go the girder an starts fiddlin with the knob.

Emmi! I yell. Are you crazy? Hang onto somethin!

Leave me alone! she yells. I know what I'm doin!

She twists to glare at me. She loses her balance.

Emmi! I yell. I start to sprint up the hill.

She throws her arms around the girder. She's safe. But she lets go of the long-looker. It flies into the air. I make a dive fer it. But I'm too far away. There's a crack as it hits a rock jest ahead of me. I land with a thud on my stummick an lie there, lookin at the shattered bits of long-looker scattered all over the grass. Nero flaps down an lands on my head.

Crap, says Jack.

Gawdammit, Emmi, I says. Look what you done now.

†   †   †

Okay. Jack slides over the top of the hill to where we're huddled outta sight. Looks like there's jest two of 'em. They're on foot. Walkin their horses in.

That's good, I says. I'd hate to hurt a horse.

But you don't mind if it's a person, says Jack.

They can take care of theirselves, I says.

Remind me not to git on the wrong side of you, he says. D'you think we made the hole big enough?

I told you, I says, I dug hunnerds of traps jest like this one. Me an Lugh used 'em all the time when we was huntin wild boar.

Emmi frowns. She says, But Saba, there warn't no wi—

Behind Jack's back, I slash my hand across my throat an scowl at her somethin fierce. She snaps her mouth shut.

My plan better work. I don't want Jack twiggin that I never actually made a pit-trap before. Lugh an me used to talk all the time about diggin one, but at Silverlake there warn't no huntin worth the time an trouble it would of took us. Jack an me's dug this one in the spot where my foot went through the ground. Right in the middle of the main track through the city. Turns out there was a pretty big hole already there. All we had to do was make it a bit deeper.

My bedroll's gonna git all dirty, Emmi grumbles.

We spread it over the hole, pegged down the edges an covered it all with grass. Now you'd never know there was a hole there.

Too bad, I says. It's yer punishment fer bustin the long-looker.

I said I'd try to fix it, says Jack.

Emmi pokes her tongue at me.

I point at her. Yer gittin way too fresh, Emmi, I says. You jest wait till we—

Shhh! Jack lays a finger over his lips. We crouch there, silent, not lookin at each other. Jest waitin.

Then I hear voices. The soft snort of a horse.

They're comin, Jack whispers.

We flatten ourselves into the side of the hill. Jack an me reach fer our crossbows an load up. Emmi fits a stone into her slingshot. My heart's poundin hard in my chest.

The voices pass by our hidin place.

Then, Aaah! They yell out as they step into nuthin. As they tumble into our trap. The horses squeal, frightened.

Go! yells Jack.

We leap up an rush over the top of the hill. We thunder down th'other side. Their horses, two of 'em, rear in fright an dart outta the way.

Hands up! I yell. We got you covered, you bastards!

Me, Jack an Emmi take up positions around the edge of the pit. Our weapons is drawn. We aim down at our captives.

I don't believe it, says Jack.

✝   ✝   ✝

278

What the hell're you doin here? I says.

Ash an Epona stare at us from the bottom of the pit where they're lyin in a tangled heap of arms an legs.

It ain't ezzackly the welcome we was expectin, says Ash. But I've had worse.

They git to their feet. Epona holds up a hand. Wouldn't mind a little help gittin outta here, she says.

It'd serve you right if we left you there to rot, I says. But I give her my hand an Jack gives his to Ash an we help 'em climb out. They start to brush theirselves down.

Hell, Ash, says Jack. That was more'n stupid. We could of shot you. You could of broke a leg when you fell in. Why didn't you let us know it was you followin us?

We wanted to surprise you, says Ash.

Well you did that all right, says Jack.

I frown. I thought the Hawks had some trouble to take care of, I says. Maev said somethin about a territory dispute on the western road.

They dart a look between 'em. A guilty look.

She don't know yer here, I says. Don't tell me . . . she left you two in charge of Darktrees an you snuck off.

Okay, says Ash, we won't tell you.

Go away, I says. Turn right around an go back. An make sure you tell Maev this was all yer idea an nuthin to do with me.

Hang on a minute, says Epona. We happen to think Maev's

wrong. That she should of sent at least some of us with you to help.

This is more important than who's got control of the western road, says Ash. From what you said—about Freedom Fields an the Tonton an the chaal—this could be about more than jest gittin yer brother back. It could affect all of us. Jest burnin down Hopetown ain't enough. We cain't stop there. We gotta stop the whole thing. Git rid of 'em all.

Listen, I says. I don't care about nuthin besides gittin Lugh back. D'you hear? That's it. Nuthin else. An I don't need yer help. I don't want it. Go home.

Why d'you always gotta be such a rudesby? says Emmi. They jest wanna help us find Lugh.

Button yer lip, Emmi, I says. I got a good mind to send you back to Darktrees with 'em.

She scowls an crosses her arms over her chest. Jest try an make me, she says.

Don't you sass me!

Now now, says Jack, let's jest everybody calm down. I'm sure we can—

Shut up, Jack, I says. I narrow my eyes. Give Ash a good hard look. You sure there ain't another reason why yer here? I says.

I glance at Jack, then look at Ash agin. She's gone all red in the face.

Of course not, she says.

C'mon, Saba, says Epona. You know we're good in a fight.

I'll say this one last time, I says. If I wanted you to come with me, I would of asked you to come with me. But I didn't. That means I don't. You can be on yer way soon's I fetch Emmi's horse. Yer goin back with 'em to Darktrees, I says to Em.

No! she says. An you cain't make me! I hate you, Saba!

I turn an start walkin fast towards where we tethered our horses while we found out who was followin us. We hid 'em well outta sight.

Excuse us fer a moment, I hear Jack say.

He sprints after me an grabs my arm. I wanna talk to you, he says.

I yank my arm away an keep walkin. There ain't nuthin to talk about, I says. They're leavin an Emmi's goin with 'em.

They wanna help, he says. They wanna do somethin. Maybe help make the world a better place. C'mon, Saba, what's yer problem with that?

I keep walkin.

He goes around in front of me.

What's the matter with you? he says. Talk to me.

While he's talkin, I try to dodge around him, right then left, but he blocks my way every time I move a foot. My temper's dancin. It's itchin fer a fight. I clench my teeth, my fists.

Git outta my way, I says.

No.

I'm goin to git the horses. Git outta the way, Jack.

Not till you tell me why you got such a burr in yer britches, he says.

Fine, I says. You wanna know what's wrong? It's this . . . crowd of people trailin along behind me, slowin me down, an I'm sick of it, that's what's wrong! I don't care about makin the world a better place. All I wanna do is git Lugh back. But I keep gittin trapped. I leave Emmi somewhere safe an she follows me. The Pinches snatch us an I end up in Hopetown in the Cage. I finally escape an, thanks to you, I ain't only lumbered with Emmi agin, but here we are in the middle of nowhere an Ash an Epona's pitched up. An why d'you think that is, Jack?

You know why, he says. They wanna help.

Are you blind? I says. They only followed us here because . . . d'you like Ash?

What kinda question's that? Of course I like her. What's not to like?

No, I says, that ain't what I mean. I mean . . . do you like her? Because she likes you. A lot.

What? He laughs. Don't be stupid.

You really cain't see it? I says.

He shakes his head. Yer bein ridiculous, he says.

Oh am I? I says.

I push past him. Head to where the horses are. My skin's

pricklin. My belly clenches. I'm hot all over, head to toe. I start to untether Joy an Hermes.

He strolls up with his hands in his pockets. Stands watchin me.

If I didn't know better, he says, I'd think you was jealous.

Jealous! I glare at him. Whaddya mean?

I mean, he says, that you want me fer yerself. You jest don't wanna admit it.

I stare at him. Then, Go to hell, Jack, I says.

C'mon, he says, admit it.

Leave me alone!

I cain't look at him, cain't listen to him, cain't think about things I don't wanna think about. Feel things I don't wanna feel. I can only think about Lugh. Nuthin but Lugh an gittin him back.

All I want from you is the fastest way to Freedom Fields, I says. I'm goin on from here by myself.

By yerself, he says. Are you sayin you don't need me?

I don't need you, Jack.

Yer wrong. You need all of us. You jest don't know it yet. The Tonton won't take kindly to their King bein killed. They're gonna want somebody to pay the price. I'd almost put money on them goin ahead with their ceremony. If yer gonna save Lugh, yer gonna need all the help you can git. An believe me, once we reach Freedom Fields, you'll be damn glad we're with you.

I lean my head aginst Hermes' side fer a moment an close my eyes.

You ain't gonna let me go by myself, I says.

No, he says.

You cain't stop me. I could jump on Hermes, right now, an ride away as fast as I can.

We'd follow you.

Trapped.

You always know best, don't you? I says.

I like to think so, he says. An that reminds me, you owe th'others a apology fer bein so rude an high-handed back there.

What? I says.

Apologize, he says. Fer bein so damn ungrateful.

I narrow my eyes. I don't learn manners from a thief, I says. Cuz that's what you are, ain't it Jack? That's what you do to git by.

I might be a thief, he says, I might not be. One thing's fer certain though. I ain't the one they call the Angel of Death.

He knows jest where to stab me.

You bastard, I says.

If it makes you feel better, he says.

He gives a little bow of his head, turns an walks away.

✝   ✝   ✝

Jack picks up the pace.

He says he ain't certain how long it's gonna take us to git to Freedom Fields. Says it depends on whether we run into any trouble on the way but it might take us a week or it might take us ten days.

Ten days. With midsummer twelve days away.

The sun beats down on us, white hot an merciless. The air shimmers, heavy an thick. It's hard to breathe. I pull my sheema down over my forehead.

Ash rides at the front with Jack an makes up to him like nobody's business. Even he must notice it by now. She rides so close to him that her leg touches his. She looks at him all the time. She leans over an says things that make him throw his head back an laugh like he never heard nuthin so funny in his life.

It's sick-makin.

Or it would be, if I cared.

Which I don't.

Liar, whispers the voice inside my head. *Liar, liar, liar.*

† † †

We pass through the Wrecker city an cover another four leagues before we stop fer the night. Jack calls this real mountain country. The trail's bin snakin around the edges of steep, heavily wooded slopes that all press in close together.

This land don't please me. Too closed in. Too dark. Not enough sky.

We set up camp inside the ruins of a big stone buildin that stands beside a stream in a little rocky valley. Nero swoops in an out through the windows, cawin with glee as he scatters the roostin pigeons. Ash an Jack bring down a couple of 'em fer supper.

They all chatter away while they build a fire an git the water boilin fer a brew of sage tea. Epona plucks an guts the pigeons with Emmi's help. Then she shoves 'em on a spit an sets 'em to roast.

I sit on my own a little ways off, pullin at tufts of grass, mullin over what Jack said to me.

After a while Emmi comes over. Mind if I sit down? she says.

I shrug. Suit yerself, I says.

She sits herself down beside me. We don't say nuthin fer a bit, then, I'm sorry fer sassin you, she says. An I shouldn't of stuck out my tongue. Lugh'd be mad if he knew.

Don't s'pose he'd be too impressed with me neether, I says. Losin my rag with you like that.

Guess we'd both be in trouble. Epona's nice. An Ash. Don't you think?

I grunt.

Well I like 'em, she says.

I don't say nuthin.

They'd like to be yer friends, you know, she says.

Huh, I says.

She kneels up an takes my hand. We're gonna find Lugh. I know it. We're all gonna help you. Me an Ash an Epona an Jack.

You would of bin safe with Mercy, I says, pullin my hand away. You should of stayed there, like I told you to.

I know, she says. But I'm stubborn. Like you.

We look at each other. Then we smile.

Yeah, I says. I guess you are at that. Listen, Em, I . . . I'm sorry. I know I ain't bin very nice to you. I don't mean nuthin by it, you know that, don't you? It's jest . . . I'm worried about Lugh. Worried that . . . that maybe we won't—

I know, she says. I worry about him too. Jest like I worry about you. I couldn't hardly stand it back in Hopetown when you was fightin in the Cage. Every day I was so afeared that you'd die an leave me.

I won't leave you, I says. I promise. I sigh. I'm gonna try to be a better sister to you, Emmi.

It's okay, she says. You don't hafta. I'm kinda used to you the way you are.

She kisses me on the cheek, real quick. She goes back to the fire to join th'others. I sit there a minute or two, till the lump in my throat goes down. Then I walk over. The conversation stops. They all look at me. Essept Jack. He stays crouched by the fire an makes hisself busy pokin at it with a stick.

I got somethin to say, I says. To all of yuz. I know I bin actin like I got a . . . a burr in my britches, bein ungrateful an cantankersome an . . . well . . . I'm sorry. An I wanna say . . . I wanna say thanks. Fer comin with me. Fer tryin to help me find Lugh. I'm grateful.

They look at me. Like they're waitin fer more.

That's it, I says.

Ash shrugs. We're doin this fer everybody, she says. Not jest you an yer brother. It's bigger'n that.

We'll find Lugh, Saba, says Epona. We'll help you git him back.

She smiles an they go back to their cookin an chattin.

I done what Jack said. What was right to do. Now I walk away from 'em quickly. But my heart feels lighter. More hopeful.

A hand on my arm stops me. Jack. That was well done, he says.

An, like every other time Jack's touched me or come near me, heat washes over me, through me, around me.

Don't touch me, I says.

He steps back, holdin up his hands. His mouth's a tight line. Sorry, he says. My mistake. It won't happen agin.

As he goes back to join th'others, I pull the heartstone outta my vest an curl it in my fist. Hold it while it cools down.

I look up at the sky. The first stars is out. An the moon.

Every night it creeps along in the sky, closer an closer to where it'll be at midsummer. There ain't nuthin gonna stop it.

We're in a race, the moon an me. An it's a race I cain't afford to lose.

Maybe it ain't such a bad idea to have some help. I'll put up with anythin if it means I git Lugh back safe. Anythin an anybody. Even Jack.

† † †

We slide offa the horses an stand on the edge of the escarpment. We look over a dry river gorge to the mountain on th'other side.

It towers above us, dark an jagged an dangerous. Behind it, more mountains stretch as far's the eye can see.

Is this th'only way to Freedom Fields? I says.

No, says Jack, I brought you this way because I thought you'd enjoy the scenery. He glares at me an I glare right back. We bin snappin an snipin at each other ever since the Wrecker city.

Them mountains look awful big, says Emmi.

They're called the Devil's Teeth, says Jack. Look. About halfways up. D'you see it? That's the One-Eyed Man. That's where we're headed. That's the plan.

He points out a buildin that clings to the side of the mountain. I probly wouldn't of noticed it otherwise. It's made of the same dark stone as the mountain. It's long an low, set well back into the rocks. A narrow white track zigzags to it from the gorge below. Smoke trickles out from a crooked chimley.

What's the One-Eyed Man? says Emmi.

A tavern, says Jack.

Epona frowns. She says, An we're goin there becuz . . .

. . . you'd like a drink? says Ash.

Jack shakes his head. The landlord's a friend of mine, he says. Ike Twelvetrees. He's a good pair of hands. Dependable. Jest the man fer this kinda thing.

I stare at him. Oh no, I says, no way. You ain't askin him to come with us.

Yer right, he says. I ain't gonna ask him, I'm gonna tell him.

An you an this . . . this . . .

Ike, says Jack.

This Ike, I says, the two of you's such good friends that he's gonna drop everythin an come with us jest becuz you tell him to.

That's right, he says. You got a problem with that? He gives me a fierce look, like it might put me off.

Yeah, I says, I do as a matter of fact. An I also got a problem with you tellin us this is th'only way to Freedom Fields. I think yer takin us this way becuz you wanna see yer friend Ike.

This ain't no social call, Saba, he says.

Oh, so you ain't denyin it!

Look, d'you wanna find yer brother or not?

Of course I do!

Then shut up an mind yer footin on this slope, he says. I'll go first.

Jack an Ash an Epona go first. They disappear over the edge of the escarpment as their horses start to pick their way carefully down the slope.

All right, Em, I says. You go now. Nice an slow. Give Joy her head.

The earth's dry, pebbly an loose. Hermes moves along sure-footed, but fer some reason Joy's playin up skittish. Em's havin trouble controllin her.

Whoa! I pull Hermes up, jump down an pick my way over to her. You better git off, I says. We'll let Joy go down on her own.

I've jest lifted Emmi offa Joy's back when Ash calls out.

Wind's changin direction!

Epona points at the sky. Thunderheads! she shouts.

A great towerin bank of brown clouds come rollin at us from the northeast. They're movin hellish fast. Lightnin forks down. I count. One Missus Ippi, two Miss—thunder rumbles. It'll be on top of us any moment.

Those are rain clouds! Jack shouts. Hurry up!

I go to take Emmi by the hand but she's gone. She's already headed down the slope on foot, holdin Joy's rope in her hand.

Joy whinnies nervously, shyin an pullin back. Her feet's slippin in the loose earth.

I start after 'em.

Emmi! I call. Let Joy go!

Jest as I say it, Emmi tugs too hard. The pony throws her head back an rips the rope outta her hands.

Joy pulls herself the few feet up the slope an gallops off, back the way we jest come from.

At that moment, the clouds crack open.

† † †

Rain pours down on top of us in sheets. In seconds, we're drenched through to the skin.

You idiot, Emmi, I says. I said to let Joy find her own way down. Why cain't you jest do what I tell you fer once?

Saba! Jack's voice. Muffled by the rain. Git offa that slope now!

Don't tell me what to do! I yell back.

I throw Em onto Hermes' back an lead him down. The ground's turnin to mud unner our feet.

You took yer sweet time, says Jack when we git to the bottom.

Don't start with me, Jack, I says. The pony's gone. Bolted fer home.

That's jest great, he says. The river's started to run. If the rain keeps up like this, we could git a flash flood. We gotta git across before we're trapped in the gorge.

We start towards the river's edge but as I lead Hermes, I feel him limp badly. His left back foot.

Jack! I shout. There's somethin wrong with Hermes!!

Okay! I'll take Emmi across! he calls.

I run around an lift Hermes' hoof. He's picked up a nasty thorn—must of bin when we passed by them hotprickle bushes—an it's worked its way in. I lever it out with my knife.

There you go, I says. That should do it.

Him an me's headed fer the river when somethin makes me pause. I frown. I feel . . . I know there's somethin not quite right, but . . . I shake my head. No time to stop an think now.

When we reach the riverbank, the thick reddish brown stream of muddy water's flowin fast. It catches on a dead tree lyin on the riverbed, turns it this way then that way, slowly, like it's makin up its mind what to do with it. Then it lifts the tree an rushes it downstream.

The riverbed's narrow here but deep. The banks ain't wide. If the rain keeps fallin like this, it ain't gonna take long fer it to overflow its banks an fill the gorge. We'll be swept downstream if we're caught in it.

Epona an Ash is almost at th'other side.

Be careful! calls Epona. The riverbed's all churned up mud!
It's hard to keep yer footin!

Jack heels Ajax an he starts to wade into the water. Emmi's
sat behind Jack, clingin to his waist.

Suddenly I know what it is that ain't right. My heartstone's
gone. I run back to where I took the thorn from Hermes' foot.
There it is, lyin in the mud. I snatch it an shove it deep into my
boot. Run back to the riverbank.

In time to see Ajax stumble.

In time to see Emmi lose her grip on Jack's waist an fall
into the river.

Emmi! I cry.

She cain't swim. Without thinkin, I dive in to save her. I
surface to see Jack haulin her outta the water by the back of
her tunic. He swings her up in front of him.

Is she okay? I call.

She's fine! he says. Jest git yerself across!

Hermes plunges past me. He's had it with waitin. He's
crossin by hisself. Looks like I gotta do the same.

The water's reached my chest now. The wicked current
wraps itself around me. I ain't took more'n four steps when
somethin bumps into me. I look down.

It's a human leg bone.

†　　†　　†

I gasp.

All around me, the dead are risin.

Another leg bone bobs to the muddy surface. Then a skull. A arm bone. They swing lazily. The current grabs 'em an carries 'em away.

Wreckers must of used the dry riverbed as a mass grave an now the heavy rain's churnin it all up.

I snatch my hands from the water, hold my arms high, outta the way. Slowly I turn in a circle, blinkin the rain away from my eyes.

Ohmigawd, I says. Ohmigawd ohmigawd ohmigawd.

The river's alive with dead men's bones. It's thick with 'em.

My breath's comin shallow an fast.

I feel somethin touch me. I make myself look down. A skellenton's wrapped itself around my chest. The skull grins up at me.

I shove it away. But when I pull my hands up agin, the whole top half of the skellenton comes with 'em. I'm stuck in the ribcage. The skull's right in my face.

I scream. Shake myself loose. Scramble to git away. Lose my footin.

I fall. I go unner.

An the current sweeps me away.

† † †

I fight my way to the surface. Spit out a mouthful of filthy river.

Help! I yell. Help!

I doubt if any of 'em can hear me over the poundin of the rain an the rush of the river. An I must be well outta earshot by now. I'm a ways downstream from where I fell, that's all I know. An I got no idea where this river goes.

I grab onto the trunk of a dead tree as it slides past me. I pull myself up so's at least my head's outta the water. I hang on tight as I go rushin along on the river of mud an bones.

Jack! I shout. Jack!

The heavy rain means I cain't see no further'n three arms-length in front of me. There ain't no way of tellin how far I am from the riverbank, but I know it's there somewhere. I gotta try to make my way over to it.

I grit my teeth an kick hard, tryin to steer away from the middle of the river, but the current's got other ideas. The moment I start to make headway, it snatches at my tree an whirls us off. I keep on tryin, over an over agin. But the current's too strong fer me to fight.

Then I start to hear another kinda roar. One that ain't the rain, but somethin else. It reminds me of . . . I cain't think what, but I know that whatever it is, I heard it not so long ago.

The river's gittin narrower an narrower. I'm bein carried towards a group of jagged rocks that stick up outta the water.

I'll try to grab holda one.

But I'm goin too fast. As I reach the rocks, the tree trunk I'm clingin to hits the first rock an cracks in two. I lose my grip. I'm dragged unner the water. My nose fills. My mouth fills. I'm chokin. My body smashes aginst stone. Once, twice, I hit the rocks, still unnerwater. I'm tumbled every which way.

I bob to the surface. Gasp fer air, spit out water. Grit in my mouth, on my tongue. I got nuthin to hang onto now. It's all I can do to keep my head above water.

The current races me downstream.

That roarin I bin hearin . . . it's gittin louder. Ever louder.

Now I remember where I heard that sound. It was at Darktrees. The day when Maev an me went bathin.

An my heart stops in my chest. Becuz I know what that sound means.

There's a waterfall ahead.

†   †   †

Jack! I scream his name as loud as I can. Jaaaaack!

The roar of the waterfall's gittin louder. The river's gittin wilder, throwin up filthy water in great sprays.

A rock lies straight ahead. Right in the middle of the river. It's wide an flat. Not too high. I could pull myself onto it. But it's smooth. Nuthin to grab hold of.

I'm there. I reach out. No! I'm bein swept past the rock! I feel the rush of the falls. Draggin at my legs. I fling my arm back. Over my head. Make a grab at the air. Grab fer anythin. There! My hand closes around somethin. My arm's near yanked outta its socket.

I stop.

I've stopped.

I wait there fer a second, gaspin, as the river roars around me, tuggin at my legs, frantic to rip me from my handhold an throw me over the edge of the falls.

I hang on. My arm's pulled backwards over my head. Whatever I got hold of, it seems strong enough. A piece of metal stickin outta the rock. Cold. Rough. Sturdy. I flip myself over, git ahold of it with my other hand too. Then slowly, fightin aginst the current with every bit of strength still in me, I manage to drag myself outta the water an onto the rock.

I lie there. Pantin fer breath.

I can feel the rain pound down on me but I hardly notice it. After a bit, I lift my head to see what it is that's saved me. A iron spike. Rough an rusted. What it's doin in this rock in the middle of this river at the top of this waterfall an who put it here, I'll never know. I'm jest damn glad it's here.

I pull myself up to sit, still hangin onto that spike. Then I cain't help myself. I peer over the side to see how close I came.

An I start to shake.

Becuz my lucky rock is hangin over the edge of the water-fall.

† † †

Below me, the waters roar as they plunge down.

My bowels clench an I scrabble back from the edge.

I'm on a rock. On top of a waterfall. In the middle of a river. With no way off.

I look down.

The water's still risin around me.

If it keeps on, I'll be swept over the falls. I got no idea how high they are.

My teeth is chatterin from the cold, or maybe shock. I huddle in the middle of the rock. Hug my knees to my chest.

Saba! Saba! Where are you?

My heart leaps. A voice. Muffled by the rain, but—

I peer through the curtain of rain, try to see where it's comin from.

Then I see him. He's in the river, swimmin an bein carried along by the current. There's a rope looped unner his armpits, tied high around his chest.

Jack! I shout. I kneel an wave. Jack! Over here!

He spots me.

The next thing you know, he's comin up right below me. I hang onto the spike with one hand an reach down with th'other.

He grabs it. I give him a pull an he scrambles up beside me. He drags the slack of the rope outta the water an plops it onto the rock.

That was close, he says. He sits there, pantin.

Jack! I throw my arms around him. I'm shakin, head to foot. I never bin so glad to see anybody in my life! I says.

He shrugs me off. Looks at me with narrowed eyes. What happened?

I lost my . . . my necklace, I says. I had to go back fer it. Then I lost my footin an . . . well. Here I am.

He don't say nuthin fer a moment. Then, Did you find yer necklace?

I can feel the heartstone burnin aginst the skin of my ankle, where I shoved it deep down inside my boot. Yeah, I says.

Good, he says. I'd hate to think this was all fer nuthin. Well. Much as I'm enjoyin sittin here . . . talkin about . . . jewelry . . . I think we'll continue this conversation somewhere safer.

He scoots around behind me so's I'm sittin between his legs. He loosens the slipknot on the rope around his chest.

At least we're even now, he says.

Even? I says. Whaddya mean?

He lifts the rope from around him an starts makin the loop bigger. The rule of three, he says. You remember, I explained it to you. You save somebody's life three times, their life belongs to you.

He slips his arm around my waist an pulls me in closer.

What're you doin Jack! I—

Shut up or I'll throw you in, he says. He lifts the rope over so it's around both our waists. As I was sayin, he says, you saved me back at Hopetown. That was one to you. Jest now, I saved you from goin over the waterfall so that's one to me.

You did not! I saved myself!

You wanna quibble? I'm happy to leave you here.

No! I says. No! Don't do that!

Well then, he says. I think we're even.

I don't believe it, I says. Rule of three. That's about the stupidest thing I ever—

He yanks the slipknot tight. My back's crushed aginst his chest.

—heard of, I says.

Stupid, eh? He whispers it in my ear so's his breath tickles. I shiver.

I hope you got somethin strong at th'other end of this rope, I says.

Ajax, Ash an Epona, he says. All right?

I nod. He gives the rope a sharp tug to let 'em know we're ready.

Then we slide down into the river.

† † †

Ash an Epona give one last haul on the rope an Jack an me's dragged outta the water onto the muddy riverbank.

We lie there, gaspin fer breath.

Saba! Emmi throws herself on top of me. Saba! I thought you was drowned! I thought I'd lost you!

C'mon, Emmi, says Ash. Give Saba a chance to git her breath back.

Thanks, Ash, I says.

She peels Em away from me. Epona gives me a hand up an wraps me in a fierce hug.

Thanks, I says.

Ash an me ain't much good at swimmin, she says. Yer lucky Jack was here.

He grins his big jimswagger grin. Would you mind repeatin that, Epona? he says. I don't think Saba realizes ezzackly how lucky she is.

I'm startin to feel stupid that I threw my arms around him like I did. Like I couldn't help myself. I didn't need savin, I says. I was perfectly fine till you came along.

He stares at me. His mouth drops open. The rain runs down his face into it.

You, he says, are insane. Truly insane. Five minutes ago, you was stranded on a rock in the middle of a river at the top of a waterfall with no way—I repeat, no way—of gittin off. Any normal person would not consider that to be fine. An—correct me if I'm wrong—but when I got there, I distinckly heard you say you was never so glad to see anybody in yer life.

Did not, I says.

Uh . . . I think we'll jest start on up to the tavern, says Ash. Her, Epona an Emmi disappear.

Jack gives me a hard look. You make my brain hurt, he says.

An yer the most puffed-up, big-headed swagger boots I ever met, I says. I got news fer you, Jack. You ain't so great. You ain't great at all. Not even the slightest bit! If it warn't fer you an yer stupid plan to go see yer stupid friend in some stupid tavern, I wouldn't of ended up in the river in the first place!

Oh, I know what this is about, he says. This is about Ash agin.

It is not! Anyways, I couldn't give two hoots about you an Ash or you an anybody else!

There ain't nobody else! he yells. It's all in yer tiny little mind! You know what you need?

Yeah! I need you to shove off an leave me alone! I yell back.

No! What you need is to lighten up! My gawd, if yer outta yer mind, I must be outta mine even more! An you know why? Fer even thinkin fer a moment that you an me could of—

Could of what?

Dammit, Saba, I thought we could have a good time together! You know . . . I'd help you find yer brother an you an me 'ud . . . you know.

No! I don't know, Jack! What the hell're you talkin about?

What I'm talkin about . . . is this!

He hauls me to him, grabs my face an kisses me.

I hold my hands away from me, stiff. At first, from shock. But now to keep 'em away from Jack. They're itchin to touch him. All over. His arms, his face, his back, his chest. I cain't let 'em.

I give him a shove. He goes sprawlin backwards into the mud.

What was that fer? he yells.

Fer kissin me! I yell. An don't you dare do it agin!

Oh don't you worry about that, he says, I'd rather throw myself over that waterfall!

He picks hisself up.

I'd rather sleep naked in a nest of scorpions! he says.

He stomps off, leadin Ajax behind him.

I follow with Hermes.

My lips is tinglin.

† † †

The faded sign creaks on its hinges. The painted head of a man glares down at us, a bloody hole where one of his eyes oughta be.

Here we are, says Jack. Welcome to the One-Eyed Man.

The dark stone tavern hunches, low an mean-lookin, into the side of the mountain. Rain sheets down its saggin roof an pours over the edge. A pale thread of smoke trickles outta the chimley.

It don't look too welcomin to me, says Ash.

I don't like it, says Emmi.

Yer jest cold an tired, says Jack. Once you git a bowl of Ike's rock squirrel stew inside you, things'll look a lot brighter.

We lead the horses to a lean-to. There's a few horses there already, includin a big piebald mustang an a sturdy little gray donkey huddled together fer warmth. They flick their ears an whicker softly as we tie our horses next to 'em.

See? says Jack. We ain't th'only ones here. We'll git settled in first, then we can deal with the gear an the horses.

There's a candle burnin in th'only window, a narrow slit set halfways along the wall. Jack rings the bell beside the battered old wood door. Right away, the candle goes out.

Looks like yer friend Ike don't want company, I says.

Probly heard you was comin, says Jack, all sour faced.

He tries the rusty latch. It don't move. He bangs on the door with his fist. Thud thud thud. Thud thud thud.

Ike! he shouts. Ike Twelvetrees! It's me! It's Jack! Let me in!

Nuthin.

Hey! Open up! I yell an pound on the door. I go to try an shoulder it open, but Jack holds me back.

Hang on, he says. There's a knack to it. He leans back, lifts his leg an gives the door a almighty kick. It flies open. He goes in an we trail behind.

We see 'em right away.

I snatch my crossbow an take aim.

Beside me, Ash an Epona do the same.

✝   ✝   ✝

Hold fire! says Jack.

My heart pounds wildly. We keep our crossbows up, bow-strings drawn, arrows ready to fly.

We stare at the men who face us, their weapons at the ready. There's at least twelve of 'em. On their feet, with blades, bows an flintsticks pointed straight at us. They're the most scurfy lookin pack of villains I ever seen in my life. A knife scar here, a eyepatch there, busted noses, missin ears, three fingers. They make the low-life scum of Hopetown look sweet as spring clover.

I do a quick sweep of the room. Take everythin in. It's one long room with a low ceilin. The fireplace in the center's got a blazin fire goin. In front of the fire, there's a large table with a stewpot in the middle an stone drink kegs.

Wooden benches lay on their sides. Kicked over when they all jumped up.

There ain't no sound but the cracklin fire an the rain poundin down on the roof.

Hello boys, says Jack. Nice to see y'all.

Jest then, a man comes through a door in the corner that I didn't notice before. He's tall, at least six five, six six. He's got a huge platter of roasted meat hefted onto one shoulder. He don't even look our way as he goes over to the table an dumps the platter down. Then he starts over to us.

Ike! says Jack. He steps forwards, smilin a big smile an holdin out his hand. Hey man, long time no see!

But Ike don't smile back. An he don't take Jack's hand.

He walks straight up to him an punches him in the face.

† † †

Jack goes sprawlin on the floor.

Jack's down. Hurt. The red hot rips through me. I ain't felt it since Hopetown.

I aim my bow at Ike an walk at him—fast—till he's backed aginst the wall with his hands on top of his head. I press the arrowhead into his throat. He gulps.

There's a quick rush of feet an the men surround my back. Without takin my eyes offa Ike, I can feel their weapons pointed at me. Hear their breathin.

It's all right, Saba, Jack calls. Don't kill him. I deserved it.

Tell these dogs to stand down, I says to Ike.

Weapons down, boys, or supper's off, he says. He don't move his eyes from mine.

There's a pause, then a clatter as guns an bows an knives hit the floor behind me.

Epona? I says.

Yer okay, she says. It's all clear.

I step back from Ike. Lower my bow. He feels his throat. Grins an shakes his head.

Gawdammit, he says. I bin waitin fer a woman like you my whole life. Jack, I think I'm in love.

Ferget it, Ike, says Jack. She's far too dangerous fer the likes of you.

Oh, says Ike, it's that way, is it?

He goes over to Jack, reaches down a hand an gives him a tug up. Jack rubs his jaw where Ike punched him.

Don't worry, says Ike, I didn't do yer pretty face no harm. I should of though. After what you done to me.

He glares at Jack an Jack actually looks shame-faced. Ike jabs him in the chest with a big meaty finger.

You left me, you sonofabitch, he says, hangin upside down, stark naked, with all them women in their—

Jack grabs his hand. Not now, Ike, he says. We'll talk about it later.

Not to mention the time you was supposed to meet me at

Pat O'Dooley's an I waited there like a stooky fer two months, with that little dog of his that's always bitin at yer ankles, an all the time you was off with that—

Ike! Jack yells, pointin at the villains at the table. Look! He's takin seconds!

Oh no, he ain't! Ike rushes off.

Jack grins at me. Poor Ike, he says, tappin the side of his forehead. Crazy as a coot.

Somehow I don't think so.

† † †

The men mutter among theirselves as they sit back down at the big table an git to work on their meal. Ash elbows through 'em an fills three trenchers fer her, Epona an Emmi. The one with the eyepatch tries to slide his arm around her an she gives him a sharp rap over the head with the stew ladle.

Then they pull three chairs close to the fire an tuck in. Both Ash an Epona keep their crossbows close. Nero perches on the back of Emmi's chair an sets about dryin hisself an puttin his feathers into some kinda order. He hates gittin wet.

I roll the stiffness outta my shoulders, let the warmth of the room soak into my cold bones.

Jack motions me over to join him an Ike at a table in a dim lit corner. It looks like the kinda spot where plots git hatched.

I pull up a stool an sit down.

No hard feelins? I says to Ike.

Naw, he says. I like yer style.

Ike's got a big head to match the rest of him. With a bushy beard an moustache an straight black hair down to his shoulders. His eyes is dark an set deep. His voice rumbles from somewhere down near his toes.

Ike, this is Saba, says Jack.

I hold out my hand fer Ike to shake but he grabs it, lifts it to his mouth an gives it a big wet smack of a kiss.

Marry me, he says. I got all my own teeth, I wash twice a year an I'll cut you in fer half the business here.

My cheeks flame hot. No thanks, I says. I try to pull my hand away, but he clutches it tight to his chest.

Maybe not right away, he says, but once we git to know each other. A week or so. I don't mind a little wait. Jest don't keep me simmerin too long, sweetheart.

I don't really think I . . . uh . . . , I says.

I shoot Jack a help-me-out-here-yer-friend's-crazy kinda look but he don't even look at me. He leans back in his chair with his hands behind his head an his legs stretched out.

Will wonders never cease, he says. Ike Twelvetrees finally

caught in the net of love. I gotta hand it to you, Saba. Name the first boy after me, will you?

The first—! I shove back my stool an jump up. I ain't marryin Ike! I ain't marryin nobody! What the—?

Then I catch the look that passes between 'em. Jack's mouth twitches an they bust out laughin. I glare as they hoot an slap each other on the back like a couple of idiots. Bloody Jack. There he goes agin, makin me look like a fool.

Very funny, I says. Couple of hyenas. Go on, laugh it up.

I turn to leave but Ike's long arm shoots out an grabs my wrist. Aw, don't, he says, wipin his eyes. Stay. We don't mean nuthin by it, do we Jack? It's jest us havin some fun. You don't hafta marry me . . . not until yer ready to, that is.

I guess that'll be never then, I says.

He clutches his heart. Wounded! he says. He drags my stool back to the table. Sit, he says. Have a drink. Tell me what brings you to the One-Eyed Man.

He lifts a jug an pours a clear liquid into three chipped mugs.

I stand there with my arms folded over my chest.

What's the matter? says Ike. You got a face on you like a slapped polecat.

I don't like people makin fun of me, I says.

Dangerous an prickly, says Ike. You got yerself quite a handful here, Jack.

I ain't his handful, I says.

She sure as hell ain't, says Jack.

Ike raises one shaggy eyebrow. You sure yer sure about that? C'mon, he says to me. Siddown. Drink.

I sit.

Jack lifts his mug. Me an Ike do the same.

To Molly Pratt, says Jack.

Ike scowls at him. Watch yer mouth, he says.

Jeez, Ike, says Jack. All I'm sayin is . . . to Molly Pratt.

Ike looks sly. Leans in an waggles his eyebrows. To Molly Pratt, he says, an her frilly red bloomers.

One helluva woman, says Jack.

One helluva pair of undies, says Ike.

Then they throw their drinks down their necks.

I take a sip. Fire races over my tongue, down my throat. Tears spring to my eyes.

Jack pounds the table with his fist. Gasps like a landed fish. That's smooth, Ike, he says. What is it?

Pine sap vodka, says Ike. Down it in one, he says to me. That way you cain't taste it.

I take a deep breath. I down it in one, like he tells me to. The fire hits my belly an starts a slow burn.

Now, says Ike, let's git down to business. I know you, Jack. You only ever show up when you want somethin. What is it this time?

† † †

Freedom Fields, says Ike. Well well. Innerestin.

What d'you know about it? I says.

No more'n anybody else in this part of the world, he says. I heard about it.

He looks at Jack before he says it. A quick flick of the eyes, that's all it is. But it's enough to make me think he might know more. I'm jest openin my mouth to ask him when a boy comes up an plonks three bowls of stew on the table. I'll bide my time.

This boy ain't seen no more'n fourteen summers. He's thin an peely-wally, like he don't ever see the light of day, an he's all elbows an ears an big clumsy feet. Ike reaches out to ruffle his hair.

Thanks, son.

The boy gives Ike a shy smile, ducks his head an hurries away. We tuck in.

I never knew you had a kid, Ike, says Jack.

Oh Tommo ain't my real son, says Ike. He showed up a few winters back. Found him one mornin, huddled in the lean-to with the horses. Starvin . . . you could count every rib.

Where'd he come from? says Jack.

No idea, says Ike. When I asked him, all he said was, "He told me to wait fer him. I waited an waited, but he never come back." I found out later it was his pa told him to wait. I took him in. What else could I do? Follows me around like a dog. He cain't hear, but he watches yer lips while you talk.

Unnerstands most things that way. He's a good boy, Tommo. A hard worker.

Cain't say I ever thought of you as the fatherly type, says Jack.

Ike shrugs. Life's full of surprises, he says. He fills my glass. Gives me a shove with his elbow. Go on, he says, drink up.

So, says Jack, Freedom Fields. Whaddya think?

I dunno, says Ike. Business is good. I don't really wanna—

Rule of three, Ike, says Jack.

Ah, says Ike. Well . . . I cain't deny that the rule of three applies here.

What? I says.

I saved Ike's life three times, says Jack.

That means my life belongs to Jack an he can pretty much call the shots, says Ike. I ain't ever heard of anybody goin that far. Usually it's more like . . . callin in a favor.

But the rule of three's a . . . a joke, I says.

A joke? says Ike, starin at me. Where'd you git that idea?

Told you, says Jack to me. So, Ike. We could sure use yer help. Will you come with us?

Sounds like it's up to you, Ike says to me. He's yer brother. D'you want my help?

I look at him. Built like a mountain, with a steady, dark gaze. A good man. Dependable. Those was Jack's words. An he knows more'n he's lettin on.

So does Jack, fer that matter. Maev was right. There's secrets in them moonshine eyes of his. Jack vexes me. He bothers me. I wish my heart didn't beat faster every time he comes near me. But I trust him. Even when I cain't bring myself to speak to him.

As fer Ike, if Jack says he's okay, that should be good enough fer me.

Ike waves a hand in front of my face. Saba, he says, I said d'you want my help?

Yes, I says. I believe I do.

He takes a big mouthful of stew an starts to chew. While he chews, you can see him thinkin. Jack an me watch him fer what seems like a long time. Finally he swallows. Wipes the ends of his moustache. Then, We'll head out in the mornin, he says. Let's drink on it.

† † †

Somethin tickles my nose. I swat at it without openin my eyes. There's a giggle.

Go 'way, I mutter. There's a poundin inside my head. My mouth's dry as a dust bowl. I groan.

Another giggle. Then somethin wet drips onto my forehead. I open one eye. Emmi's head hangs above me, upside down. She's holdin a drippin cloth over my head. I shove it away. Movin makes my head even worse. I groan agin.

Rise an shine! she says.

Leave me be, I croak.

Time to git up! she says.

I cain't move, I says. There's somebody poundin on my brain with a hammer.

That's what you git from a heavy wet, she says.

Whadda you know anyways, I mutter.

I know that you drank too much of Ike's hooch, she says. Jack says to give you this. It'll help yer head.

I drag myself up to lean on my elbows, moanin the whole time. Emmi pushes a tumbler into my hand. I sniff at it.

What is it?

Jest drink it, she says. Down in one.

Where've I heard that before? I says. But I do like she says an throw it down my neck in one. I gag. Ohmigawd that's disgustin! What is it?

Boar's blood an a raw pigeon egg, she says. Jack says it's good fer a hangover.

Jack says, I mutter. I look around. There ain't nobody in the tavern but me an Em. Where is everybody?

Loadin the horses, she says. An Ike sent all the no-good lowlife bastards packin jest after dawn.

Hey! I says. Watch yer language!

But that's what Ike called 'em.

I don't care. You ain't Ike. Now gimme a hand up.

With Emmi's help, I git slowly to my feet. I ain't never felt so vile in my entire life. Mouth like the bottom of a weasel nest, legs like soggy string an a head full of rocks. At least the poundin in my head's startin to ease some. Maybe Jack's foul brew's doin the trick.

As we shuffle over to the door, I can see it's a bright sunny mornin. We step outside an the light stabs at my eyes. I lift a hand to shield 'em. I squint to see what everybody's up to.

Good mornin, I croak.

Ike whistles. Ash laughs.

Uh oh, says Epona. Poor you.

She stops loadin her horse.

Come with me, she says. She takes my arm an leads me over to the water barrel. Sorry about this, she says.

Then, without another word, she shoves my head unner the water. I rear up, gaspin, an she shoves me unner agin.

The shock of the cold water's like a slap in the face. When I come up the second time, I yell, What the hell'd you do that fer?

Sorry, says Epona. Guess I should of warned you.

Anybody else did this to me, I'd come to cuffs with 'em, but Epona's a good-hearted soul. I know she only means to help.

It's all right, I says. Thanks. I . . . I feel a lot better.

An, to my surprise, I do.

I dunk myself a couple more times, then rinse off my shoulders an arms. Jest as I'm finishin, Tommo sidles up. He hands me a rough cloth an keeps his eyes on the ground while I dry myself with it.

When I'm done, I touch his arm. He looks at me. He's got the most beautiful eyes I ever seen—deep brown, almost black, with long dark eyelashes. Eyes like a deer. Too beautiful fer a boy really.

I smile at him. Thanks, I says. His thin face flushes pink. He ducks his head an scurries away.

Jack's voice comes from behind me, makes me jump. He ain't got a chance when you smile at him like that.

I turn around. He's closer'n I thought. My stupid heart skips a beat. He leans aginst the wall with his hands in his pockets. His eyes ain't moonshine silver today. They're darker, more like stone.

Very funny, I says. I busy myself foldin the cloth.

Tommo's a lonely boy with a soft heart, he says. Find somebody else to practice yer smiles on.

I dunno what yer talkin about, I says.

Then let me make it clear, he says. Pick on someone yer own size, Saba.

What? I says. Like you, I s'pose?

We stare at each other fer a long moment. An then I'm lookin at his lips an I cain't seem to look away an I cain't seem to think about nuthin but how they felt aginst mine. Then he says, No. Not like me. I don't want yer smiles eether.

It's like he's slapped me in the face. I cain't think of a thing to say.

He goes to load Ajax.

I stand there, starin at nuthin.

Like always when Jack's near, the heartstone floods my body with heat. But this time, I shiver too. From the coldness in his eyes.

† † †

I figgered Ike 'ud board up the tavern to keep it safe till him an Tommo come back, but he says he ain't got no intention of ever comin back. All he does is shut the battered old door to keep the weather out.

So that's it? I says. Yer leavin it, jest like that?

Oh it won't stay empty fer long, he says. Somebody'll come along an take it over. That's what happened to me. On the road, lookin fer a place to sleep one night an came on this place. By the look of it, bin empty fer years. Next mornin, I had the notion to sweep the floor an before I knew it, I was runnin a tavern. No, I bin here long enough. Me an Jack talked about it last night. After we find yer brother, him an me's gonna hit the road agin. Take Tommo with us.

He nudges me in the ribs. To be honest, he says, I got a lady waitin fer me. The most glorious creature that ever drew breath.

Not . . . Molly Pratt? I says.

He presses his hands together an raises his eyes to the sky.

Lips like ripe berries an curves to make a man weep with joy. I want her to meet Tommo. It's time I settled down. An I got a notion I might turn out to be a good family man. Don't say nuthin to Jack though. He'll make my life hell.

But . . . what about him? I says.

Jack? A family man? Ike hoots. That's a good one!

No, I didn't mean that, I—

Hey Jack! Ike calls. What is it you always say?

Move fast, travel light an never tell 'em yer real name, Jack says.

That's the boy! Ike winks at me.

I got a funny feelin inside me. A flutter in my belly. Jack gone. Not bein able to see him no more. I hadn't really thought about it before now. What might happen after we find Lugh.

Ike! calls Jack. Saba! Move it! We ain't got time to stand around yappin.

I bin so busy listenin to Ike that I ain't noticed that Jack an Emmi an Ash an Epona's already on horseback, ready to go. Tommo's on the sturdy little donkey, holdin the reins of Ike's big piebald mustang.

Nero caws impatiently from his perch on Jack's shoulder. Traitor bird.

We're comin, I says.

Ike looks up at the head on the faded tavern sign. Gives it a shove an starts it swingin.

So long, you one-eyed bastard, he says.

Then him an me mount up an we move out.

† † †

Seven days to midsummer.

I cain't stop thinkin about Lugh. Worryin about how he is. Worryin that he might be hurt. I wonder if he thinks I ain't comin. I wouldn't blame him if he did. Lugh knows I keep my promises, knows I'd grow wings an fly to the moon to git him back, but it's bin so long he might think somethin's happened to me. He might even think I'm dead. I'd hate it if he thought that.

Ike an Jack both swear that the quickest way to Freedom Fields lies through these mountains, the Devil's Teeth. There is another route, the one that's most used, but it 'ud mean retracin our steps almost back to Darktrees. So here we are, an all becuz Jack jest had to have Ike join us. He better turn out to be worth the trouble.

This may be the quickest way but it ain't well traveled an no wonder. These ain't mountains that deal kindly with people who try to cross 'em. They're steep an jagged with no way of keepin to the high ground. They force us to climb up an then lose the height we jest gained by climbin down agin.

It ain't good ridin country, that's fer sure. The goin's so hard that we mainly hafta walk the horses.

An it ain't jest the mountains. There's the fog.

It come down on us the day after Ike closed the door of the One-Eyed Man an it ain't showed no signs of liftin. It lies on the mountains night an day, heavy, dank an bone-chillin. It swirls around our legs an strokes our faces with its clammy fog fingers.

I hate it. I cain't stand it if I cain't see the sky. No matter how bad Silverlake was, at least you could count on big skies, always high an wide, comin right down to meet the earth. A person could breathe there.

We go along without talkin fer the most part, huddled in our cloaks, heads down. When somebody does say somethin, they talk quiet. Even big Ike with his boomin voice talks soft. A normal voice sounds too loud, almost shockin, in this muffled fog world. There ain't no birdsong. No rustle of animal feet. It's like we're th'only souls alive.

Emmi's made friends with Tommo.

They ride along together. He talks to her in his strange hoarse voice. Or he'll use his hands an fingers to speak. She seems to unnerstan what he means, jest like he's talkin like normal folk do. Like it ain't no different.

It's gittin so's they're almost brother an sister, Tommo an Em. I'm glad. It's good fer her to have somebody near to her own age. An she's lookin happier, not peaky like she's bin fer so long. Ever since we left Silverlake really.

But it's all changed between Jack an me.

It started at the Wrecker city an got worse after he pulled me outta the river. The last time we spoke to each other was when he told me not to smile at Tommo.

We'll say one or two words if we hafta, but he don't tease me no more or let his hand brush aginst mine an both of us make sure our eyes don't meet. It's like I only dreamed that he held me an kissed me till my spine melted.

Well, what did you especk? Every time he came near you, you pushed him away.

Oh, it's a waste of time thinkin about Jack. Soon I'm gonna be back with Lugh. Then him an Emmi an me'll find ourselves somewhere good to settle. A place that's green an kind, by runnin water. Maybe near to Mercy. An we'll be a family agin. That's all I care about.

I shiver an pull my cloak around me tighter.

It's so cold in the fog.

Even colder without Jack's smile.

† † †

It's bin two whole days of fog but it's finally startin to thin out some. It ain't lifted entirely, but the wind's picked up an it's gone all wispy, like long gray feathers driftin lazily around us. The air's still cold an dank. Hard to believe it's the middle of a summer afternoon.

That's when we come upon the hanged men.

Four of 'em. Danglin by their necks from nooses tied to the branches of a big, lightnin-black tree. They turn gentle in the breeze, their faces an hands gray where they bin covered with wet ash that's dried. The fog winds itself around their bodies.

We pull up. Fer a long moment we sit there an look. Nobody says nuthin. Epona's horse snorts.

Then Jack gits down from Ajax. He walks over to the tree an feels the hand of the nearest man. He crouches down an checks the ground. He shoves his hat back an looks at Ike.

It's Skinny Nick, says Ike, an uh . . .

McNulty, says Tommo.

That's right, says Ike, McNulty. An the two fellas who was with 'em. They was all at the One-Eyed Man the night before you showed up. Left together on foot the next mornin.

They bin dead fer at least a couple of days, says Jack.

They must of crossed somebody, says Ash.

Yeah, says Ike, that'll be it. Poor bastards. He clicks to his horse an leads the way past the hangin tree. I hold back while th'others go on. Wait while Jack swings hisself onto Ajax.

You an Ike know who done it, I says.

Yup, he says. A little nerve jumps at the corner of his mouth.

Was it the Tonton? I says.

Looks like it, he says.

Why's there ash on their hands an faces? I says.

Uninvited guest ain't ezzackly welcome at Freedom Fields, he says. Sometimes the Tonton hang you, other times they'll cut yer head off an put it on a spike. But they always put ash on the face. It's how you know yer in their territory. Wise man sees that, he turns around an gits the hell out as fast as he can.

But we ain't turnin, I says.

No, he says. Wisdom ain't a virtue I ever aspired to.

✝   ✝   ✝

Ever since we come across the hanged men, I cain't stop thinkin about Vicar Pinch. About DeMalo an the rest of the Tonton.

With every step, we git closer to Freedom Fields. Until now, I ain't gived much thought to what we'll be up aginst. Who we'll be up aginst. But now I do.

The Tonton hang people in trees. Cut off their heads an stick 'em on spikes. Fer nuthin more'n wanderin into their King's territory. Men like them wouldn't think twice about killin Lugh. All the things Helen told me run through my head. All the things I know about Pinch an DeMalo. But I need to know more. I gotta know my enemy. I need to know what Jack an Ike know.

An they know plenty, I'm sure of it. I'm gonna make 'em tell me. They owe it to me.

I wait till we're settled into camp fer the night. Epona's takin the first watch. Ash an Emmi an Tommo's wrapped in their bedrolls, already asleep. Ike's propped aginst a log. His head lolls forwards onto his chest.

Jack an Nero sit by the fire playin dice. Once Jack found out how good Nero was at countin, he carved a pair of dice an learned him how to play. Nero throws one at a time, usin his beak.

I go an stand over 'em. Nero throws two sixes.

Damn, says Jack. You beat me agin. Never thought I'd find myself losin to a crow. Think he might be cheatin.

Nero bobs up an down, squawks with glee.

If he is, I say, he learned it from you. I wanna word, Jack. With you an Ike.

He sighs. Like he's bin expectin this. But he stands up an gives Ike a nudge with his foot. Ike wakes with a grunt.

What? he says.

C'mon, says Jack. Saba wants to talk.

As Ike heaves hisself to his feet, Nero flaps up to sit on my shoulder. He rubs his head aginst my cheek. He always knows when I need somebody on my side. Like tonight.

I lead 'em away from the campsite. Climb uphill through the trees till I git to a rocky outcrop. I turn to face 'em. The fog's completely gone an it's a warm night with a high sky. A midsummer night sky. I can see Jack an Ike clearly.

All right, I says. Tell me what you know about Freedom Fields. Tell me everythin.

They look at each other.

I bin straight with you, I says. I told you everythin. What Helen told me about the midsummer sacrifice an why they took Lugh. Pinch might be dead but Lugh ain't safe, not till we git him outta there. Now you two gotta be straight with me. You need to tell me everythin you know. That way, at least we got a chance of figgerin out what we might be up aginst.

Well, you know more'n we do, says Ike. We only heard things from travelin folk. You know, you meet somebody from time to time an you git talkin an—

Ferget it, Ike, says Jack.

What?

I said, ferget it.

But I thought we said we'd—

Ike, he says. Saba's right. She needs to know what we're up aginst.

I knew it! I says. I knew you knew more'n you was lettin on. Gawdammit, Jack, why didn't you tell me before? Why didn't you tell me right away, when you found out where I was headed?

I know I should of, he says. But I didn't want you to know till you had to.

I ain't a child, I says. I don't need you to pertect me.

I know, he says, I know, I'm sorry.

Think I'll . . . head on back to camp, says Ike.

Coward, says Jack.

Go on, Ike, I says. Jack's gonna tell me everythin I need to know.

Right, he says. Well . . . if I hear any screamin, I'll send Emmi. He disappears without a sound. Not a rustle or a footstep. Fer a big man, Ike moves real quiet. Nero must be startin to feel restless becuz he takes off after him.

Then it's jest Jack an me.

All right, Jack, I says. Start talkin.

† † †

Four years ago, he says, I was in the wrong bar at the wrong time. Got picked up by the Tonton. They're always on the lookout fer strong workers. Fer slaves. That's how I ended up at Freedom Fields.

You was there, I says.

I was, he says. Let's sit down.

We sit facin each other, on a couple of rocks. A bit too close fer my likin. His feet nearly touch mine. The heartstone's hot aginst my skin.

That's where I met Ike, he says. We got slaved there about the same time. As you can imagine, him an me didn't take kindly to a slave life, workin in a chain gang in the fields. But everybody else . . . well, nuthin seemed to bother 'em. We figgered out why pretty quick. A big waterwagon 'ud come around twice a day, once in the mornin an once in the afternoon, an fill everybody's waterskins. There's chaal in that water.

Helen said it was all about chaal, I says.

It slows yer brain down, he says. Makes you stupid. A good thing if you wanna control people. But if you take too much, everythin speeds up. Yer heart races, you git all excited an aggressive, you don't need sleep or food.

I think of Mad Dog, back at Hopetown, what he did to Helen. Of the crowds in the Colosseum, bayin fer blood in the gauntlet.

I seen what it can do, I says.

Me an Ike 'ud fill our waterskins with the rest, he says, but we never touched it. We'd sneak water from the irrigation channels in the fields.

How long was you there? I says.

A couple of months. Jest long enough to collect what we needed to pick the locks on our ankle chains. Then we had to wait fer a stormy night. The dog patrols don't go out when there's lightnin or bad weather, it spooks 'em.

So you got away, I says.

An counted ourselves lucky, he says. We hit the road, layin low, keepin outta trouble. Ike eventually settled at the One-Eyed Man. But I kept on goin.

Till you ended up in the cells at Hopetown, I says.

Yeah, he says. Wrong bar, wrong time. Agin.

You'd think you'd learn, I says.

You'd think.

Whaddya know about the King? I says.

He was crazy, says Jack.

I know, I says. I seen him.

He was crazy, he was smart, an he controlled everythin an everybody, he says. Lived in a big white house up at Freedom Fields. The Palace. With the finest of food an drink. Everythin. Amazin stuff from Wrecker days. Soft chairs, big tables, lookin glasses, pictures hangin on the walls. He had house slaves who'd crawl on their hands an knees if they went into a room where he was. If you looked at him the wrong way, he'd run his sword through you. I only ever seen him from a distance. That was close enough.

I know what you mean, I says.

An over the last couple of years, he started expandin his empire. Everywhere I bin lately, I'm havin to dodge Tonton or I'm hearin about 'em. Any place where there's good water or land fit fer growin food, they're comin along an claimin it fer the King. If there's somebody already on the land, they eether work it fer the Tonton or git killed. They got spies an informers all over the place.

He don't control everythin, I says. Look at the Free Hawks.

Maybe they won't be free fer much longer, he says. The King might be dead, but somebody'll step into his shoes. His empire'll keep growin. You can bet on it.

I cain't believe Maev don't know this, I says. That she ain't heard about it.

I tried to tell her, he says. She wouldn't listen. I believe her ezzack words was, I dunno what yer game is, but as far as I'm concerned yer a lyin chancer. That desperate fool might trust you, but I sure as hell don't.

My belly hollows out. A desperate fool. That's what Maev thinks of me. Then the rest of what he said starts to sink in. I stand up slowly. Stare down at him.

So that's it, I says. That's why you came after me. Why you showed up at Darktrees. You wanted the Free Hawks to help you clear out Freedom Fields. You don't care if I find Lugh. You don't care about me. All that . . . crap about how you couldn't help it, you had to follow me . . . that's jest what it was . . . crap. Gawd, I am such a idiot.

No, he says, that was all true, I swear it was. It is!

He throws his head back an curses unner his breath. Stands up. Whatever I say now, he says, you ain't gonna believe me.

Probly not, I says.

I did want the Hawks to help me, he says. When me an

Ike left Freedom Fields, I warn't thinkin about nobody but myself. But I started to see what was goin on everywhere an I started thinkin about them poor bastards we'd left behind in the chaal fields. Then I ended up in Hopetown an saw what was goin on there, an I met you an the Hawks an suddenly there's a chance I can do somethin decent in my life . . . so I took that chance. It all happened at once, Saba. You gotta believe me. It's fate, like I said.

Jack, I says, you cain't possibly think that seven of us an a crow's gonna bring down the Tonton an their operation.

Why not? he says. Me an Ike know the layout. We can take 'em by surprise. They won't expect trouble from outside.

I'm here to git Lugh back, I says, not to change the world. I told you before. An by the way, yer outta yer mind.

C'mon, Saba, he says, if we come up with a good enough plan, we can all have what we want. D'you wanna git yer brother back an then hafta live in a world run by the Tonton? I don't. Ike don't. Ash an Epona don't neether. An if you asked 'em, I bet Tommo an Emmi'ud say the same. You might of burned Hopetown to the ground, but they'll be buildin on its ashes already. You can bet on it.

So what're you sayin, Jack? That you ain't gonna help me unless I fall in with yer plan?

No, he says. No! What I'm sayin is, we think big. We git Lugh back an take out their operation at the same time. The Tonton, the chaal fields . . . everythin. But we cain't do it without you.

You promise me that we'll git Lugh outta there, I says.

I promise, he says. I promise.

All right, I says. I'll go along with yer plan. What is it?

To be honest, he says, I never bin much fer what you'd call a plan. They're more like . . . ideas.

Jack!

I said I promise! he says.

We're gonna need more help, I says.

I whistle fer Nero. He comes in a flutter of wings an lands on my shoulder. I pull Maev's little gold ring from my pocket.

If you ever need me, if you need the Hawks, send Nero with this an we'll come. Wherever, whenever . . . you send this ring an we'll be there.

It's Maev's, I says. She said to send it if I needed her. D'you got somethin to tie it on with?

He fumbles in his pocket an pulls out a good sized piece of string.

Tie it to his leg, I says. Make it good an tight, but don't let it cut into him.

He works quick.

Done, he says, steppin back.

I stroke Nero's feathers. Look into his clever black eyes. Find Maev, I says. I touch the ring, then I touch him on his breast. Nero find Maev. Find Maev.

He cocks his head to one side. Then he caws twice an takes off into the night.

He ain't never let me down yet, I says.

I should of told you everythin sooner, Jack says. I should of . . .

What? I says. Trusted me?

Yeah, well . . . , he says. I ain't ezzackly bin in the habit of trustin people.

Me neether, I says.

We could try startin agin, he says.

He holds out his hand.

I hesitate. Then I take it. Warm. Callused. Strong.

I'm sorry I was such a ass back at Ike's place, he says. It was jest that . . . ah hell, Saba . . . I was jealous that you smiled at Tommo an not me. You was hardly even talkin to me, let alone smilin, an it was like I couldn't help myself.

Jealous? I says. You? Jealous? Of Tommo? He's a child.

I'm jealous of anybody you smile at that ain't me, he says. He takes a step closer. Reaches out. Runs the back of his hand down my cheek. A hot shiver ripples through me. You look at me with them eyes of yers, he says, an I look at yer lips . . . an all I can think about is what it 'ud be like to kiss you. You got no idea, do you? You got no idea how beautiful you are.

We stare at each other. The moon silvers his face. Shadows his eyes. Makes him look strange. Not quite real.

I step back so's his hand falls. I block out what he jest said. Even though my heart's bangin aginst my ribs. Even though I cain't git my breath an the heartstone's burnin into my skin.

I think we're gonna head back to Crosscreek, I says. Me an Emmi an Lugh. To start with, anyways. We got a friend there, Mercy. Did I ever tell you about her?

Saba, he says.

She's real nice, I says. A old friend of my ma. Yeah, I got it all worked out. I had plenty of time to think about it.

Saba, he says.

I know I'm babblin. I cain't seem to stop myself. An I don't dare look at him. If I do, I fear I'll say somethin I shouldn't or do somethin I don't mean to. I dunno what ezzackly but it's . . . I feel like I'm walkin along a narrow ridge an my foot could slip at any moment. I jest gotta think about Lugh, think about why I'm here, an everythin'll be okay.

Well, I better git back, I says.

I go to slip past him an he grabs my hand. Stops me. We're standin close. Too close. Stay, he says.

Before I can stop myself, I look at him. A mistake. Hot silver eyes. Burnin fer me. My heart lurches.

He leans his head down. Stay with me. He whispers it into my ear. Jest fer a while.

I . . . I gotta go, I says.

Please, he says.

The brush of his breath aginst my skin. The warm Jack smell of him. I feel myself weakenin. Dangerous. This . . . the way I feel whenever I'm near him . . . it's dangerous. I pull my hand from his.

No, I says. I . . . I caint. G'night, Jack.

I slip past him. Gotta git away. I cain't move fast enough.

He don't reply.

† † †

The mean white sun's bin poundin down on our heads all day. The way turned steep an rocky around noon. We had to dismount an start leadin the horses an we bin climbin ever since. We're headed fer a pass high in the mountains that's our last big crossin before we git to Freedom Fields. Jack says he wants to reach it before nightfall, but it's slow goin in this terrain.

The higher we climb, the hotter it gits, even with the day closin down around us. There ain't bin no relief from the heat, none at all. Not even a single tree to shade us on our way.

When we was stuck in the fog fer days on end, I never would of thought fer a second that I'd be longin fer its cold dank heaviness, but I am.

Em's bin bit by bit fallin behind th'others an I bin holdin back to walk with her. But she's gittin slower an slower. I look over my shoulder. She plods along on heavy feet. She looks so pale an tired. I wait fer her. The sweat runs down my face, stingin my eyes. I mop myself off with the end of my sheema.

I'm so thirsty, she says when she reaches me.

Waterskin empty? I says. She nods. Siddown, I says.

She sinks onto a rock. I unstop my skin an hold it to her lips. She sucks hard on it, gulpin the water. It runs down her chin an neck an I wipe it away with the tail of my shirt.

She looks a bit surprised. I don't ever bother with her that way, worryin about when she last had a wash or if her face is all grubby. Once Pa gave up carin, Lugh looked after that kinda thing. I ain't gived it a single thought till this moment. I stare down at her, frownin.

When did you last have a wash? I says.

She looks even more surprised. I dunno, she says.

You should wash more regular, I says. You gotta be decent.

Okay, she says.

I turn away an take a swig of water myself. I rub a drop into my dry lips.

The rest of 'em's well ahead of us. Ash turns back, sees us, waves. She cups her hands around her mouth. No time to stop! she shouts. Jack says we gotta make the pass before dark!

Emmi needs to rest! I shout back.

She can rest later!

She needs to rest now!

I can see 'em talkin amongst theirselves. Then Ike hands his reins to Tommo an makes his way back down to us. He crouches down beside Emmi.

Hey there, kid, he says. Yer doin real good. How's about a ride to the top?

She nods, not lookin straight at him. She likes Ike, but she's a bit shy of him. I think on account of him bein so big an her bein so small.

C'mon then, he says, hop on. She climbs onto his back.

Thanks Ike, I says.

We gotta reach the pass before dark, he says.

I know, I says. I heard it the first hunnerd times.

He checks the sky. The light's startin to soften, turn to gold. We're gonna be pushed, he mutters.

Ike starts up the mountain, with Emmi clingin to his back like a spider. I cain't believe how fast he moves, pickin his way around the rocks. Like she don't weigh nuthin. I guess to a man his size, she don't.

I take a last swig of water. Then I pick up Hermes' reins an follow behind Ike, fast as I can.

† † †

They're all waitin fer me when I git to the top. Emmi gives me a quick look, but nobody else looks my way. They're starin at somethin in front of 'em.

What is it? I says.

Then I see what it is. What they're all lookin at.

We're standin on the edge of what used to be a mountain lake. Back in Wrecker times it must of bin a stretch of cool clear water, a welcome relief fer the tired feet of travelers. But it sure ain't that no more.

Now it stretches away in front of us. Parched, scorched, criss crossed with great cracks an crevasses. Endless.

My heart drops into my boots. I lick my lips.

I cain't see th'other side, I says.

It's there, says Jack. We should of had it in sight by now.

We couldn't of gone no faster in this heat, I says.

I know, says Jack, I know. It's my fault. We should of set off earlier or . . . He grabs at his hair, frustrated. Gawdammit, he says, I thought we'd have plenty of time. He looks at Ike. Whaddya think?

We might make it across before nightfall, says Ike. But you can tell by his face, by his voice, that he don't think no such thing.

I don't see what the problem is, says Epona with a frown. We'll jest ride across. As fast as we can.

Yeah, I says an Ash nods.

We cain't go fast, says Jack. There's too many cracks, too many places a horse could stumble.

Well all right, I says, we'll go slow an careful then. An if it turns dark before we finish crossin, we'll jest set up camp on the lakebed.

We cain't, says Ike.

I look at Jack. At Ike. They're starin at each other, their faces grim.

What is this? I says. We gotta cross before dark, we cain't camp on the lakebed . . . I ain't likin the sound of this.

That makes two of us, says Ash.

Try three, says Epona.

I cross my arms over my chest. Fergawdsake, jest tell us, I says. Why is it we gotta cross before dark?

Ike spreads his hands. Tell 'em, Jack, he says.

Jack curses unner his breath. Looks at the ground fer a moment. Then he reaches fer the edges of his shirt an pulls it off over his head.

Emmi gasps. Beside me, I hear Ash's breath hiss in. I already seen 'em, back at Hopetown, but my stummick still clenches.

Three long pink claw marks that slash across his body from his right shoulder to his left hip. Jack stands there fer a moment. Then he turns so we can see his back. A smaller set of claw scars slash across his right shoulder-blade.

He turns around agin an puts on his shirt.

Does that answer yer question? he says.

✝   ✝   ✝

What did that to yer back? Emmi whispers.

It was dark, says Jack. I didn't git a good look.

They call 'em hellwurms, says Ike.

Wurms with claws, says Epona. An big wurms by the look of it. I ain't heard of nuthin like that before.

An you ain't seen nuthin like 'em neether, says Ike.

What are they? says Ash.

Story goes that a long time ago, back in Wrecker times, they put some kinda poison into the lake, says Ike. It killed off everythin. Essept the wurms. They grew.

You said they, says Epona. That means there's more'n one. How many more?

A lot more, says Jack.

This jest gits better an better, I says.

There's silence. Then, That settles it, I says. I'm goin on alone.

Well, everybody starts talkin all at once, even Tommo, one over top of th'other, gittin louder an louder till at last I put my hands over my ears an yell, Shut up, will you! Jest . . . shut up!

They do. They all look at me.

He's my brother, I says. An I ain't lettin none of you come with me if that's—I point at Jack—what we gotta deal with before we even git to Freedom Fields. Now, I cain't afford to go back down the hill an wait to try agin tomorrow. We're nearly at midsummer. If I start right away, I might reach th'other side of the lake before dark.

She travels fastest who travels alone, says Ike, is that it?

That's it all right, I says. Okay, Emmi, you—Emmi, what the hell're you doin down there?

While we bin talkin, Emmi's bin scrabblin around on the ground. Now she stands up an holds out her hands. She's got a pile of white pebbles in one an a pile of black pebbles in th'other.

White means we go with you, she says. Black means we don't. Whatever we git the most of, that's what we do.

I ain't got time fer this, Emmi, I says, I'm—

Shut up, Saba, she says.

An I'm so astonished that I do.

She sets the pebbles in two piles on the ground. She leaves a space in between.

Everybody gits one vote, she says. You choose yer pebble an then you put it in the middle. When we're all done, I'll count 'em up. Now, turn around so's you cain't watch what the other person's doin.

Nobody moves. We all jest stand there, starin at her.

I said, turn around! she says. Tommo, you go first.

The rest of us turn our backs. Ike's next to me. I see it runs in the family, he mutters.

Emmi directs the whole thing. I'm th'only one left.

What about me? I says.

You don't git a turn, she says. Okay, turn around.

In the middle there's six white pebbles. Not one black one.

I crouch down. Pick up the pebbles an hold 'em in my hand. They feel solid, warm. I look up into their faces one by one. An it's like I'm lookin at 'em fer the first time. Jack, Ike, Emmi, Epona, Ash an Tommo. Every one of 'em willin to walk with me across the lake. To go with me into the darkness an face what lives there.

My throat feels tight.

You don't hafta do this, I says.

Epona shrugs. We're yer friends, Saba, she says. We wanna help.

I wish you wouldn't, I says.

Too bad, she says. We're stickin with you.

If this gits any more heart-warmin, says Ash, I'm gonna start cryin. Now if we're done here, I say we git movin.

† † †

Jack gits us to muffle the horses' feet with cloth so's the wurms don't know we're passin over the top of 'em. Then we move out onto the parched lakebed.

We go as quick as we can, but like Jack said, we gotta guide the horses safely past all the cracks an crevasses, big an small, that split the earth an slow us down. We don't talk, try not to make no sound. But the horses sense somethin. They're nervy. Soon they start to shy at their own shadows.

An we don't make it. We don't make it across the lake before dark. Even though it's the season of long days, we're only about halfways across when we start to lose the light.

Jack stops. Looks at the sky. He waits fer everybody to catch up. When the light goes, he says in a low voice, it's gonna go fast. We gotta be ready well before then.

My stummick clenches. Ready fer what? I says.

Hellwurms sleep in the day, he says, deep inside the mountain. When night falls, they come up through the cracks in the lakebed. They'll be lookin fer food. It could be we git lucky. If they already got full bellies from last night or even a couple of days ago, they might stay down there an sleep it off. But if we don't git lucky—

—the minute it's dark, says Ike, wurms is gonna crawl outta them cracks an cover this lakebed faster'n you could ever imagine.

You should of told us this before we started off, I says.

I was hopin I wouldn't hafta, says Jack. But would it of made any difference? Anybody?

Everyone shakes their head.

Hell no, says Emmi.

†   †   †

We decide to let the horses go. We unwrap their feet an set 'em on their way across the lake. This way, there's at least a chance they might make it safe to th'other side. Once the wurms come out, they won't have no chance at all.

I lean aginst Hermes' head. I stroke his soft nose.

Saba, says Jack. Time to let him go.

I look into his wise brown eyes one last time. Thank you, I whisper. Then I stand back. Go on, I says.

He trots a few paces away. He stops. He turns to look at me. I raise my hand in farewell. He tosses his head an whinnies. Then he heads off after th'others.

As I watch him go, I know I'm watchin my best chance of reachin Lugh by midsummer disappear. I wanna blame somebody fer the mess we're in, but yellin at Jack or Ike or anybody else ain't gonna change nuthin. We're all in this together now.

I turn around.

So, Jack, I says, what's the plan?

✝   ✝   ✝

We work fast. We ain't got much time before the dark comes.

My hands move, my feet move. I push down the fear that's risin in me. There ain't no room fer it, ain't no time fer it.

Jack's in charge. He says to do somethin, we all do whatever it is right away. We don't ask no questions, don't ask him what his plan is. We'll be findin out soon enough.

He gits us to gather as much wood as we can find. Branches, twigs an trunks of long dead trees blown here by the mountain winds. No matter how big or small, we find 'em an carry or drag 'em to Jack an Ike.

Then we bundle together all the small bits an tie 'em with nettlecord. We break up what bigger branches we can by hand an them that's too big, Ike chops with his hatchet. Then we start to lay 'em out in a big circle.

Jack calls me over. Count how many arrows we got, would you? he says.

I empty my quiver. Lucky Maev sent me off with a full load. Then I go around an count what's in Jack's an Epona's an Ash's quivers. Ike's got a bolt shooter as well as a crossbow, but he's only got a few bolts fer ammo so we'll hold the shooter in reserve. Emmi an Tommo both got slingshots. I do a quick arrow count. Then I count agin to make sure.

Two hunnerd an eighty eight, I tell Jack.

He flashes me a tight grin. That's better'n I thought, he says. Wrap the heads in bits of cloth, whatever you can find.

I reach fer the bottom of my shirt. It's soaked through with sweat from the climb an the heat, but I should be able to rip a strip from it.

No, he says. Dry cloth. It's gotta be dry. See how many

bottles you can scare up. An ask Ike fer some of that pine sap vodka of his.

Now I know what his plan is.

Fire. We're gonna fight 'em with fire.

† † †

The wood's laid out how Jack wants it. It's heaped in a big circle ready to be lit the moment he tells us to. We've left a good-sized open space in the middle. That's where we'll stand an fight. Inside our fortress of fire.

We've made torches with bundles of twigs tied to the ends of branches. Now, with one eye on the darkenin sky, we're all workin fast to tie cloth strips around the arrowheads. We've torn up bits of our bedrolls, even our shirts an tunics. Whatever we've got that's dry.

Ike's poured some of his precious vodka into bottles, two fer each of us. As soon as we git a pile of arrows done, Emmi an Tommo take 'em away an stick 'em, head down, into the bottles. Ready to be pulled out, lit an shot. We only manage to fit a handful of arrows in each bottle, so once the action gits goin, it'll be their job to keep 'em filled up. That an slingshot duty.

Ike's workin next to me. You crossed the lake that night with Jack, I says. Where's yer scars?

Jack took the hit instead of me, he says. I wouldn't be here if he hadn't of got between me an the wurm.

Well, you was movin so slow I had to do somethin, says Jack.

You was away, says Ike. You was clear. You should of left me to fend fer myself, not turned back an nearly got yerself killed.

I'm still here, ain't I? he says. He goes over to help Tommo an Emmi.

Damn wurm nearly killed him, says Ike.

Jack's . . . different from what I thought when I first met him, says Epona.

Yeah, says Ike. There's more to Jack than meets the eye.

Jack hands his last bundle of arrows to Tommo an slaps him on the back.

That's it, he says. We're ready.

There's a hot clench of fear, deep in my belly. I know it well. I used to git it all the time, jest before I went into the Cage. An I know how to use it. A slow smile spreads over my face. I look around at everybody.

I dunno about you, I says, but I'm feelin lucky tonight.

† † †

We wait.

We sit on the ground, spaced out evenly jest inside our

circle of wood. We face across the lake. I got Jack on one side of me an Epona on th'other. Ike an Ash cover the rest of the circle. Emmi an Tommo crouch in the center next to the piles of stones they collected fer their slingshots. I clutch my flint in my hand, ready to set my section alight.

The night starts to drift in. The crimson fingers of the dyin sun bleed into dark gray. The first stars blink down at us. Not long to wait now.

If I ask you somethin, says Jack, will you tell me the truth?

Maybe, I says. Depends.

What made you come after me? he says. Back at Hopetown, I mean. How'd you know where to find me?

I'm about to give some kinda smart answer, somethin that'll keep him at a distance, like always. But I don't. The heartstone's burnin aginst my skin. An I'm feelin brave. Reckless.

I had a dream, I says. The night before the fire.

You dreamed where to find me?

We talk in low voices, so th'others cain't hear us.

In my dream, I was in the dark, I says. I couldn't see, couldn't hardly breathe. There was smoke an fire an the heat was somethin fierce. An I was searchin fer somebody. I didn't know who, I jest . . . knew I had to find him. But I couldn't an it was . . . awful. Frightenin. Then I . . . woke up.

You was . . . lookin fer me? says Jack.

I think so, I says. Yeah.

But you did find me, says Jack. You found me even though I was locked inside the Cooler. How?

I move over, kneel next to him. Feel this, I says. I take Jack's hand an bring it to the heartstone around my neck.

It's hot agin, he says.

I take a deep breath. It's a heartstone, I says. It only gits warm when I'm near you. The closer we are to each other, the hotter it gits. That's how I knew where to find you.

He don't say nuthin. It's the first time I ever seen Jack lost fer words. After a moment, he takes his hand away.

Must be kinda annoyin, he says.

I'm used to it by now, I says. Listen, Jack. I jest wanna say I—

Shh! He holds up his hand.

We wait. Listen.

Silence.

Silence.

Then. A faint rumble. Like thunder in the distance.

They're awake, he whispers.

†   †   †

Light the fires! Jack says.

I scramble to my knees, hold my flint to the tinder at the base of the wood circle.

I strike my flint. A spark arcs onto the dry tinder. It catches an I blow on it gently till I git a flame goin. It licks quickly up the twigs an branches. I check over my shoulder. Everyone else is doin the same with their own section. In no time, we got a strong fire goin an we're standin inside our fortress of flame.

We're lucky with the night. The sky's high an clear. The moon hangs low over the mountain tops an throws a wide silver path across the lakebed. We got a clear view in all directions.

I hold my bow in my hand. Two bottles of vodka-soaked arrows stand by my feet. My knife's in my boot sheath. I ain't gonna think about havin to use it. It's my last defense an usin it 'ud mean everythin else had failed.

I feel calm. Clear-headed. Even though my heart's bangin aginst my ribs.

Emmi, I says, stay close to Tommo.

Okay, she says.

Silence. Silence. Silence. Essept fer the cracklin of the fire. I dart a look at Jack. His head's lifted, like a wolfdog onto a scent.

Then a creakin noise. A slow, painful groan. The kinda noise a old rusted shut door makes when it's forced open. But it ain't a door. It's the ground.

From somewhere deep below us, from somewhere down down down in the dark heart of th'earth, the lakebed's ancient body is slowly bein forced open.

The hellwurms is awake. An they're comin up to feed.

The ground starts to tremble. It starts to shake. Then it shifts unner our feet. I stagger. Epona grabs my arm, stops me fallin over.

Holy crap in a cup, says Ash, her eyes wide.

Everybody git down! yells Jack.

Me an Epona throw ourselves to the ground. Throw our arms around our heads.

The earth groans, deep in its belly, as it's forced open. Over an over an over it moans its pain. Groanin an shriekin an shakin unner us, around us, it gits louder an louder. Till it takes me over, floodin my body, my breath, my brain till I think I'll go mad.

Then it stops.

Silence.

Slowly, we all git to our feet. My fingers is clenched tight around my bow. I look over at Emmi. She's clutchin Tommo's hand, her face white in the moonlight.

Then, over the crackle of the fire, another sound.

A rustle. The click of claws on dry earth. Somethin's movin. It stops. Hisses.

It can smell us, Ike says in a low hoarse voice.

A high pitched shriek rips the night open.

My heart leaps to my throat. My bowels clench.

It's callin th'others, Jack says. Git ready! An remember what I told you.

Aim fer the eyeholes. An don't let 'em git close enough to use their claws.

Claws. No eyes, jest dents in the skin where they used to have eyes a long time ago. No point in havin eyes, Jack says, livin unnerground like they do, so they hunt by smell. They sniff out their prey.

Their prey. Us.

Then, not more'n thirty foot away, straight in front of me an Epona, a crack appears in the ground. It splits open, starts to widen.

Here we go! Epona yells.

A claw appears.

† † †

The claw hooks itself onto the edge of the crack. It's got three long scaly toes. Each toe ends in a hooked nail sharp enough to slash to the bone with one swipe. Then another claw hooks itself beside the first.

Don't be shy, I says. Show me yer face, you scaly-toe sonofabitch.

An, almost like it heard me, a round head appears. Covered in scales an maggot-white with a dip in each side where the eyes oughta be. A long neck. The blunt head sways back an forth, the scales ripplin like tiny waves. It must be smellin us.

That's right, I says. Over here. I'm real tasty.

I pull a arrow outta the vodka. Nock it to my bowstring. Dip the arrowhead into the fire at my feet. It flames up right away. I take aim.

The hellwurm slithers outta the crack. Gits up on its hind legs.

Uh . . . Jack, I says. You didn't say they could walk.

Sorry, he says. I fergot that bit.

The wurm's three times my height. Two long arms with claws, an claws on its feet too. A wide slash of a mouth with lots of sharp teeth, good fer tearin flesh. You can see right through its death white skin to its beatin heart an other innards. It gives off the most gawdawful stench. Like a three-day-old corpse in a small room on a humid day. I gag. So does Epona.

It throws its head back an shrieks.

I let fly with my arrow. Straight at the right eyehole. A hit. The wurm's head bursts into flame. It screams an staggers backwards into the crack it jest come from.

Nice shot, says Epona.

But there's more comin. From all around us. Hunnerds of 'em by the look of it. The lakebed's alive with their scuttlin stinkin bodies.

We start pickin 'em off with our crossbows, as fast as we can. Epona an me, Jack an Ike an Ash. Emmi an Tommo fire away with their slingshots, dartin in between us to git a closer shot.

Hellfire, Jack, I says. You didn't say there was this many.

They must of bin busy breedin, he says. He shoots me a grin, but I can tell this is worse than he especkted.

The night rings with the screams of the hellwurms an our shouts. The air's filled with the filthy smell of 'em an the crackle an smoke of the fire.

I keep firin. Dip the arrow, nock, let fly, hit. Dip, nock, let fly, hit.

Around me, everybody else is doin the same. Em an Tommo run around stuffin arrows into our bottles but, no matter how many wurms we shoot, more keep comin.

There's too many, says Epona. We ain't gonna do it.

I'm gittin low on arrows, I says.

Me too, says Ash.

More arrows here, Emmi! I yell.

That's it! she cries. There ain't no more!

Jack grabs my arm as I'm about to fire. By the silvery white light of the moon, I can see his face is all streaked with smoke from the fires.

Git outta here, he says. Take Emmi an Tommo. Ash an Epona'll cover you.

My heart stops. There's a roarin in my ears. You want us to go? I says.

He nods. Ike an me'll stay, he says.

No, I says.

I pull myself free. I grab twig bundles, shove 'em into the fire.

They catch light an I launch 'em at the wurms. More screams as they burst into flame. Beside me, Jack keeps on shootin his bow.

If you leave now, he says, at least you got a chance of findin yer brother.

Ferget it, I says.

I snatch my bow agin an start firin.

Use the torches if they git too close! yells Ike. Don't waste yer arrows!

I look around. The hellwurms is closin in. Closer an closer they come. Some slither along the ground, some walk upright, their heads swayin. They won't try to cross the fire ring, but once it starts to die down, that'll be it.

Jack pulls the bow outta my hand. If you don't do this, he says, everythin you bin through to find yer brother counts fer nuthin.

I stare at him. I feel like my throat's closin up. Leave him. Leave Ike. But I gotta find Lugh. I'm so close to findin him.

You know I'm right, he says.

Okay, I says. We'll go.

Saba! yells Ash. Behind you!

I whirl around.

One wurm, bigger'n the rest, darts forwards through a dyin section of the fire ring. Jack grabs my arm an goes to yank me back but the wurm's claw flashes out. A hot pain slashes through my right shoulder. I cry out.

A blast rings out an the wurm's head explodes in a million

pieces. Putrid flesh an blood splatter down on me like rain. I look over my shoulder. Ike's holdin his bolt shooter. He gives me a little salute.

You all right? says Jack.

I close my mind to the pain. Like I used to do in Hopetown.

I'm fine, I says.

Time to go, he says. He grabs up a torch in each hand an lights 'em. Ash! he yells. Epona! C'mere!

They start to run over to us.

The ground rumbles. We all stagger an I grab onto Jack to keep from fallin.

The wurms stop. They raise their heads. Then they scatter.

Jest like that. They scuttle an slither across the lakebed an disappear back down inside the cracks.

They're gone. An all that's left is the smolderin corpses of hunnerds of hellwurms.

† † †

We stand inside our circle of dyin fire an stare. There ain't a sound but the hiss of the embers. Nobody moves. It's like we're all holdin our breath. Like we cain't believe our own eyes.

Then, Yee ha! Ash yells. Her an Epona jump around, punchin

their bows in the air. Did you see that, Jack? Hey Ike! Did you see them bastards go? They grab Emmi's an Tommo's hands an whirl them around in circles.

Somehow it don't seem right, them celebratin an makin lots of noise. I dunno why, but it don't.

I look at Jack. His jaw's set. A little nerve jumps in his cheek.

What is it? I says.

We didn't scare 'em off, he says. They was gittin the better of us.

Well, if we didn't scare 'em off, I says, what did?

Ike moves over to stand beside us. Him an Jack stare out over the lake.

The earth shakes agin. This time louder an longer.

Dammit, Jack, I says, tell me what yer thinkin.

Epona an Ash stop their celebrations. They come over, with Tommo an Emmi, an we all draw in close together.

Emmi slips her hand into mine. What's goin on, Saba?

Some people say the hellwurms got a master, says Ike.

There's another rumble.

A master? says Emmi. What does that mean?

What it means, says Jack, is there's somethin down there so big an bad, even the hellwurms run when they hear it comin.

I let that little fact sink in. Then, If runnin's good enough fer hellwurms, I says, it's good enough fer me.

An me, says Jack.

358

We stare at each other a split second. Then, at the ezzack same time, we yell, Run!

✝   ✝   ✝

We all scramble, grab whatever weapon's closest, start to run fer it. Ash an Epona take off fast, with Emmi an Tommo. But before I can take more'n a couple of steps, there's a almighty roar. The ground heaves. It lifts. It splits open at my feet. I'm slidin down into a giant crack. I scrabble wildly. I cain't stop myself.

Jack's there in a flash. He grabs my hands an yanks me out. I lie on the ground, pantin. My heart's goin like a hammer.

Thanks, I says, it jest about had me there. I—

Suddenly a long tail whips up from the crack. It wraps around my ankles an pulls me in.

Jack dives. Grabs hold of my hands agin. He's laid on the ground on his belly, hangin on fer dear life. Ike! he yells. I need you here!

Ike throws hisself down beside Jack. Now they each got one of my hands.

I feel like I'm bein slowly ripped in half. The tail pullin me down, Jack an Ike pullin me up.

I cry out. I stare into their faces. Their eyes is desperate, their faces strainin with the effort. My hands start to slip outta theirs.

Jest then, Ash an Epona appear above me at th'edge of the crack, their crossbows loaded. They aim down an fire past me. There's a high pitched scream an the tail loosens. Jest a bit, jest fer a moment. Ike an Jack heave me up an out.

Go! Go! Go! yells Ike. He scoops Emmi into his arms an takes off at a fast run, headin north. Epona, Ash an Tommo's right behind him. I snatch my crossbow but only got time to scoop up one arrow. Then Jack an me sprint after 'em.

There's a angry roar behind us. I glance back.

A giant hellwurm's jest crawled outta the crack. It stands up on its hind legs. It's twice the size of th'other ones, at least thirty foot high, with a long lizard tail.

Ohmigawd, I says. I'm still runnin but I slow down a bit to look back.

The hellwurm's caught our scent.

It's followin us! I says.

Jack takes my hand an we run faster. I shoot another look over my shoulder.

It's gainin on us! I says.

Jack stops runnin. Stops dead. Without a word, he turns around an starts walkin back towards the hellwurm. He's headed fer it an it's headed fer him.

Jack holds Ike's shooter in his hand. He must of picked it up without me noticin. As he walks, he loads it with quick jerky movements.

Jack! I shout. What the hell d'you think yer doin?

I'm sick of this bastard! he yells.

Jack! Don't be so crazy!

He keeps on walkin.

Jack! I scream. Don't!

He stops. Lifts the shooter. Takes aim. He waits till the hellwurm's twenny paces away. Then he fires.

The shot slashes the hellwurm's arm. It roars, but keeps on comin. Jack fumbles fer the pouch with the bolts while he keeps one eye on the hellwurm.

I can see he ain't got time to reload. An he ain't got his crossbow. He must of dropped it earlier. I start runnin towards him.

The hellwurm's on top of him. It rears up to its full height. It lashes out, swipes at him. Jack's thrown into the air, like Emmi's peg doll. He lands with a heavy thump on the ground. He don't move.

The red hot races through my blood. I throw down my crossbow as I run. Hold my one last arrow in my hand. The hellwurm leans over Jack. It lifts its claws, ready to swipe at him agin.

I don't even slow down. I run around behind it an right up its back. I wrap my legs an arms around its stinkin neck an I squeeze with every bit of strength in my body.

It roars with fury. Turns itself in circles, round an round, its great claws flailin at me, tryin to pick me off, shake me off. Somehow I hang on. I raise the arrow up high an then, with all my strength, plunge it into the left eyehole. It goes in hard. Deep. I pull it out an jab it into the right eyehole.

The hellwurm bellows in pain. I leap from its back as it crashes to the ground. It pulls itself up agin. It near crushes Jack unnerfoot as it struggles to stay upright. Its tail lashes out an sends Jack skiddin.

It staggers this way, then that. Then it's gone. Disappeared down a big crack in the lakebed.

I watch it fall, roarin an clawin at the air, hittin the sides as it plunges down down, deep down into the earth to die.

✝   ✝   ✝

Jack! I yell. I run to where he's lyin so still on the ground. I throw myself beside him, turn him over.

He ain't breathin. He's most awful pale. His eyes is closed. I run my hands over his legs, his arms, his neck to check if anythin's broke. They seem okay.

Jack! I pat his face. Jack! I tilt his head back, pinch his nose an blow into his mouth. I check fer his chest risin. I blow agin.

His lips twitch. He's smilin.

I jump to my feet. Gawdammit Jack, I says, what're you playin at?

He opens one eye. Yer kissin technique could do with a bit of work, he says.

I thought you was dead, you bastard! I was tryin to save yer life! Although why I should save a snake like you, I got no idea!

I was winded, he says, not dyin. You should learn to tell the difference. He pulls hisself up to sit. Shakes his head an groans. I sure hit that ground hard, he says.

Not hard enough, I says.

What happened to the wurm?

Dead, I says.

He grunts. Closes his eyes.

Don't thank me or nuthin, I says.

Thanks, he says. I make that two to you now. One fer the cellblock an one fer this. An it's two to me. Pullin you outta the river an pullin you outta that crack jest now.

I ain't playin yer stupid game, Jack, I says. Git up.

He opens one eye. In fairness, he says, Ike did help to pull you out, so that should probly only count fer half. He holds out his hand to me. All right, help me up. But go easy.

I yank him as hard as I can. A hot pain shoots across my right shoulder. I gasp. It feels like it's on fire. I bin so set on savin myself an savin Jack, I ain't even felt it till now.

You got slashed, he says. I fergot all about it. Let me take a look.

He reaches out. I slap his hand away.

Leave me be, I says, I'm fine.

Don't be so damn stubborn, he says. C'mere.

Go to hell, I says. I head back across the lakebed in the direction th'others took, collectin my crossbow on the way. I walk fast an I don't look back. I ain't waitin fer him.

Behind me, he starts to sing.

I've climbed the high mountains an sailed the wide seas
Fair faces a-plenty I've gazed on
But with one glance, her beauty sent me to my knees,
O hard-hearted Annie I never shall please.

I've roved an I've rambled all o'er the wide world
And kisses a-plenty I've tasted
But it's her wine-sweet lips that I'm still dreaming of
O hard-hearted Annie, cruel Annie my love.

I've loved many women an wooed many girls
And many soft arms have embraced me
If only she'd lie with me one fleeting night
With hard-hearted Annie I'd die of delight.

Oh many fine beauties did beg me to stay
But none until Annie did snare me
Though she hurts me an shuns me an makes my heart bleed
My hard-hearted Annie I never shall leave.

I don't think most people 'ud feel like singin jest after they'd fought off hunnerds of hellwurms. But Jack ain't most people. I should know that by now.

He's got a strong voice. It carries over the lake, clear as if he's walkin right beside me. The tune ain't bad. An he's a fair singer. But after he's sung it through once he goes back to the beginnin an starts all over agin. Pretty soon I ain't jest sick of the tune an his voice, I'm also sick of hearin about hard-hearted Annie.

What a stupid song.

I mean, what kinda fool 'ud put up with a woman that troublesome?

†   †   †

I dare a look at my shoulder while I walk. I ease my shirt away, slow an careful. Dried blood sticks to the cloth, pulls at the wound. I bite my lip so's I don't cry out. Jack's still somewhere behind me. Don't let him hear. Only one tear in the skin, but it looks deep enough. It's throbbin somethin fierce.

But the pain ain't no worse'n what I used to feel after a rough fight in the Cage. I tell myself that, over an over. That's the way to keep it unner control. I jest need to do what I did then. Cut my brain off from what my body's feelin. Make myself believe it's happenin to somebody else.

Think of somethin else.

Think of Lugh. Think how he looked the last time I seen him. Thrown over the back of a horse, wrists an ankles tied, like a beast.

They killed my father. They stole my brother.

It's the anger that keeps me goin.

I feel its heat in my belly. All through me.

Heat.

So hot.

† † †

Soon's I catch up with Emmi an th'others, I'll bathe my shoulder an pack it with . . . with bark. That's it, I'll pack it with . . . what was it now?

My feet's so heavy. Like I got somethin tied to the end of my legs. Need to keep goin. Gotta git to . . . where am I goin agin? Oh yeah. To Lugh, that's it. But I'm jest gonna hafta . . . sit. Jest fer a moment.

I sink down.

It's night. It should be cool but I'm sweatin like billy-o. I go to wipe my forehead with my sleeve but my arm . . .

cain't lift it. Now I remember. My shoulder. Must be . . .
infected.

Gotta find Lugh.

I'm jest so . . . tired. Must . . . lie . . . down . . .

† † †

I'm five year old. It's a sunny day. I'm on the shore at Silverlake.
I'm by myself. A breeze lifts my hair. The lake water laps softly. I'm
crouched down, pilin up flat stones, all white, one on top of th'other.
I count as I go.

One, two, three, four, five, six, seven!

A shadow falls over me. I look up. It's Pa. Like he used to be when
I was a kid. Before Ma died. Thick black hair, smilin eyes, strong,
handsome.

Seven, Pa! Look at that!

He hunkers down beside me. Takes my hand.

They're gonna need you, Saba, he says. Lugh an Emmi.
There'll be others too, many others, who will look to you, an you'll
hafta stand alone. Don't give in to fear. Be strong, like I know you
are. An never give up, d'you unnerstand, never. No matter what
happens.

I smile at him.

I won't, I says. I ain't no quitter, Pa.

That's my girl, he says. Then he's gone. Jest like that. Disappeared.

Pa! I jump to my feet. Where are you, Pa? Come back!

His voice echoes, drifts away, gittin softer an softer. That's my girl, my girl, my girl.

Pa! I look around, frantic to find him. But he's gone. Silverlake is dry. The ground unner my feet an as far as I can see is parched an cracked.

† † †

Darkness. Voices. Angry. Shoutin. I cain't hear the words though.

Then it all stops.

A flash of white light. An Epona stands there. Alone. Darkness all around her.

There's only the sound of my heart. Beat, beat, beat.

Epona looks over her shoulder, like she sees somethin behind her. She turns back agin. She sees me. She nods.

An it all happens slowly. So slow, I can see the blink of her eyelids. I can see her lips move as she takes in a breath.

Beat, beat, beat goes my heart.

She starts to run towards me. She throws her arms wide open an lifts her face up. She leaps.

A flash of white light.

An the world smashes into a million pieces.

† † †

Jack! I think she's awake! Emmi's voice.

There's a dull throb in my right shoulder. I hear the crackle of a fire. Somebody kneels beside me. Lays a hand on my forehead. It's callused, cool. Nice on my warm skin.

Slowly I open my eyes. I'm lookin up at rock. I frown.

It's a cave, says Jack.

I turn my head to look at him. In the flicker of the fire-light, his silver moon eyes glitter. His skin gleams. He's beau-tiful.

Welcome back, he says.

I lift my hand an touch his cheek. It's warm. Rough with stubble.

Jack, I says.

He goes still. He puts my hand back down on the blanket. I'll git you a drink, he says an disappears.

Emmi? I says.

I'm here! She grabs my hand an kisses it, over an over.

Hey Emmi, I says. C'mon now, I'm fine.

I was afeared you'd die, she says. You had a fever. You was shoutin out, callin fer Pa.

Was I? Em . . . I was havin the strangest dreams.

Jack's back. Here you go, he says. He puts his arm around my shoulders an raises me up. I wince.

Sorry, he says. He holds a cup to my mouth an I drink. It's bitter an I make a face. Willow bark, he says. It brings down the fever. I brewed it myself.

He makes me drink the cup dry before he lets me stop.

My right shoulder's wrapped tight in a strip of ripped shirt. How bad is it? I says.

A lot better'n it was, he says. We cleaned you up an put a poultice on to draw out th'infection. That wurm slashed you deep. It needs stitchin, but we had to wait till it's clean.

You bin out fer two days, says Emmi.

Two days! I says. I sit up like a shot an go to shove my blanket away, but Jack stops me. Presses me back gently so's I lie down agin. My shoulder throbs. It cain't be, I says. That means we only got . . . when's midsummer eve?

Him an Emmi look at each other. It's tonight, she says.

No! What time is it now? I try to sit up agin an this time Emmi stops me. I gotta git there!

It's okay, says Emmi, we got time.

We're here, says Jack.

What . . . ? I says. Whaddya mean . . . we're here?

Freedom Fields, she says. Saba, we're at Freedom Fields.

† † †

It's jest th'other side of this hill, says Jack. He gits up an goes over to the fire. Starts doin somethin, takin pots offa the fire an movin things around, but I cain't see what.

I don't unnerstand, I says. How'd I git here?

You passed out while you was still on the lake, says Emmi. Jack found you. He carried you all the way till he caught up with us. You would of bin dead if it warn't fer him. Ain't that right, Jack?

He grunts.

He wouldn't let nobody else touch you, she says. Then he loaded you onto Hermes an we jest kept goin till we got here.

Hermes? I says. But we set the horses loose. They should of bin long gone.

Not Hermes, says Emmi. He waited fer us. Fer you.

Remind me to thank him, I says. I lie back. We made it in time, I whisper. We made it.

By the skin of our teeth, says Jack.

Where's everybody else? I says.

Outside, he says. They're gittin a few things together that might be useful.

They're makin arrows, says Emmi.

I need to help, I says.

You can help in a minute, says Jack. Soon's I stitch that wound.

There ain't time, I says.

You ain't got a choice in the matter, he says. He starts to thread fine catgut through a thin bone needle.

Emmi says, You should of seen 'em all run when Jack asked who was good at stitchin.

Cowards, says Jack. Every one of 'em.

Ike said only a fool 'ud dare touch a prickly pear like you, says Emmi.

Is that what you are, Jack? I says. A fool?

Seems that way, he says. Now, let's take a look. He pushes my shirt offa my shoulder an unwinds the bandage. I peer at it. The oak bark poultice done its work. The wound's ugly but clean.

Yer gonna have a big scar, says Emmi.

You ain't seen me sew yet, says Jack. I do real neat work. He holds out a bottle of Ike's vodka. It's half full. Here you go, he says, drink it down. It'll help dull the pain.

No, I says. I'm gonna need a clear head later on.

He lifts one eyebrow. You sure? he says. Go on.

No, I says. I don't wanna drink.

Well I sure as hell do, he says an he takes a long swig.

Jest git on with it, Jack, I says.

He hands me a cloth. I shove it into my mouth. Then he gives me a rock fer each hand.

Emmi sits on my legs to stop me kickin. She's got a flamin torch in her hand. Don't throw me off, she says.

I'll work as fast as I can, says Jack, but this is gonna hurt like the devil. You ready?

My heart's thumpin. I bite down on the cloth. I squeeze the stones hard. I nod.

Gimme a good light, Emmi, he says. All right, here we go.

Then he commences to stitch me up.

Lucky fer me, I faint right away.

FREEDOM FIELDS

I STEP OUTSIDE INTO THE MIDDAY SUN. I BLINK AFTER THE darkness of the cave an take in a deep breath to clear my foggy head. The air's cooler'n I'm used to. It smells different. This air smells of fir, sharp an sweet at the same time.

The longest day of the year. Midsummer. This is it.

Yer awake, says Jack. He's sittin on a big rock. It's on the edge of a little clearin to the side of the cave. He finishes tyin the head onto a arrow an tosses it onto a growin pile. How's the shoulder?

I roll it around. A bit stiff, no surprise there, an a bit sore where the stitches are, but no pain. I guess I got Jack's disgustin willow bark brew to thank fer that.

Feels good, I says. Thanks. I look up at the sky. Any sign of Nero?

He shakes his head. No. My stummick tightens. I look up at the sky agin, like he might of appeared in the last two seconds. I had to tell everybody where he is, says Jack. They kept askin.

He'll find Maev, I says. I know he will. They should be here by now. C'mon, Nero.

I scan the sky.

It's outta our hands. Let's jest git on with it. Saba.

Yeah . . . yeah. Where is everybody?

If you look around the corner, you'll see, he says.

I step around him, into the clearin, an there they all are.

Ash an Epona sit side by side, strippin an smoothin down sticks into arrow shafts. They work fast. Ike an Tommo's makin slate chips into arrowheads an Emmi bobs around, fetchin an carryin an generally makin herself useful.

It looks like they ain't none of 'em had no sleep fer a while. They look up when they see me, throw a nod or a little smile, but don't stop what they're doin. Even Emmi keeps at it instead of rushin over to me like always.

It's so heavy in the air you can smell it, almost taste it. The tightness. The urgency. I feel the heat rise in my cheeks. Everybody must think I'm a real shirker, snorin away while they work.

You all right? says Epona.

Yeah, I says. I'll be okay to shoot.

Good, Ike says. I especk we might be seein a little action later on.

Gimme somethin to do, I says.

You can help me tie on arrowheads, says Jack. He shifts to make room fer me on his rock an I sit beside him. Right away, the heartstone starts to heat up. I shake my head.

What? he says.

Nuthin, I says. I take a length of nettlecord, a head an a shaft an git to work. My fingers feel clumsy to start with, slow, but after I done a couple I git into the swing of it.

Jack holds up a finished arrow. Sights along it. Whenever I make a arrow, he says, I see it in my mind's eye . . . flyin outta the bow . . . singin through th'air, headin fer the target straight an true.

Me too, I says.

Our eyes meet fer a second. We smile. Then we bend our heads to our work an really set to.

Did you know, he says, that every time you make somethin, any time you make anythin, a little bit of yer spirit goes into it?

No, I says. I didn't know that.

Well, it's a fact. So . . . you wanna make sure it's a good bit of you, not a bad bit.

I think I used up my last good bit a while back, I says.

Me too, he says. He gives me his lopsided grin an my heart turns over.

I'm sorry, I says.

Fer what? he says.

Fer always bein . . . you know . . . so—

Ungrateful? he says.

Yeah, I says.

Ornery?

I guess so.

Rude? Pig-headed? Violent?

I ain't violent!

Oh yes, you are. Very. But I like that in a woman.

I laugh. Yer crazy, I says.

I was fine till I met you, he says.

† † †

When the sun's high in the midafternoon sky, we break camp an start to gather up our weapons. I remember what Emmi said about Hermes waitin fer me an not followin th'other horses when we set 'em loose back at the lake.

Where's Hermes? I says.

There, Tommo says with a jerk of his head. We're all used to him by now an pretty much know what he means. Emmi still seems to git more outta his one or two words than anybody else though.

He means he's on th'other side of the hill already, Emmi says now. He's waitin fer us.

Tommo nods.

I knew what you meant jest fine, I says. Thanks, Tommo.

He turns bright red an hurries off.

The kid's soft about you, says Ike. An he ain't th'only one. I'm jest waitin fer you to give me the word, darlin.

You know, Ike, I says, I think I might be comin round to the idea.

He looks shocked. But only fer a moment. Then he grins.

You wouldn't be flirtin with me, would you? he says.

I dunno, I says. Yeah. I think I might be.

Be still my beatin heart! he says.

All right, says Jack, break it up. Time to go. We need to git movin.

You scouted it out, right? I says.

Completely, says Ike. Me, Ash an Epona did it while you was gittin yer beauty sleep.

What does it look like? I says.

Ike winks. No problem. Piece of cake.

Piece of cake. Ash shakes her head.

Wait, what's the plan? I says.

You know me, says Jack, I don't like to be hampered by too much plannin.

Jack!

Keep yer shirt on. I got a couple of ideas to run by you. But we won't know properly till we see what they're up to. We might hafta . . . wing it a bit.

Wing it! I says. This is my brother's life we're talkin about, Jack. I ain't wingin nuthin. You said you had a plan.

Uh . . . I think we'll head over, says Ike.

Good idea, says Ash.

They all hurry past us an turn right, disappearin back into the cave.

Why're they goin back in? I says. You said Freedom Fields is on th'other side of the hill.

It is, says Jack. But there's a tunnel that cuts through from the back of the cave. A short cut. He starts to follow 'em.

I grab his arm. Hang on, Jack, we ain't finished here. We need a plan. A proper one. Right now.

I promised you we'd git Lugh outta there, he says, an I meant it. We will. That's the main thing, no matter what. You said you trusted me. Do you? Here an now. Do you trust me?

I stare into his eyes. Searchin fer . . . somethin. Then. I see it.

I see him. Suddenly I see him. Not the Jack of the jokes an the flirtin an the shyin away. The real Jack. The . . . truth of him. The stillness at the heart of him. Like calm water.

I seen it once before, that first night we lay unner the stars. When I told him about Lugh an he promised me we'd find him. An this is the thing. The truth about Jack's bin right in front of me all along. I jest wouldn't let myself believe what I seen. Till now.

I laugh. Gawd help me, I says, but I do. I trust you, Jack.

Then let's go, he says. We turn into the cave. Now I can see there's a narrow crack at the back. The entrance to the tunnel that leads to th'other side. Jack lights a torch in the dyin fire, then I help him break it up, spreadin the ash so's it can cool.

That's it, he says, turnin to go.

I touch his arm. Jack, I says. I . . .

What?

I didn't really thank you fer . . . takin care of me. Fer fixin me up.

Don't mention it.

He starts to go, an I stop him agin. Jack! Yeah?

I might not git another chance to say that I . . . to tell you . . . how much I appreciate everythin yer doin. Everythin you done. To help git Lugh back an . . . well, everythin. You didn't hafta but you did an . . . I am. Grateful, I mean. I always have bin, it's jest . . . I guess I ain't too good at showin it, is all.

Don't keep thankin me, he says. I don't deserve it. I ain't some hero.

He turns an I follow him to the back of the cave. We slip through the narrow crack an pretty much right away it opens into a tunnel that's high enough to walk upright. My stummick's all jittery an tight. We ain't gone more'n a few steps when I says, Jack. Wait.

He turns around, all impatient. Now what?

I wanna say somethin to you. I wanna say . . . I dunno . . . more. I could bust apart with all I'm feelin inside of me right now. What with fightin off the hellwurms an gittin my shoulder tore open, an how I felt when I woke up an seen you an, now, here I am, bein so close to findin Lugh an I dunno what's gonna happen an—

Jack's lookin at me, frownin. What's the matter with you, Saba? he says.

I grab his face an kiss him on the lips.

Then I step back.

We stare at each other. All the air gits sucked outta the tunnel. The heartstone burns into my skin. The blood pounds in my ears.

Yer timin stinks, he says.

He drops the torch. He pushes me aginst the wall. Then his mouth is on mine an he's kissin me like he's starvin or dyin of thirst or somethin. He kisses my lips, my face, my neck, then back to my lips agin. His lips is smooth. Warm. The smell of him fills me.

We're pressed tight together, chest to chest, thigh to thigh. His heart thuds aginst mine. A shiver runs over me from the top of my head to the ends of my toes. I'm hot an cold all at once. The tiny hairs on my arms, on the back of my neck, tingle. My skin's stretched tight over my bones. A heavy heat settles low in my belly.

I never thought kissin 'ud feel like this.

I kiss him back. I run my hands up an down his arms, his shoulders, his back. I feel the strength of him. I press myself closer. I cain't seem to git close enough.

Stop, he says aginst my lips.

I don't. I don't want to. I cain't.

He grabs both my hands. Saba, he says. Saba. Stop.

We're both breathin hard. I'm dizzy. Dazed.

What? I says. What? Was I doin it wrong?

No, he says, no, don't ever think that! That was . . . oh boy . . .

that was . . . perfect. It's jest . . . this ain't the time or the place. An you bin through a lot. You ain't thinkin straight.

I am, I says. I swear I am.

No, you ain't, he says. An I ain't neether. But I bin wantin to kiss you like that from the first moment I seen you. You got no idea how much.

I start to say, me too, but he puts a finger aginst my lips.

Don't say it, he says. It'll only make things worse.

He kisses me one last time. Quick. Hard. Then he pushes away from me an picks up the torch from the ground. It's still lit. C'mon, he says. We gotta git movin.

Jest like that? I says.

Saba, he says. Yer brother. He's waitin fer you.

He heads off. I jest stand there. My lips is tinglin. I can still taste him.

I'm glad he called a halt. He's right, this ain't the time or place. An him an me both know there never will be the right time an place. Once I've got Lugh back, that'll be it. I'll head to Crosscreek with him an Emmi, or maybe somewhere else entirely, an Jack'll go off with Ike an Tommo an we'll never see each other agin. We both said what our plans is an that's what we're gonna do.

But I'm glad we did it. Kissed. It was our only chance. An I'm glad he stopped it when he did.

Liar. Liar, liar, liar.

Saba! he yells. C'mon! Hurry up!

† † †

It gits lower here, says Jack. Mind yer head.

The torch throws jagged fingers of light up the rough stone walls. We're makin our way through the tunnel an I reach a hand out, feelin where the top is. I gotta duck every now an agin so's I don't bang my head.

It seems to go on an on an on. I'm gittin to the point of thinkin it ain't never gonna end when I start to see light an it gits brighter an brighter, spillin into the darkness. Then the tunnel ends an we step outside, into the golden sky of a midsummer afternoon.

Everyone's waitin fer us. Emmi, Tommo, Ike, Ash an Epona. Hermes is over to one side, tearin at long tufts of grass. He lifts his head an whickers when he sees me.

What took you so long? says Emmi. We bin here fer ages.

Ike, Ash an Epona look at each other an grin. They look at me an Jack.

Pretty dark in there, says Ash. Did you git lost?

I feel a hot flush crawl up my neck. Lucky fer me, Hermes trots over an I busy myself strokin his neck.

It uh . . . took us longer'n we thought to put out the fire, says Jack.

Saba, says Emmi. Come an see! She grabs my hand an pulls me over to the edge of the ridge we're standin on. The ridge runs all around the edge of the valley, like the rim of a bowl. It's covered with thick stands of oak an tall pine trees. A wide flat valley lies spread out below us. It's covered in rows an rows of low bushes covered with shiny dark green leafs. Lots of workers in white tunics move between the rows, bendin, pickin the leaf from the bushes an puttin 'em into sacks on their back. Slaves.

Helen was one of these once. An Jack an Ike.

It's a land of plenty. Lush an beautiful. Like Pa told us it used to be back in Wrecker times. Paradise, he called it. When the air was sweet an the earth was good. When they grew so much to eat that they heaped it in mountains an if they needed some they'd jest go with their bucket an fill it up.

But this ain't no Paradise.

There it is, says Ike. Freedom Fields.

Ash points. Across the valley, on the far side, a wall of rainbow light shimmers. An that, she says, that's the King's Palace.

✝   ✝   ✝

Jack pushes somethin into my hand. Here, he says. It's half of the long-looker that Emmi broke back at the Wrecker city.

Jack fixed it! she says. Jest like he said he would!

I put it to my eye.

Be careful! she says. It's awful bright!

Directly opposite where we are, on the far side of the valley, a big house, the biggest I ever seen, sprawls out half-ways between the valley floor an the ridge above it. The walls is completely covered in shimmer discs. As the sun hits 'em, they shoot off rainbows of light. Red, yellow, pink, green, purple. The colors streak out, like shootin stars, sparkin an dancin so bright that black spots appear in front of my eyes.

Ohmigawd, it's amazin! I says. I never seen nuthin like it.

They'll be keepin Lugh there unner guard, says Jack. Ain't that right, Ike?

Yup, says Ike. An they'll be takin good care of him, seein they went to all that trouble to git him.

D'you really think so? I says.

You can bet on it, says Ike.

The Palace. I squint at it sidewise. Now I can see it's got many windows. Tall posts runnin all along the front of it. Two massive front doors made of hammered copper. Wide steps lead down to a path made of crushed white rock. It winds through a garden to the fields below. I think of Ma with her garden of stones at Silverlake. She would never of dreamed that there might be a garden like this one.

There's a great carved basin with jets of water sprayin way up into the sky. There's flower an vegetable beds laid out in fancy patterns, an a grove of fruit trees.

Lots of people movin about. Tonton mainly, in their long

black robes an body armor, but some slaves dressed in their white tunics.

See the stables? says Ike. Off to the right?

I focus the long-looker on the low stableyard next to the house. Got 'em, I says.

An the irrigation system? he says.

Runnin all across the fields, raised above the bushes on long legs, there's what looks like troughs with silvery streams of water runnin through 'em. They're all joined up together.

That's what you call them troughs? I says.

Right, says Jack. Keeps the bushes watered with a steady drip. Chaal bushes like it damp but you gotta be careful. Too much water kills 'em off real quick.

You don't say, I says.

I do say, he says. Now that plan you wanted? Gather round everybody. Me an Ike got a couple of ideas.

† † †

The afternoon drags on. Then it's early evenin. The rainbow shine of the Palace slowly dims as the sun's power fades. But it'll be light fer hours still. The longest day of the year. The longest day of my life.

There still ain't no sign of Nero. No Maev. No Free Hawks.

I never bin so twitchy. We all take turns watchin what's goin on down below. But when it ain't my turn, I cain't settle. If I flop onto the ground, I jump right up agin. I drive everybody mad by askin 'em how long they think we bin there. I comb all the tangles outta Hermes' mane with my fingers an check his teeth till he gits fed up an gives me a sharp nip. I twang my bowstring till Ash barks at me to stop or she'll strangle me with it.

Nero should of bin back long before now, I says to Emmi.

You said that a million times already, she says.

Somethin's happened to him. I know it. It ain't like him.

You said that a million times too, she says. He's fine. He's on his way.

What if somethin happened to Maev? I says. She said there was trouble on the western road. What if . . . I mean, she could of got herself killed? Happens all the time.

Maev ain't dead, says Emmi. She'll come, like she said she would. The Hawks'll be here, Saba.

You don't know that. What if they don't come? I don't think they're gonna come. We're gonna hafta do this all on our own. Let's jest do it now. C'mon, let's go. Let's move! What're we waitin fer?

Gimme strength! says Ash, as Ike groans, Tommo sighs an Jack lays back with his eyes closed an hums a little tune.

Epona's on looker duty. Saba, she says, we all agreed that we hafta wait till dark. Ain't nuthin can happen till then.

Epona. Always calm, always patient. Nuthin like I first thought she was.

Right, I says, yeah . . . wait till dark. I know, I know but . . . ohmigawd, Epona, I'm gonna go mad with all this waitin around. I jest wanna see him. Make sure he's all right.

I know you do, she says. Be patient, Saba. Wait till dark.

† † †

Darkness is gatherin. Purple an black streak the sky. Clouds drift over the midsummer moon. The moon we bin chasin fer so long.

A cloudy night, says Jack. That's good.

Then.

A high pitched noise wails across the valley, cuttin through the air. The workers lift their heads an start to move outta the fields. They all head towards what look like some long bunkhouses in the distance. Now I can see they're chained together at the ankle, six of 'em all together.

Quittin time fer the Children of Light, says Ike.

Can you believe he calls 'em that? says Jack. His Children of Light. Fond memories, eh Ike?

No, he says.

The slaves clear outta the fields an head fer bunkhouses off

391

to the left. A group of Tonton head fer a big open space in the middle of the fields.

Jack's on long-looker watch. Well well, he says. At last. This is startin to look innerestin.

† † †

Jack an me crouch on the edge of the ridge. We pass the looker back an forth. We got a clear view of the whole valley, but all the action's goin on between the Palace an the open space in the middle of the chaal fields.

Big horse-drawn wagons is rollin between there an the Palace.

First the Tonton build a big platform in the open space. Then they put together a higher platform at the back of it, with a long set of stairs goin up to it. They bring a massive chair from the Palace an use a pulley an ropes to winch it up to the higher platform. The chair's golden. With fancy carvin an studded all over with shiny stones.

Jack says, Anybody sittin on that chair would have a fine view of proceedins below.

D'you think they're gonna go ahead with the ceremony anyways? I says. Even though Pinch is dead?

It looks that way, he says.

The Tonton wheel in two sets of stairs, one on each side of the big platform. Then they disappear back to the Palace an it all goes quiet fer a bit.

Ike, Ash an Epona's gone off with Emmi an Tommo, takin Hermes with 'em. They're gittin the first bit of our plan unnerway.

Me an Jack got nuthin to do but wait. An wait some more.

It's that strange time on the longest day of the year when it's late enough to be dark but there's still some last streaks of light. Dark clouds scud across the sky. The wind's on the rise.

I look up at the moon. Must be a hour or so to midnight, I says.

Almost midsummer's eve, says Jack.

I shiver. Then I say what's bin growin on me all day. They ain't gonna come, I says. Are they?

I don't think we should count on 'em, he says.

It's okay, I says. We can do this.

Another wagon's rollin down the path from the stables to the platform. The Tonton leap down. They start unloadin it an carryin stuff onto the platform. Heavy bags of sand. Armloads of wood.

They don't look to be carryin no weapons, I says. That's strange. An I thought you said there was dog patrols.

They obviously ain't expectin trouble tonight, says Jack. But there'll be some of 'em armed. At the very least, the King's bodyguards.

There's a rustle. It's Ike an Epona. They're back. They crouch down beside us. Ike's grin flashes white in the gloom.

Emmi an Tommo on their way to the meetin place? I says.

Yeah, says Ike. They got off fine. They'll wait fer us at the tire dump an hour's ride north of here.

Was Emmi okay on Hermes? She still ain't so good on a horse. Did you—

She's fine, Saba, says Ike. Don't worry.

Yer sure they know what they gotta do? I says.

I made Emmi repeat it three times, says Epona. They wait fer us at the dump. They stay outta sight. If we ain't there by dawn, they take a big loop to the east an make their way to Darktrees. They know to give Hermes his head.

An Ash? says Jack. She's at the stables?

Nearby, says Epona. Well outta sight. They won't have no idea she's there. She'll have the horses ready an waitin fer us. Can I take a look what's goin on down there?

I hand her the long-looker. She trains it on the platform.

What's that they're puttin in the middle? Ike says, squintin.

They're spreadin out a circle of sand in the middle of the big platform, she says. Looks like they're makin a sandpit. An they're settin up a post in the middle of the circle.

What, you mean like a fence post? says Jack.

Kinda, she says. But bigger. Taller. I wonder what that's fer.

Let me see, he says. She hands him the looker. He stares

fer a long moment, then lowers it. He looks at me direct when he says, The post's about the right size to tie a man to. An a sandpit's useful if you wanna make sure a fire don't spread.

The bottom falls outta my stummick. My breath starts to come fast. No, I says. No . . . they wouldn't do . . . Jack, you don't think they'd . . . burn him. They ain't gonna burn him, are they?

No, he says, they ain't. We won't let 'em. They won't hurt Lugh, I promise you. He takes my hands in his, holds 'em tight. Now . . . listen to me, listen. Are you listenin?

Yeah, I says, yeah.

Yer gonna stay calm, he says. An yer gonna trust me. Yer gonna trust all of us. Me an Ike an Ash an Epona. Tommo an Emmi too. We all know what the plan is. This don't change nuthin. We all know what we gotta do. We'll go over it now, okay?

Okay, I says.

Okay, he says. Emmi an Tommo's on their way to the meetin point right now. They're outta harm's way. Once it's all clear over at the stables, Ash is gonna git six horses ready to go. You an Ike's gonna snatch Lugh. Then we all meet up at the stables an take off. Epona, you say agin what yer job is.

While Saba an Ike's gittin Lugh, Epona says, you an me is gonna be . . . creatin a diversion.

That's right, says Jack.

Hey, Ike says. Looks like this party's really startin to kick off.

There's bin the sound of drumbeats driftin up while we bin talkin. The noise grows louder an louder, with more an more drums joinin in. They're bein played by Tonton in their black robes. Bone flutes start to shrill. There's fires lit in big buckets scattered all over the open space.

Slaves in white tunics, unchained now, spill outta the bunkhouses an stream across to the open space. Men, women an even a few children. In front of the platform, they start to dance wildly, swayin an spinnin an leapin high over the firebuckets. The growin throb of the drumbeats fills the night.

The Tonton drummers start to chant an the slaves join in. No words. Sounds from deep in their throats. The Tonton sway an twirl. The slaves leap an spin.

There's movement around the Palace. Torches light the path from the house down to the fields.

Epona's still got the looker. She holds it to her eyes. Somethin's happenin, she says. Then she sucks in a breath. Ohmigawd, she whispers. Ohmigawd. I don't believe it.

What? I says. What is it?

She shakes her head as she hands me the looker. Her eyes is wide.

Like she's jest seen a ghost.

† † †

I train the looker on the Palace.

Vicar Pinch stands on the steps.

My heart slams to a stop. Then it starts racin. It cain't be, I says. He's dead!

What? says Jack. You don't mean Pinch? The King's alive?

Yeah, I says. But I seen him. He was dead. I swear he was dead.

The devil ain't so easy to kill, says Ike.

Pinch is dressed all in gold. Short puffy britches, stockins an high heeled shoes. Over top of it all, he wears a splendrous golden robe trimmed with white fur. The robe sweeps down to the floor an trails behind him. It's crusted with sparklin stones, bits of lookin glass an shimmer discs. He's got white hair today. Long curls reach down past his shoulders. Tower high above his forehead.

His face is painted gold too. Some kinda paint with sparkles in it. He poses with his walkin stick at the top of the steps. The torchlight plays on him. He shines in the darkness, like the sun come down to earth. The Sun King.

Suddenly I notice that he's favorin his left leg.

I crouch down, peer unner the landboat.

Vicar Pinch lies on the ground. His right leg splays out at a strange angle.

He's hurt his leg, I says. Must of happened when the landboat flipped over on him.

Four boy slaves lift the ends of his robe. Then two of the biggest Tonton come an lift him carefully. They carry him down the steps an hand him into a sparklin golden car chariot that's waitin there. The boys arrange his robes. Then six Tonton pick the chariot up by the handles an start down the torchlit path towards the chaal fields.

I track 'em with the looker as they head fer the open space where the platform is. Pinch's chariot squeezes through the heavin crowd of slaves, still chantin an dancin. They reach up their hands, frantic to touch him. The Tonton carriers kick an shove people away. They carry the chariot up the stairs onto the platform an set it down in the middle.

Then they lift him out. His shimmerin robes billow in the night wind. They carry him up the steps to the smaller platform, an sit him on the golden chair. Then the Tonton take his chariot an leave.

I'm startin to git that feelin agin. The jumpy feelin, deep in my gut, that means somethin big's about to happen. I don't know ezzackly what it is, but I'm gonna be ready fer it. I used to git it before I went into the Cage.

It's the red hot. It's on the rise.

Let's git down there, I says.

† † †

We keep low. Me an Jack an Ike an Epona run between the rows of chaal bushes. We duck unner the irrigation troughs. We reach the edge of the open space.

We crouch down behind the chaal bushes. They're so thick with leaf that they give us good cover. The slaves seem to be in a frenzy. They leap over the firebuckets. They dance an chant an spin. The drums vibrate inside me. The stomp of feet shakes the ground. The flutes squeal. The sweet smell of burnin chaal leaf fills the air.

Vicar Pinch sits in his golden chair. DeMalo stands to one side of him. There's another Tonton on his other side. Pinch is holdin somethin in his hand that looks like a big horn. He lifts it in front of his mouth. I see his lips movin, like he's sayin somethin, but there's too much noise with the drums an chantin.

DeMalo whips a shooter out from inside his robe. Shoots it into the air. Three times. The shots crack through the air with a little flash.

It's such a shock that everythin stops. Jest like that. The drums, the dancin, the chantin.

That ain't no bolt shooter! I whisper to Jack.

It's a firestick, says Jack. Stay outta its way, whatever you do.

The slaves face the platform, pantin fer breath. Their faces an bodies shine with sweat by the firelight an their eyes gleam, all wild-lookin. Pinch speaks into the horn.

Children of Light! he cries. Behold your King!

His voice rings out through the valley.

The slaves roar, punchin their fists into the air.

Your King is all powerful! All wise! All merciful!

With each thing he says, they roar in reply.

He is the fountain of life! The source of plenty! The earth herself bows to his will!

He's crazy, says Epona.

Crazy like a fox, says Ike.

Children of Light! Pinch cries. Tonight! In this place! On this midsummer eve! Our mother sun, high in the sky, reaches the height of her powers. And tonight! The life force of the Winter-born Prince reaches its peak! The sun! The moon! Their power is your King's power! Tonight that power shall be one! They will be joined by fire! And your King will be born again!

He throws his arms out wide. The slaves go wild.

Look! hisses Epona. Over at the Palace!

I jam the looker to my eyes.

A group of Tonton move down the steps an start down the path. They march along, two by two. The first four light the way with torches. The next four carry a man on their shoulders, laid out flat. The torchlight glints on a long gold plait.

It's Lugh.

† † †

It's him, I whisper. It's Lugh. He's alive.

An suddenly the tears come. I bin holdin it in so long. I bin lookin fer him so long.

Jack pulls me into his arms. Holds my face into his shoulder. My body shakes with silent sobs. Shhh, he says. Not now. This ain't the time. Stop it, Saba.

I lift my head. I was afeared he was dead, I says. I never said so, but—

I know, Jack says, I know. But he's alive an we're gonna git him outta here right now. All right?

I take in a couple of deep breaths. Push away from him. Wipe my eyes.

Sorry, I says. Yeah. All right.

Okay, everybody, says Jack, this is it. I'll take the looker now. If me an Epona's gonna create a diversion, we'll need to git the timin jest right.

As I hand it to him, he squeezes my hand. Good luck, everybody, he says. Make the most of any chance you git, but be careful. See you at the stables.

Let's git these bastards, says Ike.

Jack an Epona peel away to the left.

Me an Ike go right. We're headed in the direction of the Palace. We duck along the rows of chaal bushes at top speed, keepin outta sight. We stop where the chaal fields end an the gardens of the Palace begin. We crouch down behind the bushes at the side of the path. They're gonna hafta go right past us to git to the platform.

The Tonton party carryin Lugh is skirtin around the fountain. They start to march along the path, through the middle of the gardens, two by two. Four torch bearers at the front. Four carryin Lugh. Six bringin up the rear. They march to the beat of the drums. An they chant as they march. The same chant as the crowd of slaves.

The two Tonton at the very back of the group lag behind the rest a bit.

Those're our boys, says Ike.

The Tonton's in the orchard now. We watch as the torches bob along. They'll be with us in a minute or so. Ready? I whisper.

Ready, Ike says.

We crouch down low. We each slide a length of nettlecord rope outta our pockets.

The four torchbearers march past. Their boots shake the ground. Their chants fill the air. Strange words I ain't never heard before. Their robes brush aginst the bushes. I can feel the warmth of their bodies. I can smell 'em.

The next four march past. The ones carryin Lugh. I jest catch a glimpse of him. His eyes is closed. He moves his head from side to side, restless. My heart turns over. Looks like they drugged him.

Here come the last six Tonton.

We wait. I count 'em off in my head.

Two, four.

A pause.

Then the last two Tonton come past.

Me an Ike slip onto the path behind 'em. We move without a sound.

My heart's bangin so hard in my chest, it feels like it's gonna smash right through my ribs. I finger the rope in my hands.

Ike gives me the nod. We throw our ropes over the Tontons' heads. Yank it tight around their throats an drag 'em offa the path into the bushes. They're so surprised that they come without a fight.

Ike lifts his bolt shooter high. One, two—he coshes 'em on the head with the butt. They're out cold. The best place to git up to mischief, says Ike, is in a noisy crowd.

We strip 'em. We truss 'em up, stuff a cloth into their mouths an leave 'em in the bushes, outta sight. We pull their black robes an breastplates over our own clothes. We check that our crossbows an quivers cain't be seen. My robe's way too long.

Allow me, says Ike. He grabs hold an hitches it up through my belt.

I pull my knife from my boot sheath. Tuck it outta sight in my belt. Ike does the same with his shooter. Then we run to catch up with Lugh's escort.

Ike turns to me an grins. His teeth flash white in the torch-light. His eyes spark with excitement. He looks dangerous.

So far, so good. It's all gone accordin to plan. Me an Ike managed to join the Tonton.

But this is where the plan ends. From now on, we gotta wing it. Jest like Jack said.

† † †

We march along the path, through the chaal fields towards the platform.

We reach the edge of the open space. It's jam packed an heavin with the hot sweaty bodies of the dancin slaves. The drums beat faster an faster. The slaves stamp their feet an chant. The noise is deafenin.

The four Tonton torchbearers push their way into the middle of the crowd, shoutin an shovin the dancin slaves aside, clearin the way to bring Lugh through. Then we close ranks an ram our way through the crowd as one unit, with me an Ike bringin up the rear. Close up, the sour smell of unwashed bodies fills my nostrils. Makes me gag.

We reach the stairs to the platform. We're goin up the stairs. We're on the platform. Ike an me shrink down inside our hoods. I throw a quick glance at Vicar Pinch. At the King. He sits on his golden chair in his golden robes, starin out at the heavin, chantin crowd. No expression on his sparklin gold face.

The four Tonton carryin Lugh march over to the sandpit. As they set him down, his knees give an his head lolls back. They quickly catch him an stand him with his back aginst the pole. They tie him to it, hand an foot. Then they start to lay dry kindlin at his feet.

Lugh faces out towards the crowd. His chest's bare. He's only wearin britches an boots. His eyes is still closed. His head hangs to one side, but I can see his lips movin. Without thinkin, I start towards him.

Ike grabs me. Wait, he hisses. Watch.

There's movement all over the platform. The Tonton finish tyin Lugh to the pole. They jam their lit torches around the edge of the sandpit.

Then they hurry to line up on both sides of the pit. Two groups of seven, one on each side.

In the confusion, Ike an me manage to git ourselves on the end of the rows, closest to the pit. We're the closest to Lugh. Ike on one side. Me on th'other.

Make the most of any chance you git.

Drums beat, feet stamp, voices chant. The earth shakes.

Vicar Pinch, the Sun King, sits in his golden chair, raised up behind us on the small platform. He's flanked by DeMalo an another Tonton guard.

DeMalo an th'other Tonton help Pinch to his feet. Now!

Pinch screams. Light the fire! He flings his arms open wide. Lifts his head to the night sky.

The Tonton beside us stomp their feet. They chant an sway.

Sweat runs down the back of my neck. We need Jack an Epona to make their diversion. Now.

C'mon, Jack! Where are you?

I look over at Ike, hidden by the hood of my robe.

Light the fire! Pinch screams agin.

Ike nods. Him an me step into the sandpit. We take a couple of the torches. The crowd's still chantin an dancin an drummin. They don't seem to be payin that much attention to what's goin on on the platform.

Can you cover me while I cut him free? I hand Ike my torch. Lucky fer me he's so big. He shields me with his robes as I duck down.

Make it fast, he says. If we don't light this fire, they'll start wonderin what's wrong.

My knife's sharp. It quickly slices through the rope holdin Lugh's ankles.

Quick! Ike hisses.

I gotta free his hands, I says.

C'mon, Jack. The diversion! What're you waitin fer?

Light the fire! Pinch yells agin.

At that moment, a siren wails across the valley. The same one that called the workers in from the fields earlier.

A quick glance over my shoulder. The irrigation troughs

all over the field start to bust open. Fast. One after another. Water sprays out in great gushes, silver in the moonlight. All over the chaal fields, the water troughs an channels blast open, overflowin, collapsin.

Jack's diversion.

It's a flood.

The end of Pinch's precious crop.

I work at the ropes tyin Lugh's wrists.

Pinch screams in fury. Guards! Guards! Move, you fools! Move!

Around us, all the Tonton start to run. Rushin down the stairs, leapin offa the platform, they disappear into the fields to try an stop it.

I slice through the last rope tyin Lugh's wrists to the pole. Ike heaves Lugh over his shoulder.

Go! I says.

Then it all happens in a flash.

DeMalo an th'other Tonton's still standin beside Pinch. They suddenly notice what we're up to. As Ike sprints across the platform with Lugh, the hood of my robe falls back.

DeMalo clocks me. Our eyes meet. Then he turns away.

He turns away.

At the same time, Pinch points at me an screams, Seize her! Seize her!

Th'other Tonton guard leaps from the platform. Comes at me.

As I grab a lit torch from the sandpit an throw it at him.

He ducks.

The torch lands on the edge of Pinch's golden robe. Flames race up the material. He screams an beats at the flames.

I don't stop to see what happens next. I leap down the stairs an into the middle of the crowd. The slaves is too chaaled up to do anythin. Most of them's still dancin an chantin. Others sit on the ground or stand there, lookin confused, with foolish smiles on their faces.

Then I'm away. I race through the chaal fields. Stayin low, keepin unner cover. I head towards the Palace an the stables.

† † †

When I reach the stables, Ash's got all the horses ready an waitin. They're dancin with nerves from the shoutin an sirens an the smell from the flooded fields. Jack's already there, on the back of a fine white stallion that's nervy with excitement.

Ike's liftin Lugh up to sit in front of Jack. His head lolls forwards onto his chest. I run over an grab his hand.

Lugh! I cry.

No time fer that, says Jack.

Saba! Here! Ash tosses me the reins of a black mare an I swing myself onto her back. We did it! You got him!

Her an Ike mount up. Ike holds the reins of a spare horse fer Lugh to ride on once he comes to.

Let's go! I says.

As we wheel the horses around, Ash yells, Wait! Where's Epona?

She was right behind me! Jack says. Leave her a horse! She'll catch us up!

We cain't leave without Epona! I says.

Saba! he shouts it at me. We cain't wait! C'mon!

We all gallop outta the stableyard an up the hill behind the Palace.

I bring up the rear. At the top of the hill, I look back, espektin to see Epona hard on my tail.

She ain't there.

But down below, a mob of Tonton's runnin along the path from the fields towards the Palace. They're in the orchard, in the gardens, racin around the fountain. An they're chasin somebody.

It's Epona.

†   †   †

I pull up my horse. Wait! I yell at th'others. They got Epona!

409

They wheel around an come back. We got a full view from here on top of the hill but there's good tree cover so we cain't be seen.

Epona reaches the Palace.

I'm goin back fer her, says Ike.

Jack grabs his reins. Stops him. It's too late, he says.

I watch, my heart in my throat.

Epona makes a leap at a drainpipe an grabs hold. She starts to shin up it, real fast. Two Tonton start to climb behind her. They're heavier, not so nimble. Epona ain't armed. She must of lost her bow somewhere.

We gotta do somethin! Ash says. We cain't jest leave her, they'll tear her apart!

We all look at each other. I can see in Ike an Jack's eyes what needs to be done. I swing my bow around, take it off.

Go on, I says. I'll catch you up.

No, says Ash. No. Oh please, no.

There ain't no other way, Ash, says Ike.

Jack says, Saba, why don't you let me—

I said I'll catch you up, I says.

They hesitate, lookin at each other.

Saba, says Ash.

Go! I says.

They turn their horses an leave. I pull a arrow from my quiver an fit it to the bowstring. My hands is shakin.

Epona's on the flat roof. She runs around, lookin every

which way fer escape, but she's trapped. The two Tonton's at the top of the drainpipe now. They pull theirselves onto the roof. They reach fer their shooters. Start to move slowly towards her. There's more Tonton arrivin below. They move out to surround the Palace. Epona looks over her shoulder. Sees the two Tonton comin towards her.

Epona looks over her shoulder, like she sees somethin behind her. She turns back agin. She sees me.

Suddenly Epona spots me at the edge of the trees. The world slams to a stop. There ain't nuthin an nobody else. Jest Epona an me an the sound of my heart.

Beat, beat, beat.

She nods.

An it all happens slowly. So slow, I can see the blink of her eyelids. I can see her lips move as she takes in a breath.

She starts to run towards me. She throws her arms wide open an lifts her face up. She leaps.

Tears blur my sight. I wipe 'em away. I lift my bow. I take aim. Epona smiles. She nods.

She starts to run towards me. She throws her arms wide open an lifts her face up. She leaps offa the roof. She soars through the air. Fer one last moment, she's free.

That's when I shoot her.

†   †   †

Th'others is gone on ahead with Lugh. Ash waits fer me.

The clouds clear the moon. I see the tear tracks down her face.

Hawks take care of each other, she says. No matter what that means. It should of bin me did it, not you. But I . . . I'm sorry, Saba. I'm sorry.

She was here becuz of me, I says. I had to be the one. It's right that it was me.

† † †

The clouds lift. The wind dies down. It's a beautiful, clear midsummer night.

We ride north at a good pace. Head fer the meetin point where we sent Tommo an Emmi to wait fer us with Hermes. We move downhill, outta the mountains the whole time. As we drop down, the ground changes. It's drier, rockier. The trees is smaller now. Scrubby pine, juniper an some cottonwood.

It didn't take long fer me an Ash to catch up with Jack an Ike. Then Jack an me traded horses so's I can ride with Lugh.

He ain't woke up yet. He slumps back heavily aginst my chest. I feel his breath go in an out. My arms ache from holdin him upright.

Lugh's here. I got him. He's safe. I cain't quite believe it. I dreamed of this so many times. Lived fer this moment, only this moment, fer so long. With a cold emptiness inside of me. A Lugh-shaped space that cain't be filled by nobody else. An now he's here, back with me, everythin should be okay agin.

But it ain't.

My whole body's numb.

Epona. Fer the rest of my life, every time I close my eyes I'm gonna see her leapin offa that roof. I'll hear the sound of the arrow singin outta my bow towards her heart.

Jack falls back to ride beside me.

Are you all right? he says.

I says naught.

Nobody should ever hafta do what you did, he says. I know it don't feel like that now, but you did the right thing by her. The merciful thing.

It ain't right, I says. She'd be alive now if it warn't fer me. She should never of left Darktrees. My voice comes out thick, clogged.

Epona made her own decisions, says Jack. She wanted to come. She knew the risks. We all did. Nobody blames you.

I'm sick of death, I says. I seen too much of it.

We all have. He reaches out, puts his hand over mine. It's gonna be okay, Saba.

This ain't finished yet, I says. They're gonna come after us. I'm right, ain't I?

Most likely, he says. But me an Ike figger we got a good

couple of hours' head start. Pinch ain't gonna go nowhere till he gits the floods in the chaal fields unner control.

I set him on fire, I says. Accidentally.

Nice touch, he says. Don't s'pose you could of killed him?

What was it Ike said? The devil ain't so easy to kill? No. I don't think so.

Too bad, he says. Still, it might buy us a bit of extra time.

I take a deep breath. Sit up straighter. Let him come, I says. I ain't come all this way jest to let that bastard win.

That's the spirit, he says. That's my girl.

We ride on in silence.

✝ ✝ ✝

Saba? Lugh's voice. Hoarse. Confused. Saba? Is that you?

A jolt goes through my heart. Lugh, I says. It's me. I'm here. I got you.

Yer really here, he whispers. He takes my hand an kisses it. Tears start to my eyes.

He's awake! I call out. Lugh's awake! I pull up my horse. Him an me's ridin at the rear. Th'others wheel around an gallop back to join us. Jack swings hisself down.

D'you think you can stand? he says to Lugh. I'll help you.

Who're you? says Lugh.

I'm Jack. A friend of Saba's.

I'm another one, Ash says. The name's Ash.

Me too, says Ike. Ike Twelvetrees.

Lugh glances around. I never knew you had so many friends, he says to me. Thank you. Thank y'all.

Jack helps him down. I slide to the ground.

We'll leave you two to say hello, he says.

After they've moved away outta earshot, it's jest me an Lugh. We look at each other. We stare at each other fer a long long moment by the bright white light of the midsummer moon.

His face looks thinner. He looks older. Harder. My heart twists.

My golden brother. Still so beautiful. But changed. He ain't that Silverlake boy no more.

Are y'all right? I says.

A bit dizzy, he says. But . . . yeah, I'm . . . I'm good.

Good. I . . . Tears start to my eyes. Roll down my cheeks. I dash 'em away. Sorry it took me so long, I says. I got . . . delayed.

There's tears on his face too. He takes a couple of steps towards me. Holds out his arms.

I run at him. I throw my arms around him. I hug him to me fiercely. I'm weepin.

Lugh's arms go around me slowly. Lightly. Like he ain't quite sure I'm real. Am I dreamin? he says.

No, I says. No. It's real. I'm real. Here. Feel. I hug him even tighter. Then he clutches me to him. We hang on tight. I found you, I says. I said I would an I did. I did. I found you.

They told me you was dead, says Lugh. They said they killed you an Emmi.

An you believed 'em? I says.

Not at first I didn't, he says. At first, I kept thinkin . . . she'll be here soon. She said she'd find me. She always keeps her word, she'll find a way. So I waited fer you. I waited an I hoped an I kept on hopin . . . fer a long time. But you didn't come. An I thought . . . I know Saba. She's so gawdam stubborn th'only thing that 'ud keep her from comin is if she was dead. That's when I started believin what they told me. An then I stopped hopin. That was the worst bit. When I thought you was dead. When I didn't have no hope.

You really think death 'ud keep me from findin you? I says. You know me better'n that.

I do, he says. Guess I shouldn't of bin so impatient. Is Emmi okay?

She's fine, I says. Still annoyin.

I touch his cheekbone. His birthmoon tattoo jest like mine.

Did they hurt you? I says.

No, he says. I mean, not . . . nobody laid a finger on me. I never bin fed so well in my life.

Suddenly, it's like he properly notices me. What happened to yer hair? he says.

I'd fergot all about my hair bein shaved so short. I run a hand over it. It feels longer, softer. Must of grown some since I left Hopetown. But I won't tell him about the Cage. Or anythin else. Not now. It's a long story, I says. I'll tell you later.

It suits you. There's a pause. Then he says, You look different.

I know, I says. My hair.

No, he says. It's more'n that. It's . . . you. You've changed, Saba.

The day the Tonton rode into Silverlake, everythin changed, I says.

Guess we'll jest hafta git to know each other all over agin.

Guess we will, I says.

† † †

It's bin two hours or so since we left Freedom Fields. Now that Lugh's able to ride, we're coverin more ground.

Meetin point's jest ahead, says Ike in a low voice.

We're comin up to the Wrecker tire dump where Emmi an Tommo's gonna be waitin with Hermes. It's a big one. A hunnerd foot ahead, the piles loom high in the darkness by the side of the trail. Ike holds up a hand an we stop.

He does a high pitched squeak like a bat. It's the signal to let Emmi know it's us. When she hears it, she'll do one back. That's what we agreed.

There ain't no answer.

A shiver runs through me.

Where are they? Lugh whispers.

Ike signals agin. Nuthin.

C'mon, Emmi, Ash mutters.

Ike does the bat squeak once more .

This time, there's a soft whinny. A horse.

Somebody steps out from between two hills of tires. It's Tommo. He's leadin Hermes.

But there ain't no sign of Emmi.

† † †

My heart clutches.

We ride to meet Tommo. I'm the first to jump down an run over to him. The rest of 'em's right behind me.

Where is she? What happened? I grab Tommo's arms.

The look on his face tells me what I already know. She didn't make it this far. You can tell he's bin cryin.

You left together, says Ike. I saw you off safe. What happened?

Tell us, Tommo, I says. Go on.

Emmi made me turn back, he says. She wanted to wait. See Lugh. I couldn't make her go.

Gawdammit, I says. Why cain't she ever do what she's told?

So we see Lugh an then Emmi says let's go, says Tommo. But there's too much noise an Hermes . . . he gits skeered an he . . . takes off.

He bolted, I says. An Emmi fell off.

Tommo nods. He wipes his eyes with his sleeve. I went back, he says, but the men . . .

Men from Freedom Fields? I says.

They took her, he says. I wanted to follow an git her back, but Ike, you said—

I said no matter what happens, keep on goin till you git to the meetin point, says Ike. An that's what you did, son.

He pulls Tommo in an gives him a hug.

I'm sorry, says Tommo. Sorry.

It's okay, I says. You did the right thing.

Emmi's a good fighter, he says. She kicked the men. She yelled an punched 'em.

Relief floods through me. I look at th'others. She's alive, I says.

You mean she was alive then, says Lugh. If that bastard hurts her, I swear—

I don't think he will, says Jack. More likely he'll use her to bargain with.

Bargain fer what? I says.

Yer guess is as good as mine, he says. He looks up at the moon. Time's movin on. They'll be after us by now an they'll follow our trail easy enough. We ain't bin hidin our tracks.

I want Emmi back, says Lugh.

We all do, says Jack.

So we'll meet 'em, I says. We'll meet Vicar Pinch an the Tonton. We'll git Emmi back.

But we decide the where an the when, says Jack. We find somewhere to take a stand.

What's a stand? says Tommo.

It's when you meet yer enemy on yer own terms, son, says Ike. Not let him hunt you down like a beast.

I don't like the odds, says Ash. At Freedom Fields, at least they wasn't expectin us.

What else can we do? says Lugh. We cain't jest march up to him an demand that he hands Emmi over. This way, at least we got a chance.

You think so? she says.

There's silence. We're all thinkin the same thing. That this is a different order to anythin we've bin through so far. My stummick's squeezed tight.

No point pretendin it's gonna be easy, says Jack.

It ain't possible, says Ash.

It ain't impossible, he says. Nuthin's impossible.

Without thinkin, I glance up at the sky. As if Nero might

be flyin across the moon at this very moment. But there ain't no black crow comin to save us.

I say we do it, I says. I say we take a stand.

Where? says Lugh.

Pine Top Hill, says Jack. Due north of here.

If you gotta take a stand, says Ike, you could do a lot worse.

You can see anybody comin at you from a long way off. There's a good slope on it fer the last hunnerd foot, says Jack. An if I remember rightly, it's loose rock. Bad ground fer horses. They won't be able to charge at us uphill.

We wanna be set up there well before they show, says Ash.

What're we waitin fer? says Lugh. Let's go.

† † †

We ride due north through the night.

Jack pushes us hard. He don't let us stop till we come across a little trickle of a stream. We all slide down to water the horses an ourselves.

We're nearly there, he says.

Lugh shivers. He rubs his arms an hugs hisself. Th'only clothes he's got on is his britches an boots.

You should of said you was cold, says Jack.

He reaches over his head an reefs off his shirt. He tosses it to Lugh.

Sorry it ain't cleaner, he says. I'm a bit behind with my laundry.

I cain't take yer only shirt, says Lugh.

Go on, says Jack.

But now you'll be cold, says Lugh.

Oh I'm warm blooded. Jack grins. Anyways, Saba likes to look at my bare chest.

Lugh looks at me. Frowns. Is that a fact? he says.

I feel myself go bright red. It is not a fact, I says. You stinker, Jack.

They all laugh. All essept Lugh that is. He's still frownin as he pulls Jack's shirt over his head.

I glare at Jack an he winks at me. I go even redder.

See? he says. She cain't help herself.

I could kick him fer makin me look foolish. But I could kiss him fer liftin the gloom a little bit.

Considerin what might lie ahead, that's a good thing.

†　　†　　†

We reach Pine Top Hill as the sun's startin to break out in the east. It's gonna be another hot one. You can almost hear the tired earth sighin as it faces the day.

There it is, says Ike.

A dusty plain of red earth stretches out in front of us. Straight ahead, a round hill rises up from the plain. There's a little wood of scrubby pine trees on top an some big rocks that'll give us good cover. An, jest like Jack said, a steep slope of loose rock an slippery shale.

If they're gonna attack, they'll hafta to leave their horses an come at us on foot. An we'll be in the better position.

It's a strange place, this plain where we'll take our stand. Dry an dead lookin an everywhere you look, red. Like the heart of a fire. Red rocks, red earth.

Red as the dust storm at Silverlake on the day the Tonton rode in.

A little ways to the west of the hill, a long, craggy ridge towers above the plain.

To the east, a clutch of spindly rock fingers rises up, reachin fer the sky. There's lots of 'em, all crowded in together. Tall an thin an pointed. They look wicked. Sharp. Like teeth. Red teeth.

The back of my neck prickles.

What the hell's that? I says.

They're called the Hoodoos, says Jack.

Ash shudders. They gimme the creeps, she says.

We make our way to the foot of Pine Top Hill as quickly as we can.

What about the horses? says Lugh.

We might need 'em, says Jack.

He don't say it, but we all know he means if it goes wrong an we gotta make a run fer it.

I want Hermes with me, I says. They'll be safe hidden in them trees.

I swing myself down. I lead Hermes up the hill, criss crossin the loose shale. His feet slide an slip, but I talk to him in a quiet voice an he don't make a fuss. He trusts me. Jest like I trust him. Th'others follow on behind, an we pick our way, slow an careful, to the top.

Jack's right. We'll be able to see Pinch comin at us over the plain from a long ways off.

I give Hermes' rump a pat an Ash an Ike lead the horses off to settle 'em in the trees behind us. Meantime, me, Jack, Lugh an Tommo divide our ammo. There's a good sized pile of arrows fer each of us, but still my heart sinks at the sight of 'em.

Tommo looks at Jack. His brown eyes dark, worried. Not enough, he says.

We got plenty, kid, says Jack. Don't you worry.

I ain't got a weapon, says Lugh.

Tommo lifts his bow over his head. Hands it to him. She's a good 'un, he says. Ike made her fer me.

I couldn't, says Lugh. What'll you use?

Slingshot, says Tommo, holdin it up.

If yer sure, says Lugh. Thanks, Tommo.

Ike an Ash join us.

Jack hands Tommo the long-looker. You wanna be on lookout? he says.

How's about that, son? says Ike. Lookout's the most important job there is.

Tommo beams. Really?

Really. Now, you go pick the tree with the best view over the plain. Climb right to the top an keep watch. The moment you see anybody comin, call out. Good an loud. Got it?

Got it, says Tommo. He's turnin to go when Ike grabs his arm.

If there's any fightin, Tommo, you stick close to me. Don't go off on yer own. You unnerstand, son?

Don't worry, Ike, Tommo smiles. I got yer back. Clutchin the looker to his chest, he runs off to choose his lookout spot.

He's got my back, Ike mutters. A fight ain't no place fer a boy who cain't hear. I wish I'd never brought him.

He'll be fine, says Jack. Don't worry. You told him to stick with you an he will.

So what's the plan? says Ash.

Jack looks at me. Gives me his lopsided grin. I smile back.

Jack's silver moonlight eyes. The stillness at the heart of him. Like calm water.

We're gonna hafta wing this one, I says.

Ash rolls her eyes. How did I know you was gonna say that?

What now? says Lugh.

Now, says Jack, we wait.

We hunker down behind the big rocks at the top of the hill with the stand of pine behind us. The plain sweeps out in front of us, wide an bare.

Me an Lugh sit with our backs aginst one big rock. Close together. Our shoulders touchin.

Oh, I says, I nearly fergot. I reach into my pocket. Pull out his necklace. The little ring of shiny green glass threaded onto a scrap of leather. I hand it to him. Found this lyin by the road, I says.

I was wonderin where that got to.

Lucky fer you I was passin that way, I says.

Yeah, he says. I'm lucky all right.

We're quiet fer a bit, then he nudges me with his elbow. So, he says, what about this Jack?

What about him? I says.

Looks to me like there's somethin goin on between yuz, he says.

I feel the heat crawl up my neck, into my cheeks. There ain't nuthin goin on, I says.

Look at you, he says. Yer such a bad liar. So. You like him. Where'd you meet him? His voice sounds all tight. He's jabbin at the ground with the end of his bow.

In Hopetown, I says. I wouldn't of found you in time if it warn't fer him.

He looks at me sidewise. Do I need to thrash him?

Don't be so stupid. No. You don't hafta thrash him.

Good, he says. Cuz I'm a dangerous man now. A hard man.

Hard man, I says. As if.

We shove each other with our shoulders. Sit quiet fer a bit. Then he says, You know what I hated most? Besides bein away from you?

What?

Thinkin about Pa. Thinkin how I was with him that last day. Rememberin all them awful things I said to him. That he died believin that's what I thought of him.

He knew you didn't mean it, I says. It's my fault he's dead, says Lugh. I feel . . . It's like I killed him.

How can you say that? I says. The Tonton killed him, not you. You loved Pa an he loved you.

He says naught. Jest stares at the ground.

You didn't kill him, I says. Don't ever say that again.

The sun starts to rise.

We sit silent.

An we wait.

✝   ✝   ✝

They're comin! Tommo yells down from his lookout point high in the tree.

How many? calls Ike.

Tommo holds up three fingers.

What the hell? says Ash.

Tommo's climbed down the tree fast as a lizard. He throws hisself down beside Jack.

Jack jams the long-looker to his eyes. Lowers it slowly. It's Pinch, he says. He's got Emmi with him all right. But there's only two Tonton with him. What's his game? He tosses the looker to me. Sure enough, there's only three horsemen headed our way across the plain. They ride close together. DeMalo th'other Tonton. One on each side of Pinch.

I train the looker on Pinch. He's ridin a big white stallion. An he's still dressed like he was last night. Long golden robe with shiny stones an bits of mirror an shimmer discs. But it hangs down in burnt an tattered shreds. He holds his right leg stuck out to the side. There's metal bars an straps around it, almost like a cage. He's got his face an head wrapped in a gold sheema.

An ridin on Pinch's horse with him, tucked aginst his chest like he's got every right to have her there, is Emmi. She looks so small, so skinny, so pale. But her chin's held high. She won't show him she's afeared. My heart lurches.

Lugh snatches the looker to see fer hisself. Emmi, he says.

She looks all right. It don't look like he's hurt her.

If he did, I'll rip his head off, says Ike.

Looks like this is the showdown, says Ash.

Everybody ready? says Jack.

We fit arrows to our crossbow strings. Keep outta sight behind the rocks an wait. An wait. My heart's beatin like crazy. My mouth's dry.

They're here. says Tommo.

We raise our heads over the rocks. We take aim.

They've stopped a little ways from the bottom. Within shoutin distance.

Pinch edges his white stallion forwards. The horse tosses his head an dances a little.

Looks like he don't trust his rider.

Emmi! I shout. Are y'all right? Did they hurt you?

No! Her voice sounds thin an shaky. I'm fine!

A classic battle tactic, calls Pinch. Forcing your enemy to attack uphill. But there is no enemy here. Only your King.

You ain't no King of mine! yells Ike.

Ike! Jack hisses. Not helpful.

Well, he ain't.

You left something behind, calls Pinch. Something of value. The King has condescended to return her to you.

Let her go! I yell.

He slides a bolt shooter from his robes. He presses it to Emmi's temple.

He dislikes children, he says. So noisy. So dirty.

Let her go! says Lugh, standin up. It's me you want.

I try to tug him down, but he pulls away.

You have displeased your King severely, says Pinch. He chose you with great care but you're too stupid to realize the great honor done to you. All his years of planning . . . gone to waste. His many kindnesses to you—a guest in his royal Palace—and you repay him with humiliation. The King is not accustomed to being humiliated.

I'll come back with you, says Lugh. Whatever you want. Jest let my sister go.

You have wounded the King with your ingratitude, he says. But you are no longer of interest to him.

Cold fingers of fear start to creep along my spine.

Then take me, says Ike. I'm the one who showed 'em where to find you.

The gallant giant, says Pinch. No. You won't do either.

Git to the point, says Lugh. What do you want?

Not what, he says. Who.

He points at me.

The King wants her, he says. The Angel of Death.

What fer? yells Ike.

He wishes to speak with her, says Pinch. To have a friendly little chat.

Right away, I lower my bow an take a step forwards.

Lugh grabs my arm. What're you doin? You cain't go down there.

He's got Emmi, I says. Of course I'm gonna talk to him.

He don't wanna talk to you. Look at him. The man's crazy.

It's too dangerous, Saba, says Ash.

What does he want with you anyways? says Lugh.

She killed his parents back at Hopetown, says Jack. She nearly killed him too.

It was a accident, I says.

Lugh swears. Why didn't you say nuthin?

I didn't think it mattered, I says.

I say we take him out, says Ike. There's six of us an only three of them.

Ike, he's holdin a shooter to Emmi's head, I says. The way I see it, we ain't got no choice. I'm goin down.

No, says Lugh. We'll think of somethin else. You cain't go. I ferbid it.

She's my sister, I says.

Jack catches my hand. I look down at him. I know what he's thinkin.

If it'd bin Emmi they took, he says, Emmi an not Lugh . . . would you of gone after her?

When he asked me that question, back at Darktrees, the answer was no. If he asked me agin, if he asked me now, I'd answer yes. Without stoppin to think. Yes.

He squeezes my hand. Says, Whatever he says, don't trust him. We'll be coverin you.

Saba! Lugh says. Come back here!

I make my way down the hill, my feet slidin on the scree. I stop when I'm ten paces or so from Pinch an Emmi.

All right, Em? I says.

Yes, she whispers.

That's my girl.

How touching, says Pinch. Throw your weapons down.

I pull my quiver over my head an lay it down beside my crossbow.

Is that it?

I nod.

Check her, he says to his men.

They dismount.

DeMalo walks towards me. That closed face. Those shadowed eyes that flick over my face, jest once, as he starts to pat me down. The feel of his hands on me. Quick. Light. Cool. I hold my breath. He finds the knife in my boot sheath.

He takes it, along with my bow an quiver.

She's clean, he says to Pinch.

Take the child, he says. If Angel here tries anything, break her neck.

While the other Tonton covers me, DeMalo lifts Emmi down. Pinch slides from his horse. He lands badly, on his caged leg, an curses.

DeMalo hands Emmi back to him.

Pinch holds her in front of him, the bolt shooter to her head once agin. He takes a few steps towards me, swingin his leg. He's wet through with sweat. Must be in a lotta pain.

I can smell him from here. That sour, sweet, rotten smell.

So, Pinch says. At last. The Angel of Death. The King has a personal score to settle with you.

What? I says. That I took my brother before you could burn him to death?

Your brother, he says. Of course. That tattoo on your cheekbone. The King should have killed you then and saved himself a lot of trouble. No, it's not that.

Then what? I says.

He pulls his sheema away from his face. It's a mess. Burned. Raw pulpy skin, angry an red. His gold face paint's all flaked an melted into the flesh.

He stares at me, breathin high an fast. His black eyes hard. Full of hatred an . . . an somethin else. Madness.

Look what you've done, he says.

I says naught.

Look what you've done! He yells it.

It was a accident, I says. I didn't mean to.

The King's leg. Look what you did to his leg.

You was chasin us, I says, an the landboat turned over. I didn't make it turn over. It was a accident.

They were not! Accidents! He screams it at the top of his voice. All the veins in his neck pop out an spit flies outta his mouth.

I take a step back. Emmi stares at me with huge eyes. Her face is white.

The King requires your life in payment, says Pinch. It's simple. You give yourself to him and they all go free. Your precious brother, your innocent little sister and your friends.

I don't say nuthin.

No one is holding you, he says. You're free to walk away. But the moment you do, his finger will slip and . . . pop! No more little sister.

I stare at him. Frozen.

DeMalo's watchin me, his face blank.

Think, Saba, think!

Ah, says Pinch, so many questions going through your mind. Does he have more men? Waiting out of sight? Your friends probably told you not to trust him. You're thinking, how do I know if he'll keep his word?

He pauses. Then, You don't, he says. That's what makes this so delicious.

Let her go, you bastard, I says.

His face twists. He backhands Emmi across the face an she falls to the ground. Right away, he hauls her back up by one arm. There's a ugly red mark spreadin over her cheek.

Your fault, he says.

The red hot rushes through me. I'll do whatever you want, I says, but you gotta let her go first.

A show of good faith? He shakes his head. No.

I feel sweat tricklin down my back. I look at Emmi. I look back at Lugh, Ike, Tommo, Ash. Watchin me. Waitin. An Jack. Oh Jack.

None of 'em move.

The blood pounds in my ears. My heart's in my throat. My belly twists.

I turn back to Pinch.

You win, I says.

† † †

I hold my hands up slowly.

He waves a hand. DeMalo stays where he is an the Tonton guard runs over. He jerks my hands behind me an ties 'em tight.

Now let my sister go, I says.

Pinch don't move. He jest stands there, starin at me fer a long long moment. Then his lips stretch in his ruined face. He's smilin.

For every winner, he says, there must be a loser.

He raises a hand. DeMalo lifts a twisted piece of metal to his lips an blows. A loud noise splits th'air. A flock of birds rises up in a flurry.

I look around wildly, my heart racin.

Tonton step outta the woods at the top of the hill. Right behind Lugh an the rest. Twelve of 'em, with crossbows an bolt guns aimed an at the ready. They must of circled out to come at the hill from the north.

I hear a strange sound. Like . . . a hammer poundin a nail in. I whirl around.

Behind Pinch, from the direction of Freedom Fields, even more Tonton, at least fifty armed men by the look of it, come into view. They run towards us, across the plain, keepin in step with each other. The ground shakes as they approach.

Tricked.

Trapped.

No way out.

† † †

The Tonton line up in formation behind DeMalo.

I watch as my friends lay down their weapons. Jack an Ike, Lugh an Ash an Tommo. The Tonton on the hill make 'em all lie flat on the ground with their hands behind their heads. They git a kick in the back when they resist.

So.

After everythin we done, after all we bin through, this is the way it ends. Not even the chance to die fightin. To die together.

Twelve Tonton on the hill. Another fifty down here. Pinch ain't gonna let us die easy. My mouth's dry. The red hot's gone.

I'm small. Weak. Alone.

Saba, says Emmi. Saba, do somethin. She starts to cry.

Please, I says to Pinch. You got no reason to hurt her. Let her an the boy go. They ain't done you no harm.

Oh no, he says, they'll be the first. So the rest of you can see what's in store for you.

I go down onto my knees. Please, I says. Let 'em go.

A long pause. Then,

No, he says.

I look to DeMalo. Our eyes meet.

Help me.

My lips move. But no words come out.

Pinch strokes Emmi's face with the bolt shooter.

Slowly or quickly, he says. Cutting or shooting. He kisses the top of her head, looking at me.

Please, I says. Please.

He breathes in deeply. There's nothing like it, is there? he says. The smell of fear.

Suddenly a hoarse cry rings out—caw! caw! caw!

A black bird sails out over the red ridge to the west.

It's a crow.

† † †

My heart stops.

Time stops.

There's a low rumble of hoofs. A long line of horses an riders appears at the edge of the ridge. It's the Free Hawks. But it's more'n jest them. There must be another thirty or so riders who ain't Hawks. Maev's right in the middle. Nero swoops above me, screamin in triumph.

The red hot kicks me in the gut. Slams into action. I leap to my feet.

Nero! I yell.

A small group of Free Hawks, maybe ten of 'em, come runnin outta the woods on Pine Top Hill. They take the Tonton completely by surprise. Lugh, Jack an the rest leap up an grab their weapons. The fightin starts.

Maev comes thunderin down the ridge in a cloud of red

dust, with the riders spread out behind her. They whoop an holler as they head straight fer the Tonton lined up behind DeMalo. Arrows fly ahead of 'em. The Tonton start to reel back, scream, as they hit their mark.

What? shrieks Pinch. What is this? He looks around, frantic.

DeMalo walks towards me. He's got my bow an quiver slung on his back. He's holdin my knife in his hand.

That's it! says Pinch. Slice her!

DeMalo stands in front of me. He drops my bow quiver at my feet.

What . . . what are you doing? says Pinch.

DeMalo puts his arms around me. Holds my eyes. With one slash, he cuts the ropes tyin my hands behind my back.

DeMalo! Pinch yells.

Until next time, DeMalo says softly. He tosses the knife on top of my other weapons. He turns to go.

DeMalo! Pinch screams. Are you mad?

DeMalo swings hisself onto his horse an rides off, away from the action, back in the direction of Freedom Fields. A few of the Tonton see him go an run after him.

DeMalo! Pinch howls after him. DeMalo! Where are you going? Attack! Attack! He circles like a mad dog, wavin his bolt shooter. His lips is drawn back over his teeth. Like a wild animal in a trap. He's still holdin Emmi to his chest. She looks terrified.

I run at him, leap at him feet first. I kick his hand an the shooter flies up in the air. He yells in pain, spins away.

Run, Emmi! I yell.

Pinch lunges at me. A arrow whistles through th'air. Hits him in the chest. He screams. He staggers an falls back. I look to see who's saved me.

Maev gallops up. She's got Hermes in tow behind her. He rears up, squealin with excitement.

About time, I says. Who're yer friends?

The raiders from the western road, she says. We called a truce. They're a wild crowd. When they heard there might be a fight, I couldn't keep 'em away. She tosses me Hermes' reins. Just outta interest, do you go lookin fer trouble, or does it jest find you?

I wish I knew, I says.

See you later! she says. She rides off to join in the fight.

I swing Emmi onto Hermes. Put the reins into her hands.

I point to the ridge that the Hawks jest rode down. See that? Git yerself to the top. Stay outta the way till this is over an fer gawdsake, hang on this time.

But I wanna fight! she says. You gotta let me stay an fight!

No way! Heeya! I slap Hermes on the rump an he takes off like a shot. He'll keep her safe.

Up on Pine Top Hill, the fight's over. All quiet. Them twelve Tonton's eether dead or fled.

Lyin on the ground below, Pinch ain't movin. A arrow sticks outta his chest. He won't be gittin up no time soon.

Nero calls. He swoops down. I hold up my arm an he lands

on it. I stroke his feathers, kiss his soft black head, breathe in his dusty bird smell. Gawdammit, Nero, I says. You sure took yer time.

He's a crow that likes excitement, Nero. If there's somethin happenin, he ain't gonna hang around. He flaps his wings at me, caw-caws an flies off to watch the action from high above.

I start runnin. Head fer the thick of the fight. Hawks, western road raiders an my friends aginst the Tonton. Excitement races through my body, speeds my feet.

I snatch a arrow from my quiver as I run. Load my crossbow. I start shootin the second I catch sight of a black robe.

Ike's slashin away on the edge of the action, a wicked lookin longsword in one hand an a studded chain in th'other. Tommo's at his back, busy with the slingshot.

Ike grins when he sees me. Now this is what I call a fight! he shouts.

I wade into the middle of the battle. At one point, me an Jack's fightin back to back. Then Lugh an me. Then me an Ash.

Look! yells Ash. Pinch! He's gittin away!

I spot him. He's managed to pull the arrow outta his chest. He's climbin onto his big white stallion. Slowly, painfully.

Got him! I says. I run towards him flat out. As he pulls hisself onto the horse, I shoot my last arrow. It hits him in his bad leg an he cries out.

He tries to wrench the arrow out as he fumbles with the reins. The horse rears up. It squeals an dances as it tries to throw off a rider it don't trust.

I make a dive fer him. Grab at his caged leg. He kicks out an the cage catches me unner the chin. I go flyin back an slam onto the ground. Git the air knocked outta me.

As I drag myself to to my feet, he gallops away. Towards the Hoodoos. I look around me, frantic. Not a horse in sight.

Then I see Ash gallopin towards me. On the black mustang we took from Pinch's stable. He goes like the wind.

Quick! I yell. He's gittin away! Let me take Titan!

She jumps down right away. I swing myself on to his back.

Wait! she says, holdin the reins. We're winnin, Saba. You got Lugh back. Emmi's safe. Let him go.

No, I says.

What does it matter?

It matters to me, I says. Let go, Ash.

Then I'll come with you, she says.

This is my fight, I says. Don't tell the rest of 'em where I've gone. Promise me, Ash.

All right, if that's what you want.

She lets go the reins. Steps away.

I wheel Titan around.

Saba! Here! Ash tosses me her half-full quiver an I catch it. Good luck!

I'll be back. Heeya! Heeya! I dig my heels into Titan.

An we tear across the plain towards the sharp red fingers of the Hoodoos.

✝   ✝   ✝

Titan feels good unnerneath me. Strong an wild. He can feel the red hot burnin in me. It's burnin in him too.

Nero flies above, a little bit ahead. He'll scout the way.

The Hoodoos rise in front of us. They look even stranger close up.

Deep channels etched down their high sheer sides. Sharp points. Crammed tight together. I start to see crevasses. A few thin trees cling to the mean red dirt.

I bin watchin Pinch. He disappeared through a gap in the rocks. I walk Titan through the gap. We're on a narrow path worn into the earth that snakes its way around the rocks. Right away, I see the prints of Pinch's horse.

It's gloomy here. Like bein in a deep canyon.

An it's silent. A heavy silence. Like the very rocks is holdin their breath.

But there's alway somethin to listen to, even in silence. Up ahead, a nervous horse whinnies. Stamps his feet. There's alway somethin to smell. There it is. The faintest whiff. Sour, sweet, rotten. The smell of Pinch.

Then, a echo.

I halt Titan. Wait while it dies away. It's the sound of rocks fallin. An a faint, scrapin sound as Pinch drags his injured leg behind him.

I slide offa Titan's back. Wait here, I whisper.

There's a couple of Hoodoos rounder an smoother'n the rest. I can see a way up between 'em. I start to climb.

The earth's dry an loose unnerfoot. I move careful, tryin not to make any sound. Nero comes down to see what I'm doin. He hops an flaps from rock to rock, always stayin ahead of me. I hold my finger to my lips so's he knows not to squawk or caw.

I reach the top. Check that Pinch ain't in sight. Pull myself up. I'm on top of a flat Hoodoo. There's drag marks in the dirt from his leg. He couldn't of got far. He'll be in a lotta pain.

I slide my bow offa my back. Fit a arrow to the strings. Then I start to follow the drag marks. They stop at the edge of my flat Hoodoo.

I send Nero up into the air. Almost right away, he starts circlin. He's found Pinch. Looks like he's on the next Hoodoo to this one. It goes straight up, like a jagged chimley.

He must be on the far side of it.

There's a little gap between the Hoodoos. Maybe two foot. Only a small bit of flat rock to land on, then a narrow ledge goes off to the left an disappears around the corner.

He could be right around that corner. He's got his bolt shooter. But he's injured. He's weak. Maybe even dyin.

The devil ain't so easy to kill.

I look at Nero, still circlin above. He seems calm enough.

I jump over the gap an land lightly. I'm on the Hoodoo with Pinch.

My breath's tight in my throat. I flatten my back aginst the rock. Then I start to sidle along the ledge. To inch my way around the corner.

Be ready.

I move slowly. Feel ahead with with my right foot. I don't make a sound. I only got a chance if I take him by surprise.

Be ready.

The ledge starts to widen out. Wider. Wider. I'm turnin the corner.

Now.

I move fast. My bow at the ready.

I take it in at a glance.

I'm on a wide ledge on the side of the Hoodoo. Pinch is sittin on a rock, restin his leg.

He looks up, startled. He reaches fer his bolt shooter.

I let fly with my arrow. It glances offa his hand.

He yells out but keeps goin fer the shooter.

No time to reload my bow.

I dive at him. Knock him offa the rock.

Somehow he's managed to git hold of his shooter. He tries

to jam it unner my chin. We struggle an I knock it outta his hand.

He gits his fist unner my chin. Pushes up into the soft bit.

I cain't breathe. He's pressin on my windpipe. I grab his hand with both of mine. Try to pull it away. I kick an squirm.

But he's stronger'n I ever imagined.

The rank stink of his breath, his sweat, fills my nostrils.

No escape this time, he says.

I claw at his robes. Then I claw his burnt face.

He shrieks an rolls offa me.

I dive at my bow. I dropped my quiver when I jumped Pinch an my arrows is scattered all over. I scrabble around on my hands an knees, reachin fer one.

But Pinch is on his feet. Holdin his bolt shooter with both hands. Aimin it right at me.

I scuttle as far away from him as I can. Press myself aginst the rock.

Pinch comes towards me. His face bleedin where I clawed him. He's a terrible mess. Blood an burnt flesh an flaky gold paint.

Somethin sharp's cuttin into my hand. I'm clutchin somethin in my hand. A little bit of mirror from Pinch's robe. I must of ripped it off.

Suddenly the sun catches it. It throws out a sharp shard of light.

Pinch flings up his hand. Covers his eyes.

A chance. I got a chance.

I flash the mirror at him agin. Then I move. Quickly. Silently.

He aims the shooter where he thinks I am.

I move. Flash the mirror agin. Move.

He waves the shooter around. Stay still! he yells.

I flash the mirror. Move.

He shoots.

I duck.

The shot goes wild. Ricochets offa the rock, sendin red dust flyin everywhere.

As the echo dies down, as the dust clears, I see Pinch.

He's standin a few paces from the edge of the ledge. He looks surprised. There's blood gushin outta his neck. The bolt's ripped through it. He touches his neck. Looks at his wet red fingers like he cain't believe what he sees. Then he presses his hand to the wound.

But I'm the King, he says.

You ain't no King, I says.

They said you were the Angel of Death, he says. He takes a step towards me, blood gushin out from between his fingers. I didn't believe them.

Suddenly Nero dives at him, squawkin an flappin. Pinch's arms fly up. He staggers. Steps back into thin air.

I rush to the edge.

He's on his back. His arms an legs flung out. His eyes wide open.

Speared on the sharp point of the Hoodoo below.

Nero flutters down to land on my shoulder.

By rights, I should feel somethin. Joy or relief or triumph or . . . somethin. But I don't. I don't feel nuthin.

The wind moans among the red teeth of the Hoodoos.

The sound of birds above me. I look up at the sky. The vultures is already startin to circle.

Let's git outta here, I says.

† † †

As I ride up to the battlefield on Titan, they're clearin up.

I spot Lugh. He's sittin on the ground a little ways off, lookin exhausted. When he sees me, he raises a hand. Jack an Ash is helpin out with a few injured Hawks. Luckily, it don't look like nuthin too bad. But we lost two Hawks an one of the raiders. They're bein tied onto the backs of their own horses to go back to Darktrees where they'll be set on a funeral pyre.

Emmi rides up on Hermes. She jumps down, goes runnin over to Lugh an throws herself into his arms.

Everybody else is movin around, gatherin weapons an anythin else that might come in useful. Ike's bendin over a dead Tonton, checkin to see what he's got on him. Tommo's standin beside, watchin him.

A movement catches my eye. A Tonton. Lyin on the ground not far from Ike an Tommo. He's raised hisself up on one elbow. He lifts his bolt shooter. Aims it.

Ike! I scream.

He straightens. He turns.

I yank my crossbow around. Snatch a arrow. Load. Fire.

It all happens at once. It all happens too fast. The Tonton shoots, jest as Tommo throws hisself at Ike. They both go down.

My arrow hits the Tonton.

Ike! I scream. Tommo! I gallop over an leap off. I'm there the same time as Jack.

Tommo's lyin on top of Ike. I haul him into my arms. He lays there, limp. His eyes is closed.

No! I sob, shakin him. No, Tommo!

With a shudder, he comes to. His beautiful brown eyes stare up at me, dazed. I hug him to me, hold him tight to my chest.

Jack's rolled Ike over. He kneels beside him, feelin his neck. Dammit, Ike, he says softly. He looks at me an I know.

Ike? says Tommo. Where's Ike? I want Ike! I hold him even tighter as he tries to struggle free of me. I don't want him to see. I don't want him to know.

I feel it the moment he spots Ike. His body stills. I let him go. He stands. He walks over to Ike, sits on the ground beside him an takes his hand. No, he says. Don't leave me, Ike. Not you too. Great tears start to roll down his face. He rocks back

449

an forth, pressin Ike's hand to his heart. Sayin it over an over an over agin.

Don't leave me, don't leave me, don't leave me.

†   †   †

We build a pyre in the middle of the battlefield. A fine one, fit fer a warrior. We lay Ike on it.

Jack says a few words. Good words. About friendship. Other things too, but mainly friendship. Then him an me an Ash set the pyre alight.

We stand in silence. All of us an all of the Free Hawks an all of the raiders from the western road. We watch while the flames lick up the wood, catch on his clothes an start to burn.

Tommo's by hisself, a little ways off. He won't let nobody touch him. Won't be comforted.

Lugh puts his arm around Emmi. She cries.

Fearless, kind, funny Ike. With his big laugh an big heart. I think of Molly Pratt, the most glorious creature that ever drew breath. She'll still be waitin fer him. He wanted her to meet Tommo. He had a notion he might turn out to be a good family man.

An I cry too.

As we send Ike back to the stars.

I shake his hand. Creed. Skinny, wild-haired, tattooed. Barefoot leader of the raiders from the western road. Maev's new friends an allies.

Thanks, I says. We couldn't of done it without you.

He sweeps me a deep bow an kisses my hand. It was fun, he says. He jumps onto his horse. Gives me a big, white-toothed grin. Lemme know the next time you wanna rumble, he says.

He digs his heels in an, with a yip-yip-yip, him an his raiders go tearin off across the plain.

Sure you won't come with us? Maev says. We always got room fer one more.

I'm sure, I says.

It's good of you to take the kid, she says. She looks over to where Tommo's helpin Lugh git the horses ready to go.

Jack says Ike would of wanted it that way. An he'll be good company fer Emmi. Listen Maev, I says, I dunno how to thank you. None of us 'ud still be here if it warn't fer you.

I should of listened to Jack, she says. Come with you in the first place. But, like I said, better late than never. She swings herself onto her horse an nods at Nero. He's perched on Emmi's shoulder where she's givin him a good beak rub.

You should thank that bird of yours, she says. He's quite

somethin. If you ever git tired of him, I'd be happy to take him offa yer hands.

I don't think I will, I says. I turn to Ash. She smiles. I feel tears prick at my eyes. Ash, I says. I pull her into my arms an we hold each other tight. Thank you, I says.

She don't say nuthin. We stand there fer a moment. Then she steps away. Stay outta trouble, she says.

I'll do my best.

Lugh gives her a boost an she swings up behind Maev. With them leavin three of their horses fer us, she's hitchin a ride back to Darktrees.

Lugh holds up his hand. Maev takes it. Thanks, he says. Fer this an . . . fer helpin Saba an Emmi. Maybe we'll see you agin sometime.

You never know, says Maev.

They look at each other. My hand, she says. He's still got hold of it. He lets it go slowly an steps back.

G'bye, says Ash.

See you around, says Maev. She wheels about an they gallop away to join the Free Hawks waitin fer her on the ridge. When they git to the top they pause to look down. Then Maev rears her horse in farewell an they're gone.

Lugh's still starin after them. She's quite the girl, I says. Don't you think? Lugh?

Huh?

Maev, I says. Quite the girl.

Oh, he says. Yeah. She seems nice. He sets about gittin the Hawk horses ready to go.

Maev, nice? I mutter. Nice.

So, says Lugh, where're we headed?

What about Crosscreek? I says. It's so beautiful, Lugh, you wouldn't believe it.

No way. Lugh shakes his head. That's goin backwards. Far's I'm concerned, that's in the past. We had enough of livin in the past with Pa. We gotta move on, right?

Right, I says.

I say we head out west, he says. To the Big Water. There's rich land there. They say the air smells like honey.

Who told you that? I says.

He shrugs. I cain't remember.

I jest want us to be together, I says. Somewhere far away from here. Somewhere safe. The Big Water. I like the sound of that. Whaddya think, Em?

Sounds good to me too, she says.

Tommo? I says.

He nods.

Then west it is, says Lugh. No point in waitin. Let's head out.

Wait, I says, lookin around, where's Jack got to? Anybody seen him?

Tommo points. There! he says.

Jack's ridin away.

Across the plain on his white horse. They're headed east.

Anger rips through me. Panic. Heats my blood. Oh no, you don't, I says.

I jump onto Hermes' back, dig my heels into his sides an we take off like the wind. Nero streaks along above us.

Saba! Emmi shouts. Tell him to come with us!

† † †

I catch up with him jest after the Hoodoos. He turns when he hears us comin. Stops. Waits.

I pull up in front of him an jump down. I go over an grab his horse's bridle. The blood's rushin in my ears, my breath's comin short. My heart pounds in my chest. Git down, I says, glarin at him.

Not if yer gonna kill me, he says.

I said . . . git down!

All right, all right, he says, swingin hisself off. There . . . I'm down.

Nero caws as he settles on a nearby bush. I see you brought backup, says Jack.

Whaddya think yer doin? I says. Runnin off like that. Sneakin off like a . . . like a . . . no g'bye, no see you later, no nuthin. Jest . . . gone.

He frowns. I'm comin back, he says.

I go still. I stare at him. What? I says.

I'm comin back, he says. But I got some business to take care of first.

Business, I says. What kinda business? I thought you was a thief.

Oh! Charmin! I never said that. There's . . . a couple of things I gotta do. An Ike's got somebody waitin fer him. She's bin waitin a long time. She needs to know what happened.

You mean Molly, I says.

You know about her.

Ike told me.

But after I see her, I'll be comin back. That's the plan.

Becuz . . . becuz I saved yer life, I says. Three . . . no, two times. From the fire an then from the hellwurm. An yer the one that said it, when you save somebody's life two times—

It's called the rule of three, he says, not the rule of two. I should know, I made it up.

I knew it!

Look, he says. Two times, three times . . . this ain't about obligation. That ain't why I'm comin back.

It ain't?

No. It's about you. You. He takes a couple of steps towards me.

Yer in my blood, Saba, he says. Yer in my head. Yer in my breath, yer in my bones . . . gawd help me, yer everywhere.

You have bin since the first moment I set eyes on you.

My heart turns over. I don't dare breathe. The heartstone's burnin into my skin.

I seem to remember, he says, that first time we met, you said . . . what was it you said to me?

I said that . . . you ain't my type, I says.

Would that still be . . . yer opinion?

I look at Jack. At his strange silver eyes that go from moonlight to granite in a instant, at his crooked nose, his top lip with the little dip in it. An I says, That would . . . not . . . still be my . . . opinion.

He gives me his lopsided smile. C'mere, he says.

No, I says. You c'mere.

He steps in close. He smells of sage, summer skies an somethin that's jest him. Jest Jack. Now what? he says.

Now, I says, you kiss me.

He wraps his arms around me an hauls me up tight aginst him. He kisses my lips, my eyes, my face, my lips. An I kiss him. I breathe him in like he's air. Drink him in like he's water.

At last he pulls away, holds me at arm's length. I gotta go, he says.

You could go later, I says. We could go together when—

No, he says. I gotta go now. He starts to walk backwards while he talks. He's lookin at me all the time.

But how'll you find me? I says. We won't be here. You don't

even know where we're goin.

Yer headed out west, he says, to the Big Water. They say the air smells like honey. He swings hisself onto his horse.

Wait. Take this. I run over to him, fumblin fer the heart-stone. He leans down. I put it over his head, around his neck.

It . . . it'll help you to find me, I says.

I don't need no stone to find you, he says. I'd find you anywhere. He kisses me agin. Till I'm dizzy. Till my legs go weak. Then, See you, he says.

He tips his hat, wheels his horse around an trots away. As he goes, he starts to sing.

Oh I've roved an I've rambled all o'er the wide world
And kisses a-plenty I've tasted
But it's her wine-sweet lips that I'm still dreaming of
O hard-hearted Annie, cruel Annie my love.

† † †

Saba! It's Lugh's shout. Him an Emmi an Tommo ride to meet me.

Are y'okay? says Lugh.

I nod.

Didn't you ask him to stay? says Emmi.

He had somewhere he needed to be, I says.

I swing myself onto Hermes' back. Nero flaps over to ride on my shoulder.

Are we ever gonna see him again? says Emmi.

One day, I says.

One day soon, says Tommo.

I hope so, I says.

We turn our horses' heads to the west.

Oh! I nearly fergot! Emmi pulls Lugh's slingshot from her pocket an hands it to him. I bin keepin it fer you, she says.

He reaches over an ruffs her hair. Thanks. I'll teach you how to use it.

You don't need to, I says. She's a good shot.

Well, whaddya know? says Lugh. Guess I'll hafta find somethin else to teach you, Em.

Or maybe I'll teach you somethin, says Emmi. You dunno everythin. You jest think you do.

Lugh shakes his head. I definitely bin away too long, he says. I can see you need takin in hand, Emmi. Talkin to yer elders an betters that way . . .

I drop back a bit. I listen while they chatter on an Lugh makes us laugh. He always does.

We're together agin.

Lugh goes first, always first, an I follow on behind.

An that's fine.

That's right.

That's how it's meant to be.

Lugh turns around. Smiles.

Hey, he says, what're you doin back there? I ain't got a clue where we're goin. Git on up here an lead the way.

So I do.

ACKNOWLEDGMENTS

This book would never have been written without Sophie McKenzie, Melanie Edge, Gaby Halberstam and Julie Mackenzie. To each of them, my ever grateful thanks.

Thanks also to Julia Green, John McLay, Gill McLay, Lisa del Rosso and Roma Downey for their support and encouragement.

Thanks to Gillie Russell and Marion Lloyd for their expert guidance.

And special thanks to Elizabeth Hawkins, who showed the way.